W9-CDS-658

RECEIVED
FEB 06 2013
By

LOOSE ENDS

A Selection of Titles by Susan Moody

LOSING NICOLA *
DANCING IN THE DARK *
LOOSE ENDS *

DOUBLED IN SPADES
DUMMY HAND
FALLING ANGEL
KING OF HEARTS
RETURN TO THE SECRET GARDEN

writing as Susan Madison

THE COLOUR OF HOPE
THE HOUR OF SEPARATION
TOUCHING THE SKY

* *available from Severn House*

LOOSE ENDS

Susan Moody

This first world edition published 2012
in Great Britain and 2013 in the USA by
SEVERN HOUSE PUBLISHERS LTD of
19 Cedar Road, Sutton, Surrey, England, SM2 5DA.

British Library Cataloguing in Publication Data

Moody, Susan.
Loose ends.
1. Traffic accidents–Ecuador–Fiction. 2. Suspense fiction.
I. Title
823.9'14-dc23

ISBN-13: 978-0-7278-8227-1 (cased)

Except where actual historical events and characters are being described for the storyline of this novel, all situations in this publication are fictitious and any resemblance to living persons is purely coincidental.

All Severn House titles are printed on acid-free paper.

Severn House Publishers support The Forest Stewardship Council [FSC], the leading international forest certification organisation. All our titles that are printed on Greenpeace-approved FSC-certified paper carry the FSC logo.

Typeset by Palimpsest Book Production Ltd.,
Falkirk, Stirlingshire, Scotland.
Printed and bound in Great Britain by
MPG Books Ltd., Bodmin, Cornwall.

Dora

The body didn't surface for several days. When it finally did, drifting languidly in the oily olive water of the canal, bumping against the ancient Victorian brickwork which had for the most part withstood the test of time, though here and there over the years, it had been resurfaced with patches of concrete, it was unfortunate (not that anything, by then, could have been done in the way of first aid) that the first three dog-walkers along the tow path did not notice the raft of waterlogged clothes and bloated flesh, or if they did, simply assumed that someone had dumped their rubbish in the water and, lifting eyes mentally to heaven and condemning the way the world had deteriorated since their young days, had simply walked on by.

The fourth dog-walker that morning was a Mrs Dora Harding, recently widowed by an industrial accident at the local iron foundry and trying, not very hard, to assuage her guilt for the relief she had felt when, thanks to the compensation plan, instead of her brutish husband, Ed, a large cheque came through the front door. She saw the bundle of material now swinging out into the middle of the canal, since a bit of a breeze had got up, and recognized it instantly as a body. Digging into her pocket for the mobile phone she had not been allowed before Ed's death (*'rot your brains, them things will'*), she dialled 999. While waiting for the police and ambulance services to make their way along the narrow canal path, she let Livingstone off her lead, urging her into the rough litter-strewn grass to do what she was supposed to do, and sat down on a convenient bench some yards further down the path from where the body drifted in the little eddies stirred up by the breeze before veering back against the brick wall with a damp squelch which she found interesting, although faintly disgusting. It was – had been – a man, she could see that from the shortness of the dark hair matted above the corpse's neck and from the soggy remnant of what must once have been a good-quality thorn-proof jacket. Plus, of course, the wide-wale corduroy trousers, cherry-red, always a dodgy option for a man, she thought, gave off the wrong messages (though on the other hand, it did imply a certain self-confidence), together with the size eleven or twelve leather lace-up (she'd worked in a shoe shop before marrying Ed) which remained on his right foot, though the left one was now devoid of either sock or shoe.

Further along the water's edge, Oprah came stepping daintily along the towpath towards her, curly black spaniel ears hanging just above the ground, followed by Mollie somebody or other (Mrs Harding hadn't caught the surname when Mollie offered it, and didn't like to ask again, not that it mattered since their paths were unlikely to cross in a social sense).

'Morning,' Mollie said.

'Morning. How's Oprah – she just had a little operation, didn't she?'

'Fine, fine. The vet's very pleased.'

'That's good.'

Mollie hadn't noticed the body, and Mrs Harding decided not to call her attention to it. Mollie was, in Mrs Harding's experience, the sort who would succumb to hysterics, given half a chance, involving all sorts of tedious action on the part of those round her like pats on the back and murmurs of 'There, there,' and smelling salts being waved about. (Whatever happened to those? Did anybody use them any more? And didn't there used to be something involving feathers being burned under someone's nose, though when you thought about it, how many people had feathers lying around on the off-chance someone went into hysterics?) Mother had had a small brown bottle of salts which she kept, for some reason, in her sewing basket, but Mrs Harding could only remember them being used once, when a man walked into the back garden when poor Cora was sunbathing, and pulled down his trousers to flash his thing at her. Mrs Harding routinely thought of her twin sister as poor Cora, though Cora herself would have much resented the label; she was doing very nicely with her B&B, thank you *very* much, Dora, although she often discussed her dream, if funds were ever to permit, of upgrading her place a bit (*'Boutique, Dora, that's what I'm aiming for'*) to which end she played the Lottery weekly, and bought Premium Bonds whenever she had a spare tenner (*'Well, you never know your luck, Dora, do you,* someone's *got to win the million pounds'*).

Occasionally the body dipped in the riffled water, turned to one side and then another, and Mrs Harding was able to catch a glimpse of a torn and battered cheek, large ears and what she at first took to be a nasty cut under the chin, bleached though it was by immersion in the unhealthy waters of the canal, until she took in the fact that the throat had been slit.

Mafia, Mrs Harding decided. Not that this was Sicily, or New York, or anything like, but it had to be something gang-related, stood to reason, people didn't just go round slitting other peoples' throats and dumping them into the canal because they didn't like the look on a person's face or because someone had pushed in front of them in the queue for the cinema, did they? Unless it was drunks or druggies, plenty of those round here, and maybe the man in the water was just unlucky, in the wrong place at the wrong time. More likely a contract killing, she decided, having watched a lot of telly, the assassin up from London for forty-eight hours, casing the joint, studying the victim-to-be, then catching him from behind, forcing him to his knees, pulling out a knife and dragging it across the tender skin of his neck. Maybe there'd been two of them; you'd probably need two. Someone had beaten him up first, she was sure of it, and then you'd need help just to get him over the handrail and into the water; he seemed a fairly hefty sort of corpse, from what she could see. Probably chased him to the footbridge a bit further down (he must have run right past where she was walking now), did the deed, and over the rail he went. *Live by the sword*, Mrs Harding thought, somewhat inappropriately, *die by the sword.*

Babylon, they called this area, and very suitable too; she'd seen a reference to it in the local newspaper only the other Wednesday – *a modern-day melting-pot of vice and dissipation*, the reporter had said, making reference to the fact that gays were buying up all the over-priced loft conversions and the number of immigrants swarming into the place, not that Mrs Harding was prejudiced, far from it, her own late husband having more than a touch of the tar-brush about him, and none the worse for that, though none the better, either, terrible temper on him and his attitude to women had to be seen to be believed – slaves, in his book, *in* bed and out.

Olga and Andrei came shimmying towards her, feathers streaming behind them. He must spend hours brushing them, she thought, those beautiful white and orange coats, picking up burrs and grass seeds soon as look at you, she couldn't be doing with it herself.

'Morning, Doctor Lennox,' she said.

'Good morning, Mrs Harding. How are you today?'

'Fine, thank you. Apart from—' She was about to indicate the body, him being an educated man and unlikely to fall about alternately laughing and shrieking his head off, like poor Cora had done all those years ago, when Olga spied something in the distance and took off like a rocket, dragging Andrei and Dr Lennox behind her.

Livingstone was barking at something, on and on and on, barking mad, Mrs Harding thought, and laughed internally at her own joke, rather clever, if you asked her, rather witty. 'Oh stop it, Livvy,' she said, glancing at the sluggishly moving corpse, 'show some respect,' but the dog went on ferociously barking at something hidden among the clumps of grass and the empty baked bean tins (did they come down here all prepared, with a tin opener in their pocket?) until her owner got up to see what was agitating the creature and found her prancing around a clump of faded brown grass. Mrs Harding bent down and parted the grass-blades and there was a silver dolphin – not a real one, of course, it would have taken up most of the path and half the canal if it had been, quite apart from the fact that dolphins were a kind of fawn or beige colour, rather than silver. 'Why are you making such a fuss?' she asked Livingstone. 'It's not something you can eat.' But the dog went on yapping, jumping up at Mrs Harding's hand as she picked up the dolphin, then started licking at the red-brown stains on it.

It was about three inches long, heavy for its size, made of some kind of shiny grey metal, and attached to a key-ring with one of those flimsy little keys that came with suitcases or padlocks. Not a house key or the key to a car. She could hear sirens in the distance – the police arriving at last, better late than never – so she dropped the dolphin into her pocket. Nobody was likely to go to the police to say they'd lost a suitcase key, and anyway, they always came in pairs, those kind, so the suitcase owner would be all right. The dolphin was rather nice; she might hang on to it, finder's keepers and all that.

On the other side of the canal, old Mr Gilmour from the flats was slowly making his way along the towpath, led by Betsy, his guide dog – now *there* was a worthwhile charity if you liked, Guide Dogs for the Blind (stood to reason it was for the blind, didn't it, no-one else would need one, unless them St Bernards with a barrel of Famous Grouse round their necks could be called guide dogs, in which case someone buried in an avalanche might indeed require one, not that she'd know, avalanches being few and far between in this neck of the woods).

She sat down again as Chaz came lurching along as though he'd been up drinking all night, breathing like a bad case of asthma, studded collar round his neck, red-spotted handkerchief hanging in a jaunty V over his broad chest, followed by Jazz, shaven-headed, gold earring in one ear, ripped jeans, spider tattooed on his neck, three silver studs attached to his eyebrow and another through his upper lip.

'You all right, Mrs H?' he said. 'Don't often see you sitting down.'

'Right as rain, thanks, Jazz. And yourself?'

'Great. Doing great.' Chaz snarled, and lurched on his thick lead, leaning heavily to one side while his short pit-bull legs scrabbled around on the gravel of the path.

Mrs Harding indicated the other side of the canal. 'Seen that?'

Jazz stared at the body, taking a moment to realize what it was. 'Oh my Gawd,' he said. 'Is that what I think it is?'

'A body's what it is.'

'Blimey.' Jazz reached for the back of the bench and leaned against it. 'I never seen a dead body before,' he said faintly. At his side, Chaz snuffed and snorted, pointed face swinging from side to side as he looked for something to shred to pieces.

The body rolled slowly on to its side, letting out a distinctly audible burp, and they could both see the tattered remains of its face, shreds of white flesh fronding its eye sockets and a mouth full of horribly gleaming shards of teeth.

Jazz said, 'Strewth,' thinking it looked just like his old man on a bad day.

'It's fish,' said Mrs Harding, 'nibbling, like,' and Jazz, turning pale, indicated that he wouldn't be coming down the canal with his fishing rod any time soon.

'I called the police,' Mrs Harding added, looking past him, not wanting to admit her own ignorance of death's cold face, Ed having been removed to the undertakers directly from the factory, and having heard about his injuries, she'd elected to have the coffin sealed, which she might have done anyway, even if he'd died peacefully. Not having much enjoyed looking at him alive, she wasn't especially keen to see him dead, unless it was to assure herself he was no longer in the land of the living. 'Looks like them coming now.' She shook her head. 'Take their time, that lot do.'

Half-running towards them came two police officers, one male, one female, clad in fluorescent yellow jackets over their uniforms, and behind them, two paramedics in red gilets, though why they bothered, Mrs Harding couldn't imagine; they weren't likely to be giving the kiss of life to the sorry piece of former humanity in the water. They were followed by two men carrying a stretcher and two firemen with a ladder.

'Looks like the ruddy Keystone Cops,' Mrs Harding said but Jazz didn't hear her, being too busy slipping a muzzle over Chaz's snout before the police reached the bench.

Mrs Harding answered all the questions they asked her, although it was obvious to everyone, including herself, that she knew absolutely nothing germane to the case at all. Then she took Livingstone home to her neat little semi, washed her hands which despite Livingstone's tongue were still covered in brown stuff (where'd *that* come from?), fed the dog and looked again at the dolphin key-ring with its little key. Briefly she considered inching the key off and dropping it into the mug commemorating the coronation of King George VI and Queen Elizabeth, which had belonged to her grandmother (*'that's a real collector's piece, Dora, you mark my words'*) but decided against it as being too much of a nail-breaking fag and instead, transferred her own keys to the ring, hung them from a hook on the dresser and poured herself a nip of whisky. She brought down the coronation mug and spilled its contents on the table – a pile of golden one-pound coins she was saving up, a couple or so at the end of each day, to add to what remained of the compensation money (she'd paid off the mortgage and had the place redecorated from top to toe, bought a new bed (to replace the scene of Ed's too-frequent grunting ejaculations), a microwave which Ed always refused to buy (*'do your head in, those things will'*) and a decent washing machine ('If you want your shirts beaten against a rock down by the river, the way your grandma in Jamaica did, you're welcome to do it yourself,' she used to tell him, to no avail, so until he'd died, it was down the Laundromat twice a week, lugging the dirty washing) and a lovely new three-piece suite.) Her dream was to save up enough to go on one of them cruises – Captain's table, evening dress, drinks at the cocktail bar while being chatted up by a good-looking officer in tropical kit, her favours being sought by some handsome billionaire from Texas or the Deep South (all that Spanish moss and mint juleps on the verandah), locals crooning in the background. 'A girl can dream,' she told herself and poured another nip of whisky.

It had been quite a morning and here it wasn't even nine o'clock.

There were no distinguishing marks on the body, apart, of course, from the extensive cut beneath its chin, the stove-in head and the shattered teeth. No kind of identification: wallet, car keys, diary, all removed, no jewellery. The clothes were expensive but standard; the only hope the police had was through dental records, and that would take time. Meanwhile, the body languished in the police mortuary, waiting for someone to come in and file a missing-person report.

Kate
One

Stale air, stale smells, stale stink of toilet-freshener and old pee wafting through the bar each time the door to the lavatories was opened. Stale job, stale *life*. Kate didn't want to think about what she was still doing here, eight months – nearly nine, ever since the divorce – after she'd first seen the notice in the window and thought it would be an easy fill-in while she worked out what she *really* wanted to do and found herself a proper job. Leaning her elbows on the copper-clad counter, she looked round the semi-dark space full of thirty-somethings enjoying a glass of wine or a plateful of chicken 'n' chips. The designer hired at vast expense by the owners of Plan A had employed every wine-bar cliché in the business to make it the kind of place you'd want to come back to ('a real home from home'), though as far as Kate was concerned, she had never decorated her home (when she still had one) with such an eclectic mix of dried flower garlands, fishnets scattered with plastic shells, Chianti bottles dripping multi-coloured wax, and never would. 'Looka dis place!' Fredo, the manager, used to rant. 'Nits onna walls, rubbish shells all over da place, empty bottles onna table . . . issa not like any house I ever bin in.' But the decor must have worked, because people *did* come back, and not just once, but regularly.

Outside the windows, it was raining again. Cars threw up rainbows of oily water as they swished past, dark figures walked hunched against the cold, gutters ran with discarded paper cups and polystyrene trays.

Kate made her way across the room towards the two guys in the corner, easing between the crowded tables. One was a regular; the other she hadn't seen before. 'There you go.' She put their drinks down in front of them.

'Thank you very much.' The wine drinker was the regular: a nice-looking man, dark hair and eyes, dimples, well-spoken, with a faint foreign accent which she wasn't interested enough to wonder about. A good tipper. Open-necked dress shirt, white with a pink stripe, sleeves rolled up to the elbows, small gold earring in one lobe.

'Anything else?' she asked.

'Not for the moment.' He smiled at her and automatically she smiled back. ('They may alla be bastards,' Fredo often said, 'but they ah bastards, so be sweet.') As she turned to go, he added, 'It suits you.'

'What?' She stopped, confused.

'The hair. I like it.'

'Oh.' Kate brushed a hand below the short hairs at the back of her neck. Two days ago she'd had it cut off, reshaped, had dark highlights spun into the basic honey-blonde. 'Thanks. I thought I'd have a change.'

'A change?'

'I'm kind of hoping it'll inspire me to move on from here. Push me into doing something a bit more meaningful with my life.' From past experience, she was aware that it was a mistake to be talking to him like this: get too friendly with the punters and they think they own you, not that this one had overstepped the mark. Not yet.

He nodded. 'I know how that can be.' He lifted his glass of wine and tipped it at her. 'Good luck.'

'Thanks.'

'When's that likely to be? The moving on, I mean.'

Kate shrugged. 'Whenever the right opportunity comes along.'

'And if it doesn't?'

'Then I'll have to go looking for it, I guess.'

'You'll tell me, won't you?'

'Tell you what?'

'Where you're moving to.'

She stared at him. This was *definitely* overstepping the mark. 'Oh *sure*, I'll be taking ads out in all the newspapers. Might even have a billboard or two put up saying that I'm moving to . . . wherever. Let me know if you need anything else.'

'Oh, don't worry, Kate, I will.'

Kate made her way back to the bar, picked up another order and delivered it to another table. Back at her station behind the bar, she frowned. *Don't worry, Kate, I will* . . . His manner was a bit too bloody familiar, and it annoyed her; she should never have told him her name when he'd told her his, as though he thought she'd want to know. Anton? Gustav? Johan? Something foreign. He came in quite often, maybe two or three times a week, sometimes alone, sometimes with someone else or even a group, but always with men. He looked like he might be from one of those Mediterranean or Latin-American cultures which didn't rate women very highly. She watched him laugh at something his companion had said, his tanned face creased with amusement. The two of them glanced in her direction, then at each other, touched glasses in a toast and drank, making it obvious that they were talking about her (*'Phwoar, wouldn't mind shagging that one . . .'*). She didn't like the friend: overweight, head thrust forward like a black bull, with a mean mouth and eyes as cold as a boa constrictor's. Or, to continue the animal metaphor (or possibly simile, she'd always been vague about the difference), a fat city cat in mufti, striving for the landed-gentry look, tweed jacket, hand-woven tie and so on. Someone should tell him that on him it didn't work; he still looked like a jerk.

Meanwhile, she didn't get off work until eleven o'clock that night, and there were still two hours to go. Tomorrow she would definitely go through the appointments pages of the papers, and find another job. Anything would be better than this – anything except getting back together with bloody Brad, Brad the Love Rat, Brad the Impaler, though sometimes she was tempted, especially when tired or depressed, to call him up and suggest they try again. He would jump at the chance. Other times she knew, solidly, strongly, that she would rather undergo major dental surgery without anaesthetic than return to the life she'd led with him. It had been an endless nightmare of recriminations, bailiffs, moonlight flits, betrayals both small and large, endless listening to his ludicrous daydreams of how this time, honey-babe, finally, it was all going to come good, and the two of them would be rich at last – *if,* that is, she could see her way to one last and absolutely final loan, swear to God, darlin', after which they'd be laughing, trust him, he'd be able to pay back every red cent she'd ever given (sorry, *loaned*) him and then some. When she'd first met him, shortly after what she called in her own mind The Accident, he'd seemed like a reassuring haven in which she could moor the leaking vessel of her life, and there find time to caulk it until it was seaworthy again. Big mistake. What amazed her most was that for so long she could have fooled herself into believing in Brad's fantasies, to the extent of handing over a substantial six-figure sum – her entire inheritance, in fact – to be sunk into the bottomless pit of his unstable dreams.

From the corner of her eye, she noticed Regular waving at her and went over.

'We'll have one chicken and chips, one cod and chips, Kate,' he said, when she was standing beside him, pad in hand. Kurt, was he called? Karl? Knut?

'Anything else?' she asked. 'A green salad? Vegetables?'

'Salad, Mick?' he said to his companion.

'If you do mushy peas, I'll have them,' Mick said, barely glancing at her. He had a more cultured accent than might have been expected, given his brutal appearance. 'Otherwise, give me the veggies.'

'Say please to the nice lady,' said Kurt/Karl/Knut. Or was it Stefan?

Mick shot him a sour look. One doesn't say please to the help, Kate could see him thinking, while Stefan – yes, she was pretty certain his name was Stefan – smiled at her over Mick's head, showing the dimples, and winked.

'We'll have a bottle of white wine, too,' he said. 'Got something different from this one?' He touched his glass.

'I can recommend the Chardonnay – nice and dry,' Kate said.

'We'll have that then, please.'

She was tired by the time her shift ended. The rain was still tipping down and though she tried to keep out of the puddles, water seeped into her boots (two days ago, one of the soles had mysteriously cracked almost in half) and splashed up the back of her legs. The pavements were greasy with the rain and twice she slipped on the slick residue of city filth. Somewhere she'd mislaid her gloves and her hands were freezing. Even worse, the burn scars on her left leg were chafing. Eleven o' clock on a cold winter's night and she was bedraggled, exhausted, fed up. If she hadn't been so stupid as to throw all her money in Brad's direction, not just once but countless times, she could have bought a little house in Spain or France, all white walls and orange-tiled roof, geraniums in pots, sun streaming through the grape arbour and a bottle of chilled white wine to hand – probably France, because Spanish wines weren't as good. There might even have been a swimming pool sparkling nearby, yet instead of that, here she was, standing in the rain waiting for a bus. Admittedly, according to Peta, whose parents lived in the Dordogne, it could get pretty nippy out there at this time of year, but even so, at least the sun shone and the skies were blue – though perhaps not at eleven o'clock at night, any more than they were here.

Two bus journeys and a half-mile walk lay ahead of her before she would arrive at the house she was currently sharing with her brother. It was in a shabby part of town, slowly being gentrified by hopeful young city workers frantic to get on to the housing ladder and looking for bargains to do up with their annual bonus. Already there was an abundance of freshly painted woodwork, new shrubs in front gardens, optimistic bay-trees in blue ceramic pots beside pristine brass-furnitured doors, though her brother's house – at least on the outside – remained pretty much in its original state.

Her hands were so cold she could scarcely get the key into the lock, and when she opened the door, the hall had an arctic chill. Magnus, usually the most solicitous of brothers, had obviously forgotten to turn on the central heating, which meant a long wait before the hot bath she'd been looking forward to. As so often, she longed for some maternal pampering, a tray, perhaps, laid with a pretty cloth, a delicate china cup and saucer, some reassuring digestives on a matching plate, a Thermos of hot chocolate to counteract the discomfort of wet feet and frozen hands ('*welcome home, darling, see you in the morning*'). But her mother had died when Kate was ten, and Luisa, maternal though she might have been, had lived out in Ecuador with Dad.

Hearing her come in, Magnus came to the door of his study. 'You look tired,' he said.

'I *am* tired.' Kate shucked off her coat and hung it on the hallstand before putting her arms round his waist, resting her head against his chest, taking comfort from the familiarity of the thick oiled wool of his fisherman's jersey. 'Whacked, if you really want to know.'

'Let's have a brandy. I could certainly do with one.'

'Had a hard day at the coalface, have you?'

'I'll say. I thought I'd made all the notes I needed, then I found one of my files had gone missing, and spent hours trying to find it.'

'And did you?'

'Not yet. It seems to have vanished into thin air. I probably left it on my desk at the uni.' He walked across the hall and into the sitting room. 'Come on and get cosy. I lit the fire for you, so it's not too cold in here.'

At the sound of his voice, Olga and Andrei, the two white-and-apricot King Carl spaniels, jumped down from the sofa where they'd been snoozing and trotted across the wooden floor, claws clattering, to greet her. While she bent down to caress their soft heads, Magnus took two balloon glasses from the old-fashioned sideboard against one wall, and removed the cork from a bottle of Armagnac.

Kate took off her sodden boots and sat as close to the fire as she could get. Massaging her toes, she said, 'I think my feet are about to fall off.'

He poured a generous measure and handed it to her. 'There you are. Get that down you.' Sitting opposite her, he cupped his hands round his glass to warm the spirit. 'So, yet another awful day, huh?'

'You can say that again.'

'I really wish you'd get a job which didn't entail coming back late at night on the bus.'

'Magnus, we've had this discussion a dozen times.'

'But these are dangerous times . . . I worry about you getting mugged, or – or caught in crossfire between two rival drug gangs, or one of the many other hazards that a city this size is prone to.'

'I appreciate your concern, but I'm a grown woman, I can defend myself, I'm OK.'

'Against random bullets?'

'You want me to wear a bulletproof vest? Besides, how many times have there been gunfights in a provincial little place like this one?'

'There's always a first time. Just be careful.'

'I always am, especially when I hear gunfire.' Sniffing deeply at her glass, Kate felt the warming fumes of the cognac go up her nose and slowly begin to circulate through her blood. 'It's so *cold* out there.'

Magnus shook his head. 'Sorry to sound like a nag, but you've only yourself to blame for taking jobs with unsocial hours.'

'I know, but—'

'You've had a good education, you got to university—'

'And got right out again fairly soon after that. I never wanted to go in the first place; it was you who was so keen, not me.'

'Two years isn't all that short a time. And what with the . . . well, you had good reason not to complete your degree.'

'I only got there with your help in the first place.' If pushing and shoving and bullying and constant coaching constituted 'help'. And when she got to the red-brick place on the south coast, she'd wasted the first year, demonstrating against harsh sentences meted out to Saudi Arabian women taken in adultery, or invasions of small defenceless countries by richer bullying ones. Even though she buckled down a bit in her second year, her tutor nonetheless summoned her in and suggested she might be better suited in some vocational situation, a proposition she was only too happy to agree with. And then came The Accident. 'I'm not academic like you. Never have been.'

'You're not stupid, Kate.'

'I know. But . . .' It was easy for him to say. She smiled across at him, handsome, gifted Magnus, fair-haired, blue-eyed, so like the photographs of their father when he'd been young. And suddenly she was there again at Dad's memorial service, leaning on crutches, her arms and legs buzzing with agony behind the painkillers they'd given her at the hospital, while the ex-pat minister from the English church in Quito recited verses from the Bible. There'd been a crowd of people she didn't know, snuffling, sighing, dabbing at their eyes with white handkerchiefs, sobbing, even. Her heart was lodged in her chest like a cannon ball, round, heavy, hard, and she had done her very best not to cry, hearing her father's voice somewhere near her ear, telling her to buck up, pull herself together, big girls don't cry. He was full of such urgings. *Be a man*, he'd told her once, an odd exhortation because if there was one thing she could never be, however hard she tried (major surgery and hormone treatment notwithstanding), it was a man. And then Magnus had put his arm round her shoulders, the two of them, so suddenly, orphans, doubly, trebly, bereaved, and taken her hand with his other one, and she'd known that insofar as things could ever be all right after this, he would make them so.

She leaned back into the sofa and closed her eyes while beside her, Olga stirred, gave a small snicker of sympathy. Kate tried hard to make herself believe that her current situation was all down to Brad, but the truth was that her current situation was her own fault, for being so deliberately blind to her husband's shortcomings, especially when she'd known from the beginning that rushing into marriage with handsome useless Brad wasn't the answer to her problems. In the six years they'd been married, he'd managed, without animosity or psychological sadism, to leach away all her spirit, her backbone, her ambition, not to mention her money: when there was nothing left except a pile of debts, he'd melted away, and without even telling her, flown back to his native New Jersey. One of these days she would have to get her papers changed back from his name to her own; she had been too overwhelmed after the divorce to do anything about it.

'I know you haven't – uh – got much left from what Dad left us,' Magnus said delicately.

'I haven't got *any*thing left, darling.' Unlike level-headed Magnus, six years older and light years more sensible, who'd bought this house, and was doing very nicely, thanks to his stable job and academic salary.

Magnus took off his glasses and fiercely rubbed his eyes. 'But I could lend – even give – you some if you needed it. To start a business, I mean. I know that's what you've always wanted. Or I could pay for you to go to back to university. That's what you would eventually have done if you hadn't met Brad.'

Kate opened an eye. 'That's very sweet of you, Magnus, but I couldn't possibly take it.' (*'You have to stand on your own feet, Kate.'*)

'Yes, you could.'

'Just because I've been stupid enough to run through my lot doesn't mean *you* have to throw your money about, particularly since I must be a pretty bad risk.'

'I've thought about it a lot. Once you settle on something, I could be an investor, a silent partner. I'd like to. My books have been doing as well as history books ever do – once they become a set text in schools and colleges, you're quids in. Think about it. You could pay me back bit by bit.' He leaned forward and touched her knee. 'Remember how you were going to start a florist or a book-shop or set up as a potter?'

'Dreams, Magnus, like I said. Impractical dreams.' Not even dreams, just ideas flung off the top of her head to placate her brother. 'In any case, I don't actually want to do any of those things.' In an idle moment she'd imagined herself sitting at a wet potter's wheel, pulling up the clay into bowls and vases, the amazing glazes she would produce, Bernard Leach-style, or being declared a National Living Treasure like Shoji Hamada, carrying off prizes at Biennales. Or maybe producing such fabulous floral creations that hostesses all over the western world would vie for her services to decorate their homes before some tremendous dinner, being flown into the White House, called to the Elysée Palace, summoned by the Vatican. As for a bookshop, it was just an idea she'd had for about ten seconds . . . She sighed, working her shoulders about; as so often, they felt as though she'd been carrying a sackful of rocks on her back all day. The rocks were always the same ones – The Accident which had killed her family, the divorce from Brad, her general state of poverty – and between them they had caused her to disintegrate to such an extent that on some mornings she would wake up and seriously wonder who she was.

'The bookshop idea,' her brother was saying. 'That was a good one – I buy lots of books, and I could get all my colleagues and their families to—'

'Magnus, dear Magnus, what it boils down to is that I don't really know *what* I want to do – I'm pretty useless at just about everything.'

'Don't keep putting yourself down, Kate. I'm not Brad your ex-husband, I'm your big brother and I have every possible admiration for you, for your guts and perseverance, your humour, your – your abilities.'

'I wish *I* had,' Kate said. 'Whatever they are.'

'You just have to get yourself together again, that's all.'

'I will, I promise, but it's taking a hell of a long time.'

'OK, even though the accident was nearly ten years ago, it's only, what, just over a year since Brad took off?'

'True.' She held out her glass. 'Can I have a drop more?' While Magnus poured another fingerful of Armagnac into her glass, she added, 'So how are the imperial Russians doing?'

Magnus topped up his own glass and leaned back, happy to put contemporary matters aside. 'Those poor people – given their privileged backgrounds, it's amazing that they stood their imprisonment so well. The adults at least must have realized that they had no-one to turn to, having been abandoned by all their cousins in the Royal houses of Europe, and that it could only end in disaster, but for the sake of the children, they tried to make it all seem normal, almost bourgeois.'

'It sounds very brave of them.' She picked up one of Magnus's more precious *palekhs*, the highly lacquered papier-mâché boxes which were as much works of art as any icon, the more valuable ones having their own provenance and artist-signatures. This one showed a Snow Princess in a wood of white trees, with snow falling and a moon casting a mother-of-pearl light over everything, against a blue background.

'It was probably Nicholas's finest hour,' Magnus said. 'He certainly wasn't much cop as a tsar, in fact he was the most inept, anti-Semitic, useless . . . he was really the last of the medieval monarchs. Even so, I hate to think what those last few weeks were like in the Ipatiev house: the hottest days of a stifling summer and they were all – a family of seven, two of them semi-invalids, plus their servants – they were all forced to stay inside, only let out once a day, otherwise cooped up in a few small rooms with the windows whitewashed and kept shut. Mind you, those were small inconveniences, when you think of the atrocities the land-owners were able to inflict on their serfs, thanks to Nicholas's ineptitude and indifference, the pogroms, the disastrous attempts to put down rebellion, not to mention his high-handed attitude to political advice.'

'So in one sense, he got exactly what he deserved.'

'You could say that. Did you know that in addition to more formal titles, he referred to himself as the "owner of Russia"?'

'How very arrogant. But I don't know how I'd have handled being shut up like that,' Kate said. 'You hear these awful stories of girls kidnapped and kept inside wheelie bins, or in boxes under the bed. I would definitely go mad.'

'No, you wouldn't, you'd think of some way to escape. Remember that time we both got stuck in the garden shed because Dad locked it by mistake? You got us out, picked the lock with a screwdriver or something.'

'A kirby-grip, actually.'

'Well, I couldn't have done it – I've never been very practical, as you know, whereas you . . . enterprising in the extreme.'

Kate made a face. 'It was that or die.' Even now she could remember the hot dread which had flooded her, the incipient panic as she realized what had happened, the certainty that if she wasn't out of there in seconds she would disintegrate into a screaming heap of raw ganglia, nerves and arteries bursting like wires through her skin, eyes blinded by waterfalls of blood, fingertips dissolved into bleeding stumps. Since then, she'd never been able to travel on the

Underground; even on an ordinary train she would lose control if they stopped in a station without the doors immediately opening.

She glanced at her watch. 'Look at the time! I'm off to bed. By the way, I'll be out on Friday evening, we're having a girls' night out.' Girls' Night Out, she amended, mentally adding capitals because Jenny had summoned them together to impart some Very Important News.

'How are they all?'

'Just fine.' Kate sighed – a great deal finer than *she* was, that was for sure. 'Jenny's got something really big to announce so we're going to Fabers so she can tell us in suitably pleasant surroundings.'

As Kate stood up, Magnus said, 'Think seriously about what I said, sweetheart.'

'I will. Honestly.'

Magnus
Two

Listening to her run up the stairs, Magnus Lennox reflected how much he enjoyed having his sister's company, how satisfactory it was to have her under his wing, as it were. At the same time, having that sort of a mind, he considered other brother-and-sister combinations, Charles and Mary Lamb, for example, or Tom and Maggie Tulliver, or Dorothy and William Wordsworth. W. B. Yeats lived with some sisters, didn't he, and there were the Brontës, though perhaps they didn't count since they lived with their father as well.

Had those brothers worried about their sisters the way he worried about his? He thought not. Yeats had been a surly bugger, from what he'd read, rude and demanding; Tom Tulliver (admittedly he was fictional) was criminally careless of Maggie until the end; William took Dorothy mostly for granted while Branwell was a drunk and an opium eater. He felt himself to be much closer to Charles Lamb, who had loved his sister Mary without question, had made all sorts of sacrifices in order to care for her, even after she'd murdered their mother.

He had not been called upon to make many sacrifices for Kate, in fact so far, none. It was hard to imagine what they might be were he asked to make any, but he worried about her all the time, coming back late at night on the bus, she could be mugged, abducted, gang-raped, turned into a drug-addict and sent out on the streets to earn a living for a pimp in a sky-blue doubled-breasted suit and a salmon-pink shirt, like the ones he'd seen in the red-light district of Amsterdam. He had regarded Bradleigh Fullerton III, his erstwhile brother-in-law (supposedly the scion of a family which could trace its roots back to the first wave of Pilgrim Fathers), as little more than a successful con artist. He'd always had a sneaking liking for him (being likeable was probably the most important stock-in-trade of a fraudster) but when Brad had abandoned Kate, Magnus had been secretly relieved to have her back where he could keep an eye on her. When he said he was happy to be a silent partner in whatever business she might want to take on, he meant it most sincerely. He saw himself seated Buddha-like upon a rock, wearing only a loincloth and uttering the odd gnomic sentence from time to time, or like Simeon Stylites, never opening his mouth, simply there on top of his pillar, a mentor nonetheless, not that Kate would have heard his words if he had spoken, unless he'd used a megaphone. Simeon's last pillar had been, if he remembered correctly, sixty-six feet high. Magnus feared that at the age of no more than thirty-five, he himself was fast turning into a metaphorical stylite, set upon the pillar of a Young Fogey or even a Middle-Aged one. If, indeed, he hadn't already become an *Old* Fogey, with his patent coffee-making machines and his two pretty dogs, his collection of hand-painted *matrioshkas* and *palekhs*, his peaceable bachelor household, his *sister*, for God's sake. Not that there was necessarily anything wrong with being a fogey, old *or* young (*fogey* deriving from *foggy*, or moss-bound, he'd discovered, looking it up one evening when the Romanovs were being less satisfactory than usual, though that seldom happened). In fact, he rather liked the idea of it, a small rotundity about the middle, snuff stains on a canary-coloured waistcoat (he'd worn one at Cambridge and considered himself no end of a dog), the suggestion of rich port emanating from his jacket. It's not too late, he told himself, getting up and staring into the Venetian mirror, which long ago Magnus's mother had brought to her marriage as a gift from her Finnish grandmother (though Magnus was never to know this), in order to examine his eyebrows from a couple of inches away, thinking they were taking on a decidedly Denis Healey sort of growth pattern. Something must be done . . . but what?

In his final year at university, Magnus had seriously thought of taking Holy Orders. He'd liked the idea of a rural ministry, the Early-Victorian rectory with its many bedrooms and pretty overgrown gardens, parishioners stopping for a chat (*'Morning, Vicar'*) as he laboured with a spade or pruning shears in a short-sleeved black shirt and dog-collar, his hybrid tea or damask roses regularly winning a prize at the annual Flower Show, joining a team of rustic bell-ringers. Matins, he had thought, in some sixteenth-century parish church, his voice sonorous and encouraging from the pulpit. Dinner up at the Hall every now and then, mothers coming to him to confide their fears about their adolescent sons or daughters and himself dispensing wisdom, pointing to his own children who'd been caught in some minor transgression (*'This too shall pass, Mrs Harkness!'*) and how well they were now doing, the girl studying medicine, the boys (maybe they were twins) doing awfully well at university. There'd be an occasional peaceful death which he would attend in an outlying farmhouse, holding the dying man's hand, while his tearful widow (or about-to-be widow) wept quietly on the other side of the deathbed (*'Oh Vicar, I don't know what I'd have done without you'*) until the day of his own quiet dying, mourned by all.

He'd thought, too, of joining some contemplative order, might even have done so if it had not been for his perceived responsibility for Kate. He'd done his three years at Cambridge more to please his father than for his own satisfaction, reading Russian, because the careers master at school had told the Modern Languages Sixth that with *glasnost* and *perestroika*, it was the language of today, gentlemen; with Russian at your fingertips, the world will be at your feet. He'd always had an ear for languages, already spoke fluent French and Spanish, and he had worked hard, with a view to going into the Foreign Office or starting on the lower rungs of the ladder of the Diplomatic Service. Sitting on the low wall at the Mill between essays and tutorials, with a pint of beer in his hand while punts moved along the river below, he'd pictured himself *en grande tenue*, kissing hands, showing his credentials – in the purely professional sense, of course – perhaps with some kind of sash across his chest and a diamond starburst pinned to his bosom, bestowed upon him by a grateful monarch for unspecified services to the Crown, though he was a little unclear as to whether monarchs, grateful or otherwise, bestowed starbursts and the like upon their diplomats. Sometimes he envisioned a wife standing at his side, well-born, elegant, thin, a bit like Edwina Mountbatten during her brief post-Partition tenure as Vice-Reine of India, only with a more modern hairstyle. There'd be an ambassadorial residence, perhaps with peacocks and camellias in the garden, and staff to deal with all the tedious day-to-day matters, and the Edwina-wife throwing stylish little receptions, entertaining visiting notables and VIPs, perhaps even the younger royals, attending parties at other embassies, and being pleasant (*'Such a nice couple'* or, *'He'll go far'*).

But he couldn't really believe in it. He was afraid that once he'd got his foot on the first rung of the ladder, he would never get it any higher, it would stay there, forever poised below the second, and in the end, he decided to take the easy way out and stay on at Cambridge and do a further stretch to get his PhD. But his heart hadn't really been in that either, and he was very conscious of simply putting off some inevitable and possibly calamitous decision.

Having completed his thesis, he hadn't known where to go next and since he had the Russian, he'd decided to go to St Petersburg for a year. Once there, he flirted with Russian Orthodoxy for a while, loving all the golden grandeur of it, the chanting and the incense, the rattle of chains from the smoking censers and the Feast Days, the gilded gates opening and closing, the knee-bending and sign of the Cross in triplicate, sad cadences in the deepest of bass voices wafting upwards to the buttressed roofs, weeping Madonnas and black-faced saints. Until the day the white-robed acolytes had swung open the shining gates of the iconostasis a little too soon and he'd seen the celebrant munching on what, from Magnus's kneeling position on the stone floor of the cathedral, had looked suspiciously like a Macdonald's hamburger. Somehow, the magic was lost after that, and he was back to wondering what to do with himself.

He took a job teaching English as a Foreign Language, walking every day from his shabby room in a shabby hotel along a shabby backstreet behind Nevsky Prospekt, to spend several hours a day in an Institute of Language which was housed in part of what had originally been a grand house belonging to some archduke or other, and was in the process of being restored amid a jungle of plastic sheeting and precarious wooden scaffolding from which workmen filled in holes and scraped plaster. He taught in a room which had once been magnificent and was now filled with battle-scarred tables at which, for the most part, sat equally battle-scarred throwbacks to the Communist era, large men with red ears, plump women in rusty black skirts, the occasional very young girl in clothes so revealing of stomach and breast as to insinuate, to Magnus, at least, that she was some kind of call girl. He could scarcely imagine why his pupils were there in the first place, since none of them had any feel for language. Perhaps it was some kind of mandatory outreach programme, because the circumstances in which any of them might need to speak English was difficult to conceive. Helping tourists, perhaps, or serving behind the high glass counters at the covered market, doling out the thick cream cheeses or the multicoloured honeys, or, in the case of the (possible) call-girl, directing her foreign clients into ever-more pleasurable postures. The Director of the Institute was an oddly hairless man with the kind of shiny skin which suggested that every other week he boiled himself in depilatory wax, whose own grasp of Magnus's mother-tongue was so tenuous that for his first week at the Institute, Magnus assumed the man was talking in some kind of Russian dialect. He found himself moderately happy.

And then came the phone call. 'Your parents, Señor, your sister, also Señora Bailey, so sad, so very sad, we do not know exactly what happened but—'

'What?' he said. 'Who is this?'

'Dottore Eduardo Gonzalez, the lawyer in Quito, the lawyer of the Professore James Lennox, your father.'

'Yes. What's happened, what is sad?' He could feel the blood draining right out of his body and dared not look down in case he found himself standing with a pool of it lapping redly at his shoes.

'Your family, Señor, an accident on the road, I am very sorry.'

'My family . . .' An accident, was that a euphemism, did he mean they were all dead?

'Your mother, your father, Señorita Bailey, your sister—'

'I have another sister,' he had shouted down the phone. 'Which one are you talking about, which of my sisters is . . .' It had sounded then, and still did in retrospect, as if one sister mattered to him more than the other, though that had not been in his mind at all. He had been juggling with the horror of losing Dad and Luisa, his stepmother, the prospect of having to act as a surrogate father to his little half-sister Annie, the late and unexpected daughter of his father and Luisa, or as a rock for his full sister Kate. And who was Señorita Bailey, anyway, what did she have to do with anything?

'Your sister is in hospital, many burns,' the heavily accented voice said. 'The emergency services . . . could not, unfortunately . . . in time to save . . . so very sorry . . .'

Magnus had cleared his throat loudly. 'I can't hear you very well . . . who did you say was in hospital?'

'Señorita Lennox, Señorita Katerina Lennox.'

And for the rest of his life he would be ashamed at the relief he'd felt in the deeper recesses of his being at not being required to bring up eight-year-old Annie, a child he hardly knew. She would have required things from him he wouldn't have known how to give, though obviously, just as Dad had done after Mother died, he would have given it his very best shot ('*once a month, darling, it means you're a Woman now*'), buying brassieres and tampons for her, worrying about boyfriends and unwanted pregnancies.

'Dad . . .' he said. 'Kate . . . Oh dear God, this is terrible.'

'Yes . . .'

And Luisa, too, the pretty South American biologist his father had married fourteen years ago, plus the unknown Señora (or was it Señorita?) Bailey.

He pulled himself together. 'Mr Gonzalez, I shall fly to Quito as soon as I can make the arrangements. Is there someone I can contact, someone who could meet my plane, take me to wherever my sister is?' and he scrabbled at the drawer of his bedside table for a biro and some poor-quality lined paper with the name of his hotel stamped crookedly across the top.

Kate
Three

'We're a young company,' the woman who interviewed her – Janine Taylor – had said. 'Small, specialist, dynamic. At the moment, there are only three of us: me, Fran and you . . . if you prove to be the best candidate for the job, that is . . . plus another girl who helps out three days a week during peak times. Do you think this is the sort of work you'd enjoy?'

'Definitely.' Kate was looking as specialist and dynamic as she could. She had spent half the morning doing typing tests, familiarizing herself with the office computer, and conversing with people on the end of the phone, part of Janine's impressive interviewing techniques.

'We try to offer something a little more offbeat than your average high street travel agency. And because we're competing with the big boys – Thomas Cook's, STA, Thomsons, not to mention the cut-price people, we have to offer a more personal approach. This job is all about people skills. Are you good with people? '

'Very,' Kate said keenly. The job might end up being as boring as working in the bar, but at least she'd get to sit down from time to time, and the hours were sociable.

'Hmm.' Janine, only a couple of years older than Kate, hitched her clearly unnecessary glasses back up on to her nose and looked down at the paper in front of her. 'Well, I can't say it's a very convincing CV.'

'I know. First of all I got married, and my husband wanted me to work with him in his various . . . businesses. And since we – um – split up, I've been waiting for the right kind of job to come along, the sort of job I know I could do well.'

'And you think this could be it?'

'I do.' Kate was very definite about it, very dynamic.

Janine looked briskly at her watch. 'Well, we'll let you know no later than the end of the week.' She stood up, smoothed out her skirt, adjusted the turquoise cravat thing which she wore in the neck of her white blouse, and held out her hand. Her face softened slightly. 'I shouldn't say this, but I agree with you: I think this is a job you'd be good at.'

'Oh . . .' Kate was taken aback. 'Why, exactly?'

'You can handle a computer, which is essential, of course. You have secretarial skills and a good telephone manner. You speak fluent Spanish and French, always useful. But more importantly, you have a confident approach, which is absolutely key in reassuring our customers. They come in here to spend a lot of money on a holiday they've probably been discussing and saving up for all year, and they need to feel certain that we know what we're doing.' Janine raised her eyebrows. 'When it comes right down to it, we're peddling dreams, Kate, and it's our job to make those dreams come true.'

We're peddling dreams . . . Kate liked that. It had a curiously old-fashioned ring to it, like a poem she might have learned years ago at school, or an old song heard in another life, and she remembered Dad seated on the piano stool, Mum with her hand on his shoulder, the E-key sticking every time it was hit, causing a tiny hiatus in the music, the two of them singing *If there were dreams to sell, what would you buy?* The recollection was so vivid that it made her eyes sting.

The four girls were sitting in the window of Fabers restaurant. Across the road was a canal and beyond it a park. Despite earlier rain, the evening was now relatively dry, though the air was still full of moisture, creating a mophead glow around the street lamps, and the bare soaked branches of the plane trees lining one side of the street dribbled freezing water on the unwary pedestrians below.

They'd spent some time catching up. Finally Peta clapped her hands. 'Quiet, ladies! We want to hear what the big news is. Come on, Jenny: spill the beans!'

Jenny looked round the table, her eyes bright. 'Guess what: Don and I are moving to Australia!'

'Australia? Wow!'

'Fabulous!' Peta and Lucy seemed almost as excited as Jenny. 'When are you off?'

'In about two months. Don has to work out his notice, and there's dozens of arrangements to make, and all the packing and putting stuff into storage, you know how it goes.' Jenny looked over at her closest friend. 'You're very quiet, Katie – what are you thinking?'

'I'm thinking that I'll miss you,' Kate said. She hoped she didn't sound as quavery as she felt. Why was it that the people you loved and relied on, the people you married, ended up either being snatched away from you, leaving you or dying? 'But obviously I'm thrilled for both of you. How long will you be gone for?'

'Rest of our lives, I think. I mean, we're emigrating, not just going for a holiday.'

'Wonderful,' Peta said. 'Can I come and visit?'

'I'm expecting all three of you, soon as we're settled.'

'Just think: I might meet a nice Aussie bloke and settle down next door, Jen.'

'I'll try and line a few up for you.'

'Where are you going to live?' someone asked. 'Perth, Sydney, Adelaide?'

'Melbourne, Don's whole family's there.'

'Once you married an Aussie,' Lucy said, 'it was always on the cards that you'd leave us.'

'When we got engaged, I promised we'd go out for at least three years, see how I'd like living there,' Jenny said. 'And of course I'm dying to go. But it'll be hard to leave my family behind. And you three.'

'Good thing Don's loaded,' said Peta. 'You'll be able to come home at least once a year.'

'With any luck.'

Kate wondered what it would feel like to abandon everything you'd ever known. Apart from the clichés – gum-trees, koalas, kangaroos, kookaburras – she knew almost nothing about Australia, nor could she envisage the underside of the earth, though of course she knew perfectly well that people in the antipodes didn't walk upside-down, the way her childhood storybooks showed. 'Sydney Opera House,' she said.

'What about it?'

'It's one of the few things I know about Australia, that's all! Doesn't the bathwater run out in the opposite direction from here?'

'That's what they say.' Jenny laughed. 'I keep meaning to check it when I'm there, but I can never remember which direction it runs out at home. Anyway, they're more into showers than baths.'

Kate's attention was caught by someone passing the window, someone she recognized. Surely it couldn't be Stefan Thing, her regular from the wine bar? But it was. He stood outside, examining the menu, screwing up his mouth as though considering his options, then pushed open the door and came in. The shoulders of his well-cut navy-blue coat were wet, and raindrops sparkled on his dark hair.

Of all the irritating coincidences . . . Or was it? Could he be deliberately following her? While someone came forward to seat him, Kate turned her head away and stared out at the leafless trees, the railings separating the street from the canal, their crossbars trimmed with necklaces of raindrops. She prayed that he wouldn't notice her. She didn't want to have to speak to him; she hated the idea of her shitty job intruding on her ordinary life. Smiling at – even flirting with – a customer was quite a different matter from meeting him outside the boundaries of the wine bar.

'Girls, I've got some news, too.' Lucy smoothed her dark hair behind her ears and looked shyly down at the tablecloth. 'Robbie and I are . . .' She swallowed, then blew out a nervous breath. 'We're moving in together.'

'At last!' Kate put an arm round her friend's shoulders. 'I'm so happy for you, though I can't imagine why it's taken you both so long to get your act together.' The saga of Lucy and Robbie had been a long and arduous one. For various reasons, both of them were unusually reluctant to commit, though it was obvious to their friends that prison officer Robbie and maternity nurse Lucy were an ideal match.

Jenny said, 'Should we be ordering our wedding hats?'

'Not just yet. But maybe . . .' Lucy gulped. 'Maybe soon. Like, maybe, this summer?' She looked so apprehensive that Kate laughed aloud.

Too late, she saw Stefan Thing turn round. Then, to her horror, he was on his feet and coming over to their table.

'Kate!' he said. 'What a surprise.'

She felt a surge of dislike. 'Isn't it just?' She hoped she sounded surly enough for him to get the message.

He looked round at the others and held out his hand to Peta. 'Hi, I'm Stefan Michaels.'

'Hel-*lo*,' Peta said.

'And you are?' He addressed Lucy.

'Lucy's just got engaged,' Kate said quickly.

Peta said, 'How do you and Kate know each other?'

'We don't,' Kate said, hoping that Peta, now in full-blown flirtatious mode, wouldn't ask him to join them. She looked at her watch. 'We haven't got much longer, ladies, I have to go and . . . and . . .' She paused – what could she possibly be doing at this time of the evening? 'Visit someone. I absolutely promised I'd drop in tonight, on my way home.' To Stefan, she added: 'We'd ask you to sit down, but the four of us so seldom get a chance to meet that I'm sure you'll understand if we don't.'

'Of course.' His eyes rested on her thoughtfully. 'I understand completely.'

When he'd returned to his table, Peta leaned over and hissed, 'What's the matter with you, Kate Fullerton? I think he fancied me.'

'Go and join him, then,' said Kate. She saw Stefan call over the waiter and say something to him.

'Talk about a dog in the manger.' Thin blonde Peta, always on the lookout for, if not Mr Right, then Mr Would-Do-At-A-Pinch, and always finding her relationships foundering, seemed really annoyed. 'Just because you don't go for him is no reason to block someone else's chances.'

'I'm not stopping you; I just didn't want him sitting down with us.'

'I agree,' Jenny said. 'Men always change the dynamics.'

'And usually for the worse,' said Kate.

The waiter was approaching them, carrying a silver bucket in one hand, four glasses in the other and a collapsible side table under his arm. 'The gentleman sent this over for the lady who's just got engaged,' he said. 'Said he wanted to congratulate her.'

'That's changing the dynamics, all right,' remarked Jen.

'Gosh . . .' Lucy looked overwhelmed. 'How nice of him.'

'Go over and thank him,' said Peta. 'Or do you want me to?'

'You're absolutely shameless, Peta.' Jenny turned to Kate. 'What's the matter, Katie? You look a bit stressed.'

'I am. I don't want to get all lovey-dovey with some guy who comes into my workplace, someone whose only relationship with me – if you can call it that – is that he leaves me tips.'

'Nobody's asking you to get lovey-dovey.'

'Yes, but with Peta slobbering all over him—'

'I am *not* slobbering.'

'All but,' Kate said. 'Thing is, I don't want to get personal with the punters. I'm sure you can understand why.'

'Of course we do,' Jenny said. 'Don't we?' She smiled at the others.

'I wasn't slobbering,' said Peta. 'Just getting in touch with my inner whore.' She started laughing. 'Honestly, Kate, I don't know why you get so worked up about things.'

'What about this bubbly?' Jenny said. 'Should we accept it?'

'As long as Kate doesn't object, on principle,' Peta said.

'He'd probably be mortally offended if we didn't.'

Kate shrugged. 'Who am I to turn down free champagne? Bring it on, I say! And while we're swapping news, I've finally got my act together and given in my notice at Plan A – thanks for coming in so often, all of you – and I just heard this morning that I got the job.'

'What is it?'

'Working at that travel agency in the High Street, TaylorMade Travel.'

'Don and I'll come and get our tickets from you,' Jenny said.

'Yeah,' said Lucy. 'Robbie was talking about a week in the Canaries . . .'

Later, when they were leaving, Peta went over and leaned down beside Stefan, murmuring something into his ear. He nodded, smiled, nodded again. 'There, you see,' said Peta, as they stood outside on the pavement before their separate ways, 'He was as nice as he could be.'

'What did you say to him?'

'Thanked him on behalf of all four of us.'

'And gave him your phone number, I bet.'

'I might have done. I don't know why you're so anti the guy, Kate.'

'I'm not anti, I just don't want to mix up my work life and my personal one.'

Peta touched her friend's arm. 'Sorry, Kate. I was out of order in there.'

'That's OK.' Kate hugged her. 'See ya.' She waved as she went off to catch her bus home.

Magnus was reading in the sitting room when she got back. They sat peaceably together for half an hour while she told him about her evening, Jenny's news, Lucy's news, the irritation of Stefan Michaels appearing in the very same restaurant, plus her own news, which predictably he saw as a step in the right direction, mostly because of the reasonable hours. He told her about his Romanovs, the new information which had arrived that very morning from one of his sources in Russia, fresh stuff which even Plotnikov, in his monumental study of the subject, hadn't stumbled across.

'You sound very enthusiastic,' Kate said.

'I am. I can't tell you how exciting it is when things like this finally come right. Getting up each morning and rushing to the keyboard – it's fantastic!'

'I wish I was that thrilled about something. Since Brad left, everything's seemed kind of dull and grey. Whatever else it was, life with him was never boring.'

'There are worse things than being bored.'

'I suppose.'

'Kate . . .'

'What?'

'Did it ever occur . . . I know it's a long time since Dad died, but have you ever wondered how he came to have such a big estate, so much to leave us?'

'If Annie and Luisa hadn't died too, it wouldn't have been so much.'

'Even divided among them and us, it still seems like an awful lot of money.'

'Does it?'

'He and Uncle Blair didn't inherit anything from their parents, so it didn't come that way. And I know what his salary was – not a huge amount a year, more or less normal for an academic in an unfashionable field. Nothing like enough to have accumulated so much – even the house in Cricklewood, it was unencumbered, as they say, no mortgage. How did he manage that?'

'Perhaps the money came from Luisa.'

'Anything she had was her family's. It had nothing to do with Dad. If she'd survived the crash, she'd have been pretty well off through his insurance policies and so on, I imagine.'

'That's probably all it is, insurance policies he took out on our behalf. Or maybe Mum had something. Does it matter?'

'Not really. Just that I don't like mysteries.' He glanced at her over his half-moon reading glasses. 'Plus the worry that he might have been involved in something . . . illegal.'

'Illegal? Dad? Oh, Magnus, you always see the cloud, and never the silver lining. That's impossible. What kind of illegal, anyway?'

Magnus shrugged, rubbed again at his eyes, pinched the bridge of his nose. 'Drugs? I don't know. I'm not even saying I think he *was* doing something on the wrong side of the law, just that the possibility bothers me.'

'Can you seriously imagine Dad, our father, smuggling drugs, or anything else? And if so, where would he be smuggling them to, and how? And how would he have got involved with them in the first place? He was a scholar, an academic.'

'You're right, Katie. Absolutely right. It's just that I . . . wondered.'

'Perhaps he just made some good investments.' She looked at him sharply. 'Do you have any reason for thinking any of this?

'I suppose not.'

She got up and crossed the room to kiss him goodnight. 'I'm knackered, as usual.' Too knackered to pursue the subject any further.

He grabbed her hand as she bent over him. 'I'd give anything to make you happy again, carefree, the way you used to be.'

'I will be again, darling. I've been through all the bad things so from now on it has to be good, doesn't it?'

'How do you mean?'

'Troubles never come singly, isn't that what they say?' Kate kept her tone light. 'I've already had more than my share, what with Mum dying, Brad, The Accident – I reckon I'm in the clear, you can relax.' She waved from the doorway. 'Night . . .'

Janine

Four

'. . . *I agree with you: I think this is a job you'd be good at.*'

Whatever had possessed her to say such a thing? Watching the girl – Kate Fullerton – walk away down the High Street, Janine was amazed at herself. Never show your hand: it violated all known best practice to be so open with a job-seeker. She hadn't even interviewed all the people who'd applied – and she had no idea whether Kate Fullerton would be good at the job, but on the other hand, as soon as she had opened her mouth, Janine had known that this was the candidate she would choose. Hopeless CV, of course, but that didn't matter. She reminded Janine of her English mistress at school, that same attitude to the world, that same tacit assumption that she expected more than most people, and would get it. In other words, she had Class.

It was a slack moment, and she sat with a cup of coffee in her hand while Fran dealt with the only other customers in the shop, an elderly couple who'd come in wanting to go to India for a cataract operation. It was a holiday of sorts, Janine supposed, but not one she'd have chosen for herself, especially not with the BUPA plan she'd been paying a bomb for over the last three years.

She wondered idly whether the elderly couple would do their holidaying before or after their operations. She imagined them stumbling through the Indian jungle, tripping over creepers, pursued by tigers or hissed at by snakes, groping their way towards the white marble glory of the Taj Mahal, seeing it only through a dim blur, until their vision was fully restored. She'd never had any problem with her eyes, thank goodness; she'd bought the glasses round her neck in Boots, the same day she'd registered to change her name by Deed Poll.

She'd spent years trying to decide what would most fully express her personality, which one of the huge library of available names would resonate most, press the most buttons, and had eventually decided upon Miranda, as being both classy and feminine. And then, home from school one afternoon, she'd switched on Radio Four and heard some man on *Poetry Please* reading in an Irish voice which stirred the depths of her heart. *Do you remember an inn, Miranda, do you remember an inn?* he had asked and she decided it was *meant*, especially when she looked up the meaning of Miranda and discovered it had been invented by Shakespeare, meaning 'worthy to be admired'.

Miranda it was going to be until, idly listening to a gardening programme, she heard one of the horticultural gurus talking about the yellow garden spider, *'miranda aurantia'*, and the first faint cracks began to appear. (A *spider*? She *hated* spiders.) Then she accidentally caught sight of herself in a shop window and realized that she really wasn't a Miranda, no way, and in the end she'd gone for Janine, as being closer to her original name, and more possessed of the brisk businesslike air she wished to demonstrate in her dealings with the public, though she stayed with her chosen change of surname.

Names were funny things, shaped you in a way. She remembered telling her mother – she must have been three or four – that she wanted to change hers and Mum saying she couldn't. Why did you have to call me Jane, it's such a boring name, she'd said, I want to be something pretty. And Mum had laughed and said, Jane is what you are. Jane. Plain Jane. I like the name Jane, Dad said, a good solid name, no frills to it, you know where you are with Jane, and anyway, she's not plain, she's my beautiful girl, aren't you, darling, and she'd run to sit on his knee and burrow into the old green sweater he always changed into after work to save his shirts, and feel safe and loved.

Plain Jane. She didn't ask to change her name again. She believed her mother: looking into the mirror, she saw no reason to think otherwise. I *am* plain, she told her reflection. Plain Jane. That's what the girls at school called her, though not in a particularly unfriendly fashion, but although at first it hurt, she soon learned that she had other qualities which they didn't. She had a brain, for one thing, and she knew how to use it. And she had ambitions beyond marrying the first boy who got her pregnant, and spending the rest of her life in a council house.

She read a lot, too, gulping down books as though they were strawberries, finding small epiphanies in phrases which leapt out of the pages at her, each time giving her a jolt of pure pleasure at the precision, the rightness, yes, that is exactly how it is, the sense of exhilaration that by using words, someone could reproduce an emotion, a sensation, with such exactitude, storing them away until she had time to scrutinize them more closely. She learned many things from books, chief among them being that if she wanted something, she had to plan for it. It didn't occur to her that she might be unusual in her single-mindedness, nor lonely, nor that there was another life to be lived beyond the one she had.

She could still remember Miss Barker's voice: 'You can do anything you want to, girls. Be anything you choose to be, anything at all.' Jane found Miss Barker inspirational: no-one could call her pretty, not like the French teacher with her Parisian clothes, or newly married Mrs McCallum, the history teacher, all aglow with love and smelling faintly of sex when she came to school in the mornings.

And of course it had to be tarty Leonie Bryson who put up her hand and, looking round at the other girls for admiration at her daring, asked in a false tone of earnest desire for information, 'Miss Barker, suppose I was hopeless at everything else and decided I wanted to become a high-class prostitute,' while around her girls giggled behind their hands and looked down at their desks.

Miss Barker looked Leonie up and down, then smiled kindly. 'For you, my dear, I'd imagine that should present no problem at all.' Jane loved her for that, especially when Leonie didn't have the brains to see that she had been insulted, even if everyone else did. She much admired the English teacher, who wore suede skirts and long black boots with heels, a hand-wrought (Jane loved the word 'wrought') necklace of black and silver, bras whose outline you could see under her blouses.

After one lesson, Jane waited until the rest of the girls had gone. 'Miss Barker,' she said, 'I need some advice.'

'How can I help?'

'The thing is, I'm not particularly clever—'

'You're certainly not stupid, Jane.'

'Well, I'm not academic or artistic in any way. I'm not interested in music or art, I don't know much about painting, though I know what I like.' (Miss Barker had winced at this and Jane determined she would never use the phrase again, although until then she had felt it carried an air of sophistication.) 'And I know perfectly well I don't have looks or charm.'

Although Miss Barker privately agreed, she said, 'Who told you that?'

'My mother, for a start.'

Miss Barker drew in a deep breath. 'Don't listen to her! My mother was the same. She never believed in me, so I had to believe in myself.'

'Exactly. I'm not hugely ambitious.' (Hugely was a word Miss Barker herself used, well, hugely, and Jane had appropriated it.) 'I'm never going to be Prime Minister, I wouldn't want to be, ruling the country and everybody complaining about everything you did, but I do know what I want.'

'That's a big start. Most people spend years faffing about, trying to decide what they want, and in the end settling for something else because time starts running out. And you should know, Jane, that ambition and self-confidence in a woman are far more appealing than mere looks, so whatever your mother may have said, ignore it. Anyway, you said you knew what you wanted to do.'

'Firstly I want to get a bookkeeping qualification. That's easy, because I can do that next term, here at school. And then I need to improve my accent: I know I don't have a good speaking voice, and I wondered if you could tell me how I can make myself sound better. Ideally, I'd like to sound like you.' Crossing her fingers behind her back, she smiled at the teacher in a way that Miss Barker could see had nothing to do with sucking up, and everything to do with pragmatism. Doors always open if you have the right kind of accent, Jane had learned that long ago.

'You've got it all worked out, haven't you?'

'Well, you have to, don't you?'

'And where do you hope to end up?'

'Running my own business.' She was very clear about that. 'Not hairdressing or a café, or a florist, I've looked into all of them and they're not for me. I'm thinking perhaps an employment agency, or a party-organizer, one of those firms which organize conferences for people. It's a field which is only just opening up and I think it's going to be big. So any more advice you can give me, I'd be glad to have.'

'It seems to me, with your path so clearly before you, you don't need much advice. I take it you haven't discussed your plans with your parents.'

'There's only my mother. My father died about four years ago.'

'I'm sorry to hear that.'

'Yes, well . . .' Jane didn't want to go there, poor old Dad, twenty years older than Mum, who never let him forget it, down the pub most nights in order to get away from her, but never drunk, not ill but not well, out the door every morning quiet as a mouse, back in the evening with no more noise than a shadow, just slowly slipping away from them until the morning he wasn't there any longer, just his body lying under the covers, his cold yellow hand on the counterpane and a look of peace on his face which Jane would never forget.

Miss Barker moved on quickly. 'A Saturday job is a good way to start, to get experience.'

'I've already got one.' Jane hoped her face hadn't flushed. 'Behind the cosmetics counter at Boots.' She enjoyed that, plenty of free samples of foundation creams and lipsticks, cleansing pads and soaps. She did double shifts in order to improve the rate at which her savings increased, and she let Mr Retton, the manager, suck her breasts after hours, as well as put his fingers inside her: he paid heavily for the privilege, the disgusting perv, with his sweaty scalp and smelly shirts. Sarah Retton, his daughter, was in the same class as her at school, a fact that Jane reminded him of from time to time, while assuring him of her absolute discretion. In moments of depression, and there were plenty of those, she thought of her nest egg, or Nest Egg: it was big enough now to justify the mental capital letters. Starting out the size of a quail's egg, it had grown into a hen's, then a duck's, now it reached towards ostrich proportions. Every time she checked the steady growth in her balance, excitement flared, and the promise of the future, her own business, whatever that might be, beckoned like a lighthouse.

'And you're absolutely right,' the teacher continued. 'A course in bookkeeping could lead to all sorts of other things. You could also try further education if there are any other courses you'd be interested in: I'll look out some possibilities for you at the Adult Education Centre, if you like.' Though as she said it, Miss Barker was sure that this remarkably self-possessed young woman had already studied all the evening-class opportunities available.

'Thank you very much. Actually, I've been doing Spanish once a week for a few months.'

'Spanish? Why?'

Jane wasn't about to tell Miss Barker, even though she seemed sympathetic enough to understand, about Miranda, or that she thought that Spain, or the idea of it, at any rate, offered a romantic vision which was singularly lacking in her own semi-detached existence. She'd feel stupid trying to explain how often she dreamed of Spain, of herself (Margarita, Conchita, Isabella, *Miranda*), in the arms of a sway-backed lissom youth, a girl gone chancing, dancing, backing and advancing, to the insistent clack of castanets, her mousy hair suddenly turned long and lustrous, put up in a huge bun at the back of her head, staccato clapping from the men around and the skilful plangent notes of a guitar, a dress covered in huge polka dots, while the moon shone through the palm trees and turned the sea to silver. *Do you remember an inn, Miranda?* (*Do you remember an inn, Jane?* didn't have the same ring at all.) 'I thought it might be useful,' she said.

'As for the elocution . . .' Miss Barker hesitated. 'If you like, I could give you a couple of hours a week after school.'

Jane tried to keep the satisfaction off her face. This was what she had been angling for all along.

Thoughtfully Miss Barker watched her leave the classroom. The girl had very little sense of humour, no sense of the romance and thrill of youth, she was too old too soon, Miss Barker thought, but with that steely-eyed determination, she could go far; it was a pity that she seemed to have no wish to do so.

Twice a week, Jane went round to Miss Barker's house when school was finished for the day. It was like something out of *My Fair Lady*. The teacher showed her how to stand so that her head reached for the ceiling and her back was straight. She gave her elocution exercises to practise: *Mr Haystee the Bayker made maydes of honour and choc-o-layte éclairs*, and *Oh, oh, Antonio, over the fields you go-o-o*, opening her mouth and stretching the vowels into golden nuggets of self-improvement. She looked round Miss Barker's sitting room as she spoke, making a note of the photographs in silver frames, the complete absence of the fluffy toy dogs and shepherdesses holding out their skirts which Mum collected, the flowers in crystal vases, the single colour accent that a raw-silk cushion made against a neutrally upholstered sofa.

Miss Barker was obviously from an upper-middle-class background, and Jane didn't quite understand why she was wasting her time teaching in a comprehensive school, rather than one of the upmarket girls' schools. She understood that Miss Barker had taken her on as her personal project, and looked on her achievements with the pride she might have done had they been her own. And for the first time since her father died, Jane was conscious of something she had not even realized that she no longer had: concern, warmth, someone caring about her.

How nay-ce of you to let me come, she sang, checking her underarms in the bathroom mirror before she went out dancing on a Saturday night. *In Hhhertford, Hhhereford and Hhhampshire*, shaving her legs, wishing she looked even vaguely like Audrey Hepburn in the film. *Thah rayne in Spayne stays maynly on the play-ayne.* She couldn't speak like that at home, of course, her brother would have gone into jeering overdrive. Oh, la-di-da, he'd have said, pinching her arm in the soft place above the elbow where it hurt most, Little Miss High-and-Mighty are we? But she noticed immediately the difference in shops and on buses, when she used her new Miss-Barker-trained voice.

At school, she no longer bothered to turn up for irrelevancies such as RI or history. She worked hard at the vocational classes in secretarial studies, she continued at French, and, of course, English, more for the pleasure of hearing (and imitating quietly in her head) Miss Barker's voice than for any instruction she might receive. She would leave school at the end of the school year: she'd have several GCSEs, good grades, and she would start working immediately, in fact already had two carefully chosen jobs lined up, one as a part-time bookkeeper in a small factory making something or other out of plastic, the other part-time in Belinda's, a dress shop which would give her the chance of big discounts.

Eventually, the time came when she wanted to move on from both of these and get a proper job. She waited for the Sales and then, using her staff discount, bought a black suit, a really expensive one, designer label, which she'd seen featured in the fashion mags: short skirt, jacket flared just on the hip, narrow velvet lapels.

'You look a real treat in that,' Belinda said. 'Going for a full-time position, are you?'

'Yes.'

'Don't put on any weight. That suit is really gorgeous on you, though I say it as shouldn't.'

Jane wondered what she meant by that, why shouldn't she say such a thing, it was surely what the customers wanted to hear. And Belinda was right, she *did* look a treat, later, when she went to the interview, a plain white shell underneath, a string of pearls borrowed from Miss Barker, and a good handbag and shoes. 'Always buy the best shoes you can afford, ditto the bag,' she'd read in the fashion mags, and that's what she did.

Of course she'd got the job, no problem, not much of one, but the first step on the ladder, working in an office along with a lot of dreary old men, apart from Neville, the owner's son, fresh down from Edinburgh University, with whom she fell madly in love, though she didn't let on, having a pretty shrewd idea that if they started anything, it would mean absolutely nothing to him. Nonetheless, she let him take her out a few times, and she noted how he held his knife and fork (different from the way Mum did), how he ordered wine, how he spoke to the waiters (polite but not friendly). He had no idea of her background and she had no intention of taking him home to find out. The job lasted eighteen months, until she handed in her notice, moving on to a better-paid, more responsible position. She left the books impeccably kept, and the old boys threw a party for her, supermarket champagne, plastic glasses, olives and nuts, tiny little nibbles which they heated up in the microwave in the office kitchen. Neville even kissed her, but she could feel his heart wasn't in it, only the swelling in his trousers.

By now she had three designer suits, plus a wardrobe of good-quality separates, a shoe storage rack hanging on the back of her wardrobe door, holding six pairs of expensive shoes. Two years after she'd started working at Parties Unlimited they had a phone call from someone wanting them to organize a corporate 'do' for the parent company of the corporation he worked for, and the boss told her to handle it, she was experienced enough, she'd done brilliantly on the corporate tent at the race meeting.

'The Grand Central would be nice,' said the voice on the phone from London, adding that he wanted a three-course dinner for a hundred and fifty guests, gorgeous flowers, some kind of middle-of-the-road entertainment, no smutty jokes, no mother-in-law jokes either, not like that fat comedian on the telly, a band for dancing after dinner, but nothing too contemporary, the guests will be of a certain age, know what I mean, but the managing director wants it to be very high-class, very discreet, we want to impress our overseas customers.

'No problem.' She was already riffling through her book of contacts.

'Thank you, Janine. You have done a truly wonderful job for us.' It was the senior partner of the company which had thrown the party.

'I'm glad.'

'My customers have been so impressed, our managing director also.' Janine had met the MD at the party and taken an instant dislike to him, partly because he was a cocky little bantam in a shiny Italian silk suit and a tiepin that from a distance looked like a pair of women's legs in frilly panties and on closer inspection proved to be exactly that, partly because he had roving hands, but mostly because he reminded her of her brother.

The senior partner stepped closer and reached into his breast pocket. 'This is for you.' He handed her an envelope and winked at her. 'Don't tell your manager, OK?'

'It's all in the day's work for us to do the best we can,' she said. 'I can't possibly take it,' though she knew very well that she could – and with a little persuasion, probably would.

'Why not? It's not a bribe, it's not unethical; this is business, Janine, it's like in a restaurant: you do a good job of waiting on me, I give you a good tip. That's all this is: a tip.'

'Well, thank you, thank you very much indeed.'

'And of course we shall use your firm again.'

A week later, he had telephoned and asked for her. When she came on the line, he said, 'Will you have dinner with me tonight?'

She knew his voice at once, wondered if the 'good tip' had been nothing more than payment in advance for her favours. 'Well . . .'

'Of course you will. I'm staying at the Grand Central. I'll meet you in the Cliveden Bar at seven.'

Dressing for the evening, she analysed herself unemotionally, as she did everything: olive skin, black hair (thanks, Dad!), small boobs, thick black bush, her body, secretive and her own, not brilliant, not voluptuous, not designed to make men catch their breath, but OK. She wouldn't have time to go home and change, so in the lunch hour had gone along the High Street to Belinda's and chosen a glamorous silky top in silver and blue, very simple, with spaghetti straps, to go with her black suit. She stared down at the glass-fronted case of costume jewellery and sighed over a thick rope of tiny black, silver and blue beads. 'I love it but I really can't afford to buy anything more . . .'

Belinda shrugged. 'Look, we know you, we can trust you. Why don't you borrow it for tonight?'

'Really? Oh, you are so sweet . . .' It was a Miss Barker phrase, rather than a Janine phrase: it didn't sound quite right to her, and from the quizzical look she was giving her, she could see that Belinda also thought it a bit odd, coming out of her mouth.

At the hotel, she found him at a table in a corner of the bar, wearing a dark suit, a grey silk tie with a diamond pin, a white shirt that gleamed in the dim light of the bar. 'You look nice,' he said when she arrived. 'I like a woman with style, and you've got that in spades.'

'Thank you.' Raising her glass of white wine, she smiled, felt herself trembling on the brink of something, a flare of possibility. Why had he invited her here tonight? She half-expected that he would want her to go to his room after dinner, and had not yet decided whether she would or not. He was much older than she was, more than old enough to be her father, but he kept himself trim, he was good-looking and assured, he dressed well, he had a kind face. She hesitated not because she was a prude, or waiting for true love: she merely wanted to plan her strategy and wasn't sure if going upstairs with him was a step forward or not. Especially on their first . . . well, date, if that was what this was. She wasn't a virgin: her brother had seen to that, the bastard (though when she'd told Mum about him coming into her room at night and the things he did to her there, Mum had told her not to tell such filthy lies and slapped her hard across the face), not to mention Mr Retton, though she'd never let *him* do more than fool around, and of course there'd been other men since then.

They exchanged a few personal details about themselves over dinner. He told her about his companies (*'not* my *companies exactly, since the managing director and his wife own them all, lock, stock and barrel'*) along with their overseas links, import-export, he told her, which always seemed to her to say nothing and everything. She didn't ask what he exported or imported, though if it had been anything illegal he wouldn't have told her anyway. Looking at him over the small arrangement of yellow flowers in the centre of the table, she could imagine him – and the major shareholder, the bantam with his short little bantam legs and vulgar tiepin (she could just imagine Miss Barker's expression if she saw it!) – deeply mired in something criminal: drugs or girls or guns, or all three, or something else, something quite possibly worse. He had that look about him, as though he worked above or around the law; she found that quite exciting.

He came up from London about once a month, to oversee the importing – or possibly the exporting – side of his business. She'd looked the company up, but discovered nothing further; when she drove across town to the site of the company's local offices, there was simply a name on the gate: Import, and underneath, Export Freight. It meant nothing to her and she knew instinctively it would be hugely impolitic to ask.

It wasn't until the fourth time they went out for dinner that he suggested going to his hotel room.

'I shall be honest with you, Janine.' He picked up her hand, which lay on the table, and smoothed his thumb across her knuckles. 'I am a married man, I have grown-up children, I do not plan to divorce my wife, although we have nothing in common and though there is no more than affection between us – which is all there ever was – it is not the custom where I come from to throw off the old wife and look for a new one, it is dishonourable to both the husband and to the wife. As for you, I admire you, as you know, I find you an excellent companion, someone I am proud to be seen with, and I am also very fond of you. But that is as far as it can go. So if you do not wish to sleep with me – for that, of course, is what I am about to propose – I would quite understand, and there would be no hard feelings between us, we would remain friends and I would continue to ask you to come out to dinner with me, when I am up here.'

Janine smiled down at the tablecloth. It was not a question of wishing to sleep with him, the sexual spark between them had grown and flared over the past few weeks and was now – at least in her case – a constantly glowing ember. She liked the way he had been honest with her, and at the same time, felt a deep relief. She liked him – maybe even loved him, in a way – but marriage? She thought not: he was too exotic, too obviously foreign. She had never set her sights on the unattainable, merely on the achievable: she had wanted – still did – a nice man whom she could love unreservedly, who would make few demands, who would hold her hand when they went out together, who, above all, thought she was wonderful ('*a pearl of great price*' like it said in the Bible), a couple of kids, one of each. When she examined this wish list, it seemed a modest one, not a lot to ask for, and she lived in hope that this hand-holding man would come along one day in the not too distant future. Meanwhile, sex with a man like her handsome dinner partner had an orchidaceous allure.

She raised her eyes to meet his gentle brown ones. 'I understand completely,' she said. 'And if you were to invite up to your room for a . . . for a nightcap, I would be happy to accept.'

And that was how it had been between them ever since. That was nearly six years ago, and since then, she had moved on, leaving Parties Unlimited and, with the help of her lover, setting up TaylorMade Travel (Taylor being the useful surname she had chosen when she changed her name to Janine, hoping that Dad, wherever he was, wouldn't mind, he being so proud of his foreign heritage) which, judging by its success, seemed to be filling an unrealized desire on the part of the inhabitants of the town. At the time, there'd been a low percentage of unemployment, money wasn't too tight and there was a real craving for locations that were out of the ordinary, none of your Benidorms and Ibizas for the good citizens of the area, thank you very much. An added bonus, as far as Janine was concerned, was that twice a year she was able, for tax purposes, to write off a foreign holiday, staying in good hotels, as research for the business.

She loved those journeys abroad, her smart luggage, her good clothes, dining alone at the best restaurants which she would later recommend to her clientele, even, occasionally, though not too often, allowing herself to be discreetly picked up by some nice-looking older man, almost a clone of her lover, and enjoying a night or two of unbridled and uncommitted sex, though she'd give all that up at the drop of a Gucci bag if she could only find a man worth giving it up for.

Magnus

Five

Arrangements had already been set in train by the time Magnus came through passport control at Quito airport. Dr Eduardo Gonzalez was small and round, what was left of his dark hair slicked back across a tanned skull. He carried roses, four of them, which he thrust at Magnus, bowing his head for a moment to indicate his distress at being the bearer of such sorrowful news.

One rose for each of the deceased, Magnus realized. At least there weren't five, which meant that Kate was still hanging on. 'Can you tell me more about what happened?' he said, as Gonzalez, hurling insults at everyone who came within a ten-yard radius of his Mercedes, drove recklessly through the downtown traffic towards the familiarity of Professor Lennox's apartment.

'Very little is known. The villagers do not speak Spanish, only a few words.' Gonzalez leaned out of his window and stared backwards at the car behind them for far longer than Magnus felt was anywhere near safe, before flipping the finger and shouting words about the following driver's virility and what he'd like to do to it, which had Magnus surreptitiously curling his own hand protectively over the crotch of his chinos. 'As far as we have been able to discover, there was a tree down across the road, or perhaps it was a landslide, this is not entirely clear.'

'Why not?' Magnus tried to overcome the wooziness of jet lag and think more clearly. 'There's quite a difference between the two.'

'This is very true. *Cabron!*' yelled Gonzalez, as a small green car on the other side of the road and going in the opposite direction swerved slightly towards him.

'But surely you must know whether . . .' Magnus gave up. 'And the car went off the road?'

'Correct. Your father tried to avoid the obstacle, whichever it was, landslide – there are many landslides in the hills, Dottore Lennox – *hijo calvo de una perra!*' screamed Gonzalez at a man in a battered

red saloon, which Magnus thought was adding insult to injury. 'Because it is very wet and damp with the mist, so causing landslide or fallen tree, and unfortunately his vehicle fell over the edge of the ravine and down into the undergrowth. With, as you know, this most unfortunate and tragic loss of life. The roads are primitive up in the hills, you realize. Very steep, many, many bends. As far as we can understand it, the Professore was driving too fast, came to a sharp bend in the road and could not keep control.'

'But didn't you say he swerved to avoid a tree? Or a landslide?'

'Whichever it was, the car went down the hillside, and . . . and then caught fire.'

'I don't want to think about it,' Magnus said harshly. Burned alive. God, what a horrible way to die. He found himself praying that they had at least been unconscious by the time the car finally came to rest and before it burst into flame. 'And who is – was – Señora Bailey?'

'*Puta!*'

A prostitute? 'Surely not,' he said.

Gonzalez finished glaring at the woman driver who'd stopped at the red traffic light in front of him. 'Señora Bailey was your father's summer assistant.'

'Where was she from? Did you meet her?'

'I saw only her dead body. I have been told by your father's colleagues that she had come out from England, perhaps on a grant or bursary, to work on a special project with him, I'm not quite sure of the details.'

'So she was a student, was she?'

'Not unless she was what we call here a mature student. In her case, a very mature one.' Gonzalez chortled in an unbecoming way, while Magnus briefly considered taking up the feminist cudgels.

'Did she have a family?' he asked instead.

'We believe she had a child, or maybe children, but they were older, they had . . . flown from the nest, I think you say.'

Magnus had a brief vision of two, possibly three, nestlings, perched on the edge of some ramshackle collection of leaves and twigs, staring doubtfully down at the ground far below and wondering if they really had enough flying lessons under their belts to avoid dashing themselves to pieces, while behind them their parents, sick to death of foraging for worms and then shoving them down the throats of their offspring, twittered encouragement.

'So what has happened to her . . . um . . . remains?'

'Her husband had them flown back to England. The ashes. She was cremated . . . what was left, that is.'

Oh God. Magnus was finding this all too painfully graphic. He felt as though he were on the verge of vomiting, and wondered if he should have had so many miniature whiskys on the flight. On the way over, it had seemed the easiest and quickest route to temporarily putting the events in Quito out of his mind. Here in the downtown traffic, it looked a much less sensible solution to his problems. He hated to think what hideous invective Gonzalez would come up with, let alone what violent reaction he might have, were Magnus to throw up inside the Mercedes. On the other hand, persuading him to move over to the inside lane so Magnus could open the door and use the gutter seemed a hopeless proposition.

He listened dully as Gonzalez said, 'With regard to the funeral service for your parents and little sister, I have notified as many people as I could. And the university will of course let his colleagues know. The department is to have a small gathering afterwards, which is customary, I believe.'

'Is it?'

'So I understand. It will be closed coffins, obviously, and cremation – your father always said he wished to be cremated, if and when he died.'

'Did he?' Magnus hadn't known that. Horribly, it occurred to him that the cremation could be said to have already taken place: he swallowed hard and gripped the sides of the passenger seat.

'I have presumed that the same would be true for his wife and the young daughter.'

'I'm still not sure exactly what . . .' Magnus gulped. 'I mean, apart from this landslide or fallen tree . . .' Or perhaps it was both – that would make a lot more sense, the landslide down the side of the hill, bringing with it trees and boulders which blocked the road. 'I can't believe my father was driving so fast that he had to swerve to avoid a fallen tree. He was a very careful driver.'

'Alas, unless your sister remembers, nobody will ever be quite certain how the accident happened. And she is very . . . how do you say it?' Gonzalez rocked his hand back and forth to indicate that Kate's condition could go one way or another. 'The villagers who managed to rescue her from the . . . from what was left of the car seemed to know nothing. I believe one of the village boys said something about hearing gunshots, but I imagine that was either a mistranslation or a vivid imagination. Boys will be boys, will they not?' Perilously, Gonzalez took both hands off the steering wheel and aimed them like a pair of Colt.45s at the car in front of them. 'Pah!' he said. 'Pah! Pah!' Carefully he blew non-existent smoke from his imaginary pistols. 'Too much cowboy movies.'

Magnus looked away from the hurtling traffic all around them. 'Has this boy said anything else?'

'When the police arrived at the family house, the boy was no longer there. Sent away to an aunt in the city. The Indians don't like to be mixed up with the police, I'm sure you understand.'

Magnus did not. He'd been brought up to believe that policemen were the good guys, avuncular kindly people, upon whom you could rely to look after you if you were in trouble, who would automatically take your side and help you.

Without any signal that Magnus could see, Gonzalez turned suddenly across what seemed like five rows of honking, snarling traffic into the wide forecourt of the apartment block where Professor James Lennox and his second family had lived for many years. Small palm trees in a large concrete planter rattled in the breeze, a fountain thrust water into the air, and brightly coloured flowers – he recognized bougainvillea and pelargonium, possibly hibiscus – dripped from pots on the balconies. Coming to a gut-wrenching stop in a parking place, Gonzalez smiled sadly at Magnus. 'I'm so very sorry, Señor Lennox. This is a terrible tragedy. We shall try to make everything as easy for you as possible.'

'You're very kind.'

'I will come back for you in two hours and take you to visit your sister.'

The apartment was so exactly the same as it had always been on his numerous holiday visits that Magnus sank to the carpet, bowed down by the weight of the memories which crowded round him. He looked around him at the familiar marble-floored salon, the single sofa, eight feet long, which overlooked a view of snow-capped mountains and low-hanging clouds, the music centre, the baby grand which Luisa played in the evening, the huge bookcase crammed with books, the birdcage shaped like a maharajah's palace where Brixton, Annie's pet cockatiel, a ruggedly handsome bird, used to swing and squawk when he wasn't flying round the apartment biting things to shreds with his powerful beak (where was he, by the way? He must remember to ask Gonzalez). He buried his head in his hands. It was impossible to believe that all three of them were dead, and that Kate was only hanging on by a thread. ('*Badly burned* . . .' Would she look like a monster, her features melted down into her neck, years of skin-grafts ahead, denied all the things a pretty nineteen-year-old had a right to expect, so hideous that no man could possibly wish to go out with her, let alone marry her? He determined then and there to do the right thing: he would care for her as long as she needed him, and if he found a woman to love who wasn't prepared to take on his hideously scarred sister as well as himself, well, so be it . . .)

Luisa had taken *them* both on. He had at first been inclined to resent this new exotic woman who had been thrust into his life to take the place of his dead mother, the funeral baked meats coldly furnishing forth the marriage table, he'd thought, in the cynical way of a clever adolescent studying *Hamlet* for GCSE, until good sense prevailed and he reminded himself that his father had every right to happiness, and indeed Luisa had brought just that into all their lives. To think of her now dead, her lustrous dark hair, her huge black eyes, her loving expression when she looked at her husband or her children, Kate and Magnus as much as Annie . . . He thumbed away more tears.

He showered in the bathroom full of old-fashioned appliances – the basin big enough to bath in, the bath big enough to hold a dinner party in, the shower head the size of a satellite dish – and changed into clothes more suited to the heat, choosing them from his father's closets which contained numerous pale jackets, lightweight linen suits, short-sleeved shirts, chinos, feeling a kinship for the father he had never really – because of the vagaries of life rather than desire on the part of either of them – had a chance to know and now never would. Tears welled in his eyes as he contemplated himself in the long free-standing mirror in the darkened bedroom. He could easily have passed for his father and the sight brought back to him more than anything else just how much he had lost and how much, if Kate didn't survive, there still was to lose.

When a white-cowled nun showed him into Kate's private room, Magnus had been surprised (and vastly relieved) to see that her face on the pillow looked more or less as it always had. True there were some abrasions on her temple and her head had been partly shaved so that stitches could be inserted. One side of her face was painted purple (mercurochrome?) and both her eyes were puffy and black, providing a stark contrast to the blindingly white hospital linen. Her arms lying on the white coverlet were thickly wrapped in white bandages. Colour came from the garish red, blue and gold paintings which hung here and there along the corridors and above the beds: Christ with His head on one side, displaying His open chest and bleeding heart; the Virgin Mary with her eyes raised to heaven as though listening for the hundredth time to some tedious joke being recounted by her Son; Saint Michael the Archangel, patron saint of the sick, looking beefy and macho, more athlete than saint, perhaps intended to encourage the patients towards good health.

There was a pit of dread in Magnus's stomach as he looked down at Kate. If she died . . . if she was dying . . .

Years ago, his closest friend through school and university had contracted an aggressive cancer. John had fought hard, had gone the whole alternative medicine route, coffee enemas, acupuncture, raw carrot juice, positive thinking, but in the end, it hadn't delayed the inevitable. Magnus had gone many times to sit beside him during the final stages, watching the flesh disappear from John's face, the bones of nose and cheekbone, the brow, begin to jut, and his eyes grow ever more opaque. *Don't die on my watch*, he used to think, each time he took his seat at the bedside. *Please, John, I don't want to see you dead, I don't want to realize that the days we enjoyed together as boys, as students, are finally over, the plans you had for your marvellous future are gone for ever.* Watching the dying man, holding his hand, a gesture he would never have contemplated had there been anything of their shared normal lives left, he had marvelled at the sense that all there had ever been of John now lay crammed inside the walls of his skull, all the feelings and experiences, the joy and the disappointments, the times he had sniffed a flower or downed a pint, the taste of food on his tongue, the feel of wind against his cheek, all fined down to this body, still physically alive but in most real meanings of the word, already absent.

Was that going to happen with Katie? With the others gone, it rendered her stillness even more poignant. He sank down on to the chair beside her bed, trying to hold back tears ('*Big boys don't cry,*' his father used to say, and he'd always wanted to tell him he was wrong and that big boys did indeed sometimes cry). With Kate's hand in his, he sat in silence for many minutes, until she began to stir.

'Kate,' he whispered. 'Are you awake?'

'Magnus . . .' Kate was peering at him through the slits of her eyes.

'Kate, oh Kate.'

'Are you real?'

'Yes.' Lightly he laid his hand on one of her bandaged arms. 'Of course I am.'

'Dad . . . Annie . . .'

Magnus couldn't speak. He wasn't sure if she was supposed to know that she was the only one who had survived the car crash, that the rest were dead.

'They're dead, aren't they?'

He nodded, not sure if she could see him or not.

'I saw . . . fire. Someone was . . . screaming.'

Magnus gulped. Oh Christ . . . 'Don't think about it, Katie.'

'I can't remember much. Luisa, some men . . . I just can't remember . . .' Kate turned her head and tears welled from her swollen eyes. She breathed through her mouth, making small snoring sounds, and Magnus realized she had fallen back to sleep.

Señor Gonzalez appeared after a while, and after another nightmare journey of dangerous driving and foul-mouthed imprecation, dropped him back at his father's flat in the middle of the city, saying that he would return later and take him home for dinner with his wife and children.

'So,' Gonzalez said the next day, looking up from the papers in front of him. 'I think that is all pretty clear, is it not?'

'Thank you,' Magnus said. There had been a lot of legalistic jargon, but in view of the deaths of Luisa and Annie, the bottom line was that his father's surprisingly large estate would be divided between himself and Kate. He felt utterly helpless. He wanted to tell Gonzalez that he didn't want the money, he wanted his father back. He wanted to explain that he had in fact barely known his father, that he had been sent to boarding school at the age of ten, that until he left school, he had spent his summers in Quito – or at the research institute on Santa Cruz, where both his father and Luisa had worked when they were not at the university – but had always hoped there would be a time when he and his father would become friends, rather than maintaining the distant relationship that so much time spent apart had engendered. And now he had been cheated of the opportunity and it could never happen. In the absence of anyone else, he longed to throw himself on Señor Gonzalez's navy-blue double-breasted bosom and howl aloud his sense of loss and isolation.

Instead, he had listened in silence to the terms of his father's Will, not really concentrating, too distressed to take much in. It was not until later that he would really absorb the facts and find his brain already busy wondering how best to deal with the money, not just for himself but for his sister too. As he flew home with Kate at his side, purple-cheeked and shaven-browed, he had a Pre-Raphaelite image of himself sitting on the sofa at home with his sister in some sort of flowing white gown seated upon a footstool at his feet, her thick red hair spread across his knee (never mind that she was a blonde) while he gently but firmly advised her as to stocks and shares and prudent investments – though he dimly recognized that if this unlikely scenario was to have any chance of success, not only would he have to do some intensive and uncongenial homework in order to be in a position to advise anyone on such arcane matters but he would also have to purchase a footstool. As for Kate agreeing to sit at his feet . . . He sighed.

'Is there anything else, Dottore?'

Magnus fidgeted in his chair. 'I know it sounds a little ridiculous, in the light of the accident and so on, but do you know what happened to Anna-Margarita's – my little sister's – cockatiel? He was called Brixton—'

'A bird?'

'That's right.'

Gonzalez raised groomed eyebrows which perfectly indicated that anyone who could wonder about a caged bird at this time of grief and horror must be singularly lacking in all human emotion. Had he pursued it, Magnus would have pointed out that the brain tends to dissociate from reality when faced with grief and horror, not that the whereabouts of a cockatiel could be classed as either, but the lawyer merely nodded. 'We can ask the landlord,' he said after a pause during which Magnus tried not to feel unfeeling. 'There was also a cat, I believe.'

'Was there?'

'Cuddles?'

For a wild, and mercifully brief, moment, Magnus thought that Gonzalez was making some kind of homoerotic move on him – it was the interrogative lift at the end of the word which had caused the confusion – until he realized that this must be the name of the cat, a sobriquet almost certainly bestowed upon the unknown animal by Annie. His eyes watered again as he pictured her hugging a tiny kitten to her chest, nuzzling her chin on its soft head, pulling a length of string along the floor for it to dart after . . .

'The landlord will have removed these animals and taken them to a shelter of some kind, of this I am positive,' Gonzalez assured him.

'Good, good . . .' Was a cockatiel an animal, Magnus wondered, or, for that matter, were birds animals? Of the animal kingdom, definitely, but surely separate and distinct. 'What about my step-mother's family?'

'I have of course contacted them.'

'She was Catholic, I believe, but in any case, presumably they will wish to make their own funeral arrangements.'

Gonzalez smiled briefly. 'It is already arranged.'

'This is my colleague, Señor Carlos de Leon,' Gonzalez said, two days later. He indicated a sallow man in his late thirties, who sat sideways on to his desk, holding a briefcase on his knee. Magnus nodded.

'Señor Carlos is the landlord of the flat where your parents lived,' Gonzalez said, his eyes skittering about the room.

'I see.' There was a fan high up on one wall, which turned at a brisk rate, sending gusts of stifling air across Magnus's face and lifting his hair every few seconds.

'Papers,' Señor Carlos said. He patted the leather envelope he held. 'There are papers to sign. The rent is paid up until the end of next month, so if everything is in order, I shall reimburse this money to the estate of your late father. Meanwhile, I shall come to the apartment to check on the extent of the damage.' He spoke as if no-one was going to put anything over on him, he was fully cognisant of the ways of tenants, particularly English ones, as well as the fact that Professor James Lennox was in the habit of taking a sledgehammer to the walls, or carving four-letter words into the kitchen counters, though Magnus himself had seen nothing untoward in the flat beyond some worn-looking paint, scratches here and there on the woodwork, or cracked tiles in one of the bathrooms, which had probably been there since the apartment block was built.

'That's fine,' said Magnus. 'When would you like to come?'

'You do not have to be present, Señor Lennox. I can go in and out quite quickly. I imagine you are very occupied so there is no need for you to disturb your present arrangements.'

'I have none,' Magnus said. 'Besides, I think I should be there, don't you? In case anything goes missing – not,' he added hastily, in case the other man took offence, 'that I imagine it would, but I know my father would prefer me to be there.' Seeing the look of annoyance on Señor Carlos's face, he added feebly, 'My father's papers . . . journals . . .' Nervously he smoothed down his fan-ruffled hair.

'Very well, I shall be there at three o'clock this afternoon, if that is satisfactory.'

'Fine.'

'Though I repeat that it is not necessary for you to attend.'

The man's obvious desire for Magnus not to be present when he came to inspect the flat made Magnus all the more determined to be there. Señor Carlos might be a colleague of Señor Gonzalez (was he a lawyer? Or did the law firm have associated companies of estate agents and the like?) but that did not make him automatically above suspicion. He needed to make absolutely sure that nothing went missing – Luisa's jewellery, his father's computer, paintings or artefacts that might have some worth – though the words 'stable doors' and 'bolted' went through his mind. Señor Carlos had already had several days to search the apartment for anything he might want. If Magnus were to mention something was missing, he had only to shrug, talk about the crime rate, the ease with which burglars got in and out, and there would be nothing Magnus could do.

He addressed Gonzalez. 'I shall need the name of a firm of shippers,' he said, 'to get the important stuff back to England. And also the local equivalent of Oxfam, or the Red Cross – some charity that could make use of items which are no longer . . . viable.' It seemed an odd word but he couldn't think of any better way to put it. Annie's soft toys, for instance – her bedroom was full of them. She'd been so cute: big dark eyes like her mother's, glossy black hair, skin as smooth as coffee ice-cream. He touched a finger to his wet cheek; it was almost impossible to take in the fact that she was no longer around.

Kate

Six

Four more shifts and then she was out of here. Kate transferred her weight from one tired foot to the other, kept an eye on the punters, chatted with the people standing at the bar. Four more shifts – two double shifts, to be precise – and then she was taking a few days off before starting at TaylorMade Travel, though increasingly she wondered why she'd taken the job. It was hardly a career, and had few prospects, apart from the prospect of cheapish travel.

The door of the wine bar was pushed open and in strutted Stefan Michaels, with two men in tow, one about the same age as he was, a brother, by the look of him, the other old enough to be their father. Which he probably was, Kate thought, since there was a definite family likeness. The father was tall, distinguished, olive-skinned, his grey hair styled *en brosse.* There was something teasingly familiar about him. The brother looked much the same, only younger, while Stefan was of a smaller build and, despite a certain gym-primed muscularity, not as . . . *masculine* was the only word she could come up with, less a man who spent Saturday afternoons playing football and more the sort who enjoyed cataloguing his string collection.

She turned away and busied herself with clean glasses. Only four more shifts to go – and tonight she'd get Rachel to serve their table if they wanted anything more than a drink.

'Hello, there!' Stefan's voice was warm, genial, and she turned with a little sinking of the heart. At the sight of his complacent expression, she felt again a swell of aversion. The father – if that's what he was – had gone to find a table, and since Rachel was busy further down the bar, she had no choice but to take his order herself.

'Good evening,' she said, not meeting his eyes. 'What'll it be?'

'Don't you remember, Kate?' He spoke in a possessive sort of way, as though he and Kate were not only old friends, but intimate ones, which made her want to push her face into his and demand that he stop using her name in that overfamiliar way, leave her the hell alone.

'Remember what?'

'My usual order.'

'I'm afraid not. Far too many people come through here for me to keep tabs on everyone's "usual".'

The man beside Stefan nudged him, snickering slightly.

'We'll have something different tonight: a bottle of your best champagne.' Stefan sounded annoyed. 'My brother here is celebrating some good fortune, and we must drink to his health.'

'Congratulations.' Kate handed him a paddle with the number eighteen on it. 'Sit down and someone will bring your champagne over to your table.'

'Not someone,' Stefan said. He leaned across the polished mahogany of the bar. 'You.' He'd swapped his gold ear-stud for a diamond one, and was wearing two gold chains around his neck. There was a ring on the fourth finger of his right hand, big and ornate, like an American class ring.

Dressed for success, Kate thought. What a little ponce. 'I don't serve Table Eighteen, I'm afraid.'

'Then give us another table, one which you do serve.'

Kate could see Fredo watching the exchange. He raised his eyebrows at her, asking if she needed help, and she shook her head, indicating that she could handle it. She reached under the bar counter and brought out another paddle, number six. 'I'll be right over,' she said reluctantly.

She took her time finding a silver bucket, ice, flutes. She placed them on a tray and took the bottle over to Table Six, where she deftly removed the cork from the bottle and poured three glasses. 'There you are,' she said and turned.

Stefan seized her arm. 'You must bring another glass, Kate, and join in our toast.'

Must? 'I don't like champagne,' she said.

'Oh, but we would really appreciate it if you would.' It was the father. He smiled at Kate, his expression courteous. 'Stefano has told us so much about you.'

Stefano, eh? She raised her eyebrows. 'That's surprising, since he doesn't know anything about me.' She avoided looking at Stefan.

'I believe he knows enough.' The father had a pleasant voice and seemed altogether different from his son. 'Please join us in a toast. Tonight of all nights.'

(‘*Be sweet, Kate . . .*’) ‘Some good fortune, I understand.’

‘Indeed so. My clever son Silvio has finally pulled off a deal he’s been working on for some weeks.’ The man put an arm round the other man. ‘We are pleased for him.’

‘I see. Well, congratulations, and thank you for the offer, but unfortunately, we’re not allowed to drink while we’re on duty.’ Smiling, Kate looked at Stefan. ‘And you’re the not-so-clever son, are you?’ It was no more than a teasing remark, and one she wished un-said immediately, alarmed by the way his face darkened, especially when his father and brother broke into appreciative laughter.

‘Is that what you think of me?’ he demanded.

Only two more double shifts . . . ‘Actually, I don’t think of you at all,’ she said, with a smile. ‘Why should I?’ If that didn’t give him the message that she was, like, sooo uninterested . . . He moved his arm and she tensed, almost expecting him to strike her.

The father looked from one to the other with an amused smile. ‘That is a shame, Kate,’ he said. ‘I understood from my . . . um . . . not-so-clever son that you and he—’

‘Look, it was just a light-hearted comment,’ Kate said. ‘For all I know, your son could be a . . . a brain surgeon or something.’

‘Brain surgeon, that’s a good one!’ Father and brother laughed easily at the thought. ‘I assure you he is not,’ the brother – Silvio – said. ‘But that’s not the point. I believe he was going to ask if you would have dinner with him, one of these evenings.’

Kate stared at him. How in the world had this situation escalated to the point that some semi-stranger like this Stefan felt he had a right to discuss asking her out for dinner with his bloody family? What had he been saying about her, what had he implied? And how should she handle it? With humour, she decided. Treating it as a joke was the best approach. She lifted the champagne bottle and refilled their glasses. ‘Oh,’ she said, cucumber-cool, ‘I’m afraid I’ll be washing my hair.’

‘When?’

‘Whenever. Besides, you couldn’t afford me!’

The father and Silvio laughed again, while Stefan half-rose. His expression was grim. ‘I am not poor,’ he said quietly. ‘I offer to take you to the most expensive restaurant in London. Or I fly you to Paris, to the Tour d’Argent. To New York, or Rome or—’

‘Steady,’ Kate said, holding up her hand to stop him. ‘It’s very kind of you and I'm very flattered, but I'm afraid I have to refuse. My boyfriend would be most annoyed if I started flying off to New York to have dinner with some strange man.'

'Boyfriend?' The father looked at his son. 'Stefano, I thought you said you and she were—'

'She doesn't have a boyfriend,' Stefan said.

How did he know that? Looking at his expression, Kate felt a frisson of something close to fear. Perhaps she'd taken the wrong tack, handled the situation in the worst possible way. Perhaps the family was Sicilian and she'd violated some code of honour which could only end in vendetta, generations of Stefan's family coming after generations of hers in order to avenge the insult she'd offered him.

'Anyway,' she said, anxious to get away from his oppressive presence but trying not to make it obvious, 'I'll be off to Paris myself, very shortly.'

'A holiday?' It was the elder brother, this time.

'That's right. I can't wait.'

'Where in Paris will you be staying?' asked Stefan.

If he thought she was about to tell him, he was even more arrogant than she had suspected. 'I haven't decided yet,' she said lightly. 'In fact, I may not even go to Paris. I'm just taking off, following the wind.'

'The wind?' asked the elder brother.

Kate looked over her shoulder at the bar. 'If there's nothing else you folks want, I'd better get back to work.' She whisked away before Stefan's detaining hand could grab her short black skirt.

Back at the counter, Fredo looked at her quizzically. A short-haired grey cat sat on his shoes and he bent to stroke it. 'Whassa goin' on?'

'That guy seems to think he owns me,' said Kate. 'That we have some kind of relationship. Which we most definitely don't. Can you imagine me getting up close and personal with him? I'd rather eat a box of hair.'

'He had the hots for one of the girls who was here before you,' Rachel said. She busily polished the copper counter with a clean tea towel. 'She gave him the brush-off, too. Poor kid.'

'Why "poor kid"?'

'She was killed in a hit-and-run accident.'

'How dreadful. What happened?'

'Hell of a thing. She'd gone down to visit her mother in some village in the country – can't remember the name, Besford, I think it was called, Hampshire . . .?' She paused interrogatively and Kate said she'd never heard of it. 'Anyway, she was walking home along one of those narrow country lanes, and as far as the police could make out, this car came too fast round the corner and knocked her down.' As she spoke, she dried glasses on a cloth then handed them to Kate for a final polish, adding that the awful thing was, she didn't die for several hours. 'If the bastard had picked her up and got her to a hospital, she'd probably have been OK.'

Kate shivered. 'What a horrible story.'

'Isn't it? She and I were good friends, actually. We were going to find a place together, only she . . . died.' Rachel's eyes watered.

'I'm sorry.' Kate tried not to think of the girl lying by the side of the road in the darkness, broken limbs, internal injuries, bleeding, feeling her life seeping away, unable to move, desperately hoping that someone would find her, save her.

'Lindsay, she was called, Lindsay Bennett. She was such a pretty girl, blonde like you . . .'

'And of course they never got anyone for it.'

'They so often don't, not with these hit-and-runs. I had a friend whose brother was killed the same way, years and years ago, in some remote Scottish village. Ninety per cent certain it was someone local, but they never found out who. The brother had three young children, too.'

'Let's hope whoever it was rots in hell.'

'Trouble is, some people genuinely don't know that they've hit someone. And if it was dark . . . no street lamps on those country lanes.' Rachel shrugged. 'What can I say?'

'Just as a matter of interest, has Thingy over there . . .' Kate slightly lifted her chin in the direction of Stefan and his family '. . . ever asked you about me? My boyfriends, for example, or where I live?' She suddenly realized why the father looked so familiar: like so many handsome older men with greying hair and a tan, he was a dead ringer for George Clooney.

'No. And if he did, I wouldn't tell him. You can't be too careful. After all, you never know who's a nutter, these days.'

'Well, he's pretty close, in my book. Don't take this the wrong way,

Fredo,' she smiled at the manager, 'but I can't wait to get away from here, from people like him.' She didn't add that something about Stefan set her teeth on edge, though she'd have been hard pressed to say why.

'Yeah, I agree wizz you.' Fredo bent, his hand undulating along the back of the grey cat. 'Look out, heeza comin' over here.'

'Do me a favour, Fredo. Send me back into the kitchens – I really don't want another encounter with him.'

'Ok-igh, shweetheart.'

She laughed. 'Don't call us, *shweet*heart, we'll call you.'

'Don't letta da bastards grin' you down.'

Two days later, Fredo put his thick arm round her shoulders and pressed a kiss to her cheek. 'We gonna miss you.'

'Me too. But you have to move on, don't you?'

'Have a wonderful time on holiday,' Rachel said. 'It won't be the same here without you.'

The kitchen staff chimed in their agreement. 'You always like a laugh,' someone said. 'It makes such a difference.'

'Brave of you,' said Tina, the other waitress. 'Taking off without an idea where you're going next.'

'I thought it was time for a complete break,' lied Kate, 'before I tied myself down to another job.' She wasn't going anywhere, as it happened, but had a gut feeling that it would be better not to let anyone at the wine bar know where she would shortly be working; that way, no-one could pass the details on to someone like Stefan, were he minded to enquire.

'More champers, anyone?' Fredo tilted the bottle over the half-dozen glasses in front of him. He cleared his throat. 'On behalf uffus all, I lika say dat we wishin' you well, Kate. Watch your back and doan forgetta come in and see us.' He held his cat close to his chest. 'And tell alla your friendsa come too.'

'I already did. Why else do you think you have so many customers? In fact, now I think about it, I ought to get a bonus.'

Fredo winked at her. 'Get outta here.' He patted her on the bum. 'Enjoy your new life.'

'I fully intend to.'

When Kate got home, Magnus was out. She had a long shower, washed the wine bar smells out of her hair for the last time, and curled up on the sofa in her cuddly blue dressing gown. With Andrei and Olga snuggled in close to her side and a glass of wine on the table beside her, she felt loosened, liberated. Free at last! She ought to have been out on the town, celebrating with her friends, but this was as good as she could imagine. Warmth, companionship, clean hair, wine. What more could she want? Well, a great deal more, when she thought about it. Like money, a career, a husband and children, her own place. A mother . . .

Magnus's drawing room was a double cube, with high ceilings and elaborate cornices which he'd spent a lot of time and money refurbishing, removing layer after layer of whitewash, restoring rotten wood, cleaning marble until the potential magnificence of the place had been restored. Firelight sent gleams of gold and blue sparking from his collection of Russian icons, with their sad solemn faces of virgins and saints. In pride of place, above the mantel, hung a rare painting of Grand Duchess Maria which he'd picked up in an antique shop in Scarborough. The mantel itself was covered with photographs of their parents and of Annie. More photographs hung on either side of the fireplace, modern ones of their Uncle Blair and his family, older faded ones of grandparents, rotund in belly-filled waistcoats and watch-chains, or wearing the wasp-waisted dresses and big hats of their time. Amazing, Kate often thought, that hips and bosom should have been so flaunted, when the prevailing moral attitudes were supposedly concerned with maintaining and extolling the virtue of the weaker sex. *When lovely woman stoops to folly* . . . She herself had stooped to folly, all right, by marrying Brad, and here she was, living on her brother's charity to prove it, since she had no home of her own any more . . . She shook away thoughts of the big flat in Battersea, overlooking the Gardens, which they had shopped for and decorated together, a partially successful effort – on her part at least – to block out memories of The Accident, sold now, of course, to pay off the debts Brad had left her with.

All round the room were reminders of their parents: masks, bright-painted trays, a deeply carved side table, primitive paintings. She remembered vivid holidays with them, out in Ecuador, shadows shifting on brown skin, brilliant birds screeching in unfamiliar creeper-laden trees, waterfalls tumbling from crags, green lizards skittering about the walls of her bedroom, the stately turtles. And Annie, her dark hair pushed back from her face with a black velvet band; Annie reading *Alice In Wonderland* and *Through the Looking-Glass*, trying to see if she too could climb through the mirror into an alternative world of talking rabbits and grand duchesses; Annie eating a mango with the juice running down her chin; Annie running in and out of rainbows from the sprinkler on the lawn. She'd been so full of life and now she was gone.

Kate brushed at her eyes. It was years ago. You couldn't go on mourning the loss of something that was irretrievable. You had to move on. *Had* to.

Outside the window, something in the small frost-bound front garden creaked and rattled. Probably nothing more sinister than the overgrown holly bush in one corner, a magnet for the local birds; even at this time of night, some canny thrush or sparrow was probably raiding the larder, picking at the berries without any competition. Getting up, she stared out of the window and saw mad old Mr Radsowicz over the way leaning from the top window of his house, banging on the gutter directly above his head with a broom handle. She looked at her watch: Magnus had left a note on the kitchen table saying he would be back around midnight and it was now eleven-thirty. Yawning, stretching, she noticed an airmail envelope lying on the rosewood drop-leaf table behind the sofa. The stamps were Ecuadorean and a letter lay half inside, half out, obviously removed, read and carelessly thrust back.

Intrigued, Kate reached for it. The letter was typewritten, on a flimsy sheet of airmail-thickness A4, with the name of a law firm in Quito printed across the top. Why was Magnus receiving letters from Ecuador? It must have something to do with the death of her parents, but that had been years ago.

Frowning, she started to read further. It was written in Spanish, but her grasp of the language was more than sufficient for her to understand the information contained. The writer said that though their enquiries continued, they were still no further forward in their search. In the light of this, did he still want them to carry on or did he think that perhaps after so much time had elapsed, the quest was no longer relevant? The firm would quite understand if Dottore Lennox felt this to be the case, but before he made a final decision, he might find the following of interest.

It had come to their attention that one or more interested parties were aware of the investigations being carried out on Dr

Lennox's behalf and, or so it appeared, were actively seeking to discourage further enquiries *by any means at their disposal* (the writer had twice underlined the last six words), as Dr Lennox had suspected. The writer would await further instruction from him, and hoped that meanwhile he would rest assured of their holding him in the highest esteem, etc, etc.

Kate refolded the sheet and pushed it back into its envelope. What the hell was all that about? She examined the postmark. Sent ten days earlier . . . the letter had probably only arrived in the last couple of days. She took it out again and reread it, then replaced it, still none the wiser. And she could hardly ask for further details from Magnus, without revealing that she'd shamelessly read his personal correspondence.

She heard his ancient car pull up outside on the street, the protesting shriek of his brakes, the double slam of the door on the driver's side which never caught the first time, then his footsteps on the tiled path to the front door.

'Hi,' she shouted as he came into the house. 'I'm in here.'

'Hello, Miss Footloose and Fancy Free.' He dropped another log on the fire. 'Gawd, it's cold out there.' He turned to the drinks cabinet. 'Armagnac? Or would you rather have a nice cup of Ovaltine?'

'Do I look that bad? I've already put the brandy out on a tray with some glasses. And some crisps.' Out of the corner of her eye, Kate could still see the red, white and blue of the airmail envelope.

'Oh . . .' She pretended to catch sight of it, picked it up, examined the stamps. 'Who's this from? It can't be Romanov research, surely?'

He reached over and took the letter from her. 'Funnily enough, that's exactly what it is. Some granddaughter of a former nursemaid to the Imperial family with a not-very-interesting story to tell; nothing which really illuminates my book. You'd be surprised how many connections to the Romanovs there are all over Latin America.'

'I'm sure I would.' She arched an eyebrow. 'You've told me countless times that the vast majority of the white Russians fled to Paris or London, or even the US, because they preferred not to be too far from the Russian world they knew. Not to mention the Orthodox Church.'

'That was the aristocracy, not the common people.' The look on

Magnus's face managed to combine astonishment and hurt, as though he could barely comprehend that she might doubt him.

And I'd be even more surprised if such a descendent of an Imperial nanny exists, Kate thought drily. He was so convincing that though she had read the letter for herself, she almost believed him. Magnus had always been good at lying, or, as he called it when caught out in a blatant untruth, fabricating.

'Oh,' she said. 'Interesting.' The common people, as he put it, were too poor to do anything much except hope to be able to feed their families for one more day. She wondered why he felt the need to lie about it – but then maybe he was telling the truth: maybe a firm of lawyers *was* in fact investigating the Russian nursemaid's granddaughter's bona fides for him. As an eminent historian, presumably every fact had to be checked and authenticated before it could be used. Particularly in the case of the Romanovs, still a subject of intense interest, even after so many years – and so many books on the subject. But in that case, why should some third party be prepared to stop at nothing to prevent any information getting out? Perhaps the nursemaid had managed to escape with some of the fabled Romanov jewels and her heirs didn't want to have to give them back. Even so, it seemed a little extreme . . .

Jefferson

Seven

'Your father's papers,' Romilly said.

'What about them?'

'I think you should come down here for the weekend; we could go through them together. I don't want to throw anything out without your say-so: some things relate to your mother, and even you.'

'This weekend suit you?'

'Perfect. The children will be home and they'd love to see you.'

'Right, it's a date.'

The following Friday, Jefferson drove down to the little village where his father and Romilly had lived since his parents split up. Dad's death, a few weeks ago, had left him temporarily bereft, until Romilly had made it clear that he was still part of the family, and that he was always welcome in their warm and inviting home. His two young half-siblings felt more like his nephew and niece, and that was how they treated him, as a benign uncle. On Saturday morning, he took them for a walk through the fields which lay behind the little half-timbered cottage where they lived, mud accumulating on their wellingtons until they could hardly lift their feet, and listened while they raged their grief about the loss of their father. He told them that though he wasn't and could never be any kind of a substitute, he would always be there if they needed him, whether for money (within reason, he'd added hastily), or advice, or just an adult male to talk to. Later, in the afternoon, while they were out either playing football (Monroe) or mooching round the town eyeing up the boys and giggling a lot (Madison), he sat at the kitchen table with Romilly, both of them nursing a mug of coffee, and listened while she wept a little at her newly widowed state, reminisced about his father and the good life they'd had together.

'Truman was such a terrific dad,' she said. 'So good with the children, so full of energy and ideas – I mean, still refereeing at the local rugby club at his age! They're young to lose a parent, but I think they're going to be very special people because of his influence.'

'You're pretty special yourself, Rom,' Jefferson said.

Tears tumbled slowly down her face. 'We always knew we might not have as long together as we'd like, him being quite a bit older than me, so we always made a real effort to relish every moment that we possibly could.'

'Everyone who knew you could see that.'

'He wasn't just a great dad, but a great person.' She dabbed at her eyes with a wet ball of Kleenex. 'So many people here will miss him. He always had a kind word, always ready to help someone in trouble, he'd go and sit with old ladies in hospital if they didn't have families nearby and take flowers from the garden, let people in trouble cry on his shoulder for hours on end; he was so patient, so kind.'

Jefferson reached for her hand. 'The best thing for me was the fact that you made him so happy, after . . . well, after everything.'

She didn't say much, just squeezed his fingers. They both knew what 'everything' meant; both of them wondered how a man like Truman Andrewes had ever found himself married to a woman like Jefferson's mother; it was the most bizarre of partnerships, like a Pekinese hitching up with an aardvark, an oyster getting involved with an avocado, though no more weird, Jefferson considered, than his mother's second marriage, an even more unlikely coupling.

'Anyway,' Romilly said, after a pause which possibly she spent considering the same thing, 'your father's papers . . . They were sent to me by one of his colleagues at the Research Institute, a Dr Jens Bork, I haven't gone through the ones I'm passing on to you, but I think *you* should; your father always had his doubts about your mother's death—'

'Doubts?'

'At the time, he felt that he hadn't been given all the facts, there were some anomalies, omissions. He'd liked to have talked to her husband – Gordon, isn't it? – about it, but he wasn't very interested, said it was bad enough that she was gone but to have to imagine that foul play was involved was really too much to cope with.'

'I can understand that; the whole thing was a horrible shock to us all.'

'Of course it was, not that Truman really envisaged "foul play", but since it was no longer his concern, he didn't feel entitled to push it any further, to question your – Gordon – and in the end it was just left hanging. And then there was this nasty hit-and-run accident in the village a few months back. He spent a lot of time with the family, and it must have reminded him about your mother's death, because he got the papers out again. If you'd be willing to look into it, it would be something you could do for him, though what you could find out after all this time I really don't know. If indeed there's anything to find.' She shook her head. 'She was the most irritating, selfish, self-obsessed woman you could meet, but no-one deserves to die like that.' She sighed. 'I don't think her husband knew what to do with himself with her gone.'

'Breathe a huge sigh of relief, I should think.'

'Now, now, Jeff. That's not at all kind.'

'Neither was she. Anyway, I can't imagine Gordon at a loose end. Or perhaps all Gordon's ends are loose!'

'The thing is, none of this would have come to your father's attention if her solicitor had sent the papers to the right address, but somehow they landed up here. I'm not entirely sure why Truman kept them.'

'I'll take them away and go through them,' Jefferson promised. 'See if I can find out what was worrying him about her death, see if there's anything that still needs to be done. It's the sort of thing I'm good at.'

'You're good at most things, Jeff.'

'Except rugby.'

'Your father didn't hold that against you. He was so proud of you, you know that, don't you?'

'Well . . .'

'He was. He used to say what a miracle it was that you'd turned out so well. And the one thing he wanted before he died – I'm sure he didn't say so to you, though – was to see you married . . . properly, I mean.' Her clear gaze met his and he could see the question in them.

He smiled. 'Sorry, Rom, but for the moment there isn't anyone. But . . . I promise that when there is, you'll be the first to know.'

Back home, he parked his car in his allotted space behind his building on the edge of the canal, warehouses converted five years ago, when the economy was booming and money was less tight. Back in his loft space, he poured himself a small whisky – single malt of course; he never touched the blended stuff – sat back in an armchair, stared up into the intricacies of the steel beams and struts of the ceiling, and, as men so often do, thought about his mother.

She was a woman he could scarcely imagine agreeing to call her only child Jefferson simply because his father had been called Truman, and his grandfather, Harrison. His darkest secret, one which he felt to be not only unbecoming, but also reprehensible, showing as it did his lack of filial decorum, was the fact that he had loved his quiet father but had actively disliked his mother. Since childhood he'd always felt awkward in her presence, aware when she turned her large grey eyes on him that she was looking at a job much less than well done. In a bid to rid herself of the shackles of motherhood, which impinged too far on her feminist right to her own life, it was his mother who, over the protests of both Jefferson and his father, had insisted that he be packed off to his cheerless prep school (*'It'll make a man of him'*). Later on, she had chosen the unheated public school where he learned almost nothing and, even in the height of summer, had suffered from chill-blains and the kind of hacking cough which in a Dickens novel might have been expected to result, after a few hundred pages of mind-numbing sentimentality, in the maudlin and long-drawn-out death of some poor etiolated child.

It was his mother, too, who espoused Causes which had no resonance for either Jefferson or for his father but which, for the sake of family harmony, they had no choice but to support. Indeed, eight-year-old Jefferson's poster of a whale spouting through a green ocean pursued by a trawlerful of fishermen of indeterminate nationalities brandishing nets and harpoons was reproduced on posters across most of the Western world. A few had even made their way, via backpackers and the like, on to walls in defiantly whale-hunting nations such as Japan, causing a furore which it took all the Foreign Office's skills to calm. Some of the Causes – American Imperialism, anti-vivisectionists, global warming, endangered species, homosexual marriages and the like – she was for, others against, though often it was impossible to work out which was which.

Unlike his father, a noted amateur rugby player, Jefferson had never been 'hearty', never 'good at games'. From the age of eleven, after stumbling over a cache of old romantic novels in his grandmother's house, he had for years entertained the hope that he might at least excel at gym. He'd envisaged himself in dick-defining tights and a splendid pair of crushed-leather boots, abseiling in through high Gothic windows to fight off the unwanted suitors of pining maidens, or serenading some gorgeous creature taking her ease in the moonlight on a balcony above his head, but both dreams had failed to materialize. Firstly, he proved to be physically incapable of getting over the vaulting horse in the school gymnasium; however hard he bounced on the springboard before making his leap, he invariably landed flat on his stomach, momentarily winding himself, and killing any dreams of abseiling, in or out. Secondly, he turned out to be tone-deaf, a fact he had not been aware of until a wincing music-master informed him, after an audition, that since he appeared to be unable to carry a tune, they would not be requiring his services in the school choir, which put paid to any serenading he might have indulged in.

At school, therefore, he had learned that youthful dreams rarely came true, and in fact sometimes wondered what he would have done, once the unwanted suitor had been sent packing, and the song had been sung. '*Heard melodies are sweet*,' the gorgeous creature might have said, were she of a literary bent, poking her head over the edge of the balcony and gazing down on him with a look very similar to the music master's, '*but those unheard are sweeter*' and, really, after a snub like that, there would have been very little choice left him but to slink off into the night and find some other occupation.

When he was sixteen, he fell in love with the daughter of a man who wrote crappy pseudo-American crime novels under the pen name Bret McDermot (or perhaps it was his real name), and as a sacred duty to Love, read the man's entire undistinguished oeuvre. He wasn't impressed with the literary standard, but conceived a secret ideal of himself as a crime-buster, saving the world from itself, putting wrongs right, keeping a brown-paper-bagged bottle of hooch (whatever that was) in the bottom drawer of his desk, wearing a belted raincoat, peppering his investigations with a fusillade of witty one-liners and basking in the absolute certainty that at the end of the day, he would have tied the case up and justice, however rough, would have been done.

At school, he was able to put his powers of deduction to the test when Mrs Buonfiglio, the school secretary, whose son attended Haddon Hall on a reduced scale of fees, was attacked one winter evening and robbed of her handbag and the cellphone she used to keep in touch with her son's whereabouts. 'It was one of the boys,' she said, weeping in front of the Headmaster, something she would never have dreamed of doing if she had not taken out a large sum of money during the lunch hour in order to buy herself a much-needed winter coat and pay for her son to go on the school's skiing trip to Austria under the leadership of the games master.

The Headmaster had been intending to tell her that perhaps it was time she moved on to a job better suited to her lack of office skills but sensed that this wasn't the right occasion, especially as it appeared that one of His Boys was responsible for the large bruise on the woman's face, and the ruined tights on her legs. 'Can you be sure?' he asked. He grimaced at Jefferson Andrewes, his Head Boy, who had been the one to discover the poor woman sobbing in a flower bed beside the school gates, and even now was patting her muddy hand.

'I know it was, I could feel his blazer, that braid round the edge?'

'But you couldn't say which one?'

'No, of course not. It was practically pitch black, and he was all wrapped up in a big scarf, plus one of those balalaika things, a whatd'youcall'em, like bank robbers wear.'

'Any idea,' Jefferson said diffidently, 'which scarf?'

'Which scarf? How could I tell?'

'I mean, was it a rugby scarf, or the new bug scarf, or the swimming scarf?' It was less a sartorial question than one of genuine curiosity: the school had an arcane system of differently striped scarves for boys who had achieved some kind of sporting or personal success or were in their first year or second years.

'Oh, I see what you mean . . . there isn't much light down by the gates but I believe, yes, thinking back, I'd say it was an athletics scarf, you know, with all those whatd'youcall'ems, round things . . .'

'Hoops,' Jefferson and the headmaster said simultaneously.

'Hoops?' It was clear that she regarded hoops as something her grandfather might have bowled along a cobble-stoned alley with a wooden stick.

'There are quite a few boys with the right to wear such a scarf, including your own son,' the headmaster said soothingly (or perhaps not). 'But I'm sure we can track the culprit down.'

Two days later, Jefferson knocked at the Headmaster's door. 'Sir, could I have a word?'

'Shouldn't you make an appointment with my secretary?'

'In this instance, sir, I'd rather not.'

'I see. You'd better come in.'

Jefferson coughed a little, hesitated. 'Sir, I know who attacked Mrs Buonfiglio.'

'How did you manage that?'

'I . . . I observed, sir.' Just as he had observed the chaplain's hand on the arm of one of the prettier choirboys, the bottle of something alcoholic (hooch?) hidden in Matron's linen cupboard, the chicken legs which Crutwell, brilliant Latin scholar, stole from the refectory table and secreted in various greasy pockets about his person.

'And what, Andrewes, did you observe?'

'Someone in the athletics squad who seemed to be spending a little more freely than usual. Someone walking round with a new mobile phone, sir. Someone wearing brand-new Nikes.'

'I'm supposed to know what those are, am I?'

'Running shoes, sir. Expensive ones. The . . . uh . . . perpetrator was also carrying a new Walkman, sir.'

'Which is?'

'A small pocket-sized device which plays music and so on.'

'Wonders will never cease, Andrewes.'

'Yes, sir. Or maybe no.'

'And who is this delinquent character?'

Jefferson came closer to the headmaster's desk, looked over his shoulder at the door behind him, bent closer and said, very softly, 'Buonfiglio, sir.'

'Good God! You mean to say this wretched lad assaulted and robbed his own mother?'

''Fraid so, sir.'

'And she isn't aware?'

'No, sir.'

'Let's keep it that way. What are we to do?'

'I've got the money back, sir.' Jefferson reached into the breast pocket of his blazer and pulled out a thick envelope. 'It's all there.'

'I'm not going to ask how you managed that, Andrews. I assume a certain amount of pressure was employed.'

'Sir . . .'

The Headmaster smiled. 'I'll see to it that Mrs Buonfiglio's money is returned. What about the skiing trip? In the light of your discoveries, it doesn't seem quite appropriate for him to come along.'

'Funnily enough, sir, only this morning Buonfiglio intimated to me that he'd decided he didn't really want to go, after all.'

'Well done, Andrewes. Discreet as well as clever, eh?'

'Sir.'

Discreet and clever or not, Jefferson poured the tiniest second nip into his glass and contemplated the cobwebs again. It was time to do some more observing, he decided, observing which could only be done at close quarters, which unfortunately were some distance away. But he had accrued some holiday leave, and he'd always believed, cliché though it might be, in striking while the iron was hot, though in this case, the iron was nearly ten years old, and unlikely to be still hot, or even lukewarm. Still, he owed it to his father to at least take a look.

Kate
Eight

Before she left that Friday morning Kate peered carefully from her bedroom window. Perhaps she was being paranoid, but it didn't hurt to take precautions, and if she'd caught sight of Stefan Michaels lurking in the vicinity, she'd have been down the stairs and out the front door so fast that he'd have no time even to blink before she'd slapped his stupid face, slammed her knee into his groin, torn his throat out.

But as it happened, she could see nothing that aroused her suspicions. No loiterers, no-one bending down to tie a shoelace or leaning unnaturally against a garden wall with an open newspaper. Only mad Mr Radsowicz across the way, banging on the gutter with a broom handle, shaking his fist at the startled morning sparrows who'd presumed to build their nests on his roof, though by now they were used to him and didn't bother to fly even temporarily away. Finally, she came out of the front door and walked rapidly to the bus stop, fists clenched, peering unobtrusively about in an attempt to check whether someone might be following her. As far as she could tell, no-one was. Nonetheless, the anger simmering at the base of her stomach was diluted by a sense that at last she was up and running, moving forward instead of marking time. Janine had told her a few days ago that her flatmate was moving out to live with her fiancé, and was Kate by any chance interested in taking her place. Kate was interested; Kate was *very* interested, though she asked for some time to consider the proposal, mainly because of Magnus and his possibly injured feelings.

When she got off the bus, she walked quickly in the wrong direction, took the first turning to the right, crossed the road, took another turn, this time to the left, then dodged back across the traffic and ran down a short alleyway until she reached the back of TaylorMade Travel's premises. If anyone was following her, they'd have had a hard time keeping up, let alone figuring out where she was headed.

When she pushed through the door Janine was already there, checking figures, running over arrangements on her computer.

'Everything OK?' Janine asked.

'Fine, thanks. At least, there's this guy . . .' Kate outlined her worry about Stefan and ended by saying, 'So, although I'd really like to move in with you, maybe we should delay it for a while. I don't want to be the cause of possible trouble. I mean, if the guy really is a stalker or something.'

'A friend of mine was stalked once,' Janine said. 'It was pretty terrifying while it lasted, and he eventually went to prison for it. Your guy doesn't seem to have done much at all, whereas this other one used to ring my friend all through the night, send thousands of emails, have flowers delivered, send letters and cards. It was only when he started breaking into her house that they could finally pin something on him. It's not much comfort, I suppose, but the police told her not to worry, since most of these obsessional guys are actually quite harmless.'

'But not all.'

'Right. But what you're describing doesn't sound anything like that.'

Kate shrugged. No-one else seemed to think that there was anything to be worried about. Maybe she was exaggerating. And to be fair to him – not that she wanted to be – she remembered that she had sort of implied that she'd let him know when she moved on. 'Well, if you're up for it, I'd love to take you up on the offer to share your flat.'

'That's great!' A customer came into the shop to enquire about travelling across the Australian desert by camel, and Janine lowered her voice. 'We'll talk about it later.'

At about three fifteen, Kate was thinking about slipping into the tiny kitchen at the back of the premises, in order to enjoy a ten-minute coffee break, when a man wandered in and took the vacant chair in front of her. He was maybe five years older than she was, wearing a three-piece suit under a broad-shouldered woollen topcoat, and carrying a briefcase of such soft leather that it looked like black butter. Banker, Kate surmised. Accountant. Insurance.

He stared at her for a moment, as though someone had whipped out a kipper and proceeded to belabour him with it, then smiled, showing white teeth. 'My name's Jefferson Andrewes, and I need to . . . um . . . go on holiday.'

'Then you've definitely come to the right place,' Kate said.

'Good. Now, a couple of my friends went on an amazing holiday organized by your company last year, and couldn't recommend you more highly. So . . . what can you do for me?'

'That depends on where you want to go, and whether you'd be travelling alone or with someone else, or children. We don't really cater for family holidays.'

'Oh heavens, no children. Just me.'

'Did you have anything specific in mind?' Kate asked. 'Any places you've always wanted to go? Any dreams you want to fulfil?'

It was as though, having delivered his introduction, Jefferson Andrewes had forgotten what he'd come in for. 'Dreams? Plenty of those . . . but whether they'd ever come true . . .' He tugged at the collar of his shirt, pulled down the points of his waistcoat. 'But we're not here to discuss the metaphysics of . . . um . . . the unconscious mind, are we?'

'South America? India? China?' prompted Kate. 'Iceland? Nepal? Australia?' She smiled at him. 'The world's a big place.'

He smiled right back. 'Tell you what, why don't you have dinner with me tonight, and we could discuss it further?'

Kate laughed. 'So that's what this is all about! That has to be the smoothest chat-up line I ever heard!' How different he was from the smirking little creep who'd asked her out the other day.

'Chat-up line?' His smooth brow wrinkled like a puzzled schoolboy's. 'It really wasn't meant to be. So what do you think?'

'What about?'

'Dinner with me tonight.'

'It's a bit unorthodox.' *In fact*, she thought, *it's bloody stupid going off with a total stranger.* On the other hand, Jefferson Andrewes breathed safety, reliability, responsibility. 'But as long as you see it as a strictly business appointment, I'll accept.'

'Excellent.' Andrewes leaned back in his chair.

'Where shall we meet, then?' Kate said.

'For this . . . um . . . business appointment? Let's say Benito's, at seven o'clock.'

'I'll meet you there.'

She watched him leave, despite the gum-chewing, ear-ringed, shaven-headed bloke who took his place, with a brochure for one of their more expensive holidays in his hand. Jefferson's broad shoulders only just got out through the door. He must be at least six three, and built like a rugby player. Tight-head prop, she thought, rather vaguely, wing-three-quarter, envisioning Andrewes on the rugby pitch, tackling a forward on the opposing side, strong as a train, body muscled under his clinging team jersey, mmm, yes, lovely, but somehow she couldn't really see it. She remembered those endless games of soccer (*'it's called football these days'*) which Brad used to watch on the TV every Saturday – and any other time there was a match on. The boredom of it, the incomprehensible stupidity of it, the moronic . . . but it was only a game (why did they call it 'the beautiful game'?) and not worth getting worked up about. She saw Andrewes cross the road and stand on the pavement opposite the agency, clamp his briefcase between his legs, fish a mobile from his pocket and press in a number. As he spoke into it – work colleague, girlfriend? – he nodded and smiled, rock-like among the afternoon crowd of shoppers, mums fetching children from school, besuited stragglers returning to offices after overlong lunches.

As she discussed the pros and cons of getting married in the Bahamas (*'my girlfriend's Mum's from there'*) with the gum-chewer, she couldn't help wondering what exactly she was doing, fantasizing about a complete stranger, when for all she knew, he had never played anything more strenuous than chess or bridge.

'Janine,' she said later, during a break in the stream of customers coming in to discuss their holiday plans. 'I said I'd have dinner tonight with that big guy who came in this afternoon – don't know if you noticed him?'

'You could hardly miss him.'

'He wants us to custom-make a holiday for him . . .'

'Go for it, girl.'

'I'd be glad to but he doesn't seem to have the slightest idea what he's looking for, though he must do, really, when you think about it. Hence the dinner. Is that OK?'

'What, to have dinner with him? Of course it is.'

'I just wondered if I was breaking some travel-agency code of ethics. Having inappropriate relations with a punter or something.'

'Sweetie, I've no idea how appropriate or not your relations with this guy are likely to be, but as far as I'm concerned, if it means another commission, you can do what you like. Is he nice?'

'I'd imagine he is, though there's something slightly unusual about him, as though what you see is definitely a lot less than you get.'

'Well, watch your back, as they say. And keep me informed, Fullerton.' Janine adopted a sergeant-major pose, and Kate came to attention, clicked her heels, saluted.

'Yes, *sah*.'

She called a taxi to pick her up at the back of the TaylorMade offices, giving her time to redo her face, brush her hair and change out of her working clothes (that awful turquoise cravat!) into something more suitable for dining at one of the best Italian restaurants in the town.

Andrewes was waiting for her at the bar, a glass of wine in front of him.

'You look lovely,' he said, eyeing her up and down. 'But since this is a business meeting, that probably counts as sexual harassment in the workplace.'

'I'll overlook it this time.'

Once they had been seated, Andrewes picked up the menu and scrutinized it. 'My friends tell me that the *osso buco* here is particularly good, and all the fish dishes.'

'You seem to rely an awful lot on other people for information.'

'My friends, my colleagues.' He grinned at her and spread his hands in a gesture that made him seem more continental than English, as though any moment he might burst into a verse or two of *Nessun Dorma*.

'So, about your holiday . . .'

'The truth is, Kate – may I call you Kate? I noticed the name on your desk this afternoon – the truth is, this trip isn't really going to be a holiday, more of a fact-finding mission.'

She half-rose. 'So this isn't a business meeting after all.'

'It is, it is. I mean I could easily be persuaded to include the holiday bit, if you can make it sound interesting enough.'

'OK, Mr Andrewes—'

'Jefferson, please.'

'All right. Now, Jefferson, I need more information before I can do anything useful for you.'

'Ecuador,' he said. 'I want – I *need* to go to Ecuador.'

She stiffened. 'Ecuador . . . why?' Was this some kind of an elaborate joke?

'It's a place I've always wanted to go to.'

'There's more to it than that, isn't there?'

'This . . . um . . . mission, like I said, plus a . . . um . . . kind of family connection.'

Kate raised her eyebrows. 'Really?' She wasn't going to tell him about her own connection, bring Dad and Luisa and Annie out into the open and display them for a stranger's momentary curiosity, his fake concern. She felt a sudden longing for the singing air of Santa Cruz, alive with the songs of finches and warblers.

'Not so much Ecuador in general as the Galápagos Islands in particular,' Andrewes said.

'Oh yes?' He *had* to be having her on.

'I want to tie a red scarf round my neck and run with those turtles.'

'It's bulls that people run with, not turtles. In Pamplona, not the Galápagos.'

'Really?'

'Take a red scarf with you by all means, but turtles don't do a lot of running, though I'm quite sure you knew that already.' She leaned towards him and lowered her voice. 'How do you feel about naked men?'

His eyes, the exact shade of chocolate fudge, narrowed slightly. 'Are you trying to find out if I'm gay? Because I'm not – *not* that there's anything wrong with being gay, of course. Lots of people are, some of my best friends, all that, five per cent of the population, isn't it? Hell, I even live in Babylon, and very nice too, if that's—'

'Ssh.' Kate put her finger across her lips to stop him. She adopted a serious expression. 'It's just that if you're not dead set on the Galápagos, there's this Shinto religious festival in Japan that you might find interesting. Ten thousand more or less naked guys, all pissed as farts, racing after someone called the Spirit Man, who's this kind of Judas Goat – if they can touch him, he absorbs all their bad luck.'

'Why would I find it interesting?'

'It's unusual, you have to admit.'

Andrewes looked apprehensive. 'Would I have to be naked too? Or – Lord! – be the Spirit Man? Because leaping along the Great

Wall of China in my birthday suit is not really the kind of holiday I had in mind.'

'The Great Wall of China isn't in Japan.'

'*I* knew *that.*'

The idea of a jay-bird-naked Andrewes pursued by a horde of skimpily clad Japanese was so absurd that Kate threw back her head and laughed. As she did so, she caught sight of someone peering in through the window of the restaurant. The laughter died instantly. It was Stefan Michaels, and from where she sat, it looked as though he was staring directly at her, just as he had the other night, looking grim. Looking ragingly *jealous*. What right did he . . . She gritted her teeth; this was no coincidence, the man was definitely stalking her.

'What?' Andrewes reached across and put a hand on top of hers. 'What's the matter? You've gone pale.'

'I *feel* pale.' Kate took a gulp of wine from her glass. 'That bloody man . . .'

'Which one?'

'The one staring in at us.'

Andrewes leaned back, let his napkin slide off his lap, bent to pick it up. 'What's the matter with him?'

Kate looked at the window again, but Stefan had gone. 'He's following me.'

'Do you know him?'

'Only as someone I served a drink to in a bar . . .' She explained about Plan A and her job there, told him of her fears about Stefan, the way he seemed to show up wherever she was, like tonight, though as she talked, the story seemed increasingly thin, almost negligible.

'You know there are laws to protect you against this kind of harassment,' he said.

'If that's what it is. Trouble is, so far he hasn't done enough for me to go to the police. All in all, it doesn't add up to much.'

'Well, for tonight, don't worry, I know the head waiter here pretty well,' he said soothingly. 'When we're ready to go, I'll get him to call us a taxi round at the back. If your friend is waiting outside, he'll be foiled.' He had assumed quite a different persona, in command, knowledgeable, solid.

'Thank you.' Kate took a more measured taste of her wine and was glad to see that however shaky she might feel inside, at least her grip on the stem of her glass was firm. 'Now, since this is a business meeting and we've established that your destination is the Galápagos Islands . . .'

'I've always wanted to watch those huge megalithic creatures lumbering up from the ocean to lay their eggs, the way they've been doing for thousands and thousands of years.'

'There are many more types of turtles than the big ones – and a lot more to the Islands than just the turtles.' It was all so clear in Kate's head. 'There's . . . oh, where to start, flamingoes, volcanoes, lava formations, forests. Wildlife like boobies, birds with sky-blue feet and legs and marine iguanas, found nowhere else in the world, the only ones adapted to sea water. And, of course, Darwin's famous finches, the little birds which sparked off the whole theory of evolution.'

'Should I know about this?'

'Darwin formed his theory of evolution after sailing into the Islands on the *Beagle* and noticing that although these finches all looked and behaved the same – they all build identical nests, for instance – the thirteen species which existed there had all adapted to the different food sources available to them.' She could feel a shift of excitement in herself. 'So, just as an example, there's the cactus finch which has developed a long pointed beak in order to feed off the cactus plants without getting speared to death on the thorns, and the tree finch which has a beak like a parrot to get at the insects. And the woodpecker finch which uses its body to hammer at tree bark in order to dislodge insects and larvae and so on, and climbs up and down the tree branches.' She leaned forward. 'The amazing thing about the woodpecker finch is that it's developed a tool-using mechanism – very rare among birds – by using a cactus spine which it snaps to the length it needs and then holds in its beak so it can probe for grubs in the deeper cracks in the wood.' She paused for breath, then added, 'Sorry, am I going on a bit?'

'Absolutely not. I'm riveted. There's a famous research institute there too, isn't there?'

'That's right.' Kate was going to mention her father, but bit it back. 'How come you know so much about it?'

'I wrote a paper on it when I was at school.' It was part of the truth, but not all. 'Anyway, the Islands are near an area of subterranean activity, and developed really from volcanoes which eventually pushed through the surface to form land from the constant streams of lava flows.'

'Volcanoes . . . are they still active?'

'Most of them, most of the time, no. But you never know with volcanoes, do you? And two of the islands actually consist of seven huge and active volcanoes – you absolutely have to go and see the extraordinary patterns made by the lava flows.'

'You wouldn't like to come with me, would you?'

'I'd love to go to the Galápagos, I must say.'

'So that's a no?'

Kate smiled at him. 'I can guarantee that you'd enjoy it if that's where you decide to go.' She didn't tell him how many times she'd visited her family there in the school holidays, that she spoke Spanish, that she'd spent her gap year living and working in Guyaquil. Nor did she tell him about The Accident, though at the thought of her little sister, she bit down hard into her bottom lip. Funny how although she missed her father and Luisa like crazy, it was the loss of Annie which made her weep.

'Now,' she went on briskly. 'The thing is, do you want us to do the lot for you – airline tickets, hotels everywhere, individually hosted tours of the major sights and so on – or do you want to retain a degree of autonomy so you can take off suddenly if you see something which looks interesting that you didn't know about until you got there?'

As she spoke, Kate kept glancing at the window. In the safely normal company of Andrewes, she felt less certain that she had actually seen Stefan Michaels glaring in at her. It could have been someone with a vague resemblance to him who was simply checking out the ambience, or the menu.

'I'll come in sometime next week and we can sort out the details.' Andrewes beckoned for the waitress and ordered cappuccinos for them both. While they waited for the coffee to arrive, he said, 'OK, that's the business part over. Are we allowed to get a little more personal now?'

'How much is "a little"?'

'For instance . . .' He glanced at her left hand. 'If you don't mind me asking, are you married?

'No.' Kate wasn't about to drag in Bradleigh Fullerton III. 'Are you?'

'Er . . . no.'

'You don't sound too sure.'

'I was, once.'

'What happened?

'She . . . died.' He shrugged. 'These things happen.'

'I'm so sorry. What happened?'

'Actually, she killed herself.'

Kate tried to imagine the guilt a person would feel if their partner committed suicide. The dark hours of wondering what signs you'd missed, what cries for help had gone unnoticed, whether you could have done something to change things, whether it was your fault. 'That must be much worse than . . . than cancer or an accident.'

'Yes. She'd tried several times, long before she met me. I loved her, but I really don't blame myself. Anyway, it was some time ago now . . .' He took a deep breath. 'Do you have any family?'

'A brother, who I'm living with at the moment. An aunt and uncle and a couple of cousins, up in Edinburgh. Otherwise, no.'

'No parents?'

'They died, a long time ago. My father and stepmother, actually. I lost my mother when I was very young, I don't remember anything about her.' A scent, the softness of hair on her skin, murmurs of love which came back to her when she lay half-awake in the early morning. Nothing else. 'Any girlfriends?'

He raised an eyebrow. 'Are you always this direct?'

'I find that being direct avoids confusion.'

'OK . . . there have been girlfriends since my wife . . . died. But none at the moment.'

'What about your family?'

'Stepmother, two half-siblings, a . . . um . . . stepfather.'

'Where's your mother?'

His face twisted oddly. 'She's dead, like your parents.'

'What about your father?'

'They were divorced.' He swallowed. 'And he . . . um . . . died a short while ago.'

'I'm sorry – I know what it's like to lose a parent.'

'It's because of him, really, that I need to go to Ecuador.'

There was a silence between them, then Kate said, 'You know what my job is, what about yours?'

He grinned. 'I used to work for the SAS . . .'

Kate felt a familiar weariness close over her. Brad had told her the same thing when they first met, although he'd never been closer to a combat weapon than watching *Dirty Harry*. If there was one thing Jefferson Andrewes didn't look like, it was SAS. It must be some kind of macho wet-dream that guys had, especially the dodgy ones.

'. . . just a summer holiday job, then I did . . . uh . . . a degree, and now I mostly do . . . research, I suppose you'd call it, working for a big international company. Pushing bits of paper around the accounts department, for the most part.' He laughed self-deprecatingly. 'I probably look like an accountant, too, in this get-up.'

A huge yawn was building up inside her. Accounts! Jeez! 'Is it an interesting . . . uh . . . occupation?'

'Sometimes, if you like that sort of thing. It sounds safe and boring – but there are times when a job like mine can be tremendously exciting.'

'Really?' Rebellion in the typing pool? A senior partner showing up in – gasp! – a pink shirt?

'Sometimes even downright dangerous.'

'Wow!' Death by a thousand paperclips? She surveyed him. 'If I'd had to guess, I might have put accountant in your top three most likely occupations.'

'Nothing wrong with that, though, is there?'

'Of course not,' she agreed, a little too heartily. 'Can you really work for the SAS as a holiday job?'

'It's a joke. Can you really see me in the Special Air Service?'

'Actually . . .'

'Don't answer that.'

'Well, you've got the build.'

'It was a kind of joke. During university vacations, I worked in the offices of Scandinavian Airlines, my father knew someone, adding up figures mostly.'

The conversation drifted pleasantly off to other subjects as they skirted round each other, mapped each other's territory: favourite books, favourite films, music, interests, very few of which they had in common. One thing she learned about her dinner-companion was that the diffident air he had worn earlier in the day was a deliberate mannerism, and that he was in fact decisive and quick-thinking, both qualities she liked.

'I'll think about what we've discussed, and come in after the weekend to make some definite plans,' Andrewes said, an hour or so later, when Kate said she really had to go.

'Good. I'll have some ideas lined up for you.' She stood up, then sat down again. 'What about that taxi?'

A taxi was ordered. 'Sure you don't want me to come with you?' Andrewes said, as he settled her inside.

'Absolutely. And thank you . . . uh . . . Jefferson. I've enjoyed this . . . business evening.'

'Me too. Maybe . . . maybe we can do it again sometime.'

'Mmm, yes, that would be fun.' Her tone of voice held out very little hope of a repeat performance.

It wasn't much more than eleven o'clock when the taxi pulled up outside her house. Most of the neighbours still showed lights from behind curtained windows, including her own. She reached into her bag to find her wallet, but the taxi-driver waved her away. 'Already settled,' he said. 'And the gentleman said I was to see you safely through the front door.'

Kate smiled as she walked up the tiled path. Very thoughtful of him . . . but then that's how he came across: thoughtful, kind, safe. The exact opposite of Brad. As she opened the door, she turned to wave at the driver and watched him speed away.

A few minutes after she had shut the door behind her, the phone rang. She picked it up and heard a voice speaking through the kind of static which indicates that someone's mobile is in an area of bad reception.

'What?' she said. 'I can't hear you.'

The voice came again, interleaved with more static. There were voices in the background, someone having a coughing fit, a sudden whistle repeated a couple of times, as though the call was coming from a railway station.

'I can't hear you,' she said again. It sounded vaguely as though someone was saying something like 'Mineyore, mineyore,' over and over again. After a moment, she realized that was exactly what it was.

'I don't know who you are,' she said briskly, although she had a very good idea. 'Or what you want. But sod off, will you, you miserable little dick?' She slammed the receiver down as hard as she could, and went across the hall to Magnus's study.

'This is getting ridiculous,' she said angrily. 'It's that man again, the stalker. I swear I saw him outside the restaurant where I was . . . entertaining a client to dinner tonight. And then the minute I enter the house, he phones me up with some drivel about me being his. It's absolutely intolerable.'

'You've had punters coming on to you before.'

'Yes, but most of them take "no" for an answer, and if that doesn't work, you use stronger language. This guy doesn't seem to get the message that I don't agree with his own estimate of himself as Mr Wonderful.' She picked up Magnus's cordless phone. 'I'm calling the police.'

'Can you be certain that it was this man on the phone?' asked Magnus. 'Could you swear that you recognized the voice? How could he possibly have got hold of your phone number?'

She stared angrily at him. 'He could have followed *you* to the university. Asked someone who you were, how he could get in touch with you. Or asked bloody Peta – I know she gave him *her* phone number. It doesn't matter: I *know* it was him. And how could he tell I'd only just got back? He must have been hanging around outside, waiting. How does he know where I live if he hasn't been following me?' Her knees trembled and she sat down hard on the nearest chair. 'Look, this is beginning to really annoy me.' And alarm her, though she wasn't going to tell Magnus that; he'd probably try to impose a curfew, or lock her up in an impregnable tower, or something equally Victorian.

'If you're that sure it was him, why don't you go and confront him, tell him to stop playing silly buggers?'

Her shoulders drooped. 'That's the trouble, isn't it? As you say, I can't prove anything, and all he has to do is deny it.'

'Just ignore him – if it *is* him,' Magnus said.

Jefferson

Nine

'Mmm, yes, that would be *fun*.'

He had to laugh. It was that or weep. Or was it, 'That *would* be fun . . .' with an edge of sarcasm? It was a brush-off: perfectly civil, but he'd had enough of them in his time to recognize one when he saw it. And he hadn't even told her what he really did, though from the look in her eye when he said accountancy, he wasn't likely to get far enough to reveal the truth.

At least he would see her again, after the weekend. He thought about her conviction that someone was following her and wondered whether he should apply his powers of observation again, either give the guy a warning to lay off, together with a bloody nose, or find something more concrete for her to take to the police.

Looking about him, he wondered if he was growing out of the stark minimalism with which he had originally decorated the loft, beige linen (*'taupe, sir, if you don't mind,* not *beige, the perfect complement to almost any room, nothing like a neutral background, sets all your conversation pieces off beautifully, know what I mean?'*) not being compatible, judging by the homes of those of his friends who had children, with the raising of a family. When Jefferson queried the term 'conversation piece', the salesman had twittered a little and begun referring to clusters of willow-pattern dishes or hand-painted pottery jugs, which seemed odd to Jefferson who had never, as far as he could recall, had a conversation about hand-painted pottery jugs and if he had, wouldn't have dreamed of purchasing two sofas to 'set them off'. He sighed a little, thinking of the family who might one day soil those pristine 'taupe' covers, a contingency which although it had so far failed to materialize (first catch your family) nonetheless might eventually do so, were he only able to engage the attention of the 'object of his affections' (for part of Jefferson still clung to the dreams engendered by his grandmother's library of romantic novels) if only he had one. Which reminded him that it was time the remains of Mary-Jane – not the *remains*, obviously, so much as the last items which linked him to what now seemed almost a Mills & Boon dream, despite its distinctly *un*Mills & Boon ending – were finally disposed of.

What would Kate Fullerton have said if he had confided to her his youthful ambition to be a detective, or, for that matter (and more realistically) a policeman? When he'd informed his mother that he had decided to leave school to become a full-time police cadet, she'd thrown a teacup at him. 'Are you crazy?' she demanded.

'Maybe.' He nearly added that if anyone in the family was crazy, it wasn't him, but being a kind person he refrained, reminding himself that maybe she had just cause. Or just Cause.

'Police! Pshaw!' She was given to such unidentifiable expressions of disapproval. 'State instruments of repression! Racist, corrupt, stupid . . .' She threw him a look in which he read her sudden realization that since he was, or might well become, all three of the latter he would therefore fit in very well.

'It may sound like a cliché, Mother,' he said, trying to sound both dignified and righteous and failing badly before her unwavering stare, 'but I'd like to do my bit in some way or another, try to see that justice is done, the weak are protected, that sort of thing.'

'The weak protected?'

'Yes.'

'Talk about the blind leading the blind . . .'

It had been more than adolescent idealism, but owing to an unfortunate tendency to feel nauseous at the sight of blood, he knew he could never be a doctor working in appalling conditions in far-off African states, or even closer at hand in the countries of the former Soviet Bloc. Nor did he think he had what it took to become a missionary, preaching the Bible to the heathen: he wasn't at all sure that people did that any more, and not only did he have little belief in a benign Entity, he had never understood why missionaries were so insistent that if the heathen let Jesus into their hearts, they were from then on obliged to wrap themselves in cheap cotton, instead of remaining in the state of nature to which God and their habitat had, presumably, called them.

Approached about the cadetship, his Headmaster told him he was making a gross error. 'I shall keep your place for you, Andrewes,' he said. 'You'll be back.' His father agreed, phoning from rural Hampshire.

'I don't often find myself on the same side as your mother,' he said, 'but I have to say I think you're making a bit of a cock-up.'

Even before he started his first day, he was fairly sure his father was right, and so it proved. Apart from the thick navy-blue woollen sweater, it was too macho for him, too all-male, too reminiscent of Haddon Hall, where if you weren't good at rugby or at least cricket, you might as well slit your throat. There was no respect for intellectual achievement, and one evening after their supper, when he suggested a board-game ('*Anyone for chess*?'), he was greeted by raucous laughter. He had longed to be rugged and manly, whatever that meant, craggy-jawed and steely-eyed, a real bloke – even the weediest of the other cadets seemed effortlessly to achieve these desirable qualities – but somehow, despite his size, it all seemed too difficult to pull off, especially as he didn't swear easily, his jaw was rounded rather than craggy and however much he narrowed them in the mirror, his eyes remained quite incapable of steeliness.

After a few weeks, he resigned and returned to school, thanks to the benevolent string-pulling of the headmaster who was delighted to have him back. Eventually, he'd gained a scholarship to Oxford to study pure and applied maths. At university, he took up real tennis, seduced by the vocabulary (*hazard, tambour, dedans, penthouse*) as much as the mathematical calculations involved in judging where the ball would go, and fell in love again. For three years, he and Felicity wandered around the ancient city hand in hand, punted along the slow green river with a picnic basket and lay kissing among tall grasses in river meadows populated by dormice and larks. They were a couple, an item, their future fair and mapped out, until just before Finals when, at a party, she met a Rhodes Scholar from Pretoria, and that was that ('*It's not you, Jeff, honestly, it's me, I just don't think we work, not any more.*'). He'd tried to shrug off Felicity's defection, but she had bruised his heart almost beyond repair, or so he often thought. Occasionally he wondered how she was faring, whether she and the Rhodes Scholar lived behind high walls topped with electrified barbed wire, whether she was kind to the black servants who ran her huge ranch-style house, what crop they farmed, whether he would ever see her again, whether he wanted to.

He'd ended up with a high-powered job at one of the merchant banks in London. He proved to be adept in whichever department they put him; people admired him for his skills and gradually his mother's constant expression of regret whenever she looked at him, as though she'd been given the option to drown him at birth and had declined it, began to fade away. He'd learned the hard way that most women found the whole idea of accountancy a total turn-off. The remaining few nearly always started behaving like human calculators when he told them what he did. He could almost see them weighing up the chances in their heads: three to five years of boredom on the debit side, maybe a couple of kids, which would later be balanced out on the credit side, divorce = alimony + child support + half the house + lawyers' fees + (if his earning capacity ran to it) any number of further expenses when the children got older. Yeah, they'd be prepared to take the risk.

Call me a cynic, he often told himself, opening the newspaper and immersing himself in the crossword or the Sudoku. *I'd rather not have anyone than a woman like that.* He'd read about them in the newspapers, women who did nothing at all except spend their husband's money, didn't cook or clean or look after the children or the husband, didn't use their minds but spent their time going to nail clinics and hairdressers and gym clubs and so on. He could not have described exactly the kind of woman he wanted, but thanks to his grandmother's library, when he met her, he would know her immediately.

As indeed had happened when he met Mary-Jane Callaghan. Mary-Jane, cute and tiny, barely five feet in her pop-socks, made him for the first time in his life feel all the things he'd wanted to feel: rugged and manly, a real bloke. After a year of going out together, they had married at the little church in Cornwall where her parents lived. She went on being cute and tiny, an adorable little creature who fluttered her eyes at him and touched him with small soft fingers. Their sex life was all he could ever have hoped for. He was, for the first time in his life, truly happy.

One night he came home to find her lying in the bath, eyes open, staring up at the ceiling, small breasts flat on her chest, the rest of her body submerged in a weasel-coloured mix of blood and water. She was quite cold to the touch: he estimated that she must have taken the Donormyl as soon as he left for work, then slipped off her rose-pink silk robe, which lay like an overblown flower on the bathroom floor, and climbed into the bath where she had slit her wrists.

Later he learned from her parents that she had tried to kill herself before, once at school, aged sixteen, and again at teacher training college. He wanted to know why no-one had told him, not given him the chance to take better care of her, but it seemed pointless to get angry with them, to add to their pain at the loss of their daughter.

Although he left a message on his mother's answerphone, asking her to call him urgently, it was his father and Romilly who drove up to London from Hampshire and held him in a collective embrace, let him weep, cooked him scrambled eggs and baked beans on toast, all he felt able to get down.

'It's not your fault, son,' his father said.

'If I'd taken better care of her,' Jefferson sobbed, 'this wouldn't have happened.'

'Yes, it would,' said his father. 'Sooner or later, it would.'

'There are always people who want to kill themselves,' explained Romilly, the social worker. 'And mostly they succeed. These preliminary stabs at suicide are nearly always botched attempts, rather than cries for help.'

'You must not blame yourself, son.'

'But I do.'

'That's the cruellest thing about suicide: all the people left behind who feel that they could have prevented it.'

'In my experience,' Romilly said, 'and it's admittedly fairly limited, thank goodness, there is something already dysfunctional about people who kill themselves. Afterwards, you think back and say, yes, that was always a little weird, or, I always wondered why he or she reacted like that.'

And in the weeks and months which followed, Jefferson began to reassess the short time he'd spent with his wife, and saw that possibly Romilly was right. This did not make him any the less devastated at the loss of Mary-Jane, but did help him to stop blaming himself, come to terms with her death, though he continued to harbour a strong feeling of resentment against her family.

He weighed up the pros and cons of staying on in the little house he'd bought for them both, a cottagey place in a cul-de-sac not far from Liverpool Street Station, which he had seen as a nest, a drey, a burrow in which she could curl up like an adorable kitten and watch him with her huge childlike eyes, and which now contained all that was left of her. The pros of staying on more or less matched the cons: keeping memories intact, preserving the remnants of his marriage, and so on, but in the end the bank took control and sent him up to a subsidiary branch (*'Just to get you away, Jeff, fresh woods and pastures new, we want you back a.s.a.p.'*) which coincidentally happened to be in the same city where he had gone to school, though back then, thanks to school regulations, he'd seen little of it beyond the station and a couple of shops which made a living out of schoolboy pocket-money. He carried Mary-Jane (recently he'd been appalled to hear himself refer to her as Mary-Anne) with him and even now, in the big warehouse loft, he sometimes caught the ghost of her scent in the folds of a curtain or the softness of a cushion. He had intended eventually to return to London but in the event, found he enjoyed the somewhat slower tempo up here after the hectic pace of the capital, and without being aware of it, embedded himself in the city's life, buying a season ticket to the concert series at the town hall, becoming a Friend of the art gallery, joining a French conversation evening class and so on. After eighteen months, he had asked for a permanent transfer.

His life took an unexpected turn when one of the local partners had called him in for a 'consultation'.

Pansy, his assistant, had relayed the news with a look of apprehension on her face. 'I hope . . . oh God, they're not going to send you back to London, are they, Jeff? Or make you redundant.'

'I very much doubt it,' he'd said cheerily, though for a fraction of a second his heart had plummeted into his expensive (non-crushed-leather) boots, before he reminded himself that good financial consultants were unlikely to be got rid of, and if they were, there was always work at the next big company. In fact, he'd occasionally thought of setting up on his own, sometime in the not-too-distant future, maybe taking Pansy with him – he was fairly sure she would come – and one or two others who had expressed a certain discontent with their working conditions.

This particular partner wasn't one for beating about the bush, a trait upon which he often informed his colleagues that he prided himself.

'Someone's pulling a fast one,' he said gruffly.

For a moment, Jefferson thought this was some recondite sporting term, the partner being one of those men who liked nothing better than wallowing in mud on the rugby ground or hitting balls across nets, or even speeding along rivers in small unstable craft. 'A fast one?' he said. A cricketing term, wasn't it? He was fairly confident he'd heard Christopher Martin Jenkins ('CMJ') or someone similar use it on Test Match Special. Or was it something to do with motor racing?

'Absolutely correct. Someone, in other words, is trying to pull the wool over our eyes.'

'The wool?' Jefferson had found in the past that a kind of vague echoing murmur was the best way to advance any conversation with Mr Pritchard until such time as he should choose to divulge what he was really trying to say.

'Precisely. And I for one won't stand for it.' He grinned ferociously, causing Jefferson to smile back, though he wasn't entirely sure what the joke was.

'Mmm,' he said knowingly.

'Now, after consultation, Jefferson, we – that is to say, *I* – have come to the conclusion that you are far and away the best man to handle this. Quite apart from your considerable expertise, you have . . . erm . . . perhaps fewer ties than some of us. It'll require going down to head office in London for a month or so – naturally we'll cover all expenses – and looking into the matter. It's fraud, to be frank with you. We are in the process of being fleeced.'

This last statement, coming so soon after the one about wool being pulled over eyes, had Jefferson so hopelessly lost in the remembrance of things past – a holiday in Australia, to be more specific, and a trip to see a demonstration of sheep-shearing, the smell of Antipodean sweat, the batting away of flies, corks dangling on the end of strings, coarse male laughter, the overpowering stench of frightened sheep – that he hardly knew how to respond.

In the end, 'I see,' seemed to cover most of the bases, although he didn't, but by now he had gathered that the firm was in some way being defrauded, though how and by whom, he had yet to discover.

'I'm sure you do,' Mr Pritchard said heartily.

'I'll need a full dossier, of course,' Jefferson said, pulling himself together inside his good suit, straightening his silk tie, standing more upright. 'List of current personnel, an itemized rundown of all the details in our possession. Are the police involved?'

'I knew you were the right man for the job, Jefferson. Hit the nail fair and square on the head.'

How had he done that? 'Good . . .'

'The thing is, it's an inside job and the last thing we want is the police butting in. There's the firm's reputation to consider, absolutely top priority, so I want you to be circumspect, discreet. When we have the proof we need, then we can pounce.'

Two and a half weeks later, Jefferson did indeed pounce, almost literally, on the floor manager who had been trying to pull a Leeson, and lining his own pockets in the process. While the sums involved were nothing like Leeson was playing with on behalf of Barings, if left undetected they could have caused considerable damage to the prestige of Jefferson's own bank. The job had not been difficult, but it had entailed many long hours poring over financial reports, fitting two and two together and coming up with seven or eight. After some intense discussion (shades of his schooldays) with the pseudo-Leeson, most of the money was repaid, and the bank's reputation remained unsullied.

Since then, he'd found himself involved in other matters requiring the kind of logical putting together of fractured pieces of information, one involving more missing funds at the bank, a second involving the disappearance of a Rolex Oyster watch from a meeting of the French club.

By now he had acquired a flat and a decent car, was able to afford foreign holidays, had built up a substantial portfolio of shares. Pain from the loss of both Mary-Jane and Felicity had begun to grow less fierce, though as yet, no-one else had taken the place of either. There had been a few one-month stands, once even a girl he'd thought of asking to move with him, until he'd seen her collection of Lladro figurines and realized that whatever he felt about living with the girl, it would be impossible to live with *them*.

Kate

Ten

This was to be Kate's final night in Magnus's house. They had spent the previous weekend filling his ancient car with her suitcases, the pink dog with the lolling tongue which she'd given Annie on her eighth birthday and packed into her luggage after The Accident, some favourite bits and pieces, and driving them across town to Janine's flat. Janine herself was away, but she'd given Kate a key and told her to settle herself in.

'Nice place,' Magnus said, prowling about on the Sunday night. 'Bit different from ours.'

'Only because your house – thanks for calling it ours! – lacks a woman's touch.'

As I do myself, Magnus thought. 'Don't think I don't appreciate the things you do,' he said. 'Flowers and cushions and things. I do notice.'

'Your house is full of lovely things: you only need to dust it occasionally – and for goodness sake buy some new curtains, something light and bright. They'd transform your sitting room.'

'Perhaps you and this Janine person – where is she, by the way?'

'Gone down to London for the weekend. I think she might have a Man down there, though she's never said.'

'Oh. Oh well . . . that puts paid to my little idea that the two of you might come with me into the city one Saturday and choose some curtains. I could take you both out to lunch afterwards.'

'Sounds like a plan.'

'Not if she's got a . . . a boyfriend.'

'You can't believe that having someone in her life means she never speaks to another male again, do you?'

'Maybe not, but she's unlikely to want to spend time in the company of an old fogey like me,' he said, looking hopefully at his sister.

'Don't be ridiculous.' Kate frowned at her brother. 'You don't really think that's how you come across, do you?'

'A bit.' Magnus looked down at himself. 'I'm never going to be asked to pose for those glossy magazines about men's fashions, am I?'

'But you do scrub up well, darling. Maybe you just need to scrub up more often. And get a haircut now and then. A good one. And your eyebrows are getting a bit . . . overgrown. Maybe you should buy a hedge-trimmer.'

'That's more than enough about me, thank you.' Magnus handed her a small package. 'This is a house-warming present.'

Kate tore off the paper. 'Oh, how lovely she is.' She held the little painted box in her hand, tilting it to left and right to catch the gleam of mother-of-pearl behind the Snow Princess in her fur-trimmed hat and coat. 'Is it really for me?'

'With love from me to you.'

'I'll treasure it more than you can imagine.'

The two of them looked at each other, both remembering the family they had lost, the beautiful Ecuadorian woman who had been all the mother they had really known, the little long-gone sister, their Dad.

After so many wasted months, Kate was feeling buoyant, almost light-headed: as though she'd finally thrown off the depression caused by Brad's departure and the subsequent divorce, and was on her way to starting an independent life again. She was looking forward to sharing with Janine: her flat was light and roomy, the middle floor of a large converted Victorian semi, set opposite a park. If there was a downside, it was that Janine appeared to be excessively orderly: when Kate had gone round to view the place, the brightly coloured silk cushions were plumped up, the bathroom was immaculate, the kitchen counters were tidy and shining – no half-empty teacups in the sink, no jars of marmalade with the top left off, no bread crumbs congregating round the toaster. But with any luck, Janine was as much a slob as Kate, and had just tidied up in order to make a good first impression.

She got off the bus much later than usual: Janine had suggested they go to the restaurant round the corner from TaylorMade Travel for some quick *dim sum*, which had included two pitchers of warm *sake*. 'Tomorrow,' Janine suggested, 'we'll have dinner at my place – '*our* place,' corrected Kate, giggling a little – '*our* place,' agreed Janine, 'a celebration, a bottle of something nice,' she said, 'I'll have something ready when you arrive.'

Standing on the pavement as the bus lumbered away, Kate wondered if Magnus had remembered to buy fresh milk, decided he almost certainly hadn't, then recalled that in any case, Magnus wasn't there, having flown off to Boston to do some research at Harvard and then attend a conference in California on some piece of Romanov esoterica or other. There were still lights on in the mini-market on the corner, so she walked along the pavement, past three or four shiny yuppie cars, a white van, Mr Radsowicz-across-the-way's small red Fiat, a parked taxi. She exchanged a few words with the tall black figures of the two Somali brothers who stood like hieratic statues behind the till, tucked the carton of milk into her big leather shoulder bag and turned back towards home.

Afterwards, it was the suddenness of it all that she remembered most clearly, the smoothly efficient process of her abduction, kidnap, hijack, as though they'd practised the moves over and over again until they ran like clockwork. A figure stepping out from between two cars, an arm round her neck, a hand covering her mouth, her helplessness as she was lifted off her feet and bundled like a roll of carpet into the back of the white van she'd noticed earlier. Then a masculine presence – she wrinkled her nose against the smell of some cheap aftershave overlaying a body not washed often enough – kneeling beside her in the darkness as the van lurched into movement and took off down the street, tape over her mouth, hands secured behind her, legs fastened together with rope. A blanket shoved under her head, some kind of mattress under her body, another blanket thrown over her, stinking of stale onion bhaji and motor oil.

The van slowed, turned a corner, then came to a stop while whoever had tied her up got out, slammed the rear doors closed and climbed into the front. The whole operation took fewer than ninety seconds.

There were no windows in the van, and only a thin band of light where the two doors met. She lay in the darkness, trying to piece together what had happened, though it was obvious really: she'd been abducted, taken hostage, and the person responsible had to be Stefan, it was far too much of a coincidence if it wasn't. The bastard. My God, she thought, I've got proof enough for the police now, all right. Oddly enough, she felt very little fear. Stefan was such a loser that she was sure she would come off best in any encounter they had, as long as the driver, whoever he was, wasn't included in whatever plan sodding Stefan had for her, in which case, the odds of her coming out on top were considerably lessened.

Magnus had called her 'enterprising'. Dad had advised her to keep a stiff upper lip. OK, guys, that's what she would do. She would be enterprising and stiffly upper-lipped, though she'd often wondered why it wasn't the lower lip that was mentioned in trying circumstances, since she'd noticed that was the one which usually quivered. *Stiff lower lip, Katie . . .*

She dragged herself into a sitting position by working her back against the side of the van, then tried to pull her taped wrists under her bottom so that she could bring her ankles through the circle of her arms. At first she got nowhere. She kept falling sideways, and the movement of the van made her feel nauseous, so that she needed to lie down until her stomach settled. Too much *dim sum* and warm sake on an empty stomach, since there hadn't been time for lunch.

At last she was able to contort her body sufficiently to achieve a sitting position with her freed legs out in front of her. She lifted her taped hands to her mouth and tore off the duct tape, wincing as what felt like half the skin of her face came with it. Then she gnawed at the tape around her wrists with her teeth until she succeeded in pulling it off. Finally she bent towards her feet and worked away at the rope until it fell away from her ankles.

So far, so free. She had no idea how long it had taken, but now what? She had no idea where they were, though the fact that the van kept slowing down and idling indicated that they were still in an area of town controlled by traffic lights. There was a screen between the back of the van and the front seats, but she could hear male voices and occasional laughter, and once, the throaty concupiscence of Mick Jagger singing the opening lines of 'I Can't Get No Satisfaction', quickly cut off as one of the men in front answered his mobile, barking incomprehensible responses to his caller. When he'd finished his conversation, the other one said, 'You want to be careful, mate, you know they've got their eye on us, don't you?'

'You always say that,' said the first one, laughing.

'I say it, you little twat, because it's bloody true.'

'Who is it who has the eye on us?'

'The cops, just for starters. But don't think your dad hasn't got enemies, so watch it, that's all I can say, don't draw attention to yourself, don't drive that stupid car of yours over the speed limit, don't get drunk or diss a cop, don't do anything – they're just looking for a reason to bring us in, doesn't matter what for, any excuse will do, so for Chrissake keep your nose clean.'

'I always do, don't I?' The disdainful tone was definitely Stefan Michaels', and she was fairly sure she recognized the other voice as belonging to his friend with the pseudo-gentlemanly accent. Mick, wasn't it?

While they talked, she was edging over to the rear doors. The darkness inside the van was almost total as she felt around for some kind of release mechanism. Halfway up she found a spring-loaded lever which she was able to manipulate up and down. Carefully she pushed at it and found that the steel rod which held the doors closed moved. Would it open the doors? Next time the van slowed down, she would try it and see.

A small interior voice told her it couldn't be that easy. A slightly louder voice asked why the hell not? She leaned the side of her head against the doors: she could hear almost nothing except a murmur of what she took to be traffic, and the creaks and groans of the metal sides grating against the bed of the vehicle. She thought of Magnus, soaking up the Californian sunshine, sitting outside some Mexican restaurant and scarfing down *fajitas* or *burritos* slathered with jalapeño sauce. She remembered Jefferson Andrewes' good-natured face, his kindness, the holiday – no, the fact-finding mission – he intended to book. She wished she could join him in watching the turtles make their slow progress up the beach while the waves hissed on the sand and seabirds mewled and screamed.

The driver stepped on the brakes and slowed the van down. Traffic lights! Breathing through her mouth, terrified that at the last moment everything would go wrong, Kate bore down on the lever and pushed at the doors. They opened but as she prepared to climb out, the van suddenly accelerated, throwing her back into the interior.

Shit, shit, shit!

Through the open swinging doors, she could see they were driving along a shopping parade in one of the seedier parts of town, shuttered storefronts, a dimly lit fish-and-chip parlour, closed for the night, shops which during the day sold cheap jewellery, saris, takeaways, carpets. Two or three bookmakers. A cheapjack's, windows stuffed with orange plastic buckets and cubes of foam covered in hideous green or purple plush. In the half-light from the street, she looked around for her shoulder bag but it didn't seem to be there; maybe it was still lying in the gutter and someone would find it, call the police, use her mobile to speed-dial someone – one of her friends, or Janine. And maybe not.

At this time of night, nobody seemed to be about. They were travelling so fast now that she dared not jump out, though sooner or later the two men in front would realize that the doors had opened and she would be trussed up again. She prayed for more traffic lights. A police car. A taxi. Another vehicle to appear behind them so that she could signal for help. But the street was deserted and if there were traffic lights, her captors were driving straight through them without slowing sufficiently for her to risk the jump.

And then, once more, the van slowed. She didn't wait for it to come to a full stop but got a leg over the sill and felt for the tarmac before tumbling awkwardly into the road, hanging on to the back until the last moment, but nonetheless hitting the ground with a thump which painfully jarred her shoulder. The van remained still, engine idling, and for a moment, she thought they must have realized that their prisoner had escaped. She took a nanosecond to memorize the number plate – hopeless at maths, brilliant at numbers – then she was up and running, as fast as she could, heading for a pub where there were still lights showing.

Damn and blast! The doors were locked. Peering through the ornately etched glass of the door, she could see tea towels draped over the porcelain beer pulls, scruffy vinyl seating mended with duct tape, small round tables with laminated tops scarred with cigarette burns. Behind the bar, the lights were turned low, causing translucent reflections in the mirror of green bottles of gin, red Campari, whiskys in various shades of brown, blue Curaçao. It was difficult to believe that in a neighbourhood like this, anyone drank Curaçao.

Behind her, she heard a car squeal to a stop. Glancing over her shoulder, she saw the white van, by now some distance away, making a U-turn and then roaring back down the street towards her. She opened her mouth and screamed; at the same time, she ran round the corner of the pub and right-turned down the alleyway behind it. Still screaming at the top of her voice ('*Help! Help me!*'), she found herself in a maze of narrow bisecting passages at the back of the close-packed houses. She turned left, turned right, ran straight when she saw street lights shining ahead.

Her screams did not seem to have had any effect on the neighbours. Were they all watching television with the sound turned up? Or asleep in their beds wearing earplugs? Someone must be able to hear her. On the other hand, in a run-down area like this, they were probably used to drunken girls shrieking, and had learned to take no notice.

It occurred to her that screaming was not only useless, but might be giving her pursuers some idea of where she was. She ran on, looking at the houses for a passage into a back garden, a lighted front window, a doorway where she could conceal herself while – with any luck – the owners responded to her frantic knocking.

But she was in a part of town where the houses were terraced and front doors opened straight off the pavement. Looking at the mean little houses, her heart sank: nobody here was likely to take her in and help her. She ran on, looking for more side passages she could duck down, back alleys where she could lose herself. If she could find a rear garden to climb into, she might be able to get into a tool shed until daylight came, or find a bush to cower behind. Either way, she'd probably freeze to death before morning, but it would be preferable to being in the hands of Stefan and his sidekick. But there were no obvious gardens, and in any case, these were back-to-back dwellings with courtyards bounded by high walls which she would have no hope of scaling.

She ran on, turned a corner and then another – and was abruptly transposed into a different world: an affluent suburbia, big detached houses with mature hedges shielding them from the road. She reached a house with a gateless bush-lined gravel drive and, before she could think about it, had raced inside and pushed into the concealing evergreens of a shrubbery. There was a gate at the side of the house, leading into the back garden; the entrance to the house was fronted by a slate-roofed porch with benches on either side. Panting, she crouched like a hunted animal on the frozen soil, and paused, her breath ragged, sending plumes of smoke into the freezing winter night. There were no lights on in any of the windows, but that didn't mean the house was empty. The owners might be sitting in a room at the back, or were already in bed, cosy under their feather-filled duvet with empty cocoa mugs on the night-stands and a book lying face down on spread pages.

Could she risk leaving her hiding place and hammering at the door? If no-one came, she would be a sitting duck. She heard a car engine further up the road, brakes being applied, the soft pad of an idling engine. Then, though she strained to listen, nothing else. Nothing except a dog yapping somewhere inside a nearby house, water gurgling down a drainpipe, a distant train rattling across a bridge.

Nothing . . . and then light footsteps, rustles, a voice whispering, 'Katie, Kay-tee, where are you?' Teasing, sinister, like a Stephen King movie.

Despite the chill air, sweat broke out under her arms. God, they must be no more than a few feet away from her. She breathed into her cupped hands, hoping to hide the give-away signs of her presence, and heard it again: 'Kay-tee, we're coming for you, you can't get awa-a-ay.'

A tell-tale waft of aftershave and cigarette smoke, the soft slur of trainers on pavement. Surely they could hear her heart banging inside her chest. Were they passing by? Had they gone? How long must she wait before she dared emerge? Her bruised shoulder ached; her fingers were numb with cold. And then she heard the slam of doors, the idling engine starting up, moving slowly down the road and past the house. She was safe.

Cautiously she pushed her way between the damp foliage of whichever shrub had sheltered her – euonymus, was it? – her ears feeling as sensitive as a bat's. No engine creeping back down the road, no light footsteps, no more of the hateful whispering. She reached the edge of the drive and dropping to her knees, peered carefully round the edge of the low wall to check that the road was empty.

Suddenly, he was in front of her, lashing out with his foot, catching her in the chest so that she overbalanced and went sprawling on the gravel. She opened her mouth to scream but he grabbed her hair with one hand and pulled her up against him while with the other he shoved something – a scarf, a rolled-up tie – viciously into her mouth. She twisted her head and saw the second man, now recognizable in the street lights as Mick, Stefan Michaels' sidekick, racing towards her from the other direction, his trainers making no sound at all on the pavement. She couldn't see how they had managed to come upon her so quickly, without her realizing how close they were. She tried to spit out the gag but she was held so tightly, her head pressed so hard against Stefan's chest that she couldn't get her mouth free.

'I'll hang on to the bitch,' he said. 'You bring the van.'

Desperately, Kate struggled, making mewling sounds in her throat. This couldn't be happening, it just couldn't. Fight or flight, Dad used to say, so since she couldn't fly, she fought, kicking out at him, trying to bring her knee up to his groin. But he was far stronger than she was, and had her in such a tight grip that she could barely move.

'No hope at all, Kate,' he said in her ear. 'Why did you think you could get away from us?' They must have been watching her, maybe for weeks, learning her routines. They must have discovered where she worked, followed when she and Janine went out, made their way back to her house and simply waited until she showed up. If she could only get her head free, she could head-butt him or something. 'And nobody's going to come and save you. I told you that you were mine – and you are.'

The van reappeared. Mick stopped at the kerb, jumped out to open the rear doors, helped Stefan to shove Kate into the back of the van again, then climbed once more into the driver's seat and pulled away, moving slowly along the road while Stefan repeated his actions of last time, tape over her mouth, tape round her wrists, rope at her ankles. Before he was able to subdue her, she raked her fingers down his face, kicked out at him as hard as she could and felt the satisfaction of connecting with his ribs.

He cried out, clutching at his side with one hand. 'You fucking bitch!' he said. 'You'll pay for that.' He slapped her hard across the side of the head; his vulgar gold ring caught the top of her ear and, she was fairly sure, split it. Blood poured down the side of her face and she lay back on the mattress feeling faint and queasy.

Suddenly there was a stinging sensation in her arm, just above the elbow. She jerked her head up and saw Stefan withdrawing a syringe. Oh God, he wasn't trying to turn her into a drug addict, was he? Apart from the odd joint, she'd never tried drugs and never wanted to; she'd seen their effect at far too close hand with the disintegration and eventual death of a friend from uni, found some weeks dead in a former crack-house, her face bitten raw by rats, her clothes soiled by bodily fluids of various kinds. With tape over her mouth, it was impossible for Kate to scream, to beg, to offer anything they wanted, but the thought of being forcibly initiated into a drug habit (Heroin? Crack? Oh *God* . . .) made her insides dissolve with terror. She was helpless. Her limbs relaxed, her body grew drowsy and unconcerned, the place between her legs melted into mellowness as though she'd just had good sex – which for a moment she wondered about . . . Please God, no, surely not, not with Stefan Michaels, and besides, he'd only just stuck the needle in her arm, and until then she had been perfectly *compos mentis*, at school her English teacher, long-skirted, whiskery, halitotic Mrs Gardiner, had always insisted that if they used foreign phrases in their essays, they must be italicized, a habit she'd never dropped, partly because of an atavistic fear that if she didn't, Mrs Gardiner would appear once again behind her shoulder and release a toxic cloud of bad breath. For a moment, or perhaps for hours, images drifted across her mind like clouds on a summer's day: Magnus, Lisa, Janine, a blue silk cushion on a white rug, Mrs Gardiner, flowers of apricot and peach spilling from a green glass vase, the cold unblinking gaze of an iguana, scarlet birds with . . . and then there was nothing.

Janine
Eleven

Her face concealed behind a visor of green gunge, Janine lay back on her bed, wrapped in a thick towel, her pillows covered in another, with slices of lemon laid over her eyes. She had a plastic bowl of warm water laced with Fairy Liquid balanced on her chest with her fingers soaking in it, prior to a home manicure, since she hadn't had time over the past week to go to Nails 'R' Us.

The phone rang.

She dried her hand on the towel behind her head and groped for the phone. 'Hello? Janine here.' She spoke without moving her lips as far as possible, not wanting to crack the face mask, which still had eleven minutes to go for maximum effect.

'What is the matter? Your voice sounds very strange.'

'Oh, hi,' she said carefully.

'I'm in town for a couple of days.'

'Oh.' Removing the bowl of water so that she could sit up, she forgot about facial cracks. 'That's wonderful!'

'Dinner this evening, eight o'clock? I'm at the Grand Central, as usual.'

'I'll be there. Are we eating out, or in the room?'

'Which would you prefer?'

She wasn't sure. Eating out was always exciting, being his partner in public, however briefly, staring at each other over the rims of their glasses like an ordinary couple, exchanging looks, the excitement building. Eating in the room was more intimate, the touching and interconnecting more immediately sexy, the promise of bed easier to fulfil. 'I . . . don't mind.'

There was a pause which she interpreted, from long practice, as less than impressed. He didn't like her to be undecided: it was her certainty about things – where she was going, what she wanted out of life – which had attracted him in the first place. She added quickly, 'Out, I think.'

'Out is good. But so is in.'

'Out.' She said it firmly. 'I like playing footsie under the table.' She lowered her voice. 'Are we going to sit side by side, or across from each other?'

'Which do you prefer?'

'Side by side. I like you to put your hand under my skirt, inside my knickers, and no-one can see.'

He chuckled. 'I bet the waiters know exactly what we're up to. And what we'll be up to when we get back to the hotel.'

If he had walked into her flat right then, she'd have pulled her clothes off before he'd even closed the front door behind him – having wiped off the green gunge first, of course. 'Can't wait.'

She got up, ran a bath, and poured in a lavish amount of the expensive bath stuff he'd given her not long ago. She had half an hour, plenty of time to get ready.

'*Cara* . . .' He rolled away from her across the wide hotel bed and lay on his side, looking at her.

'Yes?' She'd been anticipating this moment, knowing that sooner or later he would tell her that, for whatever reason, it was over, they wouldn't be seeing each other again. She raised herself on to an elbow and drew the sheet over herself. If a man was about to eject you from his life because he was no longer sexually interested, it was more dignified to be covered than exposed.

He pulled the sheet down a little to expose her breasts, and ran a finger over her stomach. 'I wish you to do something for me.'

Disappointment spread thinly across her mind as she understood that (this time) he was not giving her the push; she really wouldn't mind too much if he did, he was a good companion and they'd had fun together but there was no future with him and recently the future was beginning to seem shorter than it used to. 'What would that be?'

'You are a good business woman. You have done so well with the travel agency, you are a trained accountant, yes?'

'Not an accountant,' she corrected. 'A bookkeeper.'

'But you know how to read accounts, add up the columns, check out the figures?'

'I can do all that.' She seized his hand and pressed it against her breast. 'And more.'

'I know, I know.' Gently he pulled away his hand. 'But I wish to be serious. I want you to go through my books, and report back to me. See if you find anything . . . strange.'

'Strange? What do you mean?'

'Someone is cheating me, cheating the organization, my employers, skimming money off the top, and I would like to find out who it might be. And I can trust you to be discreet – for many reasons, I don't want to go through my usual accountants.'

The main reason being that his company or companies was or were engaged in some kind of illegal activity, she guessed. 'I'd be glad to,' she said warmly.

'It may be that my suspicions are wrong.' He swung his legs over the side of the bed and walked naked (good tight buttocks) across the room to where his leather briefcase sat on a table. 'I would be very happy to know this.'

'And if you're right?'

'If I am right . . .' For a moment his handsome features went rigid, his mouth tightened, the warmth in his eyes vanished. *Oops!* she thought. *Whoever it is – if somebody is cheating him – I would definitely not like to be that person.* 'If I'm right, it will be very much the worse for him.'

'Well,' she said, 'you know you can trust me.'

'I know that, Janine.' His warm gaze rested on her body and he smiled in a way that made her feel more than a little shivery inside. She had no illusions about him. If she was granted access to his private accounts, could she be certain of her own subsequent safety? Easy enough for him to arrange the sudden shove under a bus, the fall from a bridge, the drop overboard from a boat. If he was serious about her checking his accounts, she would have to have some kind of insurance, a letter to her lawyer, with photocopies of his accounts, perhaps. But he might seek her out, torture her until he'd extracted the lawyer's name, worse still, might eliminate (wasn't that the word they used in crime movies?) the innocent lawyer. Suddenly, she wondered what she had got herself into with this relationship, and more importantly, how she was going to get herself out.

'I can't say for certain that I'd be able to pinpoint exactly what's going wrong, or who's responsible, but I'll certainly do my best,' she said. 'How long have I got?'

'As long as you need, *cara*. But sooner is better than later.' Once again he smiled. 'I will make it well worth your while. I can promise you a really good . . . reward, if you come up with the goods.'

'I don't need a reward,' she said. 'You've already done more than enough for me.'

'So now you will be doing something for me.'

'Just one thing – are you sure that someone is cheating you?'

'Absolutely one hundred per cent certain. I even have a suspicion of who it is; maybe you can confirm the name for me.' He pulled on his clothes then watched appreciatively as she put on her own. 'Now, let us go downstairs and eat a little supper, maybe dance a little, then come back and . . .' He ran his hand up and down her arm. 'It has always been a pleasure to spend time with you, Janine.'

As they ate thick steaks, matchstick potatoes, a green salad, cheese, danced for an hour or so (he was a lovely mover, like one of the professionals off *Strictly Come Dancing*) and finally ended up in his room again, she pondered the meaning of that last sentence – *it has always been a pleasure* – and thought that maybe, once she had gone over his books for him, their relationship would come to a natural end. If not, she might start not always being available when he called. If that was still going to be an option.

If there was one thing Janine prided herself on – though in fact there were several; plain Jane she might be (or more correctly, might have been once) but she had a reasonable confidence in her own good points – it was her ability to read a person's character. Kate Fullerton's failure to turn up on the Sunday she was due to move finally into Janine's flat, without so much as a phone call, was strictly unlike her. Janine tried to forget the dinner she'd organized for the two of them, a nice cloth on the round table in the bay window, flowers, silver candlesticks (only plate, but they looked like the real thing), linen napkins. She'd done avocado with prawns as a starter, followed by pasta – spaghetti carbonara – with a good green salad on the side, some cheese. And then no Kate, no phone call, nothing. Something was definitely odd about it, she'd felt, as she dug into the Ben & Jerry's Chocolate Chip Cookie Dough ice-cream (God, that was good!) she'd planned for pudding from its cardboard pint container which, she'd read somewhere, was eco-friendly in some way she couldn't quite recall.

Could Kate have changed her mind, decided Janine wasn't

someone she wanted to share with after all, but was too embarrassed to say so? Had she sussed out the fact that beneath the good clothes and the nice flat, Janine was a phony? Had she dismissed her as a social-climbing impostor and decided to stay on with her brother, just not turn up again at the travel agency out of pure embarrassment at her change of heart? Janine shook her head. No way, not Kate, she wasn't the sort, Janine just knew she wasn't. Besides, only the other day, she'd said how she wished her brother could meet someone exactly like Janine, someone pretty and smart, with her head screwed on right. 'He's so impractical,' she'd said, 'so vague, I love him to bits, of course, but he would drive most people absolutely mad; he seems to spend half his time in an alternative universe. What he needs is someone practical, someone to love him for the way he is, not the way he ought to be, but he just can't seem to find the right person. It's not as if he didn't like women, and they seem to go for him big time, but somehow nothing ever seems to come of it . . .' She wouldn't have said that if she hadn't thought Janine was good enough for him, would she? It stood to reason.

A pity she'd been down in London when the brother was helping Kate move in. The way Kate told it, he sounded like a bit of an old fogey, quite frankly, not that there was anything wrong with that but still, when you thought of Mr Right, you kind of wanted him to be a bit further up the scale as far as looks, not to mention personality, went. She thought a trifle wistfully of her estate agent days, two or three of her clients back then had been distinctly promising husband material, if she'd felt like following it up.

When Kate hadn't shown up by Monday evening, not at the flat, not at work, Janine really became alarmed. The fact that it was an exceptionally slow day, though Mondays were usually very busy (people read the Sunday travel sections and came up with all sorts of ideas for their holidays), simply added to her fears, though she told herself she was being really paranoid. There was probably a perfectly rational explanation, though she couldn't think what that might be except something bad which prevented Kate from using her mobile phone – or even a callbox if, say, she'd dropped her mobile into the canal or down a drain or something. But where had she spent the Sunday night? Surely she could have found a phone and called.

She racked her brains to remember what Kate had said about the 'stalker' and remembered her own dismissive remarks, intended to be comforting, about her friend, Michelle Watson-as-was, the one who'd had the stalker who eventually was sent to prison. He'd been much more in-your-face than Kate's person, which is why Janine hadn't felt that the situation was particularly worrying, though now, of course, she thought differently.

She didn't even have Kate's address, and although she knew that people – private detectives and the like – were able to find addresses from numbers, she didn't think that happened any more for normal citizens like herself, what with security and anti-terrorist laws and the like. Besides which, for once being less than efficient, she had mislaid the number Kate had given her.

When there was nothing from Kate on Tuesday, she went down to the police station. 'I want to report a missing person,' she said.

'And who would that be?' The woman behind the counter had eyes that were less than engaged, as though she'd seen enough of the world's depravity to know that its denizens did not deserve much benevolence.

'Her name's Kate Fullerton.'

'Address?'

Not knowing the address of Kate's brother, she gave her own. 'She's my flatmate,' she explained.

'And when did you last see her?' The police officer took her through all the relevant details, including some which she did not seem to consider relevant at all but which Janine insisted she incorporate, such as her absolute conviction that someone like Kate would never let other people down, unless she was constrained in some way.

'Vengeful ex-boyfriend?'

'Sorry?'

'Has she recently ended a relationship with someone who might feel he wanted to get back at her?'

'Not as far as I know. At least . . .' Janine outlined the possible stalker, though she knew so few details that the officer wrote only the single word 'stalker', followed by an exclamation mark.

'Any clothes missing, any suitcases gone, did she have her handbag with her, her passport?'

'What? Passport, no, she didn't have her passport with her, I'm sure, why would she? We went out to have something to eat and then she went back to her home for her last night; she was moving in with me the next day—'

'So you weren't so much flatmates as about-to-be flatmates?'

'I suppose you could put it like that.'

'And you've no idea where she was living with her brother?'

'No.'

'So she might still be in the house?'

'She could be.' Janine cursed herself for her complete ignorance of Kate's details, due to what she had seen as her own delicacy in not asking personal questions until Kate was ready to volunteer them, which in retrospect looked more like indifference than discretion. Now she saw Kate lying at the bottom of a staircase, blood seeping on to geometric tiles of Edwardian red, blue and beige, one leg twisted beneath her at an unnatural angle, or slumped across a bed or—

'Seems odd that you don't seem to know anything about this woman, even though you were planning to share a flat together.'

'Maybe it does . . . but I knew she was OK, she was a nice person, a good person, someone who wouldn't let me down.'

'What about paperwork?'

'She was planning to bring all her personal papers with her when she arrived the next day. There's nothing among her things in the flat, I've already had a good look.'

'What about papers to do with her employment?'

'We hadn't got round to it yet, not properly, and for the things, the forms, she had to fill out, she used our – my – address. And she wouldn't be paying tax just yet, so we just . . .' She shrugged. 'Just let it go.' Oh God, if only she'd been more efficient, more on the ball.

'See, the thing is, if we knew her address, her old address, we could go round there, check that she's OK, hasn't fallen down the stairs or something, can't get to the phone and so forth, but with this complete lack of any details, you'll appreciate that we have just about nothing to go on.'

'Yes,' Janine said humbly, 'I do see that.' She had tried so hard to remember if Kate had given any information at all that might be of use, but couldn't come up with anything. There was that wine bar, where she used to work: had she ever mentioned the name? She rather thought she had, if she could just recall it.

'Not even a phone number?'

'She gave it to me once but I'm not sure where it is.'

'Have a look for it, dear, and let us know.'

'Yes. Yes, I'll do that.' Janine had already dug deep into the memory banks, but could not think where she might have put Kate's phone number.

'Look,' said the officer, her face suddenly changing into that of kindness, of someone who understood Janine's concerns and felt sorry for her. 'Keep in touch. If anything comes back to you, let us know immediately, and meanwhile I'll circulate the description you've given me, all right?'

Jefferson

Twelve

Jefferson woke with a sense of excitement he hadn't felt for years. He lay in his huge custom-built bed (seven foot square and sadly underused; he'd originally bought it for himself and Mary-Anne – Mary-Jane, that is – envisaging weekend mornings with little kids snuggling up while he read them a story, drinking tea and going through the Sunday newspaper, commenting on England's disastrous loss to the Wallabies in the World Cup, perhaps, or listening to Mary-Jane murmuring about the latest must-have handbag or hand-built country kitchen), debating which would be the best time to show up for his rendezvous – if you could call it that – with Kate Fullerton. He wanted to be early enough to ask her for dinner again that evening, before anyone else could chance upon the scene and invite her, but didn't want to be too early, in case he looked overly puppy-with-tongue-hanging-out eager.

In the end, he settled for eleven-thirty, coffee-break time, and strolled in, trying hard to look nonchalant. The agency had that particular smell of warm printed matter and anticipation that he associated with travel, filled as it was with the promise of anything and everything, from palm-fringed lagoons and grinning dolphins to hot-air balloons and snow-filled landscapes dotted with penguins and glaciers, plus small tours designed for 'discerning customers' possessed of 'intellectual curiosity' which seemed to mean an interest in 'Classical Civilizations of the Aegean' or 'In the Steps of Alexander the Great'. Kate Fullerton was nowhere to be seen so he examined brochures offering him trekking holidays in Kenya, cruises down the Loire, adventure trips to Nepal and Peru, sailings to Iceland with a promise of whales and puffins. Kate did not show up after ten minutes, so she was either taking an extra-long coffee break, or . . . or he didn't know what. After a while, he approached one of the other women behind the long counter and asked for her.

'Uh, Kate's not . . . she hasn't – just a moment, will you, I know

Janine will want to talk to you.' The girl – Fran, according to the little black plastic thingy in front of her – got up and went over to a slightly older woman, presumably Janine, who made 'just-a-moment' motions at him. She was dealing with a client – Jefferson eavesdropped avidly – who had always dreamed of white-water canoeing in Colorado and knew that if he didn't do it now, it would be too late and he never would. Janine was trying to explain that at his age and given the bad knee he'd complained of ('*it's my arthuritis*'), it didn't seem quite the sport for him since for a start it involved kneeling in a canoe rather than sitting. It took her another ten minutes to persuade Arthur Itis that sadly it was indeed too late and that if he insisted on a really active holiday, he might enjoy a guided cycling holiday in France much more. Jefferson wanted to suggest the naked race through Japan, but perhaps Mr Itis wasn't into that sort of thing.

Finally Janine was finished. She held out her hand and Jefferson shook it. 'I'm Janine; you're looking for Kate, I understand,' she said.

'That's right. We arranged that I'd come in and fix up my holiday to Ecuador – the Galápagos Islands.'

'I see. Well, um . . .' Janine looked round the room and led him to a table at the rear of the room which was covered in price lists and plastic files. 'The thing is, Mr . . . um . . .'

'Andrewes.'

'The thing is, Kate seems to have gone missing.'

'Missing?'

'She was supposed to move in to my flat on Sunday – we're going to be sharing – and never showed up, still hasn't. And she didn't arrive for work yesterday or today. I know she could be ill, or unexpectedly called away or something, but she's much too reliable not to have let me know.'

'Have you been to the police?'

'I went in to file a Missing Person report, but they weren't terribly interested.' Janine screwed up her face. 'I feel we ought to be contacting her brother, but I don't know how since he's away at a conference in California. Like I said, she could just be sick. And then, I don't know her that well – maybe she often takes off without letting anyone know where she's gone, but from what I *do* know of her, it seems extremely unlikely.'

Jefferson frowned at his hands, which were clasped on the table. 'Have you ever heard of someone called Michaels?'

'No.'

'Stefan Michaels?'

'It doesn't ring any bells.'

'Has she ever mentioned a stalker?'

'Yes, she has, a couple of times.'

'Do you have any information on him?'

'None at all. Why? Do you think he could have turned violent, kidnapped her or something?' Janine's face paled and for a moment he glimpsed in her eyes everyone's darkest imaginings: chains, whips, rapes, torture, death.

'Almost certainly not,' he said, without the slightest authority for saying so. 'Much more likely she's . . . uh . . . gone down to London for the day. Or up to Edinburgh, I think she told me she had an uncle up there.'

From Janine's expression it was clear that whatever bizarre scenario he could conjure up would be more likely than Kate just taking off without telling her. She shook her head vigorously. 'Never. Some emergency might have come up, but she'd never not let me know, she's not like that.' She bit her lip. 'Should we go to the police again?'

He liked that 'we', that conjoining of the friends of Kate. 'Any idea *when* she might have disappeared – if indeed she has?'

'We went out for *dim sum* on Saturday, after we'd closed up. I waited with her for her bus, then I went home. She was supposed to move in to my place the next day, Sunday, so she could finish putting her things away and settle in, and then . . . then we were going to have dinner quietly at home and she n-never arrived.'

'So she must have gone missing – if she did – between Saturday night and Sunday night.' He thought about it. 'Could she have been in a car accident or something?'

'She hasn't got a car.'

Jefferson tried to imagine Kate, whom he didn't know in any meaningful sense of the word, helping an old lady across the road who turned out to be a white slaver and stabbed her with a syringeful of Rohypnol, or rushing into a burning house to rescue a babe-in-arms, only to succumb to smoke inhalation or licking flames. Was she a helper of old ladies, however suspect? A dasher into blazing buildings? He had no idea and, he suspected, neither did Janine. 'In case he's involved, we need to get a handle on this Michaels guy, the stalker,' he said. 'Find out where he was late on Saturday.'

'Even if it was something to do with him, we don't know where he lives, or what he does.'

'True . . .'

'The one thing I'm certain of,' reiterated Janine, 'is that she wouldn't willingly have gone anywhere without letting me know.'

'Which suggests that she might not be a free agent.'

'Oh, my God.' Janine got up and twitched at the cravat thing in her white blouse. 'I'm going back to the police.'

'I'll come with you.'

She frowned. 'What's your interest?'

'Um . . . well, we . . .' Jefferson's mind soared into fast-forward. 'We're getting married,' he said.

'Who to?'

He gazed at her with all the conviction he could muster. 'Each other, of course.'

'She's never said anything to me about getting married,' Janine said. 'She hasn't even got a boyfriend at the moment.'

'Well, that's what I meant . . . I'm her new . . . um . . . partner.'

'No, you're not. You're the man who came in on Friday afternoon and invited her out to dinner.'

In the humiliation stakes, this was right up there with the time Melvin Buonfiglio had kicked in the door of the school bogs, where he was sitting reading *Playboy* and having a quiet wank; half the school seemed to be crowded outside the door, jeering and laughing, Jefferson Wankscrewes, they called him, until he started handing out detentions like they were pizza parlour flyers. He spread his hands. 'OK, what can I say? I only met her for the first time last week, but that doesn't stop me being as concerned as you are.'

'How can you be? You don't know her.'

'Maybe not *know* know, but I *know* her, if you know what I mean.'

'I do know the meaning of "know", thank you.'

Jefferson was reprimanded. Now he came to think of it, Janine looked a bit like Buonfiglio: same dark hair and black eyes, currently staring at him with both suspicion and dislike. 'Look, let's just go to the police, shall we?'

The police station was unlike anything Jefferson had seen before, being nothing more than a converted shopfront (he was pretty sure it had been a greengrocer's back when he was a schoolboy here, riding past in a taxi on his way from the station), with the words THE COP SHOP painted along the fascia-board where it used to say J & F Kenyon, Fruiterers & Greengrocers. Whatever happened to good old-fashioned police stations? THE COP SHOP . . . it sounded as though the police weren't taking themselves seriously enough, pandering to the lowest common denominator, like the Church of England trying to get all matey and playing pop music on acoustic guitars or using colloquial version of the Lord's Prayer or the Bible, which seemed to produce no discernible gathering in of the sheep which had gone astray, and merely served to alienate the sheep which for years had been faithful attenders on Sunday.

A desk sergeant, if that's what he was, listened to what they had to say, turning a felt-tipped pen between his fingers as though ready to use it whenever it seemed worthwhile, though thus far it hadn't. Behind him, at a different desk, sat a woman leafing through a buff folder in a way which suggested that she couldn't give a toss about the contents. *What was I thinking*, Jefferson wondered, looking back at his idealistic sixteen-year-old self and his wish to join the force. He imagined some poor defrauded widow who'd given away her life's savings to a cowboy builder assuring her that if she didn't have immediate and costly renovations done, the roof would fall about her ears any day now, possibly that very night, or some old boy with a tobacco-tinged moustache and trousers stained yellow at the crotch being tormented by yobs on a sink estate, a guy whose car had been stolen and torched, a woman assaulted: none of them worth more than a passing interest. He knew this was the wrong image, that generally the police were caring and efficient people who went about their distasteful enquiries with stern resolve, but judging by the atmosphere in THE COP SHOP, it was hard to believe.

'Sorry.' The man sat up straighter. 'Maybe your friend's just decided to take a day off.'

'She wouldn't do that,' Janine insisted. 'She's not the kind of person to let people down; it's totally out of character.'

'It takes all sorts,' the sergeant said.

'Meaning what, exactly?' asked Jefferson.

'Meaning, sir, that people don't always do what you expect them to, that they often surprise you by acting out of character.'

This was so patently true that neither Jefferson nor Janine could think of a response. 'If you haven't heard anything in another couple of days, come back,' the sergeant said, more kindly.

'It's already been three days,' said Janine, 'and meantime, Mrs Fullerton could be lying dead in a ditch.'

'Then – with all due respect – there wouldn't be a lot we could do for her, would there? Besides, if that were the case, someone would have found her by now. A dog-walker, probably, you wouldn't believe how many bodies are discovered by people taking the family pet out for a walk.' He seemed prepared to expand on the theme of dogs and their ability to nose out corpses, but Janine cut in on him.

'She could be in need of help,' she said.

'I can't see what we can do.' The sergeant spread his hands. 'We'll keep a look out, mind you . . .'

'What would you be looking out for exactly?' Jefferson, as a detective manqué, genuinely wanted to know (Bodies? SOS messages chalked on a wall? The word HELP! scrawled on a piece of cardboard and held up to an attic window?) but the man seemed baffled by the question and, in fairness, Jefferson could see why. The information he and Janine were able to provide was minimal, giving the police almost nothing to go on, even if they were interested at this early stage, and he knew that, at least for the moment, the current whereabouts of Kate Fullerton were a lost cause.

As they got up to leave, Janine asked him if he knew that forty-six per cent of complaints against the police were down to either indifference or rudeness.

'Are you accusing me of—?'

'I'm not accusing you of anything,' she told him. 'I'm just saying.'

Jefferson and Janine walked down Eastgate Street, towards the canal, then turned away from it into the heart of the town. After a few moments, they passed a wine bar full of thirty-somethings, many of whom, eager for the pale early-spring sunshine, had spilled out into the street and were standing with glasses of Chardonnay in their hands, or seated at the three wooden picnic tables with integrated benches which had been behind a hedge, growing in a long black wooden box, somewhat similar to a coffin. He saw two of his colleagues there, chatting up one of the women from Mergers and another from Trading, but didn't make himself known.

'Hey!' Janine said. 'I'm pretty sure this is the place where Kate used to work.' She stepped back and looked up at the sign above the door. 'Plan A. Yup, this is it.'

'Let's go in, then. They might know something.'

Janine looked at her watch. 'I really ought to be getting back – we're short-handed enough, without Kate there.'

'Tell you what . . . I'll drop by later and tell you if I find out anything useful.'

'Fine.'

Inside, the bar was dark and cool. Jefferson approached the older man chatting to one of the girls behind the counter. 'I'll have a glass of Sauvignon Blanc, please.' He pointed to the slate on the wall advertising the day's Specials.

As it was being poured, he turned to the girl. 'Did you know Kate Fullerton?'

She looked at the older man and then back at him. 'Why do you ask?'

'She seems to have gone missing, and we thought maybe you had some idea of where she might have gone.' He was proud of that anonymous but embracing second person plural, which implied a perfect right to be asking questions, without exactly telling lies.

'Issa da Stefan person, Tina,' the man said. 'I tellin' you issa him!'

'You mean the one who's supposed to have been stalking her?' said Tina.

'Dassa bastard. Now he kill her too, I bet.'

'One of our regulars had been following her,' Tina said to Jefferson. 'Stefan someone.'

'When you say regulars . . .'

'Frequent repeat customers – not that he's been in for a while now, not since Kate left, actually. I think she was the draw and now she's changed jobs.' She shrugged. 'He's obviously off to bother someone else.'

'He fancied her,' said the second girl, 'like he did poor Lindsay.'

'Did he look like someone who would try to harm her?' Jefferson asked.

'Not really, he was kind of wimpy, pumped on steroids, I had a boy friend like that once.'

'That other one, his friend,' said Tina. 'Nasty bit of work . . . I wouldn't put anything past him. Sell his own mother down the river, he would.'

'Do you know *his* name?'

She shook her head. 'Sorry.'

'Issa bastard,' said the man. 'Issa all bastards.'

'Would you have an address for Kate?'

They all shook their heads. 'Somewhere in the Highfields area, I think,' Tina said. 'Near the canal, I think she said once.'

They all looked at him anxiously, as though afraid he might start demanding to see records and income tax returns, making it obvious that these were probably a little incomplete, if not downright dodgy.

He left, emerging into the cool sunshine of an early-summer day, not much wiser than when he went in. He stopped in at TaylorMade Travel, and told Janine his lack of further information. And for the moment, that seemed to be that.

Kate
Thirteen

Her lips were cracked and dry; her tongue had swollen to fill the entire cavity of her mouth. If she didn't drink immediately she would die of thirst. Feebly she raised her head and waved at a passing camel-train but they didn't see her and she lay down again on the sand, her tongue rasping against her flaking lips. Water, for the love of God, *my need is greater than yours*, so many references to water, *water, water everywhere and not a drop to drink*. An oasis shimmered beneath waving date palms, *cool clear water*, she could hear the clatter of their leaves, and she knew she'd have to get to it if she was to survive, before her tongue turned black and her eyes dried out and her heart stopped, *keep a-movin', Dan* . . .

She tried to sit up, and immediately lay back down. Under her dehydrated cheek, the sand moved and shifted, whispering of death and desiccation, cow skulls with eye sockets picked clean by bald black vultures, smell of hot desert, Bedouin tents, stink of goats, those rattling palm leaves . . . enough to drive you insane, rattle, clatter, iron striking metal, churns full of goat's milk . . .

Again she tried to sit up and this time was able to remain upright. Her head felt heavy and twice as large as normal, like a medicine ball which had been blown up with a bicycle pump. She put her hands up and clasped her ears, but her head seemed the same size it always had been; something fluttered like tiny moths to the sheet on which she lay and she realized it was flakes of dried blood. Her ear was tender where Stefan's ring had cut it. Although there was very little light, it was enough for her to see that she was lying fully dressed on a bed in an almost empty room. The tape had gone from her mouth; the restraints had been removed. Nor were there any black Bedouin tents, nor camels, nor date palms. Just the consuming thirst. She got to her feet and staggered on legs that bent under her like cooked spaghetti towards a peeling wooden door set into one end of a wall. Someone had long ago installed a washbasin and a loo, both rust-stained, both filthy. She turned on the tap and shoved her mouth under it, swallowing huge gulps of water until her stomach felt bloated and she had the sudden urge – *need* – to throw up. She dropped to her knees and vomited copiously into the filthy lavatory bowl, watching *sake* and *dim sum* and, in the end, when her stomach was completely empty, a thin brown slime, splash into the water. Disgusting, really, but she felt a lot better as she depressed the chrome fitment and watched the whole mess swill away.

What the hell was going on?

Sitting on the edge of the bed, it all came back to her: the abduction, the syringe, Stefan Michaels' triumphant expression. Weak tears broke from her eyes. Where was she, where was *he*, what was he playing at, though play was about as far away from her current situation as it was possible to be. What did he want? Did he plan to keep her here until she died? There was that book, years ago, *The Collector*. There was that poor girl in Germany recently, or was it Austria, whose own father had imprisoned her for twenty-seven years. Unimaginable, horrific. Don't think about it, Kate, or about them. She got up and rattled the door handle.

'Let me out!' she screamed. She hammered at the locked door. 'Please let me out!' Although the room was semi-dark, with outside shutters closed across a dormer window, she was able to see stripes of light. It must be daytime. The morning after the night before, or had she been there longer, days maybe, even weeks? She thought not; she didn't feel weeks older. There were beams across the low sloping ceiling – so she was at the top of the house, in the attic. No carpet, one bed, one chair, and a small table, all made of metal. She tried to open the window, but it had been padlocked shut. She couldn't break the glass, either: a strong steel mesh had been screwed over it.

Outside the door, footsteps echoed on bare wooden stairs, coming nearer, stopping outside the door. Instinct made her curl up on the bed, pretend to be still drugged, weaker than whoever was coming expected.

The door was unlocked, opened, locked again. She heard keys being removed, a faint metallic rattle as they were stowed in the pocket of either a jacket or trousers. Footsteps across the floor, stopping beside the bed. 'Get up!'

She didn't react.

'I said, get up.' It was Michaels. 'I know you're awake, I heard the toilet flushing, heard you shouting.'

No point pretending. She pulled herself up. 'What the fuck are you doing?' she demanded.

A smile curved across his lips. 'You'll see.' He was wearing a black leather jacket over an open-necked striped shirt. The gold stud glinted in his ear. Even in this situation, she had to concede that he was good-looking. Small, but perfectly formed.

'Why are you doing this?' she said.

''Cos nobody disses me and gets away with it.'

'I don't know what you mean.'

Suddenly he was whirling across the room, arms lifted, standing on the tips of his toes as though about to perform a *pas seul*. '*You can't afford me, Stefan. I'll be washing my hair, Stefan . . .*' He spoke furiously, in a high-pitched falsetto which she realized was meant to be an imitation of her own speech. 'In front of my brother, my father, they were *laughing* at me.' Again his voice rose. '*And this is your not-so-clever son . . .* You made me look like a total moron.'

Which is exactly what you are, Stefan, a total moron. 'It was meant to be a joke.'

'Some fuckin' joke. I could have killed you right then and there.'

'And instead you kidnap me, drug me and imprison me in some empty room.'

'It's gonna get worse.'

'Do you think you'll get away with this?'

'Yes, I think I will.'

She shivered. He sounded much too sure of himself. 'What do you want?' she said.

'I'll show you in a minute, but first I'll describe it for you, tell you exactly what I'm going to do to you, so you can enjoy the anticipation.'

'You have no right . . .'

'I know.' He bared a mirthless smile at her. 'That's what makes it such fun.'

'You can't keep me here.'

He looked around, at the door, the windows. 'Want to bet? Take your clothes off.'

'What?'

'You heard. Take them off.'

'You're mad.'

'Take them off.

'NO!'

He pulled a knife from his belt, grabbed her by the arm in the soft hurtful place above the elbow and pulled her upright, then slit her shirt and trousers from throat to crotch, so that the two halves fell down her arms and legs, and she stood there in her underwear. She folded her arms across her breasts. Her Armani trousers bought in a sale . . . thank goodness she hadn't paid full price for them, she thought irrelevantly, though the MaxMara shirt had cost a fortune . . . 'If you think you'll get away with this . . .' She lashed out at him, using both hands fisted together. She caught him high on the cheekbone and he cursed, grabbed her nipple through the lace of her bra and twisted until tears of agony ran down her cheeks, then slapped her so viciously across the face that she felt teeth loosen along her jaw.

'Shut up, bitch.' He pushed her backwards on to the bed, held her down with one hand while he shrugged out of his jacket. 'Undo my shirt,' he commanded.

'Undo it yourself, you bastard.' She swung her knees up, leaped up at him again, but he grabbed her breast again, the same one and she fell backwards, the pain almost unendurable.

He laughed. Still holding her down, he pulled down his zip, pushed his jeans to the floor and stepped out of them. He wore no underpants; she could smell sexual urgency on him, like spilled whisky. He pushed a vicious knee between her legs and fell on top of her.

Every woman at one time or another has imagined what she might do if she were raped, how she might win the battle. She'd seen it simulated so often, discussed the subject with the girls many times, batting theories back and forth over the best way to deal with it. Nothing, no amount of debate, could have prepared her for the reality. He tore her pants away, grabbed her crotch and squeezed. There was no time to consider any theory, animal instinct simply took over. She kicked and screamed, yelled obscenities, tried to butt him with her head, tried to jab her fingers into his eyes, but although he was slightly built, he was too strong for her, punching at her stomach, her breasts, her ribs while she tried vainly to stop him. Eventually, he glanced at his watch and got up.

It was only while he was belting his trousers that she realized he had not actually done anything remotely sexual, not even by proxy, no fingers forced inside, no foreign objects introduced. She wanted to say something cutting about his performance, or lack of it, but was too shocked, in too much pain, to think of any smart-ass remark, and besides, she didn't want to provoke him into further displays of violence: he obviously got off on pain and distress, and she'd be damned if she would show him any signs of either.

She read his watch from upside-down. Twelve fifty-one. Had anyone missed her yet? This was Sunday – at least, she thought it was: she wasn't even due to Janine's place until this evening.

'I'll be back later,' Michaels said, smoothing down his chest, preening.

'You're insane,' she said wearily.

'I. Am. Not. Insane.'

He didn't like that. She stored the fact away. Did she dare say anything more? Perhaps not. Not this time. She turned away from him and curled up, pulling the sheet over her.

He approached the bed, tugged down the sheet, told her when he returned, he might use a knife on *her* rather than on her clothes, she was too plump here, and here, and besides, he was always excited by the sight of blood, he knew ways to inflict pain, he said, he would have her pleading for mercy, and then he would use her like the piece of filthy scum she was, use her in every way it was possible for a woman to be used. The stream of smut grew repetitive after a while, and she drifted off into a painful doze.

Janine
Fourteen

It was Janine's day to visit her mother in Kelsford, one of the little villages five or six miles from the town, with a tiny post-office-cum-general-store, bakery, two pubs (one of them with a stream flowing past the back of it, with willows weeping into the water, picturesque enough to feature in *This England* calendars from time to time), a chapel, a primary school. Every fourth Sunday of the month, she packed a basket with several glossy magazines ('*Ooh, look at that dress, you can see right up to her wotsit*'), two pounds of best fillet steak ('*red meat's ever so good for the heart*'), two bottles of wine, one red ('*so's red wine*') and one white (so there could be no cause for complaint about the wrong colour), a bunch of grapes (one red and one white), and a round of Stilton. She used to take flowers or chocolates, but when she arrived she would always find that her brother had just bought a bigger box, a more expensive bouquet, and long ago had decided that she wouldn't even try to compete, instead choosing things he would never think of buying. The image of her macho brother buying a copy of *Vogue* was one she particularly enjoyed.

She bent to kiss her mother's cheek, relishing as always the smell of fresh-baked bread which rose from the older woman's hair. After trying various jobs at which she had proved distressingly incompetent, she had been serving behind the counter of the small local bakery for seven years or more and was beginning to take on the look of one of the items on the shelves behind her, a crisp baguette, perhaps, or an empty brandy snap. 'Hi, Mum. How are you doing?'

'I'm fine, Jane. Let's have a look at you.'

Janine stood in front of the armchair where her mother sat, and pirouetted slowly. 'Very nice. Nice pair of slacks.' Her mother sighed. 'Slacks is a good idea; I often used to wonder how you was ever going to get through life with legs like yours.'

Thanks, Mum . . . 'They're Jaeger. You can never have enough pairs of good wool trousers, or so they say.'

'That's a nice top, too.'

'Cashmere.'

'Well, no-one can say you don't make the best of yourself, especially given what you started out with.'

If I ever have a daughter, Janine vowed fiercely, I shall tell her from the very beginning that she is the most beautiful, gifted, gorgeous child that ever was, even if she is as ugly as a changeling, though since she herself was getting closer and closer to thirty-four with no man – no possible *husband* – in sight, let alone a daughter, repulsive or otherwise, the chance to do so seemed to grow further and further away. She had a friend up in the Lake District who'd been so desperate to find a husband that she and her mother had gone into a church together and prayed that she would meet a nice man and that same evening, travelling down to London, that was exactly what happened ('*there* is *a God!*'). Maybe I should do that, she thought, opening both the bottles of the wine she'd brought and pouring a glass from each, though she could hardly conceive of a situation where she'd be able to tempt her mother into a church, let alone in order to pray for a husband.

'There you are, Mum.' She handed one of the glasses over, knowing that whichever colour wine she gave her, she'd want the other.

'I think I'd prefer the white, thanks, Jane.'

'Oh, *Mum*.' More irritated by her mother than usual, Janine passed her the other glass. Kate's continued absence was growing increasingly nerve-racking, even more so given the apparent lack of interest shown by the police, and she'd been finding it hard to ignore the grotesque images of Kate which continually rolled through her mind: Kate bound, Kate gagged, Kate subjected to unspeakable torments. At the same time, she was promising herself that one of these days she would make her mother sit down and tell her that she was no longer called Jane, make her accept that she was Janine now, had been ever since she left home, even had her name changed by deed poll, that there were people who wouldn't know who her mother was talking about if she referred to her daughter as Jane, that she'd also, while she was at it, changed her surname, much too complicated and foreign-sounding (sorry, Dad), chosen something as innocuous as she could – *Janine Taylor, like it or lump it, Mum*, that's what she would say. One of these days . . .

For no apparent reason, unless she had spent some time developing her thought-reading skills, her mother started chuckling. 'Funny little thing you were, Jane, and no mistake. A stick insect, that's what I used to call you.'

'I remember, Mum.'

'And your brother said a stick insect with attitude would be more like.' Her mother laughed with fond reminiscence. 'A stick insect with attitude – I like that.'

'Ha, ha, very funny, and he was the exact opposite, wasn't he? A pig, a real porker, bloated, obese, fat as a barrel but with fewer brains, if he lay down on the beach, the Save the Whale people would come running up and try to drag him back into the sea.' She didn't say it, of course. What was the point? Mum would only get upset and angry. And anyway, since she hadn't seen him for years, he might well have slimmed down now (yeah, right), double-chinned, multi-bellied, man-boobed, fat-arsed slob that he was, or had been – though if truth be told, he hadn't been *that* big, she was exaggerating, enjoying herself while Mum went on and on about her darling son.

'Want me to do the steak, Mum?' she said, after a while. 'Or did you make something?' As if . . . her mother might stir herself to cook a casserole or a steak-and-kidney pie for her boy, but not for her girl.

'That would be nice, dear. There's some of them new potatoes in the larder. You put them on and I'll set the table.'

The kitchen was exactly as it had been when she was still a schoolgirl, the same round-cornered fridge in cream enamel, the pea-green enamel stove with the black burners, the knick-knacks here and there on the windowsill: a double egg-cup with black boots and yellow socks, a crocheted tea-cosy in the shape of a crinolined lady, photos of long-past holidays at Whitby or Scarborough stuck to the shelves with yellowed sticky tape, earthenware containers for tea, sugar, flour, rice, a picture of her brother in his school uniform. There was a photograph of her dog, too, which Dad had given her for her birthday. She'd called him Cary after Cary Grant in *To Catch A Thief* (not that Cary the dog ever caught a thief or even a ball), which she'd loved and her brother hadn't. (*'I hate that ruddy animal, hairs everywhere, licking its balls like it was starving then sticking its filthy tongue right down your throat if you aren't careful, if I want to French-kiss someone, it wouldn't be a bloody dog, I can tell you.'*) One summer evening, she'd looked out of her bedroom window and seen him in the fading light at the end of the garden, seen him hack Cary apart, splitting the animal like a kipper from anus to nose. Cary had barked, yelped, whimpered, fallen silent, the two halves of his little body spread like an opened book on the bloodied soil, his eyes gradually filming over. She could see his heart still faintly beating, until it slowed and finally stopped, and her brother tossing the corpse behind Dad's garden shed and then washing his hands under the outdoor tap. She'd never told anyone, cried in bed that night, gone out the next day and covered poor Cary with grass cuttings.

Removing her own piece of steak, draining the potatoes, adding cream to the steak drippings and a little brandy, shaking the pan until they'd all amalgamated into a sauce, adding salt and pepper and shaking again, she wondered why it was that she didn't hate her brother, was conscious only of a kind of neutrality about him, on the one hand a cruel and despicable person, on the other, her brother, blood is thicker than water and all that. He'd been good to Mum, at any rate, bought her this house, new washing-machine, microwave which Mum was convinced would cook her brains like sweetbreads in a frying pan if she used it, cordless phone. She hadn't seen him for years and hoped she never would, perhaps at Mum's funeral. Would she invite him to her wedding if she (ever) got married? Probably not, she didn't want to frighten the horses, as Miss Barker was always saying, though she would definitely invite Miss Barker, still distinguished-looking, married to a surgeon at the hospital, with nine-year-old twin girls who went to the same school as Janine had done – funny that, you'd think they'd be able to afford private education.

Behind her, an owl hooted very loudly, once, and she jumped, looked up at the bird clock over the kitchen door. When she was still at school she'd saved up for four months to buy it for Mum's birthday, a different bird for each hour, the worst one being twelve o'clock, which was an endless stream of cuckooing, though four o'clock, the blackbird, was nice and so was the thrush at seven. The clock had been up there for years and she always replaced the batteries when they ran down, even though she did not care much for the clock. Perhaps she was just pleased Mum had kept it, though probably it was only from sheer inertia; with her dodgy knee, it would be difficult for Mum to climb on a chair and take it off the wall.

Over lunch, they spoke of nothing very much, or rather Janine did, while Mum banged on about her wonderful son. 'He's doing ever so well, your brother is, starting up businesses all the time, making money hand over fist, to hear him tell it.'

'What does he do, exactly?' It was a question Janine had often posed and one to which she had never had a satisfactory answer.

'He's a big businessman, Jane, ever so successful, *you* know that.'

'But what *kind* of business?'

Her mother shrugged. 'Property, I think. I know he's just bought a house, says I'm too old to go on working, wants me to move in with him, but I don't want to, I like it here, and besides, I'd miss my friends, and my garden.'

Janine glanced out at the patch of ragged grass outside, some sticks which would later bloom into untidy sheafs of golden rod, a crab-apple tree, the ugly tool shed, a shrub which no-one had been able to identify since it never sprouted leaves or blooms, just quietly faded, year by year, rather like Dad, Janine thought. 'Mmm,' she said.

'Here,' continued her mother, 'you should have seen the coat your brother was wearing the other day, he looked like a millionaire, someone out of those fashion pages for men, I felt ever so proud.'

'Do you ever feel proud of me?'

'Of you?' Her mother stared at her, a fork laden with grey, overcooked steak (*'I don't like eating my food raw, Jane,* you *know that'*) halfway to her mouth. 'Of course I do. But you're a girl, aren't you?'

'What difference does that make?' Janine said tiredly, swallowing her own perfectly done mouthful of fillet in green pepper sauce. Vying for her mother's affection wasn't a question of sibling rivalry. Her brother was so far ahead in the maternal-love stakes that he wasn't even playing in the same league as she was.

'Well, you know . . .' said her mother.

'I don't actually. Why don't you explain it to me?'

'Well, for a start, girls don't need the same support as boys, do they?'

'I'd have thought they needed more.'

'Boys have to get on, make a living so they can support a wife and children.'

'Oh, is that what it is?' Janine snorted into her wine glass. 'Mum, do you have any notion what I do for a living?'

'You?' A shifty look came into her mother's eyes as she desperately tried to remember, if she had ever known. 'Some kind of an agency, isn't it? Parties or something.'

'I run a travel agency, actually.'

'Well, there you are, then. Didn't I say so?'

'I don't just run it, Mum, it's mine, I own it, it's called TaylorMade, I started it completely from scratch.' With a little help from her silent partner, her lover, but Janine wasn't about to mention that.

'That's nice.' Her mother looked over at the cheese dish on the sideboard. 'What about a bit of Stil—'

'We cater for holidays with a difference,' Janine plunged on. 'Out-of-the-ordinary vacations to places you wouldn't necessarily think of going.'

'Shouldn't think you make much money if people wouldn't think of going there.'

'We *show* them, Mum, we tell them about exciting alternatives to Benidorm and the like.'

'We had ever such a nice holiday in Majorca once, your dad and I. Or was it Minorca? I always get the two muddled up.'

'They're both in the Balearics, Mum.' What was the use? She could end up as Pope, Queen, Prime Minister and American President all rolled into one and her mother still wouldn't be impressed, wouldn't even be interested. Janine had a fleeting vision of her father in his grey suit, coming through the door, having a beer, ruffling her hair, asking how her day had been at school and listening with real interest to her tales, before shuffling off to the pub. *They are not long, the weeping and the laughter*, she thought, remembering Miss Barker with warmth, thinking there'd been plenty of weeping and not much laughter when she was growing up.

Jefferson
Fifteen

'Hi, Gordon, it's Jefferson here.'

'*Jefferson*!' The voice was warm and friendly. 'How're they hanging, old son?'

'Old son' was stretching it a bit; 'new' son was more like it, but taking this to be an enquiry into his general state of well-being, Jefferson indicated that things were fine, thanks, and that he'd like to drop by, or, rather, down (since Gordon lived some hundred and fifty miles further south) as he had one or two matters he'd like to set out for Gordon's consideration whenever it would be convenient, but sooner rather than later if that was possible.

Gordon was his 'stepfather', though the man had come into his life far too late to be any kind of father to him, step or otherwise. A more unlikely partner for his astringent mother it would have been hard to imagine, so the union had left both Jefferson and his father completely baffled. 'People change, I suppose,' his father said once, 'but the amount of change that woman's gone through is so enormous as to make me wonder whether we're talking about the same person as the one who gave birth to you.'

The improbable thought of his mother as a gangster's moll was sometimes the only thing which prevented Jefferson from suspecting that Gordon operated very close to the wrong side of the law, knowing as he did from his intensive study of the works of Bret McDermot that gangsters' molls chewed gum, wore fishnet tights with a crimson silk garter, had a black bandeau round their head with a red rose stuck into it and were improbably blonde, none of which attributes came anywhere close to a description of his mother. Gordon owned a series of betting shops which Jefferson felt should have pressed almost every one of his mother's disapproval buttons (cruelty to animals, exploitation of the poor and the oppressed, abuse of the vertically challenged, among others), though Jefferson often wondered whether the betting shops were no more than a (semi-) legal cover for any number of criminal pies into which Gordon's beefy thumbs were constantly dipping, Jack-Horner-like, and pulling out illicit plums.

'Jefferson! Come in, come in!' The man was welcoming in a slightly overdone manner which Jefferson, while trying hard not to be judgemental, had long ago labelled Bullshitter Bluff. Gingery hair, ever-expanding gut, Hitlerian moustache, five foot six or less, built like a bollard, Gordon wore cowboy boots, heavily tooled, with bits of bone and turquoise set among the stitched leather curlicues. Jefferson had always wanted to tell him that the heels emphasized rather than diminished his lack of height.

Gordon reached up and banged Jefferson painfully on the shoulder. 'Good to see you, mate, long time no see!'

'Same here.' Jefferson walked into the richly over-decorated house, with its state-of-the-art alarm system, its huge squashy furniture covered in red plush with purple swirls, its shiny tables, its two life-size ceramic leopards sitting on either side of a faux-stone fireplace, its ankle-deep carpeting. On the plus side, although it was decorated in a style which Jefferson associated with bordellos and other houses of ill repute (not that he'd ever entered one, nor had any intention of so doing), it was a warm and comfortable place, and his 'stepfather' was never slow in bringing out the booze in heavy crystal decanters and urging guests to help themselves, to make themselves right at home. 'How's it going, Gordon?'

'Oh, you know . . . your sainted ma . . . I get a bit down now and then, but what can you do?' Gordon said unconvincingly, going over to the bar which stood in one corner of the room, a pseudo-frontier-style roof hanging over it, and shelves behind holding all manner of expensive booze, interspersed with fake wooden boards saying things like **Leave Your Gun At The Door** in lettering supposedly reminiscent of a Wild West saloon. He poured stiff measures of a hugely expensive single malt for them both. 'I'm through in the study, come and park yourself down.'

Jefferson followed him into a dark, consciously masculine room, hung with artefacts testifying to the fact that in his younger days, Gordon had spent much time in Australia and the Far East. His study (Jefferson was never quite clear what Gordon was studying: form, perhaps, or porn videos, judging by a glance or two at the top shelves of the bookcase) was lined with panelled wood (*'gotta mate with a panelling shop,'* Gordon had told him once), and had tartan carpet (presumably the Campbell one) on the floor, with red leather club chairs studded with brass-headed nails. There was a boomerang, some many-armed Hindu goddesses, a platypus under a glass dome, which Gordon claimed to have caught and stuffed himself (if true, that must have been so illegal as to warrant a long prison term) and numerous fat-bellied Buddhas, all of which unnervingly resembled Gordon himself when stripped of his clothes, a sight Jefferson had been privileged to view only last summer when Gordon invited him down for a barbecue and swim in the pool which glistened azurely outside the study window. ('And bring along those kids of your Dad's, if you like,' he'd said generously, which Jefferson had done, to the great delight of Monroe and Madison.)

Gordon put on a sincere face. 'Now, Jeff, what can I do you for?'

'Probably nothing. I . . . it seemed awkward to ask over the phone . . . I just wondered whether my mother . . . Mum . . .'

'I know who you mean.'

'. . . whether, after the . . . accident, you ever had any worries about whether it really was an accident and not something else.'

'Such as?'

'I don't know . . .'

'No worries, Jeff, believe me. None at all. There were too many witnesses who saw the whole thing.' Gordon spread his large hairy hands. 'From what I've been told, the weather at the time was atrocious, and the driving conditions not too wonderful; it could have happened to anyone.'

'I know my father was worried about it.' Whether Gordon had genuinely exercised his taxonomic skills on the thing, or found it in a junk shop, the duck-billed platypus had been given incongruously large blue eyes, which caught and held Jefferson's gaze in an unnervingly friendly manner.

'Yeah, he rang me up about it when it first happened, wanted me to look into it a bit more, seeing as how I had a connection or two in the area. Know what I said? I said, "Truman, old boy, won't make a pennyworth of difference to either of us, no point stirring up trouble, best to just let the poor old girl be."' Gordon glanced piously up at the ceiling.

'You think there might have been trouble to be stirred up?'

'No way, mate. I just thought, you can't bring her back now, let's leave it, get on with our lives.' He sipped his whisky and eyed Jefferson with more than a little pugnacity. 'What's your interest, anyway?'

'Nothing, really. I don't know if you heard but my father died two or three weeks ago—'

'Sorry to hear that, Jeff, he was a decent sort, your dad.'

'And there were some papers—'

'Papers?'

'Mostly concerning Mum's accident, I think. His wife asked me to have a look, since he'd been bothered about it when it happened, slightly dubious circumstances and so on.'

'Tell the truth, I had the same thought when I got the info from the local police.' Gordon leaned back and crossed his short legs, displaying a pair of silk socks featuring at ankle level a golfer who'd just teed off. 'Can't trust the buggers further than you can throw them, really. So I not only had a good old gander at the papers myself, I even got my lawyers to go through them, fine-tooth comb sort of thing, and we figured it was all pretty straight up and above board, nothing fishy about the affair, all seemed hunky-dory. Show you their report, if you like.'

'Well, that might be a good—'

'Mind you, it was a long time ago, got no idea where it'd be now, but I'll take a shufti through my files some time, see if I can dig it out.'

'Probably not worth it, I'm sure there's nothing to worry about,' Jefferson said.

'Point is, you got to move on, Jeff. We all have, not just you, no point crying over spilt milk, know what I mean?'

Jefferson might not have been overly fond of his mother but it seemed hard on her to be equated with a toppled jug of Gold Top. 'I suppose so,' he said reluctantly.

'So, Jeff, what're you up to these days?'

'This and that, the usual, you know . . .'

'Money-making, that it?'

'I suppose that's what it boils down to.'

'You know what they say, no-one can be too rich or too thin.' Gordon laughed expansively and patted his belly. 'I'm not doing too well on the thin stakes but on the other . . .'

'Business good, then?'

'Strength to strength, old son. Signed up a couple of deals last week that should see me right for the next few years, and I'm just about to finalize a couple more that should make my fortune.' He sighed theatrically, Gordon Gecko finally overwhelmed by success. 'After that, it's off somewhere on holiday – haven't decided where yet. I'm looking into something really luxurious, just for a change – I had my fill of budget hotels with your mother, God rest her soul. Thinking about that Atlantis Hotel in Dubai in that palm-shaped thing they built off the coast. What about you, got any holiday plans?'

'As a matter of fact . . . a friend of mine was recommending the Galápagos Islands.' Jefferson's heart shifted as he thought of Kate; there had still been no word from her and it was five days now, where could she be? Other unfortunate women who'd disappeared and never been seen again raced screaming through his brain, no, that hadn't happened to Kate, he was absolutely sure of it.

'Galloping whats? Never heard of it.' Gordon stared at him, eyes the colour of sucked cough-drops, round with ignorance.

'They're islands off the coast of Ecuador.'

'Ecuador? Heard of that, course I have. Means equator in Spanish, I think it was your mum who told me that before she . . .' He groaned, placed a hand over his heart. 'God, I miss her. How long you staying out there, what you going to be doing?'

'Bit of sightseeing, really, before I move on to the Islands.'

'And what've they got to interest a townie like you?'

'Masses of wildlife – finches, volcanoes, giant turtles and, I'm reliably informed, blue-footed boobies.'

'Boobies?' Gordon chortled. 'Now you're talking.' Despising himself, Jefferson laughed alongside him. 'Doesn't sound like my sort of thing at all,' Gordon went on. 'South America, isn't it, godforsaken hole, nothing but bag-snatchers and cheap whores, like as not.'

'That's a bit sweeping, Gordon.'

'They're all the same, these places. Give me white beaches, blue swimming pools, flushing khazi and a floating bar, and I wouldn't call the king my uncle.'

'You can probably get all that in Ecuador,' Jefferson said mildly.

'So, when are you off?'

'Haven't got my ticket yet, but . . .' Again Jefferson tried not to think of Kate . . . 'Beginning of the month.'

'Got a hotel fixed up?'

'Not yet. I'm hoping the travel agency will—'

'Give me a bell when you've booked your flight, old son. I got a mate runs a place out in Quito . . .' Gordon looked at Jefferson and frowned. '*Think* it's there, unless I'm mixing it up with Peru—'

'Bit of a difference, Gordon.'

'No, no, I'm sure I'm thinking of the right place, anyway, let me know; my mate owes me one, I'll get you a really good price, rock-bottom, better than any agency could come up with, all that lot's after is their commission.' Gordon levered himself out of the yielding sofa he had sunk into. 'Look, don't want to rush you, Jeff, and I really appreciate you dropping by, but I got a friend coming round, a special friend, know what I mean?' He winked obscenely, raising in Jefferson's unwilling mind images of his stepfather on the job. 'We're going out for a drink first and then meeting people at a restaurant. Nice girl, you'd like her, might even take her on holiday with me.' He winked again. 'Can't mourn for ever, can you?'

. . . and besides, the wench is dead, Jefferson thought, hauling himself to his feet, though the last thing anyone would have accused his mother of was being a wench. 'Garden's looking good, Gordon.'

'Even better when summer finally comes. Want a quick look round?'

Not really, Jefferson thought. 'Love to.'

To the accompaniment of some kind of constant buzzing noise which Jefferson took to be a distant neighbour giving his grass the first cut of the season, they strolled beside wide flower beds to the end of an immaculate lawn, where a couple of drooping willows, tiny leaves just bursting out of yellow branches, formed a natural fence between the two halves of the garden. Beyond them lay a large pond with lily-pads round the edges, and bulrushes at the far end. The source of the noise was revealed as dozens of tiny frogs hopping and croaking, leaping from leaf to leaf, clinging on to bits of bark and watching Gordon with shiny golden eyes. 'Noisy little buggers, aren't they?' Gordon said admiringly. His mobile phone chirped into life, and as one frog, they plinked into the water.

Gordon glanced at the number of the caller and turned away. ''Scuse me, Jeff, old son, I ought to take this, unfinished business.

Back in a tick. You just walk round, nice view at the end of the garden, you'll like it.' He turned away and pushed back between the fronds of the willows.

Jefferson tried not to listen, a task made easier as the frogs climbed back on to the flat lily leaves and began croaking again. 'Your problem, matey, you solve it,' he unwillingly heard, '. . . I don't care . . . can't be doing with . . . look, buster, guy's a loose cannon . . . deal with it . . . unless you want . . . OK, that's good . . .'

Jefferson concentrated on a lilac bush, raised a branch to his nose and sniffed at the blossom, feeling faintly foolish. Jeez, what the hell was he overhearing here? It sounded ominous, it sounded dangerous.

Gordon came pushing back through the willow curtain. 'Gawd, no rest for the wicked, can't trust anyone these days to do what you want, considering the salaries some of my guys get . . .'

'Nothing serious, I hope.'

'No way. But I'll tell you something, Jeff, you ever find yourself in any kind of business, watch out for the loose cannons of this world, there're more of them about than you realize and they can bring an organization down, just like that.' Gordon snapped his fingers and the frogs leaped again for the safety of the water, from which they stared at the two men with their tiny brilliant eyes.

'Hope I didn't interrupt you.' Jefferson began to walk back up to the house.

'Not at all, Jeff, any time, me old son, any time. Don't forget to call me before you take off for Ecuador, I'll see you right, a quick bell to my associates.' Gordon led him towards the front door. 'And if you want my advice, which you probably don't, re your mother's accident, I'd just leave it lay, as the Yanks say. Never does any good to rake up the past.'

'You're probably right.'

As Jefferson started up his car, another one pulled up and as the occupant got out, he caught a glimpse of a hatchet-faced (what did that mean, exactly?) blonde-haired woman done up to the nines in a high-collared red suit, froth of white blouse at the neck and white stilettos to match, gold chain round her left ankle, the complete antithesis of his mother. One of these days he was absolutely going to take the bull by the horns and ask Gordon what in the world had drawn him to her, since a more unlikely couple it was difficult to imagine, though it was perfectly possible that when Gordon wasn't running his betting shops and whatever other businesses he owned (or murdering defenceless Antipodean wildlife), he could be seen on the picket lines over the flouting of human rights in China, or manning the barricades to protest against the dumping of nuclear waste. Seemed unlikely, though.

And perhaps Gordon was right. What could possibly be gained by looking into a long-ago car accident, even supposing Jefferson was competent to do so? Only the thought of his father, plus images of Philip Marlowe in the *Big Sleep* (the 1946 version set in Los Angeles, rather than the 1978 one) and a more poignant one of Romilly's sad face kept him geared up to continue scanning the papers which had set his father speculating as to whether justice had been done and the true facts of his former wife's death had been uncovered.

Kate
Sixteen

Because of the drugs he fed her, not all the time, but often enough, her memory jumped and faltered. The hours passed hazily, a constant hallucinatory loop of dreaming and enduring, threats and degradation.

She wanted to show him that whatever he did to her, he couldn't break her spirit, wanted to spit and curse at him, but she feared that if she did, he would grow more violent. At least he did not – could not? – actually rape her. A mercy, though a small one. Often she drifted away, back to the safety of school, to the rented many-verandahed house on Santa Cruz, to moonlit beaches and waving palms, shrieking parrots and the chirp of finches, not sure, sometimes, exactly where she was, whether she had left this ugly room and gone elsewhere or was still lying on the smelly sheet he had spread over the mattress. Over and over again, she lived through the sequence of events which had led to her being here and thought, *even if I'd known what would happen, how could I have deflected it, how else would I have responded?* If it hadn't been that night, it would have been another, all because she'd 'dissed' that strutting little inadequate.

She dreamed. The past returned. Places she no longer belonged to, people she no longer knew, memories she did not know she owned. Observing them, spotlighting them, she saw clearly that we are always moving forward and can carry only so much of the past accumulation with us into the present, that in order to survive, it is necessary to forget, to leave behind. But one piece of memory, incomplete but still horrifying, would not be discarded. She had spent nearly ten years trying to push it away, and had succeeded to a certain extent. But here in this dreary room, it replayed itself, not once or twice, but many times, herself sitting in the back of the car with Annie and Luisa, staring out of the window at a parakeet, red and yellow and green, its long tail feathers brushing the leaves as it flitted between the creepers. Cloud hung over the leaves, the forest, dampened the roadway which led straight along towards the village they were coming up to at Dad's usual steady driving pace, his summer assistant in the passenger seat beside him. One minute she was idly watching a group of men standing at the side of the road watching their approach, not Indians, more like men from the city, the mainland, talking together as the car approached them, some kid peeping at them around the edge of a white wall. The next, she was lying on her back, blinking up at the sky through the car's roof, which looked as though someone had taken a tin-opener and peeled it back. Beyond the jagged edges, she could see brilliant birds fussing, emerald feathers distinct as jewels among the leaves. Palm fronds pressed against the hot white sky. Shards of glass powdered her arms; her face and hair felt sticky. Only much later would she realize that she was covered in the brains and blood of the two in the front seats. One of her arms was pinned under something, she could see Annie's leg, her white sock and brown sandal, directly in front of her, unattached to anything else, she could smell fire and scorching flesh, the heat of flame on her skin, burning, her arm, her leg, oh, her leg; Dad's summer assistant lying against the front window, mouth open, teeth lying like an unstrung necklace on her navy blue shirt, a mix of other smells: gasoline, faeces, blood. Far away, she could hear voices, quick and urgent. She'd wiggled her fingers and felt something soft, silky, and realized after a long while that it was Luisa's hair. 'Mummy?' she whispered, though her mother had died years before. 'Daddy?'

It happened so quickly. The iron curtain crashing down between Before and the Rest of her Life, changing everything, irreversible and immutable.

There were few thoughts, mostly images flashing past, and behind them, the question which had never been answered: why? Why then? Why them? Dad had lived and worked in Ecuador on and off for years, so what had changed?

She had times of lucidity, and in these she walked around the room where they kept her, clutched at the bars which covered the shuttered windows, rattled the handle of the locked door. By now she *must* have been missed. Even if Magnus wasn't back from California, there was her job at the travel agency. Janine: she had to have gone to the police. But although she was fairly sure she had spoken of Stefan, Kate feared that she had never told Janine his name, so even if she *had* alerted the authorities, they would have little to go on.

She had no idea where she was. No real sense of time passing, though through the edges of the shutters she could faintly see the change of light from night to day. But there were days she might have missed, and sometimes she felt herself fragmenting, receding like a mirror hit by a bullet, pieces of herself spinning away into the distance until they disappeared.

Hatred, and the thought of revenge sustained her, kept her strong. That and the certainty that sooner or later, she would find a way to get out of here. Meanwhile, it was important that she maintained her self-respect, kept up her strength. She tried to exercise by pacing up and down, lifting the metal chair and then the table in alternate hands many times a day, did sit-ups and press-ups, ate whatever he brought her even though she knew that sometimes it must be drugged. And she waited. Escape and revenge. The two occupied her thoughts, got her through the wavering days. Revenge was easier. It would be long and slow, the death she would inflict on Stefan, the man who believed he had only to ask and she would fall into his arms, the one whose humiliation and pride was the cause of all this. There'd be blood and tears and more blood. He would beg until he saw that there was no hope, and then he would fall silent, sensing death somewhere close by – but not close enough. Occasionally this thought would cause her such pleasure that she would smile, sometimes even laugh aloud. In her more lucid moments, she knew this was nothing more than a fantasy, that she would be incapable of such actions, but it was one she clung to because it gave her something to keep focused on.

She could discover very little about her location. The house was obviously empty; no-one was living there, at least for the moment. Was Stefan an estate agent? A property developer? Did the house belong to a friend? At night, the darkness was total: no indication of street lamps or lights from passing cars, so probably somewhere isolated. She lived on the takeaway food he brought her: pizzas, Chinese dishes of vegetables and rice, Indian curries, bags of apples and oranges, water from the filthy tap.

She could hear his footsteps echoing on uncarpeted wooden steps as he came upstairs to where she waited. Stefan worked out at the gym: muscles like bowling-balls congregated at the top of his arms;

when he held her down on the bed, the veins popped and crawled under his tanned skin. She looked at his taut jaw line, and knew that he was far too strong for it to be worth struggling. Would he let her live? Almost certainly not: after this, he couldn't simply let her go – not only could she could identify him, but she would. She did not want to die, not yet, not here. The Stockholm Syndrome was where victims gradually felt sympathy, perhaps even love, for their captors. No way was that going to happen here. If – *when* – she got out, she would feel nothing but hatred and contempt. But she'd read somewhere that the more some kind of relationship was built up, the harder it was in the end for the captor to kill his prey, so at first she tried to personalize things, use his name, thank him for the food he brought, but her hatred wouldn't lie down, and it seemed a pointless charade. She was here so he could hurt her, not because he saw her as a bargaining chip, except that so far, despite his tedious sadistic fantasies about what he was going to do to her, the different disgusting ways he was going to abuse her, he had done nothing except punch her around, and throw himself on top of her, force his fingers inside her, until slowly it had dawned on her that he was unable to get it up, or at least, unable in circumstances like these.

This was both pleasing and empowering.

'I have to brush my teeth, it's been days,' she said firmly. It wasn't a question, or a plea, but a statement. Her mouth tasted foul, her breath must smell, though sometimes he left chewing-gum along with the takeaways.

'You can't have a toothbrush.'

'Why not?'

'Mick says you'd stick it in my eye if you had one.'

How right Mick was. 'Then at least bring me toothpaste. I can use my finger as a brush.' She watched him consider, wonder if she could use the tube to harm him in some way.

He was wavering. 'All right,' he said. She guessed that he was beginning to feel anxious about what he and Mick had done, were doing, whether he would really get away with it. She guessed that the plan had been Mick's, feeding Stefan's macho fantasies of dominance, of getting even, and she guessed, too, that if and when Mick showed up, things would be horribly different. She had to get out of here, and she saw the toothpaste as a victory of sorts.

She spent hours wondering how she could fashion a weapon. Although they had obviously planned and prepared for her abduction and imprisonment in detail, she knew that they could not have thought of everything. She was cleverer than either of them, and she could outwit them, especially Stefan on his own, if she only focused on the problem. She examined the table, chair and bed many times, testing the strength of joints and legs, tearing at the fabric which covered the bed's base to see if she could wrest a spring free, but she didn't waste energy on it, knowing she wasn't strong enough to pull the furniture apart. The walls were thick and solid; there was no chimney breast. He'd provided her with a sliver of soap and a towel, plus sheets and a blanket, but taken away all her clothes.

By now she knew the room as intimately as a lover: every crack in the walls, every stain on the ceiling, the scuff marks on the floor, the paint peeling from the woodwork, the dry-rot in the window-sill and skirting boards.

After much consideration, she had reached the conclusion that her only weapon was Stefan himself.

Stefan would be easier to manipulate than Mick, the thug, the bottom-feeder, if and when he finally appeared. Her mind groped its way through the sludge they had filled it with, offered her blue-footed boobies, Annie dancing in the garden sprinkler, thirteen finches chirping. She worked on a plan, though it was difficult with such meagre resources at her disposal, and a brain which wheeled and drifted inside her skull.

Each day, head swimming, she forced her body off the bed and marched round the room ten, twenty, a hundred times. She swung her arms up and down and in front of her. She brought her knees up to her chin, one after the other, ten times, twenty times, fifty times, determined not to let the drugs control her. And she worked on her plan. There was no mirror in the room, but if the light was right, she could sometimes make herself out in the glass of the windows, behind the screen. She draped the sheet seductively over herself, pulling and folding until it resembled a dress, she preened this way and that, forced her mouth into a smile, dragged her fingers through her hair since she had no comb.

'I need shampoo,' she said coldly, next time he arrived, and saw his eyes shift from side to side. Shampoo, shampoo, did he dare allow her to have some? She was winning, she could tell. 'Look at my hair.' She grabbed a handful. '*Feel* it. You used to like my hair. I can't go on washing it with soap. Besides, there's only a sliver left. Bring me shampoo. It doesn't have to be a big bottle. You needn't let Mick know.'

The next day, he brought her a small bottle of shampoo. She tried not to show her triumph.

He was in a suit today, with a tie and colour-coordinated shirt. Good, she thought, good, excellent. He undid his belt, lowered the zip, let his trousers fall to the ground and stepped out of them. He walked over to her, semi-erect, his penis poking out from under his shirt, waving like the branch of a tree, a drop of moisture at its tip; something had finally turned him on. Maybe he'd been in touch with Mick again, Mick the Mentor, Mick the Monster, been fired up in some way. For the first time in days she felt real fear.

'Let me go,' she said softly.

He ignored her, pulled off his tie, undid his shirt, dropped his jacket over the chair, watching her all the time in case she launched herself at him, attacked him.

'You don't really want to do this,' she said.

He shoved her back against the pillows so hard that her head smashed against the wall. 'Wanna bet?'

'I thought you fancied me.'

'I used to. Not any more.' His mouth sneered. 'Have you looked at yourself recently?'

'How would I do that? You haven't left me a mirror.'

'If I did, you'd break it into pieces and stab me.'

'Why would I do that, Stefan?' she said flirtatiously, though the words stuck in her mouth like under-baked bread. She reached under his shirt, trying not to shudder. 'Oh, man,' she said. 'Wow!'

He looked at her suspiciously. 'What do you mean?'

'I hadn't realized how . . . *big* you are.' She leaned back against the pillows, feeling the bruise at the back of her head. 'Ever done it with the girl on top?'

'Hundreds of times.'

'OK, then I won't bother showing you how good that can be.' She turned away from him, let her body sag. 'Better get on with what you came to do.'

She felt him hesitate. Then his fingers on her naked shoulder. 'Let's try it,' he said.

She grinned fiercely before moving to face him. What a stupid conceited self-satisfied moron! 'Lie down here,' she said, moving over a little.

She positioned herself above him, moved seductively a couple of times, let her breasts caress his chest. 'See,' she said. 'Isn't that good?' If she absolutely had to, she would take him in her mouth, though the very thought brought nausea jumping to the back of her throat. 'Isn't that nice?'

'Mmmm.' His mouth hung open, drool pooling in his lower lip. He nodded, closing his eyes, groaning softly with pleasure. She circled one arm around him, held him tightly, pressing her body down over his chest. 'That's marvellous,' she whispered. 'Magnificent. Stefan, you're fantastic.'

'Mmm,' he murmured. 'Oh God, that's so . . . so . . .'

'Yes,' she said, moaning. 'Oh, yes, yes.' Moving lightly above him, she reached one arm down to the floor, felt for the open plastic bottle she'd put just under the bed then in one movement brought it up, squeezed shampoo deep into his mouth and then, as his eyes flew open with shock and he began gagging, into his eyes as well.

'Bastard!' she screamed. 'Filthy disgusting *bastard*!' She pulled herself off him, squirted more shampoo into his face, down his throat, slammed both her fists as hard as she could into his groin, sliced at his windpipe with the side of her hand.

He shrieked, choked, curled into a ball, tears and snot all over his face.

As she had rehearsed so many times in her mind, she grabbed his shirt and pulled it on, stepped into his trousers (no underpants, *yuk*!), pulled them up around her waist and quickly buttoned them. Picking up his tie and belt, she went back to the bed where he was still thrashing about, coughing, retching. His eyes streamed, his mouth foamed, one hand cradled his balls as he moaned in pain. She lashed the tie as securely as she could around his wrists, and using the belt, she strapped his feet together. Squeezing the last of the shampoo from the bottle into his streaming eyes, she cleared her throat, gathered saliva into her mouth and spat into his face. 'Scum!' she screamed. 'Insane moronic *impotent* piece of shit!'

His jacket held a wallet, heavy with notes and coins, a bunch of keys, which she pushed into the trouser pocket. She picked up his mobile phone and smashed it down into his groin, three or four times, enjoying the sound of his muffled screams. Still carrying the phone, she pulled the key out of the lock, left the room and locked the door behind her so that he was imprisoned, just as she had been. Then she was down the stairs – three flights, passages stretching off to right and left, empty rooms with their doors open, dust lying in corners, no curtains at the windows – and in the front hall. Cautiously she opened the door on to a broad drive curving away from the house between tall trees. For a single delicious moment, she stood outside and let the breeze caress her uplifted face. There was a long-unused marble fountain in front of her, its wide basin caked with dried green algae, a short flight of steps guarded on either side by square plinths, vistas of trees and fields. How could you ever fully appreciate the wonder of breathing fresh air, looking up at the blue sky, watch leaves trembling on newly budding leaves, unless these simple privileges had been denied you? She would never take freedom for granted again.

In front of the house was a flashy Italian sports car, dark red, with white leather seats and walnut fascia, personalized number plate: SEM 123. Fingers steady, she searched through the keys she'd taken and found one attached to a leather tag, with an enamelled badge matching the one on the bonnet of the car. She got in, started the engine, sailed off down the drive. There were open gates at the end of it, and a small lodge house on one side, with a man working in the garden, pruning dead rose stems. He raised his hand as she passed, and she smiled at him, checked that there was no traffic coming and paused. Behind her were two high stone gateposts with flat tops: Dewsbury was incised into one, Manor on the other. Dewsbury Manor.

Should she go left or right? What did it matter? Sooner or later she'd find a village, a town, a petrol station from where she could call the police.

Exhilaration flooded her. She had beaten them at their own game. She was free. And ranging for revenge. Like Caesar's spirit, she seemed to remember. 'Cry "Havoc!"', she screamed, pounding on the steering wheel. 'And let slip the fucking dogs of war!'

The countryside was unfamiliar; she drove through green lanes banked high on either side, fields fuzzed with the growth of early summer, ponds where budding willows drooped. What signposts there were said things like *Martin's Well 1⅓ miles*, Martin's Well turning out to be nothing but a couple of houses and a church. Eventually she hit a T-junction where signs pointed left to Harbury, five miles, right to Chennington, three miles. She turned towards Chennington, which proved to be a pleasant country town, catering to the rich middle classes, if the shops were anything to go by: designer clothes, hats, expensive books, speciality cheeses, high-class grocers. She pulled into a parking place and waited for a woman in a pink tweed suit and a Gucci bag to come alongside.

'Excuse me,' she called. 'Could you tell me where the nearest police station is?'

'Nice car,' the woman said. She stroked the finish as though it was an expensive race horse.

'It's my husband's,' Kate said. 'The police . . .?'

'Mmm, let me think. There isn't one at Harbury, and there's certainly not one here, not any more. I think your best bet is to keep going until you hit Barbridge.'

'Is it far?'

'About six miles. Just keep going straight ahead, and you'll see the signs.'

'Barbridge.'

'That's right.' The woman smiled. 'Really nice car.' As she drove away, Kate had the feeling that someone was going to be badgered by his wife into upgrading her current car to the same model as Stefan's. She could picture his annoyance, the G&Ts being poured, his mood mellowing, something soft and enticing on the music centre, seductive with an undertone of sexuality, the negligee flung off in the bedroom, a shag like he hadn't had for a long time, followed by gentle steely persuasions. You're selling your soul for a mess of pottage, buddy, she wanted to tell him, waste of time. On the other hand, he could probably afford it. She wished momentarily for a rich husband – or at least a job good enough for her to afford such a car.

The police at Barbridge were sympathetic. They took her to a small interview room and sat her at a long table. Someone brought her a cup of sweet tea and listened with concern while she told her story and handed over the wallet, the keys and mobile phone. 'My name's Kate Fullerton.' Voice wobbling as she spoke; she found it hard to believe she was finally free, that this room would not suddenly disappear like a shifting mirage and she would find herself back on that vile bed in the shuttered room, her body no longer hers, reduced to a piece of meat.

A more senior man came in and sat down opposite her while a colleague set up a tape recorder which whirred quietly between them, before taking a chair at the far end of the table.

'I'm Detective Inspector Edwards,' the first man said, 'and this is Detective Constable Hunter.' Gently he took her through her ordeal once more. 'We've been looking for you,' he said finally.

'You knew I was missing?'

'You were registered as a missing person about four days ago.' He looked down at the slim file in front of him. 'A Ms Janine Taylor and a Mr Jefferson Andrewes have been down at their local police station every day since you disappeared . . .' He looked away from her, and she knew he didn't want to think about the ordeal she must have undergone at the hands of the man who had abducted her.

Jefferson Andrewes . . . how did he get involved? 'How long ago was that?' she said faintly. 'I've no idea how long that bastard kept me there.'

'Five days,' he said.

Nearly a week of her precious life gone because of Stefan's twisted notion of revenge. What could he possibly have hoped to gain from what he had done? 'Five days,' she echoed, her voice fading.

'Believe me, Mrs Fullerton, I have daughters of my own. If we ever catch up with these people . . .' He shook his head. 'And you don't know where you were imprisoned?' He was fatherly, kind, compassionate. He had bushy black-and-white eyebrows and grey hair cut very short, though he didn't look remotely like George Clooney.

'I could show you the way there. It's a big house, in its own grounds, called Dewsbury Manor.' She drummed on the table with her fingers: was anybody doing anything to ensure that Stefan didn't escape? She was coming down from her adrenalin high now, shaking, shuddering, her bruised, misused body feeling as though it was about to shake apart, but she held on.

'Dewsbury Manor? Good Lord. You've been right under our noses all this time.'

'Trouble was,' said DC Hunter, 'we had so little to go on. Even though we had a probable perp and even a possible name, we couldn't tie him in to anyone else, find an address for him, nothing. And then the motive . . . was it just . . . um . . . sexual gratification—'

'It wasn't rape,' she said. 'He's impotent; I was spared that.'

'That's something to be grateful for, I suppose.' Edwards tapped a pen on the edge of his notebook. 'You're sure the place was called Dewsbury Manor?'

DC Hunter said, 'Somebody bought it, end of last year.'

'Do we know who?'

'Far as I know, it was some foreign company, Italian, Spanish, not one of us, at any rate.'

'Italian?' said Edwards. 'The rest of the world is taking us over and we just sit back and let them get on with it. Places like Iceland and the Arabs—'

'The French own our electricity,' said Hunter.

'Now the Italians are buying up the shop. I don't know . . .' Edwards turned back to Kate.

'The Manor's been waiting for planning permission to convert it,' said Hunter. 'It's been empty for over a year.'

'That's obviously why they took me there,' said Kate impatiently. Why were they sitting there, gossiping about local property sales? Couldn't they see she was disintegrating, so many little pieces of her breaking off that she was surprised to see the floor wasn't littered with them.

'I t-told you, I was in this attic room, but when I . . . um . . . esc . . . when I got away, I could s-see there was no furniture in the . . . um . . . in the rooms.' Words were falling away from her, even her hair seemed to be trembling. Now that she no longer had to hold on to herself, every part of her hurt.

Edwards stood up, went to the door of the interview room, and shouted for someone called Tommy.

'Look, I'd hate this bastard to get away,' Kate said. Her teeth were jittering inside her mouth, the separate parts of her body finally allowed to admit to the abuse she had tried not to acknowledge for five (*five!*) days: was Stefan going to escape before they could nail him, just because of red-tape, an insistence on doing everything by the book?

'So would we.' He put his hand over hers. 'Don't worry, Mrs Fullerton, Kate, there are police cars already at the scene. We'll get him, and when we do . . .'

'Don't you need to examine me? DNA or something?' Her mouth puckered. 'And I need to get out of these disgusting clothes.' When this was over, she would run a hot bath, fill it with some hugely expensive bath gel, and lie there for a week, a month, forever.

'It's being sorted,' he said.

There was a knock at the door and a woman officer came in. 'Tommy,' Edwards said, 'this is Mrs Fullerton, and she needs all the help you can give her.' He nodded and raised his eyebrows. 'You've been very, very brave, Kate.' He got up and came round the table to take both her hands in his. 'And very clear-headed. I'm sorry to have to put you through this inquisition when you must be exhausted, but the sooner we get the facts, the easier it is to get a successful conclusion. So, thank you: I can promise we're all doing our best for you.'

Tommy, large-boned, high-complexioned, took Kate's arm in one of her hands. 'Come on, dear, we'll see you right.'

The relief was too much for Kate. Her lower lip quivered. The lake of tears which had been rocking inside her ever since Mick and Stefan had snatched her, suddenly overflowed. Apart from tears forced from her by pain, she hadn't cried during her ordeal, but now she buried her head in her hands, while a cataract of weeping shook her. 'Oh God,' she sobbed. 'It was . . . so unbelievably horrible . . . so, so never-ending.' The terror she had refused to let herself give in to now swept over her. 'And the whole time, I knew he'd never let me go, he would have to kill me because I knew who he was.'

'You're all right now,' Tommy soothed. She put her beefy arms around Kate and held her close. 'You're OK, you'll be fine.'

'I honestly thought I was going to die.'

And as she said it, Kate wondered if indeed to a certain extent, she had.

Magnus
Seventeen

Magnus arrived at Heathrow, got into Central London in time to catch a train north and pick up the dogs from their luxurious kennels. He'd been back in his own home no more than half an hour when the bell began to peal, at the same time as someone repeatedly pounded at the door. He put down the cup of coffee he'd just brewed on his newest machine, purchased in Boston during a free afternoon, which he'd spent very pleasantly with an extremely attractive historian from the University of Oklahoma with one of those weird hard-to-remember American names that in any ordinary country would be surnames or small county towns, something like Bristowe or Godstowe or Plaistow, who was planning a book on the Romanov Princesses (*'the ones who got away'*) and to whom, in a moment of unusual spontaneity, he had offered the flat at the top of his house when she told him she planned to spend several weeks in England during the summer, researching at the London Library.

As soon as he had opened the door, a small dark-haired woman hurtled into the house and planted herself in front of him.

'Where on earth have you *been*?' she screeched.

'What?' Magnus stepped backwards, keeping a wary eye on the door, taking note of the nearest exit, as he had conscientiously done on the flight back from the States when requested to do so (*'do not forget that your nearest exit may be behind you'*). He had long prepared himself for a contingency plan of action were any one of a number of worst-case scenarios to 'eventuate' (a word he particularly disliked and one the historian from the University of Oklahoma had used several times) and what he would do should he find himself confronted by a mad person, possibly armed with a knife (though until now he had always assumed it would be a mad*man* rather than a mad*woman*) with the possibility of violence being offered – this woman was even now approaching him with clenched fists – maintaining a clear line of escape taking first priority.

'I've been coming round every *day*, knocking at the door, you're never *in*, where the hell have you *been*?' she demanded again, in a rising crescendo of anger.

'In the States,' he said, reasonably enough. 'Though I can't really see that it's any of your business.' He had a feeling he'd met the woman before somewhere. Was she one of Kate's close little quartet? Petra, Jenny and um . . . someone else whose name he couldn't recall, perhaps she was the 'um' one.

'Of *course* it's my business,' she shouted. 'Nobody's been able to get *hold* of you, and naturally, typical bloody man, it doesn't seem to have *occurred* to you to telephone home while you were *away*, does it? Or to pick up your phone messages via your mobile.'

'I haven't got a—'

She glanced at the telephone, which was blinking redly, and the pile of letters which had been pushed to one side when Magnus opened his front door. 'Don't you ever *listen* to your *answering* machine, for heaven's sake, or read your *mail*? Once I found out where you lived, I must have put at least *five* notes through the door—'

'Just a minute.' He seized the woman's arm – she was small enough for him to feel reasonably confident of overpowering her, should the need arise – trying to steer her towards the kitchen. 'I only got back from the States about thirty minutes ago. I certainly haven't had time to listen to messages or even get started on the mail.'

'Well, you *should* have, for God's sake!'

'Calm down, will you, it's Lucy, isn't it? I've just made some coffee, want some?'

She wrenched her arm away. 'No it is *not* Lucy and no, I do *not* want any bloody coffee. Haven't you any idea what's been going on while you've been away?'

'Well, I caught CNN in my hotel room,' he began. 'Recessions all over the place, we lost to the West Indians, I'm afraid I never pay much attention to home news when I'm—'

'Just to bring you up to date,' the not-Lucy woman said sarcastically, 'while you were gone, your sister Kate was only kidnapped and imprisoned by a total *pervert* for nearly a *week*!'

'What?'

'If you'd bothered to *call* her while you were—'

'What?' Magnus said again, squeezing his eyes shut and opening them again in the hope that the woman would have disappeared and he would not have heard what she'd just told him. 'What did you—?'

Suddenly the woman (not Lucy) was weeping, bending like a sapling, falling against him and clutching at the sweatshirt which the Oklahoman historian (Marlow? Sligo?) had bought him as a memento of a good time together, her eyes promising him that with any luck there would be many more of them, and not just T-shirts. 'Kate, it's Kate, she's been, she's . . . oh, those *bastards*, they – they . . .' She began sobbing and snuffling, her head lying somewhere around his heart.

Taking the (possibly risky) decision that she was not in fact mad (the tears could be a ploy to bring him within striking distance), he set his coffee cup down on the hall stand and put his arms round her, patted her back, smelled the lemony tang of her hair. 'Tell me exactly what's happened,' he said, as he might have done to an hysterical PhD student, had in fact done (heart in mouth – a few years ago one of the chic black-suited lecturers, a medievalist, if he remembered correctly, had taken him to see *Oleanna*, at the National and ever since, he'd been very, very careful with female students, kept the door of his office open, encouraged them but tried not to touch them, even if they cried, which they seemed to do with distressing frequency), on three occasions over the years, though his heart was pounding with already-anticipated denouncement, shame, dismissal. Kate? Abducted? Raped – did she say *raped*?

'Is . . . is my sister . . .?' He swallowed. Whatever vile thing he was about to hear, please, God, please let Kate be OK . . . 'Is she all right?'

'Depends what you mean by "all right".' The girl, woman (he could never keep up with the changing fashion in acceptable ways to refer to females) gulped down the coffee he handed her, wiping away her tears with the back of her hand, smearing mascara over her face so that he wanted to whip out a handkerchief and tenderly clean her face, as she managed to describe what had happened and the presence of mind which had allowed Kate to escape from the house where she was being held prisoner.

'Oh, my God,' he said, when he finally understood (not raped, at least). 'Where is she, what's going on, did they get the sods, have they—?'

'She's OK, as OK as anyone can be after an ordeal like that . . .'

the woman choked again. 'Those fucking bastards . . .' She too stood and came round the table to him. 'It's Magnus, isn't it? Listen, Magnus, she's at my flat at the moment, asleep, doped up to the eyeballs, but she needs you badly, she needs something, someone, come on, I'll drive you to my place.'

'You're Janine,' he said, pennies dropping at last, as they climbed into the silver sports car parked haphazardly outside his door and the woman (definitely not 'girl' he seemed to remember, though this one didn't look much over eighteen and surely that was still a girl, wasn't it?) flooring the clutch, pulled away in a squealing of tyres and a blast of exhaust reminiscent of Señor Gonzalez in Quito. 'You're the travel agent, where Kate works, it's you she's sharing with, I've been in your flat, haven't I?'

'Yes.' She seemed to have calmed down a bit.

'When you were away.'

'That's right.'

'Nice.' It was nice, too, quite different from his own style, showed a modern sensibility, he told himself, or else that she didn't have enough money to purchase antiques.

'Thanks.'

Her tone was dry, rightly so, he thought, curling his fingers into his palms until they hurt. What *was* he doing? Kate was hurt, damaged, and all he could do was talk about interior decoration. Nonetheless, the image of a purple cushion juxtaposed with a pink one persisted in his mind, a way to blot out this new impairment to his dearest, his unfortunate sister.

Kate lay on her side, facing the doorway, so deeply asleep that she could have pricked her finger on a spindle fifty years ago and still have half a century to go before she woke up. There were oyster-coloured shadows under her eyes and her face was rough, unhealthy-looking, like her hair. Magnus bent to kiss her gently on the forehead, breathing in the sour smell of desolation which rose from her skin. She was clutching a furry pink dog which he recognized immediately as one of Annie's; she must have salvaged it all those years ago from the apartment in Quito.

Outside the bedroom, he gently closed the door and leaned his forehead against it. What Janine had told him was so shocking that it was almost too big to encompass. Abducted, imprisoned, tortured, all for the sake of some little wanker's pride, as far as anyone could make out. His rage was so huge that it seemed to have inflated him to the size of one of those blow-up figures tethered outside Californian fast-food joints, a sombrero-wearing Mexican waving a *taco*, twelve feet tall and eight feet wide. He wanted to drive over to the gaol where the man was being held, bend back the bars of the cell with his bare hands, haul him out and kill him. He remembered with a stupefying sense of guilt that Kate had wanted to go to the police about the man, the stalker, and how he himself had dissuaded her, saying it was nothing.

'The awful thing is,' Janine said, as she set a tray of coffee in front of him, 'she told me about this guy, told me he was stalking her, and I told her he wasn't really. If only I'd taken it more seriously . . .'

'Me too.' Magnus said. 'I did exactly the same.'

'But even if she *had* gone to the cops, they likely would have done nothing, which is what I told her, because according to them, until he *does* something, breaks the law in some way, there's actually nothing they can do.'

'There were two of them, though, where's the other one?'

'The second one only seems to have been there when they were actually grabbing her, lucky for her, though the first one – he's called Stefan – kept threatening her with him, told her all sorts of vile things he would do to her when he finally arrived. No-one knows who the other one is or where he went, according to the police, and the one in prison isn't talking.'

'Is Kate coping?'

'Just about. She's been very brave, very level-headed, but she'll be so glad to see you when she wakes up.'

Tears welled in Magnus's eyes and he bent his head so Janine wouldn't see. She came over and sat beside him, took his hand in both of hers, just held it, so kindly that he could not hold back the sob which worked its way up from the pit of his stomach. 'Poor Katie,' he said. 'Poor sad Kate.'

'It's all right,' Janine said, 'it'll be OK.' Kate had been coming in to work every day, she went on, she's trying to be normal, as though nothing had happened, doing a fantastic job, even though sometimes it was obvious that the strain was beginning to tell, she's hugely strong, she'll get over it. 'In the long term, she'll be all right, it's just getting her through the short term,' she finished.

'You're probably right.' Magnus took a sip of his coffee and flinched. Dear God, instant coffee, and not even one of the more expensive brands. He couldn't remember when he had last experienced such an assault on his taste buds. The historian from Oklahoma had shared his taste in coffee, had agreed with him on the importance of getting the right beans, using the very best machine, in fact she'd been even more inflexible than he was, insisting that there were only two coffee-makers in the entire world that were capable of delivering the perfect, the ultimate cup, and what kind of a monster was he anyway that he could even care what he was drinking at a time like this?

'I hope you don't mind instant,' Janine said.

'Not in the least.' Magnus took a valiant swallow. 'Look, we've met before, haven't we?'

'I think so.' She put her head on one side and looked at him more closely. 'Why am I thinking of nurseries?'

'Um . . .'

'I know what it was. I sold you your house!'

'That's it!'

'I was working in an estate agent's at the time. You've made it so hugely different, I didn't recognize the place. You must have done an enormous amount of work on it.'

'You'll have to come and look at it some time.'

'I'd love to.'

They gazed at each other for a moment, thinking back eight or nine years, and then, because both of them had been blessed with good teachers at school, thinking of water passing under bridges, of winged chariots, of ever-rolling streams, then looked away at the same time, Magnus considering that after all this time, his wish to show off his house to her seemed likely to be fulfilled, and realizing that she'd been lying through her teeth about the investment potential of the property, not herself believing a word of the spiel she'd handed him, thinking that she wouldn't have lived there on a bet (estate agents were the second most hated group of people in society, weren't they, after journalists, or was it politicians?), what she said had nonetheless come to pass, as witness the neat little bay trees up and down the street, the fresh paint, the ceramic pots, the good cars parked at the kerb.

'Magnus! You're back.' Kate appeared at the door, staggered into the room and sagged down beside him. 'It's so wonderful to see you.'

'And you. How—?' He put his arm round her and pulled her closer; he could see she was trying very hard not to dissolve into tears.

'God, I feel awful, I hate those pills the doctor gave me.' She glanced at the mug Magnus was holding then looked over at Janine. 'Oh, Jan*ine* . . .'

'What?'

'You *haven't* given him instant coffee, have you?'

'Why not? He didn't seem to mind.'

'He's very well-mannered.' Kate looked at her watch. 'Six thirty . . . it might be quite a good idea for you to discard your cup, Magnus, and break out that cognac I bought.'

'Good idea.'

'It's what he likes best,' Kate said to Janine, 'and it'll make up for the so-called coffee.'

'I'll certainly try to remember that,' Janine said tartly. Nonetheless, she found two thinly beautiful brandy balloons and a bottle and poured Magnus a shot and, as an afterthought, one for herself, adding, 'None for you, Kate, I think, not with that medication.'

Under her brother's arm, Kate vibrated, giving off a faint humming sound, like a fridge. To Magnus, it seemed a long time ago since she'd laughingly pointed out that she'd already had more than her share of terrible blows so was unlikely to have another. Now that it had fallen, would that be it for the rest of her days? Would she lead a charmed life from now on? If only she could meet a nice man, a decent man who would love her and look after her. Wishing the same for himself (though a woman, in his case, not a man, naturally), he smiled faintly at Janine, a woman who, despite evidence all round the room of her 'good taste', nonetheless actually thought it acceptable to serve instant coffee to a guest. Was she married? Hard to imagine the kind of man who would drink the stuff on a regular basis, and somewhere at the back of his head a jeering voice muttered 'Fogey, fogey'. Not everyone shared his esoteric tastes, why should they, though Ms Briscoe (Glasgow? Truro?) appeared to have done – or had she simply been taking the piss, mocking his stick-in-the-mud English ways, tongue-in-cheek in a particularly American manner?

'So what are you going to do, Katie?' he said. 'From what Janine's been saying, you need to get away, do nothing for a while.' He was amazed at how 'normal' she seemed after her ordeal, though looking closer, the signs of distress were there at the back of her eyes, a certain droop in her shoulders.

'Laze around on a beach,' Janine said. 'Blue skies, white sand.'

'I'd go mad,' Kate said. 'I don't like sunbathing, anyway.'

'All right, adventure holiday, trek across the Australian desert with a camel, climb Mount Kilimanjaro, swim with sharks, the Arctic experience, African saf—'

'Stop! I've got the brochures, I'm not sure I didn't *write* the brochures,' Kate said. 'Actually, there is a place I'd really love to visit again.' She looked up at her brother. 'We haven't been back to the Galápagos since . . . since The Accident.'

'That's where Mr Andrewes just went,' Janine said.

'I know. It suddenly brought it all back to me, Ecuador, the Islands . . .' She looked wistful. 'It's probably changed completely from when we were younger, and for the worse.'

'Not necessarily,' Magnus said.

'I saw a news item in the paper the other day; they've found a pink iguana—'

'Maybe he's gay,' said Janine.

'—which only exists on Isabela, on the edge of Volcano Wolf, apparently Darwin missed it – that should be worth a visit.'

'Maybe you could get Mr Andrewes to invite you out for another "business lunch",' said Janine.

'Do I know Mr Andrewes?' Magnus looked from one to the other.

'No.'

'He's a customer,' explained Janine. 'Took a fancy to Kate—'

'And who wouldn't?'

'—and invited her out for a so-called business meeting, to discuss his holiday plans.'

When Janine laughed, which she did quite often, Magnus noticed that she had a dimple, not quite a dimple, a sort of depression in her cheek, which he had to say he found utterly charming. The strains of Big Ben chimed from her leather bag and she fished around in it for her mobile, a tiny little instrument fashioned from purple plastic which Magnus instantly coveted. His students were always telling him to get a life, Dr Lennox, buy a mobile, learn to text, whatever that was; he was often aware that he had failed to get a handle on contemporary life and *mores*. Tomorrow, he would go out and buy one for himself, a purple one just like the one Janine was now flipping up the lid of, scrutinizing the message which he could see appearing on a miniature screen, sighing and replacing the phone in her bag. 'Right, folks,' she said. 'Time to eat. Do you want to eat with us, Magnus? We could have takeaway, or go out or anything.'

'Why don't you give me your orders and I'll go out for takeaway?' Magnus asked. 'I noticed a Chinese place about a block away.'

'We can telephone.'

'OK. Then I'll go and get it when it's ready.'

Janine looked uncertainly at Kate. 'Don't worry,' Kate said. 'He spends most of his waking hours in Russia, at the beginning of the last century. He doesn't know about deliveries, or mobile phones, or iPods, or DVDs. He calls the radio the wireless, and given his druthers, would still be playing records on a wind-up gramophone.'

'I think that's rather sweet,' Janine said. He could see that she really meant it, which pleased him; maybe there were still woman around who didn't despise anything that hadn't been invented in the last twelve months, women who still made their own pastry and grew herbs in the garden and made patchwork quilts out of scraps, cooked casseroles and lamb shanks and cauliflower cheese, who didn't care whether a man was a fogey, as long as he was good and faithful and true.

'Listen,' he said, surprising himself, 'why don't you two come to my place for supper – not dinner, not tonight; I'm too tied up with university things – but soon, maybe at the weekend?'

'Love to,' Kate said. 'Janine?'

'Yes, please.'

'Magnus is a terrific cook,' Kate said.

'That's good, because I'm not.' Janine, red-faced, got up very shortly after saying this and went into the kitchen while Magnus tried to hide the pleasure this announcement gave him, with its promise of a future where he cooked and she didn't. He fiddled with the third button of his cardigan, or rather, the place where the button used to be, it having somehow gone missing. 'Then I could show you round the house,' he added.

'I've *looked* round it,' Kate said, pretending bewilderment. 'Why would I want to . . . I lived there for a while, remember?'

He squeezed her against him. 'I didn't mean you, obviously.' His heart shifted. She seemed so fragile, so . . . lonely. If only she would allow herself to be vulnerable, for if she went on pretending she was all right, she would never heal.

In bed that night, and in an effort not to dwell too long on what had happened to Kate, Magnus thought back to the terrible days shortly after his father's death. A still-traumatized Kate had dropped out of university, taken up with Brad, and set off backpacking to India and Tibet, while he (safe, dull, fogeyish) decided to buy a house. Ten or twelve properties in, he found himself shaking hands with an estate agent in front of the garden gate of his current place. 'It's an up-and-coming neighbourhood, Mr Lennox,' she assured him as they walked up the path to the door.

You could have fooled me, Magnus thought. 'Really?' he said. He and Kate had agreed that they couldn't bear to keep on the house which, even though rented long-term to a family from Florida, had once been the family home, before Dr Lennox had headed for Ecuador. When the agent had, with some difficulty, unlocked the front door, the once-handsome, now neglected three-storey house had reeked of rot, both dry and wet; when wrenched open, the cellar door emitted the kind of stench which suggested that several carcasses had been butchered down there not long before and left to decompose; there was no kitchen to speak of, just a few cheap units from which the doors had long ago been ripped and a shallow stone sink with one cold-water tap.

Despite the cobwebs big enough to use as hammocks, the reception rooms were wide and handsome, the plasterwork miraculously seemed mostly intact, egg-and-anchor friezes round the cornices, ornate ceiling-roses, marble fireplaces, chipped here and there but otherwise undamaged. He followed her up the creaking staircase to the first floor where there were four good bedrooms, a box-room, an apology for a bathroom. Up another flight of stairs were three airy attic rooms, each with its original black-painted iron fireplace, each with an entrancing roofscape view, the tops of trees, and, in the distance, low blue hills.

'This would have been a maid's bedroom, back when the house was built,' the agent said, as they entered the first of the attics.

'Or a nursery.' A rocking horse, Magnus thought, a little boy in a sailor suit, riding back and forth, a smiling young wife, nothing like Edwina Mountbatten, someone not dissimilar to the agent herself, with a baby girl on her hip. (*'Darling, I think Isabella is teething . . .'*)

'You'd never regret buying this, Mr Lennox.'

She was a chirpy little thing, not exactly pretty, but nicely turned out. He particularly admired the way her dark hair had been twisted up at the back of her head, with a fountain spray of hair springing from the bejewelled comb thing which secured it. 'It's in a truly appalling condition,' he said.

'Admittedly it'll need a little work to fix it up but—'

'A little? It'll cost thousands, not to mention the upheaval involved.'

Imagination saw him five years later, a lot of hard work and money down the line. It could be really something . . .

'The price is ridiculous,' he said boldly, startling himself. It was the sort of thing his father might have said. He started back down the rickety staircase.

'Property is my business, Mr Lennox, and I can promise you that whatever it costs you to do up will be money well spent. Five years from now, the houses in this area will have trebled in value. Trust me.'

Magnus didn't. There were a great many people he didn't trust, among them politicians, journalists, solicitors, conspiracy theorists, wild-eyed enthusiasts who held convincing proof that Anna Anderson was the real Anastasia Romanov. But especially not estate agents.

'I don't think it's for me,' he said. 'Nor for anyone else, for that matter.'

She looked astonished that he could be on the verge of abandoning this amazing one-in-a-lifetime opportunity. 'But think of the investment potential.'

'I can see a lot of investment, and very little potential,' he said. 'Sorry, it's practically derelict. It'll cost a fortune to bring round, a fact which doesn't seem in any way to be reflected in the price.'

'I suppose you could always put in an offer.' She sounded dubious, as though putting in an offer was a laughably daring notion, unlikely to be taken seriously.

Which Magnus had done, a ridiculously low one, and was barely surprised when it was accepted. He imagined the vendor laughing all the way to the bank at the fool who had been parted so soon from his money. Ten years later, the area hadn't yet upped though, like a hesitant groom on his wedding night, it could be said to be constantly on the verge of coming, *vide* the yuppies and their bay trees necessarily chained to the walls of their houses to thwart vandals and thieves, but by now Magnus was used to the traffic, the wheelie-bins which seemed to still be overflowing even when the garbage truck had just passed, the empty beer cans thrown into his bedraggled little front garden, the used condoms which decorated the holly tree. Outside, the house still looked neglected but inside, over time, he had turned it into a highly desirable gentleman's residence.

During the necessary renovations, he had taken the advice of his builder and turned the attic rooms into a self-contained flat, a small kitchen, a bedroom with an en-suite shower-room, a reasonable sitting room. The idea was to have let the flat to someone appropriate ('*suit professional couple*') but somehow he had never got round to finding anyone appropriate, shades of his Cambridge digs haunting him, smells of curry, overflowing baths, rubbish bags on the stairs, thumping music of the kind which gave him a migraine. Arctic Monkeys, he thought (fogeyishly) or Babyshambles (where *did* they find these names?), the sort of thing he didn't wish to have to contend with, the role of landlord definitely not one he was suited for. (*'There seems to be some mix-up about the rent this month, I'm afraid you'll have to leave at the end of week.'*) And suppose the tenants turned violent, started threatening him, the woman fish-wifeing in the background while her husband bunched his fists and swung them at Magnus, or worse still, picked up a poker or something (not that there would have been one handy since the heating was electric), Magnus's ideas of 'professional' couples being hazy at best.

He thought sadly of Anabel, the cousin of a lecturer in economics at the university, introduced at a faculty party because, so everyone said, especially Anabel, she would suit Magnus down to the ground. While bearing no resemblance whatsoever to Edwina Mountbatten, he was aware that Anabel (slim, tailored, lots of red lipstick) would nonetheless have thrown many a stylish dinner party, had he been able to bring himself to propose to her. But in his heart, he knew she was too brisk for him, too organized, unlikely to allow him the hours of dreaming he needed to write his history texts, even though they would be bringing money into their joint household. The mere prospect of Anabel moving in with him, changing the paint colours (magnolia), stripping off his chosen wallpapers (Sanderson's William Morris *Pimpernel* in his bedroom, *Willow* on the top landing, *Golden Lily* in the attic bedroom, a bit eighties, but they suited the period of the house), modernizing the kitchen, buying new furniture, *chivvying*, had been too much for him. For the most part, he liked his house the way it was, and so he had kept silent, though he knew she had expected him to suggest that they get married.

He would have loved to show the estate agent around it, but when he dropped into the agency's High Street premises on some pretext or other, he was informed that she was now working elsewhere and it was obvious that no way were they going to tell him where that might be. A pity. He'd envisaged a light-hearted drink somewhere, while they laughed over the ludicrous price the owner had originally asked, and he'd conceded that to a certain extent she had been right about the potential of his property. And then he might have suggested supper somewhere, or arranged a second meeting on another evening – dinner, a film, a concert at the Arts Centre – and who knew where that might have led to? In his secret heart, he'd hoped it might have led, however circuitously, to bed, and now she had turned up again, sharing with his sister, *caring* for her because for all Kate's talk of independence, she *needed* to be taken care of.

What would he give Janine (and Kate too, of course) when she came at the weekend? Something simple – soup, maybe, he could make that butternut squash soup, good on a cold night, or what about, since there were only three of them, a cheese soufflé? (He'd heard someone on *Brain of Britain* deriding soufflés – *'so Eighties'* and couldn't see why food should come in and out of fashion, a soufflé was a soufflé, after all, and very nice too). He could follow it with tiny lamb cutlets marinated in port and rosemary, with peas except you couldn't get those at this time of year, unless he went for *petit pois*, have to be out of a jar, but that's how the French eat them, or he might go for green beans, never mind that they came from Kenya and exploited the local farmers, new potatoes (ditto), home-made mint sauce, not that bilious green stuff you got from the supermarket, followed by some of the pastries from the *pâtisserie* around the corner, with proper coffee. Excellent. And he'd better check that everything was dusted and looked at its best before Janine saw it, get some flowers from Happy Days Florists (it seemed such a short time ago that he and Kate had discussed the possibility of her setting up as a florist, God knew why, she'd never had a clue about arranging flowers), put them here and there around the place, a vase in the hall, a couple in the drawing room, another on the bureau in his bedroom, another in the first-floor passage.

Despite the ache he felt on behalf of his sister, he found himself excited at the prospect of Janine (nothing *like* Edwina, apart from being thin) viewing his home, making assumptions about the kind of man he was. Oh Lord, would it look too prissy to have flowers all over the show? He wouldn't want her to think he was gay, *not* that there was the slightest thing wrong in being gay, he didn't mean that, just that if she thought he was, she'd be less interested in him as a . . . as a friend, even supposing she was interested in the first place, which was of course, entirely unlikely, when he considered, and anyway, what about the Oklahoman woman, whose name he could scarcely remember now except that it ended in *o* – what should he do about *her* if she should get in touch wanting to use the flat, an idea for which he now had no taste at all, though at the time of offering he had felt a considerable excitement, but given that . . .

Trussed in a labyrinthine coil of subordinate clauses, Magnus finally fell asleep.

Kate
Eighteen

She found the days relatively easy to get through. Settling back into the normality of her job at TaylorMade, the undemanding work involved in helping people to choose a holiday, the fact that it was her own courage and skill which had released her, was beneficial. The physical damage healed, and so did some of the psychological. She thought that perhaps her hatred of her abductors had helped her survive reasonably unimpaired.

The nights were more difficult. It had been three weeks since she had broken out of her prison, but the drugs they'd given her, plus those at the hospital to help her sleep, were still raging round her body, playing havoc with her physical systems. Even without the nightmares, she couldn't sleep, would wake convinced she'd slept for hours only to find that it had been for forty minutes. She would lie in bed, staring up at the ceiling stained apricot by the council lighting outside the curtains, her mind filled with a shifting kaleidoscope of vivid scenes from her past, Luisa's dark hair, lava formations on the Galápagos, moonlight shining on the loch in front of the croft near Inverness, a beetle waving its antennae as it slowly walked up her arm, the wrinkled grey skin of Brixton's cockatielian feet, Annie.

Not every night, but on more than enough of them, even in a medically induced sleep, she found herself envisaging the scenario if she had not managed to escape. The images of her own death at the hands of Mick – it would have been him who carried out her execution, assassination, murder, not Stefan – flashed in front of her, time after time. However hard she tried, she could not escape the vile pictures in her own head: Mick with a knife, slicing her flesh; Mick with an axe, cutting off her hands, her feet, her breasts; Mick forcing her to drink acid, enjoying the sight of her agony as the corrosive liquid slowly dissolved her interior organs; or thrusting her head into a bucket of water, over and over again; or poisoning her with radiation like that poor Russian guy – Litvinenko, was it? – who took days to die, all the time knowing there was no cure, no hope, or Mick imprisoning her in a deep freeze cabinet with a glass door – she'd seen it in a film once – watching the icicles form while the blood froze slowly in her veins, and him laughing, raising a glass of whisky at her as her gradually congealing eyes stared helplessly out at him.

She spent hours in the bath, scented candles everywhere, expensive bath gels poured in by the gallon, soothing music playing softly (Mozart, Chopin, Tchaikovsky, nothing too demanding), washing away, over and over again, all that had happened, trying not to think about Stefan who was safely locked away, on remand and awaiting trial, and Mick who had managed to disappear before the police were on to him. Stefan wasn't talking (too afraid of retribution from Mick's pals on the inside, according to the police) and so far, three weeks later, no-one had any idea where to look for him ('*but we'll get him, never fear*'). She lay awake at night wondering if he was lurking outside the flat, waiting to break in and kill her, so that she couldn't talk, couldn't condemn him to a prison sentence, just as Stefan would be condemned once his trial began. In the daylight hours, she knew this was irrational: the last place Mick would lurk would be somewhere the police might expect him to lurk, but at night, irrationality became entirely rational, almost expectable.

'Go away,' Janine told her. 'Have a holiday – I'll come with you, if you like, look out for you, you'd be safe, I swear it, we could go anywhere in the world.' But Kate felt more secure in her own familiar environs than roaming the globe in an effort to escape her demons. Magnus urged her to go up to Uncle Blair's in Edinburgh; they would so love to have her, he told her, they had come down at once when they heard what had happened, but she felt it unfair to saddle them with her griefs.

At her urging, Jefferson Andrewes had gone on his holiday to the Galápagos. (Why did she have to urge him, when he was no more to her than a client, a business acquaintance?) She smiled slightly in the dangerously teeming darkness of her bedroom, remembering how he'd talked of running with the turtles. He had suggested several times that they have dinner together but she always declined, turning away her head, not wanting to look into his eyes and see pity there or, worse still, a prurient curiosity. *Damaged goods . . .*

the phrase rang perpetually in her mind, damaged goods, like a London street crier – *walk up, walk up, buy your damaged goods here* – except of course no-one knowing her history would now want to buy her, even at a knock-down price. She tried to walk tall, pretend she was the same as she had always been, but she wasn't. However, gradually, she began to put back together someone similar to but not exactly the person she had once been and from the fog of the past few years, determinations took hold. Magnus was right: she had to go back and complete her degree, she had to return to the Galápagos and face up to The Accident, she had to put Brad Fullerton the Third or Fourth behind her for good.

'Look,' she said to Janine. 'If you want to find another flatmate, I'd quite understand.'

'Don't be silly . . .'

'And if you'd rather I handed in my notice at TaylorMade, I'd understand that too.'

'I want you to stay exactly as you are.' They were drinking coffee after work. 'In the end, you really only have two choices – you can either cave in, let it break you, or you can ignore it, as far as that's possible, and go forward. I haven't known you long, Kate, but I would guess that you'd opt for the second choice. And I can tell you that as far as I and TaylorMade Travel are concerned, we want you to stay on board.'

'Thanks, Janine.' Kate bit her lip, sensing the tears which came so much more easily these days ('*stiff upper lip, Kate*').

One Sunday, she drove down to Besford, the village in Hampshire where Lindsay Bennett had died. She'd spent some time on the Internet, looking up the White Pages and reading newspaper reports from a couple of years back, had read the full story of Lindsay, winner of a Fulbright Scholarship, waiting to travel to the States to spend a year at the University of Tennessee in Knoxville, working at a London bar to earn some extra cash. Home for a few days with her family, she'd walked down to the pub, no more than five hundred yards from her home, to meet long-standing friends. On her way back, a car had hit her from behind, knocked her half into the ditch along the road, and left her to die. The person responsible had never been found.

Kate parked along the grass verge in front of the house and

walked through the five-barred white gate, from where the sound of a lawnmower chugging up and down at the back of the house was clearly audible. They probably wouldn't hear her if she knocked so she went round the side of the house. In front of her was a large stretch of lawn, striped in darker and paler bands of green where a man steering a ride-on mower up and down had already passed. A woman in a straw hat was sitting in the shade of an enormous Cedar of Lebanon reading the *Guardian*. Another woman, younger, was strimming the edges of the herbaceous borders which lined both side of the brick-walled garden. The greatest of personal tragedies sweeps across your life, but you go on, thought Kate, strimming and trimming, just as you always have. At the straw-hatted woman's side was a weathered teak garden table covered in an embroidered linen cloth and holding an assortment of tea-things, a plate of sandwiches, scones which appeared to be home-baked, and a cake on a glass stand.

Kate advanced across the lawn, hoping someone would notice her before she could scare them, and would at the same time turn off all the noise. The woman eventually looked up and raised a hand to shade her eyes.

'And you are?' she said loudly, above the lawnmower and the strimmer. Then added, 'Look, would you mind going and asking my husband to turn that darn thing off, my daughter too, and to be civilized enough to come for their tea.'

'All right.' Kate walked over to the girl and waited until she was in her line of vision, then mimed switching off.

'Oh,' the girl said, doing so. 'Have you come for tea?'

'Not intentionally,' Kate said. 'My name's Kate Fullerton.'

'I'm Sarah Bennett. Are you a friend of my mother's?'

Kate looked over her shoulder at the man, still obliviously churning up and down the grass. 'I'm a complete stranger, actually. Look, before your father – is it? – turns off the mower, could you . . . I don't want to bring up matters which I know must be painful, but would any of you mind if I talked to you and your parents about – about your sister?'

Sarah's eyes narrowed. 'Which one?' she said. 'There are three of us.' And Kate wondered whether she meant that there had once been four girls, but were now only three, or that there had always been three, even though one was no longer around.

'Lindsay,' she said, awkward now, wishing she hadn't come, but she had to know, had to do something, not sit there inactive, as though Mick and Stefan had the right to violate her and then get away with it, even though Stefan was now under police surveillance, awaiting trial.

A subdued light showed in Sarah's face, not exactly eager, no-one would be eager to hear further news about a murdered sister, but at least involved. 'Are you from the police? Have you found out who killed her?'

'I'm sorry, no. It's just that I've been the vic . . . I've been attacked too, and for a number of reasons, I'm wondering if it could possibly have been by the same person – or people – who was responsible for your sister's death.'

'I see.' Sarah waited until her father had reached the end of a long strip of grass and manoeuvred his machine round in a curve. 'Dad!' she screamed, waving her hand and when she'd caught his attention, made flicking motions, at the same time taking Kate's arm in a tightish grip and moving her towards the woman in the straw hat who was now pouring tea into cups and rattling teaspoons around.

'I'm Janey Bennett,' she said, when Kate was once again in front of her, 'but I haven't the slightest idea who you are.'

'She's called Kate Fullerton and she's come about Lindsay,' Sarah said, adding quickly, 'she's not the police or anything; I think she's got some information . . .'

'Why don't you let her speak for herself? How do like your tea, may I call you Kate?'

The sandwiches were smoked salmon spread with some kind of piquant green sauce and layered between variegated slices of multi-grain and white farmhouse bread. The cake had been made, so Mrs Bennett informed them, with ground almonds instead of flour. The tea was Lapsang Souchong, and she hoped Kate liked it, otherwise she was sure her husband – Michael, who by now had joined them, his old cricketing shirt bespeckled with tips of green grass, which also decorated his short grey beard – would be happy to go and make a pot of black tea; they had English Breakfast, Darjeeling or Assam or various assorted herbal teas if Kate liked or else—

'Oh, do shut up, Mummy!' Sarah said. 'She's perfectly fine with what she's got, aren't you, Kate?' And when Kate said she was, Michael turned towards her and said that perhaps she'd better let them know whatever it was that she had come for, he was aware that it was . . . difficult for everyone but . . .

'She's been attacked herself,' Sarah said, 'and she wondered if it was by the same guy as Lindsay.'

Kate explained about the wine bar, about the Regular – Stefan – his apparent infatuation with her, the phone call and the notes. 'But that's exactly what happened with Lindsay!' Sarah exclaimed. 'Ringing up all the time, sending her ridiculous little notes. That's why she came home, to get away from him.'

Her father, nodding, added that Lindsay had never told them the guy's name, maybe she hadn't even known it, but she *did*, said Sarah, something vaguely foreign-sounding, I'm *sure* she did, and Kate wondered if it might have been 'Stefan', at which Sarah frowned in doubt, said she wasn't certain but it could have been, and he'd asked her out for dinner, in this really arrogant way, as though there'd be no question of her not accepting, and then he got really mad when she said no way, thank you.

'Is that what happened to you, Kate?' asked Mrs Bennett.

'More or less.' Kate hesitated, thinking that maybe she didn't want to tell them about the whole hateful thing, nor did she wish to see a lurking thrill or perhaps a tad of revulsion in their eyes, watch them glance at her and then away, embarrassed, not knowing what to say, how to behave ordinarily when faced with extraordinary circumstances. But these people had suffered far more than she had, so she took a deep breath and explained, as briefly as possible, what had happened.

'Bastards!' said Sarah. 'Buggering bastards!' Mrs Bennett put her hand on Kate's arm and murmured soothingly, 'So dreadful for you, so horrifying,' and Michael Bennett pressed his lips together for a moment, then said that hanging was too good for people like that. No revulsion from any of the Bennetts, only the kindest sort of pity.

'Anyway, the point is,' Kate said, 'it was the Stefan person and his vile friend, Mick, who did . . . what they did, and it appeared to be a reaction to my refusal to go out with . . . with Stefan' - she hated saying his name, as though they knew each other - 'and it occurred to me, when I heard that he'd put the moves on your daughter and she'd turned him down just like I did, that it could have been one of them – or both – who came here and – and ran her down.'

'Revenge, you mean?' asked Sarah. 'For refusing his invitation?'

'That's right. I'm sure the police asked, but did anyone see anything like a car they didn't recognize, a stranger walking about?'

'This is a small village,' Mrs Bennett said. 'Most people aren't out late, there's not a lot to do except go to the pub, and of course though the police made all sorts of enquiries, nobody saw anything, or heard anything which could identify whoever did it.'

'The way we see it,' Sarah said, 'he must have followed her—'

'Stalked her.'

'—so he knew where she lived, and obviously he couldn't have afforded to hang about during the day, waiting for her, in case he was noticed,' and Michael added that the worst thing, for them, was that the police were pretty sure that once he hit her, he stopped the car and got out to check on Lindsay, 'though we don't know whether that was to see if she was alive, or if she was dead.'

'We all assumed it was a random thing. And now you're saying that it might not have been random, but a deliberate act of revenge, a . . .' Mrs Bennett pressed her forefinger against her upper lip and closed her eyes tightly. 'A deliberate execution?'

'I'm wondering, that's all.'

'There's so much ugliness in the world.' Janey's head turned from side to side as she spoke, her voice rising. 'So much evil.'

'So much good, too, Janey, don't forget the way the village all rallied round, and Lindsay's friends, and kind Truman, who spent so much time with us when it all happened, and now he's gone himself.'

'Yes, I know you're right, but still . . .' Janey Bennett stared darkly into some personal abyss.

'Robbie insisted that he'd seen "one of them fancy cars" driving through the village around six o'clock that evening,' Sarah put in briskly. 'A sporty thing, he said, sort of dark, or maybe red, but he couldn't pick one out of the pictures they showed him, thought it might have been foreign, like an Alfa or a Ferrari or something.' All three Bennetts gazed at Kate as though she might magically be able to pin down the vehicle used and bring the criminal to justice, so she described the red car she'd driven away from the house where they'd kept her (SEM 123), in the hope that it might help the Bennetts: though she had no idea what kind of a car Stefan might have been driving eighteen months ago, when Lindsay was killed.

She watched the three of them reliving the pain they must have endured, knowing that if Lindsay had been helped in time, she would almost certainly have survived. At first sight, they seemed a normal, happy family, but under the surface emotions must constantly be seething, especially when they thought – as they must so often do – of the 'if onlys' attendant on their daughter and sister's death, the fragility of everything that we take for granted: one moment you're strolling home from the pub on a summer evening, and the next you're gone, obliterated. After two years, did the pain die down a little, did it start not to matter who was responsible, did the fact that she was dead become the paramount thing? She guessed not, was certain that, as in her own case, which was now more than ten years ago, they still burned for what these days was called 'closure', not just for her father but for Annie and Luisa as well.

She opened her mouth to say something of all this, then decided that it would look as though she were trying to muscle in on the Bennetts' grief. 'Thank you for the tea,' she said, getting to her feet. 'I need to get back. I'm sorry if I spoiled your Sunday afternoon, raised old ghosts.'

'Oh, but you didn't,' said Janey, her face bleak. 'The ghosts are always with us.'

Jefferson
Nineteen

Gordon had certainly done him proud. The 'associates', whoever they might be, had secured him not just a room but a whole suite on the fifth floor of what might not have been the grandest hotel in Quito but certainly felt like it. He was the temporary master of an enormous bathroom with the most modern of smoked glass and chrome fittings, a kitchen with a fridge crammed with goodies (patés, smoked salmon, things in small jars, things in bigger jars), a sitting room with a view over the city towards cloud-topped mountains and full of grandiose furniture and modern gadgets, including a state-of-the-art TV which was approximately two inches thick, and a hand-held keypad which, when he pressed buttons on it, variously opened and shut the drapes, switched on the heating, started the shower in the bathroom and locked the door, though he only discovered this when he tried to leave the room. There were various elaborate flower arrangements ranged here and there, a gorgeously carved table in the centre holding a bowl sculpted from volcanic rock piled high with exotic fruit, a silver bucket with a bottle of champagne cooling in it, another flower arrangement.

It was more than Jefferson could possibly have afforded, or would have spent, even if he could, since he preferred to spend his money on other things than a few nights in an hotel. It was like travelling first class, which was very nice indeed (Head Office had sent him to Singapore several times), truly a different experience, but nonetheless, Jefferson would never personally have forked out for the cost of a seat that was three times as expensive as economy class. Fatalistically, he hoped that Gordon's promised 'rock-bottom prices' meant that the room – the suite – would end up vaguely within a range he could manage.

The champagne came with a small card propped against it on which were typed the words *With the Compliments of the Management*

Please Inform Us if there is Any Way We Can Be of Service! Well, Jefferson thought, looking at the luxury which surrounded him, maybe you could send in a dusky maiden to drop peeled (and de-pipped, please) grapes into my mouth before giving me an erotic massage, but apart from that, there isn't really anything much I need. The thought of the dusky maiden triggered memories of Kate Fullerton as he'd last seen her, her over-emphatic cheeriness as though trying to insist that there was nothing wrong, nothing, thank you, the droop of her shoulders, how she hadn't been able to maintain eye contact for very long. Perhaps she was afraid that either he'd get some kind of gleeful thrill out of imagining the cruelties which had been heaped on her, or else that he'd treat her with condescending pity; it would be hard to choose which was worse.

What he'd really like to do would be to hold her close against him and stroke her, smooth her fur; she reminded him of a dog he'd acquired when he was at university (his mother hadn't 'held' with pets when he was growing up) which had been stricken with some virulent form of cancer, and which the vet had told him it would be kinder to put down. Holding it in his arms as he waited for the injection to take effect, he'd seen the same resignation in its eyes, as though it knew very well how difficult the rest of its life was likely to be and that there was no point in struggling against it. His hatred for the two men who had abducted and abused Kate was so deep that he had to get up and walk about the room to ease his agitation.

He wanted to tell her that for her, unlike his dog, there was every point in struggling, if only to prove that the bastards hadn't broken her spirit. He had wanted her to come to the Galápagos with him, but of course couldn't ask, though it had been obvious from the way she had grown so animated when describing the place to him that she knew the Islands well, and loved them. One of these days he hoped she would describe more of it for him, maybe travel with him; it would make an ideal honeymoon destination, even if they couldn't afford a hotel like this, though if he was ever lucky enough to be marrying Kate Fullerton, he'd pay whatever it took and hang the expense.

His guide book had warned him that pickpocketing was a major growth industry in the capital, and tourists should take all precautions, so he set off on his first jaunt outside the hotel with his passport and money in a zipped bag purchased at Heathrow hanging round his neck inside his shirt. It was less comfortable than he'd have liked; the pull of the zip rubbed awkwardly against his skin and his chest hairs caught in the metal teeth at every step he took. Nonetheless, he strode confidently across marble-flagged squares, past impressive fountains and magnificently grand public buildings, secure in the knowledge that only the most brazen of pickpockets would be able to get at his valuables, unless he found himself caught in a honey-trap, a phrase which always made him think of the jars smeared with jam and half-full of water and drowned or drowning wasps which his mother used to set here and there in summer (*'wasps have rights too, Mum'*). Despite its magnificence, he was acutely aware, as always in a major city, of the darkly seething underbelly lurking round the corner or down the alley, not just lurking but in some cases brazenly advertising itself: whore houses calling themselves massage parlours where every kind of carnality, straight or deviant, was available at a price and sometimes even included a massage, dealers and gun-runners, forgers, moneylenders, people-smugglers, bars which were little more than pick-up joints, places where, if you knew the names and had the money, you could buy a heroin hit, or rent a guy who, for the price of his next joint or meal or woman, would kill a person of your choice.

He walked down a street lined with market stalls selling miscellaneous items: fruit and vegetables, porcelain hand-wash basins, woven baskets, rusty tools, colourful blankets, straw hats. Buy, buy, the poncho-wrapped Indian traders kept urging him, lovely basket, fresh fruit, nice chisel very cheap, hats, Englishman, buy a hat, and one of them, his accent noticeably different from the others, called out, 'S mad dogs and Englishmen, innit?' In summer, his father never went out of the house without his Panama hat, in honour of his namesake, President Truman, so when Jefferson saw a hat which closely resembled his father's he picked it up off a pile of others (*'Iss President Truman, innit?'*) and handed over what seemed like an incredibly large sum of money which he humiliatingly had to fish out from the front of his shirt, painfully yanking at his chest hairs as he did so. The hat-vendor informed him that he'd spent three years working in the East End of London, England, for someone he called Meesta Beeg, but came home in the end firstly because he missed his mum and secondly because he was wanted by the police for murder. 'Murder?' Jefferson said, stepping backwards into a mess of orange peel and rotting flower stems.

'Not really murder, ees my mate, he fall down in street and bang head on curbstone and is dead in one second, innit?'

But this abrupt demise wasn't, so Jefferson gathered, the fault of the hat-vendor, who had only pulled out the knife in order to frighten his mate, and he wasn't really to be blamed if the mate had misunderstood his intentions, was he, though the English police hadn't seen it like that, but Jefferson could appreciate that it was impossible for him to go back to England, where he could earn much money, much more than here, and if Jefferson wanted a guide or an interpreter, he only had to return to the stall and he, Jaime, would be delighted to be of service, take him up into the mountains (and bring him back? Jefferson wondered), out into the countryside, see volcanoes and lakes, byootiful countryside, or wherever else he might wish to be conveyed.

Jefferson promised to return if he found himself in need of guiding and strolled on, reconciled to the irritation of the pouch inside his shirt and feeling as debonair as hell in his new hat with its black band round the crown, exactly like his father's had been. When he finally returned to his hotel, and had endured a certain amount of unwelcome forelock-tugging and general smarminess from the lobby personnel, he took the lift up to the fifth floor. Opening his door, it was obvious at a glance that someone, or maybe several people, had been through his possessions. He stood in the middle of the room and slowly turned 360 degrees, observing the minute changes which became apparent as he did so. The bed had lost its original smooth-as-a-billiard-table look, one of his jackets now hung crookedly on its wooden hanger, a ripe kumquat had rolled under the table, and unless his hair had changed colour since his arrival in Quito, someone had made use of the silver-topped hairbrushes which had been a twenty-first gift from his father, had utilized the loo without flushing it afterwards and had plundered the contents of the fruit bowl. What's more, the file of papers, which had been lying on a marble-topped side table with goat-shaped golden legs, was no longer there.

Was this the work of Gordon's 'associates', or had a random

fruit-loving sneak-thief gained access to his room without the knowledge of the hotel staff? If the latter, what would a random sneak-thief, fruit-loving or not, want with his papers? He envisaged the intruder finding the file, choosing a couple of pieces of fruit, sitting down on the edge of the bed, leafing through the pages and then, catching sight of himself in the mirror, deciding his appearance needed tidying up and while he was at it, he might as well try on the gringo's jacket, first searching the pockets for any forgotten valuables, and actually, taking a leak as well. *Talk about brass neck!* his father would have said, a term which always made Jefferson think of the *National Geographic* and photographs of women with dozens of metal rings stretching their necks until they looked like human screw-in light-bulbs.

Upper lip circumflexed with distaste, he flushed away the contents of the loo, afterwards vigorously washing his hands. He wondered whether he should pretend not to have noticed any signs of intrusion, or whether he should complain to the brown-nosers on the reception desk. He made himself a cup of what the label described as tea but which tasted more like boiled snapdragons, and considered the question, finally deciding he would be a step ahead of the opposition (whoever they might be) if for the moment he acted as though he had noticed nothing untoward. If Kate had been with him, they might have sat down on the balcony with a glass of chilled champagne, gazing at the cloudy peaks in the distance while they discussed whether to tell or not to tell. 'Discretion isn't necessarily the better part of valour,' Kate might have said, looking at him fondly, and he would have murmured sagely, 'Least said, soonest mended,' at the same time wondering what discretion had to do with valour in the first place, and they might then jointly have come to a decision, before pouring a second glass of champagne prior to going out somewhere nice for dinner. He could have arranged for the champagne to be in their room when he booked the hotel, and the card might then have said *With the Compliments of the Management and Congratulations on Your Marriage!* or something similar. He opened the complimentary bottle, poured himself a glass (*Cheers, Gordon!*) and sat alone on the balcony looking at the view. There were two active volcanoes outside Quito, he'd read, when he had been mugging up on Ecuador prior to arrival. Suppose one of them erupted during the night, ash silently floating down like black snow while he innocently slept, covering the city and smothering its inhabitants . . . He would hate to end up like the people of Pompeii, caught *in extremis* and preserved for ever in the postures of an agonizing death; ash could reach temperatures of over a hundred degrees, he'd read somewhere.

He realized glumly that he would never marry Kate, never even get to first base, because even if he asked her out again, she would assume he was only doing so out of pity, and she would reject him with contempt. She was, he knew instinctively, that kind of girl. How many years would he have to serve before she accepted that pity didn't come into it? Jacob served seven years for Rachel, didn't he, plus one week, according to the chaplain at his college, but by the time he, Jefferson, had waited seven years, with or without the odd week, he'd be pushing forty and Kate might be quite old to have a first child, even with the miracle of modern science, even if she could be persuaded of his love. He sipped his champagne and thought that if, by some lucky chance, he were ever to get Kate to agree to marry him, and if by the time he'd won her trust she wasn't too old to want kids, he would definitely not name his child after an American president. Come on, guys, five generations was enough for one family, especially with Monroe and Madison already named; why should he continue someone else's tradition, anyway?

Later, when the evening was cooler, he went out into the streets again to find a restaurant where he could eat dinner. There was one in the hotel, but he suspected the waiters would be fawning all over him, constantly refilling his glass, being over-attentive, just because he was a connection of Gordon's. Several streets away, he found somewhere which looked clean and friendly and went in. There were two rooms, linked by a wide archway, and furnished with wooden tables and chairs. He would be leaving tomorrow afternoon for Guayaquil, more sightseeing and the flight to Santa Cruz island, so intended to make the most of his time here. He'd already done countless churches and cathedrals, taken a tour to see a monument purporting to mark the middle of the world, walked through the Old Town and was, quite frankly, exhausted. He ordered a soup of cheese and potatoes and, after consulting his pocket dictionary and realizing that one of the meat dishes on offer was roasted guinea pig, he opted for the fish with peanuts. (*Guinea* pig? They'd had a guinea pig in a cage at his primary school, a soft brown thing with small sleepy eyes, which they were allowed to take out of its cage and stroke. He could still remember the feel of the warm furry body against his grey school sweater . . . how could he possibly eat a guinea pig?) As he called for the bill he saw, through the archway leading to the second room, three men, two slim Latin-Americans in sharp-shouldered suits, one a plump and unmistakable Englishman, flushed face, big belly, crumpled linen jacket, of the same general type as Gordon, which was probably why he seemed familiar, though this guy was dark where Gordon was ginger, wearing a beard so big and bushy that it looked false. For a moment, Jefferson debated approaching the guy, finding out if he did indeed know him but asked himself if he'd want to be approached by a complete stranger when he was on vacation. Much as the English loved to herd together when they were abroad, it negated the whole idea of a holiday, the getting-away-from-it-all feeling of freedom from routine. So he left the restaurant without speaking to the man, pausing only to peer cautiously through the window on to the street. Yes, he had definitely met the bloke, he was quite sure of that, though he had no recollection of where or when. Not that it mattered.

He nursed a glass of wine and, staring out of the big windows of his warehouse loft, watching the sun descend behind a cityscape of silhouetted black roofs, television aerials, chimney pots and, further back, the gaunt scarecrows of cranes. He'd been back from the Galápagos a week and was still uncertain as to what he should do next.

'Definitely we thought it strange,' the man from the Research Institute on Santa Cruz had said. Dr Jens Bork, who had hair of a yellow so pale as to appear almost transparent, and very light blue eyes, was a marine biologist who had agreed to see him when he came to Santa Cruz. He sat turning in his hands what appeared to be the skeleton of a small marine animal and probably was. On one side of his desk, next to a photograph of a blonde woman in jeans with her arms round two white-haired children, stood a miniature wooden flagpole flying a small red flag with a white cross on it, which made Jefferson, who had once learned the flags of all nations for a Boy Scout badge, fairly confident that Dr Bork was from Denmark. On the wall hung a portrait of what was probably the Danish queen and her husband, flanked by what might have been her son and his wife, but could equally have been her daughter and her son-in-law (Jefferson, a staunch republican, knew little about royalty and cared even less, especially the Scandinavian kind).

'Did you conduct any kind of enquiry?' he'd asked.

'We could not do so. We had no sort of authority. Besides, the police seemed to be very convinced that they knew exactly what had happened. A simple road accident, as far as they were concerned. And then the whole thing was disposed of so quickly, really before we had time to assimilate what had happened.'

'The . . . uh . . . cremation, you mean?'

'Precisely. Almost before we were aware there'd been an accident in the first place, the . . . uh . . . remains were gone, cremated, as you say. We attended the funeral, there was a small gathering of colleagues and friends, and that, most regrettably, seemed to be that. It was only afterwards that we began to ask ourselves whether it was something quite different from what it appeared to be.'

The man spoke far better English than Jefferson did himself. 'And what exactly did you think was strange about it?' he asked.

'For a start, there was the character of Professor Lennox himself. A charming man, but also a most careful one, checking and rechecking everything, driving always as though there might be danger round the next corner. I will be frank with you, Mr Andrewes, sometimes . . .' Bork paused, looking dubious.

'It's all right, I didn't know him.' Hastily Jefferson waved away the assumption that he might be insulted by what the other man was about to say.

'Sometimes we who worked with him found this irritating, the over-methodical way in which he approached each problem as it arose. Looking back, it seemed quite honestly inconceivable that he would have driven off the road, unless forced in some way. And then there was this extraordinary talk of gunfire . . . you have heard of this also?'

Jefferson nodded. The testimony, though inconclusive, had been among his father's papers. 'A small boy spoke of it, didn't he?'

'A small boy who later disappeared.' Bork breathed deeply through his nose and relinquished the skeleton, picking up instead a ridged shell which had been lying beside a china mug commemorating the recent marriage of some Scandinavian royal couple, possibly the same crown prince or princess who featured in the photograph on the wall.

'Yes, the report I was given mentioned gunshots . . .' Jefferson nodded at the file which lay in front of the scientist. Luckily, before leaving England, he had taken the precaution of secreting a copy of everything inside the lining of his suitcase and had subsequently found a copy-shop which had Xeroxed the pages again so that both he and Bork were working from the same papers as those in the file which had been stolen.

'My colleague, Dr Chambers,' Bork said, 'who had worked closely with Professor Lennox, and was a particular friend of his, actually took the trouble to drive up to the place in the hills where the accident occurred. He said it was inexplicable; there was no bend in the road, and no signs of a recent landslide. Most of the people he questioned denied that the incident had even taken place, but there was one family who lived on the very outskirts of the village . . . after some persuasion, they spoke of hearing two shots just before the car went over the edge of the ravine. But they refused to say anything more.'

Jefferson, too, had driven up to the same village with even fewer results. If the family was still there, they did not come out to greet the gringo. His trip into the hills had begun in hazy sunshine but by the time he reached his destination, the area was shrouded in low-lying cloud which hovered wetly between mist and rain. As the fog descended further, muffling sound and reducing sight to a minimum, he was taken back to a similar afternoon somewhere in the Lake District, unseen sheep baa-ing, a bird cawing sharply every now and then, the feeling that he and his father had been transported to another planet (*'Beam me up, Scotty'*) where the sun never rose because of some galactic transgression by Earthmen, a war of the worlds about to commence. The coldly astringent scent of the fog invaded his nostrils, his face was webbed with it, and every now and then, a small clearing of the air enabled them to glimpse a group of people who might as well have been aliens, bulkily clad in wet Barbours and Wellingtons, protesting against the erection (or possibly the demolition) of a silo or maybe a nuclear reactor, neither he nor his father was quite clear. Companionably silent, the two of them ate soggy sandwiches made of some indeterminate meat paste, and drank Ribena from little boxes pierced by a sharp-ended plastic straw, which collapsed as they sucked the juice and air from them. Jefferson's spirits had soared from his usual guarded contentment into pure happiness as he stared about him at the waterlogged fields, the dripping bracken, the bird (*'A lapwing,'* his father explained. *'Also known as the green plover, or the peewit, because of its call.'*) standing on one leg below a hand-built drystone wall, green back feathers glistening with damp, one beady eye kept on Jefferson and his father, ready to go into its broken wing routine if either of them made any kind of move in the direction of the nest which lay invisibly somewhere among the clumps of wet grass.

After his driver had made enquiries, Jefferson was shown the point at which Dr Lennox had driven off the road and plunged down into the undergrowth, but, all these years later, there was nothing to see, no indication of the tragedy which had left four people horribly dead.

'What you're implying is that this wasn't an accident,' he said to Bork.

Bork had dipped his head at the papers in front of him. 'Precisely. Quite honestly, I think Dr Lennox was . . . eliminated, if that is the word I want.'

'How about murdered?'

Bork's eyebrows lifted. He nodded. 'That might well be more appropriate.'

'And if it was elimination, murder, whatever . . . do you have any idea who the target was, or why this should have happened?'

'None whatsoever. Nor were we given any satisfaction at the time, the autopsies, if that is the word, being conducted so speedily, followed almost immediately by cremation.'

'So if bullets were involved, you have no idea who might have been aimed at?'

'No. I can only say that Dr Lennox was highly thought of here, as was his wife. As for your mother . . .' He hesitated.

'It's all right, please be honest, I know she could be, in fact usually was, a pain in the butt.'

'Yes, perhaps. She could be . . . awkward. But not so much that anyone would wish to kill her, even if they might . . .'

'. . . sometimes think of it!'

A pale and cautious smile lingered for a moment on the Dane's long face. 'Besides, she was only here for six weeks, after which she intended to return to England, so she was unlikely to have been the target – if target there was.'

'So you can't think of anything at all which might have led to a possible attack on someone who was in that car?'

'It was very unlikely indeed that either of the two daughters was involved in anything which might have led to this. Katerina Lennox was here on holiday with her father, and Anna-Margarita was only eight.'

'So it has to be one of the adults, and probably not my mother.'

'That's what we think.' The Dane spoke in a guarded fashion, as though he was weighing up every possible consequence of his words.

'Which leaves Dr Lennox or his wife?'

'That is correct.' Bork set down the shell and straightened the little Danish flag. 'Though as a scientific thesis, that might be making too big an assumption, in that though unlikely, it could quite easily have been your mother who was the intended victim.'

Jefferson frowned at the file in front of him. 'Was there any trouble that you can recall? Any incident?'

'Not really, not that I remember.'

'A former worker dismissed for some reason? I realize this is a scientific foundation, but someone who was causing problems that might lead to – I know it sounds wildly improbable – to revenge of some kind?'

'There was nobody. Many of us have been here for years and are friends. Researchers appear and stay for shorter or longer periods, but people are not dismissed; they leave of their own accord or – as in my case – spend most of their working lives here, these islands providing so many utterly absorbing grounds for scientific research.'

'I can see that.'

'Besides, if revenge . . .' Bork shook his head with an expression of mild amusement. 'So unlikely . . . but if that was a possible motive, why here, on this island? Professor Lennox lived in Quito most of the year, he held a position at the university, there must have been easier ways to . . . kill him – if indeed that is what happened – than arranging an accident.'

'When I asked if there was any trouble, any kind of incident, you said, "Not really", what did you mean?'

Bork produced again his pale smile and leaned back in his chair.

Behind him was a vista of grey sea with random outcrops of rock. 'Do you know anything about sea-cucumbers?'

If Jefferson had been given an unlimited supply of paper, pens and time, he still doubted if he would have come up with 'sea-cucumbers' if asked to guess what Dr Bork was about to ask. As for knowing anything about them . . . 'No.'

'Sea-cucumbers – I shall spare you a detailed discussion of this creature, but basically, it is highly prized in the Far East, especially in China, because of its supposed aphrodisiac qualities.'

There must be a great deal of erectile dysfunction in China, Jefferson reflected, since they seem to scarf down almost anything in the search for sexual gratification, powdered rhinoceros horn and tigers' penises, oysters and shark fins and fresh snake blood. Now sea-cucumbers. 'Uh-huh,' he said.

'Not only that, *holothuroidea* is considered to possess particular medicinal properties, such as assisting in tissue repair and reducing scarring. Today, scientists all over the world are working on this, but even as short a time as ten years ago, only the Chinese seem to have known about this attribute. In short, the sea-cucumber was of considerable value to anyone wanting to make a quick profit. It is different now, of course, and the whole industry has been rationalized – you can buy sea-cucumber in pill or powder form, many countries have legalized the harvesting of the creatures – but back then, although this area had been declared a marine reserve, people – poachers – were stealing the native sea-cucumbers because the area was not properly patrolled, the population was very small, and the sea-cucumbers were in relatively shallow waters, and therefore easier to get at.'

'And Professor Lennox was trying to stop this poaching?'

'We know that he had had more than one brush with one of the known smugglers; he used to complain bitterly about it, he had even threatened the man with police intervention if he did not stop his illegal activities. It probably would not have done much good, since the police felt firstly that they had better things to concern themselves with than sea-cucumbers – you must understand that back then, environmental matters were not generally considered as important as they are today – and secondly, many of them were being paid off by the criminals and for the most part had no interest in putting stop to a trade which enriched themselves as well as the poachers.'

Jefferson sat up straighter. 'And you think it might have been this "known smuggler" who was responsible for either killing or causing to be killed Professor Lennox and his family, and, incidentally, my mother.'

'I am saying only that all of us here felt that it was a distinct possibility.'

'Do you have the name of this man?'

'We did, but the police told us shortly after we had voiced our concerns, that the man had been killed in a shoot-out, or evading arrest – as always, the exact details were a little hazy.'

'Did you believe them?'

Bork shrugged. 'Whether we did or not, it was clear that we were not going to get any further.'

'Well, thank you for your time.' Jefferson stood. 'I'm grateful.' He hesitated. 'Is there any point in giving me the name?'

'I doubt it. Even if he was still alive, not dead as we were told, it was almost certainly not his real name or, if it was, he would have changed it long ago. In fact, the chances that he is still in this country are very slight. They tend to move about a lot, these professional crooks.' Holding the door open for Jefferson, Bork added, 'Has something come up recently in relation to this accident? There's been nothing for years and now yours is the second enquiry about the matter that we've had in the past couple of months.'

'Really? Who was the other person?'

'It was through a lawyer, so I can't help you much. The lawyer would certainly not be of any assistance to you. But I could give you the address of Professor Lennox's son, if you think it might be of use. As a matter of fact the gentleman was in touch with us not long ago, about the same incident. He might have further information which could help you.'

Was it too much of a coincidence, Jefferson thought now, sipping his wine, that the son lived in the same town as he did himself? It was this which had held him back from contacting Dr Magnus Lennox; he felt he needed to consider things before he did so. Three times he had driven along the street where Lennox lived, slowing down considerably as he passed the address he'd been given by Jens Bork. Unexceptional, a gentrified late-Victorian terrace, a glimpse of an orderly, charming drawing room, and twice a man with a thick thatch of lightish hair wearing a grey cashmere cardigan over a shirt and tie, not a mode of dress to which Jefferson himself was drawn, speaking as it did of bachelordom, anoraks hanging in hall closets, train-spotting, 'twitching' and other nerdy pursuits. But the painting over the mantelpiece was fine and so was the jardinière on it – Meissen, if he wasn't mistaken, and distinctly un-nerdy – and there were some good-looking books on the visible bookshelves, in so far as a book could be considered good-looking, so perhaps the man was simply a scholar, an academic, a little fusty, maybe, nothing the love of a good woman couldn't cure.

Thoughts of women, good or bad, took him inevitably back to Kate Fullerton. Last time he'd casually walked past the travel-agency, he had seen that she was not there and so carried on down the High Street, past the bookshop next door (not in there either), stopping in at the little café round the corner for a coffee (and in the hope that she might be taking her lunch-break there) and then strolling equally casually back, to find that she was still not around.

Kate

Twenty

Good news can usually wait for a while. Bad news can't. Nobody is going to call you in the middle of the night to tell you they've just got engaged or they won a Pulitzer Prize or the Lottery, at least nobody Kate could think of, including herself, but bad news doesn't keep, so when the phone rang just after midnight – green seconds folding over in front of her as she reached for the handset – Kate knew something terrible had happened. She dragged herself out of sleep (*'I'm going to have an early night'*), still dripping dreams, to lift the receiver, her heart banging around in her chest like a trapped rat.

'Kate, I'm so, so sorry . . .'

'What's happened?' But she already knew the answer.

'You won't believe this but he – he's out.' It was Lucy's voice, wandering the octaves, close to tears. 'Robbie rang from work to tell me.'

'How long ago?'

'Three or four hours. He faked pains that sounded as though he'd got acute appendicitis. The prison hospital's been closed down for refurbishment, so they rushed him to the local hospital.' A blown breath. 'Kate, what will you do?'

'I don't know. I don't – damn . . . I thought I was safe.'

'They'll be looking for him. Robbie says he fractured the skull of the ambulance attendant and then beat up an officer. They don't stand for that, not when it's one of their own.'

As Lucy talked, Kate was thinking, thinking, options rattling round her head like a stick run along the railings of a cage. She felt like a rat in a trap. A bird in a net. 'He fractured someone's skull? Doesn't sound very much like him.' He was stupid, he could be violent when manipulated into it (as she suspected Mick had manipulated him into her abduction) but she wouldn't have put him down as murderous.

'Robbie says he definitely had help, both inside and out. Robbie says he's connected. Take care, Kate.'

'I'll do my best. Thanks, Lucy.' Kate hung up. Her hand trembled.

So he was out. And probably heading straight for her, a raptor plummeting from the sky. He was coming for her and he would be thirsting for revenge for the fact that she had fooled him, made an idiot of him.

If his 'connections' had engineered the escape, would they have been following the ambulance transporting him to hospital, ready to pick him up? They must have been. If not, he'd have to find a car, get to a railway station, get some money; he'd be without cash, credit cards, clothes other than those he was standing up in. He wasn't a criminal in the sense that he had lock-picking, car-breaking skills, nor would he want to draw attention to himself by carjacking. On the other hand . . . Kate shivered. He might well force his way into a car and coerce some hapless car-owner into driving him to the town, or getting her to take him to an ATM so she could draw money out – though if he'd had help, none of those logistical problems would exist.

By now he was probably on the way. He could be turning the corner at the end of the street at this very moment; he might be watching the building, he could already be standing outside the front door, waiting for her to emerge. And then what? Would he use a knife, a gun, a ligature? Would he overpower her, drag her downstairs, bundle her into his stolen car and take her somewhere to enjoy his revenge, or worse still, would he call in his mate, Mick (if he knew where Mick was) and let him kill her slowly and painfully?

She woke Janine to explain, called Magnus, and, stopping only to throw a few items into suitcases, the two women drove to her brother's house to spend the rest of the night there.

'The police know, I assume,' Magnus said, pouring hot chocolate from a copper-bottomed saucepan into three mugs.

'They must do.'

'I think you ought to call them and tell them you're here,' Janine said. 'If they come round to my – our – place and there's nobody home, they won't know what to do.'

'This is very true.' Magnus made a call to the station. 'They know all about him getting away,' he said, returning to the table. 'They'll be in touch with you in the morning, Kate. Said not to worry, he won't get far – and that it's quite possible he won't even try to come up here, he might prefer to get out of the country, go back to wherever he came from.'

She thought of Stefan's swagger and self-conceit. 'I wish I could believe you.'

'Mrs Fullerton?' The couple followed her into the little café round the corner from TaylorMade, where she had gone for her lunch break, and stood at the end of the booth where she was sitting.

'Yes?' Who were they, what did they want?

'We're from CID.'

'CID?'

'I'm Detective Sergeant Tessa Faber and this is Detective Constable Jack Prince. May we sit down?' When Kate nodded, they eased themselves into the bench opposite her, the woman first, sliding along the slippery red vinyl until they were both snugly seated. They both brought out badges and showed them to her, something she'd thought only happened in American TV series. 'Didn't want to come into your place of work,' one of them said. 'Less obvious if we talk to you here.'

'What's this about?' she asked. Less obvious? Every customer in the place could see they were cops.

'Do you know a place called Plan A?'

'I used to work there.'

'And Alfredo Lucanelli, the manager?'

'Yes – though I only knew him as Fredo.' What had Fredo done, to have the police conducting enquiries about him?

The woman – DS Faber – pulled out a photograph and slid it across the table towards her. 'Do you recognize this man?'

Kate stared down at the features she'd come to know and hate. Stefan looked strangely remote, as though he was thinking of something, somewhere quite different from the camera he was facing. 'Yes,' she said. 'I do.'

'Do you know his name?'

'He went by the name of Stefan or Stefano Michaels.'

'I understand from our colleagues here that you are aware that he escaped yesterday evening from the prison officers escorting him to hospital.'

'Yes. A friend of mine telephoned me as soon as her partner heard – he's a prison officer himself.'

'Did you also know that Stefan Michaels' body was found round the back of Plan A early this morning?'

Kate's eyes widened in shock. 'Did you say his *body*?'

'That's right.'

Stefan was *dead*? That vile creature was *dead* . . .

'Someone hit him hard across the back of the head several times and dumped him there,' DC Prince said.

'*Very* hard,' said DS Faber.

'Didn't stand a chance.'

'Are you sure?' What she meant was, are you absolutely certain that he's dead, that he can never come back into my life again, that I am safe, at least from him?

'Reasonably, given that you've just identified him, Mrs Fullerton.'

Repulsed by the realization that she had probably been gazing at a photograph of a corpse, Kate pushed the photograph away from her across the table. 'I hate to say this, but I wish I could feel sorry for him.' The news had filled her with a distasteful, despicable elation. 'Any idea who did it?'

'That's what we want to ask you.'

The Detective Sergeant added, 'Just a formality, but where were you last night, between ten-thirty when he first escaped, and five-thirty this morning, when he was found?'

'I was at home. First in the flat I share with a friend, then, after I heard that he was out of prison, round at my brother's house.'

'And where's that?'

Kate gave them the address of Janine's flat and Magnus's house.

'They'll both vouch for you?'

'I'm sure they will.'

'How did you feel when you heard that he was no longer safely tucked away in prison?'

'Dead scared. I was convinced he was coming straight after me.'

'Why would he do that?'

'Because he's an insane, conceited . . .' She gulped coffee-flavoured air. 'Because he wants – wanted – revenge . . . I was the one responsible for having him arrested; I managed to get away from him and his friend and set the police on him. I made him look like the moron he is – was. And if he was found right here in town, wouldn't it kind of prove I'm right?'

The DC nodded.

Kate looked from one to the other, then laughed. 'You can't seriously imagine that I did it, can you? I didn't know he was going to escape, and even if I had, I certainly wouldn't have been hanging around outside Plan A in the middle of the night on the off-chance he'd show up there, why would I? As for beating his brains out . . .'

Neither of the officers laughed back at her. 'Unlikely, I admit,' said the DS, 'but stranger things have happened.'

'The . . . erm . . . body was found just after three this morning,' said DC Prince, looking down at his notebook, 'by the said Alfredo Lucanelli, who came out of the back door of the wine bar when he'd shut the place up for the night, in order to put out a saucer of milk—'

'Fredo likes cats.'

'—which is when he noticed the . . . erm . . .'

'Body,' the DS said.

'Getting back to who might have wanted to get rid of him,' said DC Prince. 'Do you have any suggestions, Mrs Fullerton, as to who might have had it in for Mr Michaels badly enough to attack him with a blunt instrument?'

'Quite a few, actually. Starting with me, closely followed by the family of a girl who used to work at Plan A, Lindsay Bennett, any one of whom would be happy to dispatch him, given half a chance, but if that half involved hanging about outside Plan A in case he managed to get out of jail, it was one they were extremely unlikely to take, quite apart from the fact that they had no real proof, beyond what I told them myself, that Stefan was in any way involved with the fatal hit-and-run of their daughter. But in any case, none of us are the sort to take the law into our own hands, however much we might want to.'

'What about the other man who helped Michaels to pull you off the street?'

'Mick?'

They both sat to attention, looked at each other and back at her. 'Did you say Mick?'

'Yes. Why?'

'Would you have a surname to go with that?' DC Faber asked carefully.

'No.'

'Ever hear him called anything other than Mick?'

'No.'

'Could you describe him?'

'I should bloody *hope* so, after . . .' Almost choking, Kate gave them a brief description of Mick.

'Remind you of anyone?' DS Faber said to her colleague.

'Definitely.'

'It's got to be him, hasn't it?'

'No question. Our Mel always was a scumbag.'

'Mel?' Kate looked from one to the other.

'Mel, Melvin, Mick, whatever.'

DC Prince chuckled. 'It was Martin once, wasn't it, Sarge?'

'That's right. Martyn, with a "y", thought it would look classier.'

'Our Mel, classy? That's a laugh.'

'Do you think he had something to do with . . . with this murder?' Kate jerked her chin at the photograph still lying on the table, remembered the disdain with which Mick (Mel) had spoken to Stefan and his warning that the police were keeping an eye on them. She wished they had kept a closer eye than they obviously had, so that she might have escaped them much earlier. She wondered why she found the very idea of him so terrifying; she'd only really seen him once, at Plan A, yet what and who he was seemed lucidly clear. Behind the two officers, she could see the café owner watching her, a striped linen tea towel in his hand, the avid expression of the waitress, the rigid way in which those with their backs to her table sat with ears quivering, so as to miss as little of possible of what was going on at her table.

'Possibly,' said DC Prince. 'No honour among thieves and all that.'

'More than likely,' said Faber. 'If we could lay our hands on him, we'd ask him, but we still have no idea of his whereabouts. Over the years, he's been responsible for half the crime in the area—'

'Not exactly half, Sarge.'

'A good percentage then – but we've never been able to touch him for any of it.'

'Except the one time . . .'

'That was way back when. He's got the contacts now.' DS Faber looked wistful. 'If only we could lay our hands on the men behind him, the connections.'

'Red letter day down the nick, that would be,' said DC Prince. 'Break out the champagne, we would – I'd pay for it myself.'

'If it wasn't this Mick, Mel, whatever, who killed Stefan, what about the man he and Stefan worked for?' asked Kate. She could hardly believe she was sitting there, calmly discussing murder like a witness in a cops-and-robbers programme on TV, a pretty poor one at that. At the same time, the strengthening knowledge that Stefan could never harm her again – and she had no doubt that he would have tried – was like draining an industrial-strength elixir (*'Will restore you to life'*). 'Maybe he saw Stefan as a threat in some way.'

'Our colleagues at the Met are interviewing the other members of Stefan's family, the father and brother, that is,' explained DS Faber.

'If you want my opinion, I don't think either of them had anything to do with this murder,' said DC Prince. 'According to the London guys, Don Carlos seemed genuinely upset to hear the news, actually cried real tears in front of them.'

'Aaah, poor baby,' said DS Faber. 'You're too kind-hearted for your own good, you are.'

'What about *you*, Sarge, made of stone or something?'

'No, Jack, I've just seen more of these villains than you have. But I agree it's unlikely that he was responsible for bumping off his own son.' She turned back to Kate. 'They won't be able to hold them for anything, of course. They've had their eye on the father for quite some time, as a matter of fact, a really nasty bit of work, but they haven't wanted to pull him because both the Met and we are hoping that eventually he'll lead us to the Big Boss.'

Kate thought of the Clooney-clone, the man she'd seen one evening with Stefan. 'The father's a criminal too?'

'Long-time. Always manages to wriggle out of things, always acts respectable, got himself way up the food-chain, nice house in Bishop's Avenue, respected businessman, all that crap, retains top defence lawyers when things start to look dicey for him, just like our local snot-rag, Martyn-with-a-Y.'

'And of course Don Quixote can always go back where he came from, if he wants,' said DC Prince.

'If he *dares*. Far as I'm aware, he's got a record as long as your arm, plus being wanted on suspicion of several murders out there.'

'Out where?' Kate asked.

'Colombia, Ecuador, somewhere like that.'

'Ecuador?' It seemed as though all roads led inexorably to Ecuador.

'Not that they'd ever indict him; way I've heard it the police there are as corrupt as they come.'

'Cross their palms with silver and they'll follow you anywhere,' murmured the DC. 'Not to mention let you off a murder charge.'

'Just a minute, are you saying that Stefan Michaels' father is a *murderer*?' He'd looked 'nice', the only time she'd seen him, a nice man with a kind face. But didn't people always say, when someone's been caught for a string of hideous crimes, 'ooh, he was ever so nice, kept himself to himself, but always had a kind word for the kiddies, we thought he was really *nice*, whoever would have thought it?' (Though later, they were perfectly ready to believe the worst, however *nice* they'd considered him at the time, always thought there was something a bit off about him, 'know what I mean, wouldn't look you in the eye, didn't I always say so, dear?').

'Murder's only part of it. Charlie Lyons, or Carl Peters, or Don Carlos Pedro de Something-or-other y Léon, to give him his full name, is into everything – extortion, blackmail, prostitutes, gun-running, smuggling, nicking top-of-the-range cars, etc, etc, how long have you got?' said DS Faber.

'Him and his boss,' chimed in DC Prince.

'Look at it this way, Mrs Fullerton, at least we know for sure that one of your assailants has had his comeuppance. All we have to do now is find the other, young Mick.'

'Eliminate him from our enquiries.'

'Or not, as the case may be.'

'I expect his mother loves him,' said DS Faber. She laughed cynically. 'There's rumours coming through the grapevine that he's trying to go straight, trying to set himself up as a bit of a gent, going all posh on us. That'll be the day.'

'Give a dog a bad name,' the DC said.

'This particular dog chose his name for himself.'

'Of course we knew him back when he still called himself by his given name, but that was several changes ago.'

'Doesn't it seems a bit coincidental that Stefan Michaels manages to escape from prison, and that very same evening, he's murdered?' asked Kate.

'Of course it does; you might almost suspect it was planned that way.'

'My friend who's engaged to the prison officer told me that he must have had help.'

'Oh, he definitely had that, all right,' said the DS.

'If you can call it help,' added the DC.

'Get him out, get him up here, whack him,' said the DS, unemotionally.

'You think someone was waiting up here to . . . whack him?' Kate said.

'Almost certainly. Probably hired specially to do the deed.'

'By whom?'

'Ah well, that's where we came in, isn't it?' The two of them thanked Kate for her help, not that she felt she'd been of any use whatsoever, and went outside, followed by the gaze of most of the café's customers.

'What the hell did they want?' someone asked and everyone glanced at Kate and then away, as though she was somehow tainted with crime, that it sat on her face like a birthmark that you couldn't help noticing but had been brought up not to stare at.

'There was a murder last night, didn't you hear?' a voice said helpfully.

'What, here? Small place like this?'

'Some drunk outside a wine bar, way I heard.'

'Hanging's too good . . .' someone ventured, and was shouted down. The general consensus among the café's clientele was a complete, and several times repeated, lack of knowledge as to what the world was coming to.

Kate meanwhile pushed away her plate, and sat over her coffee. Why did everything slant towards Ecuador, from Jefferson Andrewes going there for his 'holiday' to Magnus and the mysterious letter from the lawyers in Quito, to her own family, even Janine, who only the other night had let drop that her secret lover (*'married, thank God!'*), the silent partner in TaylorMade Travel, was originally from Guayaquil. Now it appeared that Stefan Michaels and his family were also tied in. If only she could observe it carefully enough, might she finally see a pattern emerge, where all the pieces would finally fit together?

Magnus
Twenty-One

'Will you be at home this evening, Dr Lennox?'

The voice was unknown to Magnus, and he wondered if he should casually drop into the conversation, if conversation there should ensue, some mention of the four beefy brothers or three stalwart sons who lived with him, plus the collection of guns in a locked (of course) case (which could easily be unlocked), in order to forestall any impromptu turnings-up on the doorstep. These days you never knew what you were letting yourself in for, and the world was, as Padhraic O'Brien, one of his more brilliant students, had told him only last week, full of nutters, not to mention drunken yobs, who'd glass you soon as look at you, O'Brien had said. Hitherto, Magnus had always pictured O'Brien, when he pictured him at all, bent over his books or drinking tea from a mug featuring a leprechaun and labelled *A Present From Cork*, not out in the local pubs in imminent danger of being *glassed*, whatever that was, by drunken yobs.

'I might,' he said cautiously, trying not to crunch too loudly the piece of toast he had just popped into his mouth.

'You have no idea who I am, but my name is Andrewes, Jefferson Andrewes—'

'Ah, the famous Mr Andrewes.' Magnus swallowed hastily, the toast scratching painfully at the soft tissues of his throat, and spoke in the kind of hearty voice he never normally used, and despised in those who did. The man certainly didn't sound like either a nutter or a drunken yob, but you couldn't be too careful.

'You've heard of me, then?'

'Yes, indeed. The . . . er . . . woman (girl, lady, salesperson?) at the travel agency mentioned you.'

'The thing is, I've just returned from a trip to the Galápagos, and I was given your name by a Dr Bork who works at the Research Station there. I wondered if I could drop by and discuss something with you.'

'I . . . er . . . yes, why not. What's it in connection with?'

'My mother's death, mostly. Dr Bork thought you might be able to clarify one or two matters for me.'

During the day, Magnus did not have time to wonder why Andrewes thought he would know anything about the death of his mother, whom he pictured as a round sort of person, the way mothers so often were, perhaps in a tweed skirt carrying a pair of secateurs for dead-heading roses, or alternatively – these days – like one or two of his colleagues at the Department, a smart older woman in black suit or trousers with a white or magenta silk shirt and high-heeled black boots, short smartly cut hair, some kind of leather briefcase under her arm. The thought of his prospective visitor re-occurred to him while he was doing the bulk of the shopping for the evening after next, when Kate and Janine would be coming for dinner, and again while he made a cheese omelette for himself with a tomato and avocado salad, and while he brewed coffee. What 'matters' did Andrewes think he, Magnus, could possibly clarify about the death of his mother, a woman he'd never met and knew nothing about?

Andrewes, when he showed up at the front door, was big, an obvious rugby-player, the kind of man by whom Magnus, though tall himself, was always vaguely intimidated. The two men sat down in the drawing room, which Andrewes inspected with admiration. 'Very nice,' he said, '*very* nice. I live in one of those converted warehouses, a huge flat there, not exactly a family home like this, I'm afraid, very modern, sort of minimalist, I'm not sure I really like it very much. Taupe sofas,' he inexplicably added.

'A family home . . .' Magnus repeated, deciding not to pick up on the sofas, and he remembered a remark about nurseries that Janine, in her estate-agent incarnation, had made, which had puzzled him at the time, but which now came back to him, the fair-haired little boy on the rocking horse, the non-Edwina with baby Isabella on her hip. 'That's a compliment,' he said, 'though as yet I'm afraid there is no family.'

'I haven't got anyone, either,' Andrewes said, which wasn't quite what Magnus had intended to convey, what with Bisto the Boston Historian, and a colleague (one of the black-suited ones) at work who was always coming in to his office and perching in a manner which could only be described as provocative on the corner of his desk, and who had just that very morning asked him if he wanted to go to a concert at the Arts Centre with her, since someone had given her tickets.

'So tell me about your mother,' he said.

Andrewes laughed. 'How long have you got?'

'But why do you imagine I would know anything about her?'

'The thing is, she was killed in a car accident – except that there's more than a little suspicion that it might not have been an accident.'

'Like my father,' Magnus began, then frowned. 'Where was this?'

'Sorry, didn't I say? In Ecuador, about ten years ago, in the Galápagos Islands.'

Magnus raised enquiring eyebrows. 'What was she doing there?'

'Working, as far as I can make out, with your father.'

'Was she by any chance . . . are we talking about Rhoda Bailey?'

'That's the one. She went back to her maiden name after she split up with my father.'

'You mean my father's summer assistant, who was in the car when he and my stepmother were killed, is – was – your mother?'

'Yes.'

'How very extraordinary.' Magnus got up. 'Tell me, Mr Andrewes, do you believe in coincidence?'

'Not really.'

'And do you drink cognac?'

'When it's offered, most certainly. My name's Jefferson, by the way.'

'I'm Magnus.' The two men smiled at each other.

'I'm going to ask you a strange question,' Jefferson said. 'Do you know anything about sea-cucumbers?'

'Not a lot. Medical properties attached, aren't there? Pills – I've seen tubs of them on shelves in the health-food shops, and I know some people eat them.' A small seismic upheaval took place in Magnus's memory. '. . . I believe my father may have had a . . . there was some kind of fuss connected with them . . . aphrodisiacs, aren't they?'

Jefferson laughed. 'What isn't, if you believe in it strongly enough?'

Well, teacups for example, thought Magnus, or paving-stones, though perhaps there were people for whom a paving-stone was an erotic object liable to send them into transports of lubricious delight, which could be awkward if you simply wanted to go round the corner for a pint of milk. 'Quite.' He had little use for aphrodisiacs himself, sadly, though given the circumstances where he might have required one, he doubted whether he would need further stimulation. The image of Janine spread on his bed suddenly jumped into his mind, and he would have liked to linger there a little, but Jefferson Andrewes was speaking further about sea-cucumbers, detailing facts he must have learned at the Institute where Magnus's own father used to work.

'It seems to me quite obvious that foul play of some kind was involved.' Andrewes leaned forward, ticking points off on his fingers. 'One, this boy who heard gunshots, and subsequently disappeared into the big city, was almost certainly paid to keep silent – if not silenced himself. Two, the distinct absence of any sharp bends in the road which might have caused a vehicle to go over the edge of the ravine, leading to three, the fact that your father was by all accounts a meticulously careful driver, and likely to have been even more so with his wife and daughter on board, not to mention my mother. Four, the illegal harvesting of sea-cucumbers from protected waters, which your father stumbled upon, thus theoretically bringing to an end a lucrative trade in smuggling the things to the Far East. Five, the fact that the bodies were cremated in what, even for a Latin-American country, was indecent haste, before, that is, anybody could examine them for things like bullet wounds.'

'Six,' Magnus said, 'the fact that there seems to be absolutely no paperwork available in connection with these deaths. At the time, my father's lawyer told me he'd been quite unable to get hold of anything at all, and though I've had him write to the authorities several times since, I've still seen no details, in fact he's intimated that there are people actively interested in suppressing any details there might be. After a while,' he added tiredly, 'you start to wonder why you're bothering, it's nearly ten years ago now.'

'Exactly. But if we're right, this was cold-blooded murder, and I for one intend to see, if at all possible, that someone is brought to book for it.'

'I'm with you on that one. Anna-Margarita, my little sister, was only eight when it happened; she never had a chance to live her life at all.'

Jefferson frowned. 'You say you've never seen any papers, but just before I went out there my stepfather . . . my mother's second husband would be more accurate . . . he told me he'd seen some kind of police report about the incident, that he'd gone through it quite carefully with his lawyer and that it all seemed, as he put it, hunky-dory.'

'Do you think he'd let us have sight of it?'

'I can't see why not, if he's still got it, that is. I'll call him, ask him to have a really good look for it, as a matter of urgency, say I'd be glad to go down and collect it.' He swallowed a little cognac. 'You could come too, if you liked.'

One of Magnus's students had told him just two days ago that he ought to get out more, and now here was an opportunity to do so. 'Sounds like a good idea.'

'I'll call Gordon tonight.'

'Maybe we should rope my sister in on this. She was actually in the car when it went over the edge of the road and plunged into the ravine.'

'Jeez, that's tough.'

'She was lucky to get away with nothing more than some scars on her leg, and a touch of amnesia. She can't remember anything more than a few sketchy details about the accident.'

'Poor girl.'

'She's had a lot of . . . troubles.' Magnus wondered whether to confide further in this more-or-less stranger but decided that Kate would hate to have details of her recent abduction tossed into the public arena, though he was aware that leaving the sentence in its unfinished state might imply nothing more to Jefferson Andrewes than that his sister was one of those slightly hysterical women who suffered once a month from what he thought of as Women's Problems, but he decided that if he tried to deny this he would only land himself in a welter of explanations of a far too intimate nature, so kept silent, the unnamed 'troubles' hanging in the air like so many slowly fading smoke signals.

Janine

Twenty-Two

Seated at the small round dining table in her flat, Janine pored over the ledgers which had been delivered to TaylorMade Travel by DHL from London. She'd pushed back the green glass vase of narcissi which she'd bought at the market that morning, a small tight bunch of green stems and tissue-paper petals curved around hearts the colour of the egg-yolks she remembered from when she was a child but hardly ever saw these days, heavenly scented, *'harbingers of spring'*, she'd read that somewhere, although the dreary winter had long since receded, and even spring was well advanced. The night they'd spent at Magnus's house, there had been snowdrops in the front garden of the house, hiding under a rather unkempt holly bush, and little yellow things she'd looked up on the Internet and discovered were aconites. There was a scrubby little bush of forsythia, a plant she didn't like – was it the absence of leaves, at least in its early stages – and the remains of crocuses, too, on the lawn. She didn't like crocuses at all, the only time she'd got the point of them had been a planting she'd seen in front of a castle in Copenhagen, a great sheet of purple and white, like a carpet. She'd root the forsythia out if it was hers, replace it with mock-orange and lilac, plant lavender along the border, anything with a nice smell, like the scented garden for the blind she used to take her grandmother to, all those years ago, curry plant and mint in pots, and lemon verbena and geranium.

As soon as she'd stepped through Magnus's front door, she had experienced a sense of coherence, as if it was here that everything came together, all the loose ends of her existence meeting in this hallway and connecting into a life of happy ordinariness. It was the kind of house she'd always dreamed of, rather like Miss Barker's, with its antique furniture and good pictures, nice wallpapers, wonderful linen sheets (had Magnus chosen those?). She had felt a great longing to live there, a desire to look out of the windows at the back garden and plan its so-much-needed reorganization, to move through the pleasant rooms and over the Persian rugs and know that it was hers, to cook in the daffodil-yellow kitchen, pull out a copper-bottomed pan here, or a hugely expensive Japanese chef's knife there. She wasn't kidding herself, it was never going to happen, but in the time she'd spent there with him, she had briefly glimpsed the multi-layered meaning of the word 'home'.

Normally, handling numbers gave her a kind of interior glow, like a superior wood-burning stove, one of those Jotel things, if that was the right name, something Scandinavian spelled with either an *ø* or an *ö*. She loved working with figures, adding them up, multiplying and subtracting, watching them click accurately into place, reach the conclusions that she wished them to, the logicality of them, like music, the way they might soar into incomprehensibility on one side of a page and fall inevitably into their allotted position on the other. Tonight, though, she could not stop thinking of Magnus, the button missing on his cashmere cardigan which it wouldn't take more than a minute to fix (she must remember to put a needle and thread into her bag before they went to have supper with him, because she was pretty sure he would have neither in the house), the shaggy eyebrows which given half a chance she would gladly trim for him (she'd occasionally worked in a hairdressing salon as a Saturday job when she was still at school) and his eyes, his really lovely eyes which most of the time seemed to be fixed on something only he could see (jewelled eggs and *dachas* and fur-piled sledges racing through snowy forests?) and above all, his love and concern for his sister. She tried to imagine her own brother being as protective as that, being protective at *all*, but it was impossible. It was probably a bit sad that she had no idea where he was, her own flesh and blood, nor what he did (though it was almost certainly something which sailed far too close to the wind) and quite honestly she didn't want to know, not after he'd spent time in prison for something which Mum insisted wasn't his fault ('*well, he always was too gullible for his own good, Jane,* you *know that*'); not after he'd murdered her little dog. Dad knew it was he who'd done it, even though he hadn't watched the crime take place like she had.

During the last three evenings she had gone over her lover's books, the lists of employees, the records of the various companies they worked for under the umbrella of one holding company, with a

Board of Directors consisting of only two people, a married couple, she presumed, since they had the same surname, though they could have been father and daughter, or brother and sister. Or aunt and nephew or . . .

There were half a dozen of these companies, all with the kind of anonymous names that gave no clue as to the business activity each company conducted – Management Supplies Ltd, Communication Services Ltd, Britec Systems, Overseas Affiliates Ltd, among others – non-committal enterprises which could have been dealing with almost anything you cared to name from property to paper napkins. Meticulously, she went through the sales records, the expenditures, the pay roll, the money laid out for vans and cars and stationery and office furniture; she checked and rechecked, went over everything three times. Now she had completed the task and would shortly type into her computer the information they clearly gave her, after which she would print the pages out, take the whole lot to the all-night copy-shop and make two or three copies of everything, keeping one for herself, naturally. Her lover was right, the organization *was* being cheated, someone had been skimming off the top and then trying to manipulate the figures, quite cleverly, too, though as soon as you knew what you were looking for, it was obvious, and she hoped that whoever it was wouldn't have to pay too big a price for the wrongdoing; she didn't want to picture what the penalty for double-crossing him or his associates might be.

Kate was out that evening. Encouraged by Janine, she had gone with friends to see the new James Bond, so Janine was alone in the flat. Closing the ledgers, finally, she decided that she had to say a permanent goodbye to her lover. She hadn't decided which approach to take, but she fancied that telling him she was getting engaged might work best, him being such a proponent of marriage. She figured he would take it in good part, there never having really been any obligation between the two of them – in fact, when she thought about it, their arrangement had really been little more than a mutually satisfactory business agreement. And now it was time to move on.

Her eyes were tired from poring over figures for so long, so she flicked on the television, hopped from a football game between two European sides to a football game between two more European sides to a programme about removing all the plants from your back garden and filling it instead with white pebbles and mirrors, which seemed moderately boring but less so than soccer, and was about to pour herself a glass of wine from the bottle standing in the kitchen when the buzzer went.

She felt a frisson of apprehension. Earlier she'd told her lover on the phone that she had finished the task he had given her: now she wondered whether he had come to first collect his incriminating evidence and then to remove her. She had no reason to imagine anything like that – he had never, in all their time together, shown any kind of violence, either verbal or physical, though she remembered a call he'd taken in his room once, speaking in Spanish which, thanks to her long-ago evening classes, she had had little difficulty in following, his voice changing from genial to steely as she listened. *'I told you to chat her up, find out what she knows, not fall in love with her, you are stupid, no, no, you are already promised elsewhere, do not go on being stupid, you will begin to annoy me, life is not about love, love is not important, family is important, work is important.'* And then, just before slamming down the telephone, *'You will do as you are told, or answer to me for the consequences.'*

Janine had pretended to be doing something in the *en suite*, waiting with the door open until he came back into the bedroom and called out to ask if she was ready. 'What?' she'd said, as though she could barely hear him, and hoped that he would feel sufficiently confident that she had not been eavesdropping, though even if she had, he would surely not have expected her to understand what he was saying or the import of his words.

The buzzer sounded again and this time she answered it. 'Hello, who is it?' she said and when the muffled voice answered, asked again, 'Who?' though she had perfectly understood that somehow she had managed to conjure up Magnus Lennox who even now was outside the main door of her building, causing her body to do all the things that happen to girls in Barbara Cartland novels, such as her heart beating so rapidly she could almost see the rise and fall of her snowy bosom (though in fact her bosom was a fairly attractive olive-brown, thanks to her genetic inheritance from her father), such as the blood staining her damask cheek a crimson-red, such as the electricity of the moment coursing thickly through her secret parts. 'Just a minute,' she fumbled, placing her mouth as close to the speaker as she could so that Magnus, three stories below, could not make the mistake of assuming that she was not going to let him in. 'I'm pressing the button, just push the door and come on up.'

She rushed into her bedroom, squirted Miss Dior behind her ears, brushed her hair and let it sit on her shoulders, contemplated changing out of her sweatshirt into a demure blouse but decided none of her blouses were all that demure in the first place, and besides, Magnus had come to see Kate, not her, so what she wore was immaterial, and she'd look ridiculous if she hurried herself into one of her smarter outfits when she was supposed to be spending the evening alone, by which time he was knocking at the door of the flat. She peered through the peephole (really *lovely* eyes) and opened the door. 'Come on in,' she said. 'I'm afraid Kate's gone to the cinema with some friends.'

'I knew she was out, and in any case, I didn't come to see her,' he said. 'I wanted to talk to you.'

'You did?' For a moment her heart did the Cartland thing again, until he added, 'Yes, to . . . er . . . ask your opinion about how she's getting on, while she isn't around.'

'Oh.' What else had she expected? That he'd throw himself on to one knee, bring out a small box of navy-blue leather, open it to display a ring lying in a bed of crushed velvet, and cry *'Marry me!'*? Well, yes, in some tiny crevice of her perfectly sensible brain, that was precisely what she'd, if not expected, then at least hoped. She led the way towards the kitchen. 'Coffee?'

'Lovely . . . though actually, on second thoughts, if you don't mind maybe I'll—'

'It's all right, Kate's bought all the makings for the real stuff,' she said, trying not to laugh at the alarm on his face. 'Or there's your cognac. If you choose coffee, you'll have to make it yourself.' Such a performance, she thought, all that steaming and hissing, that grinding of beans and pushing down of plungers, that boiling of water and so on, when personally she couldn't spot the difference between the end result and instant, except that the real stuff was so much more bitter, not that she'd ever tell him that.

Later, settled opposite each other, he said, 'As I explained, the reason I'm here is that I wanted to find out how you thought Kate was doing.'

'Like I said before, she's very strong. Psychologically, I mean. What happened to her was hugely traumatic, but I honestly think she's going to get through it about as well as it's possible to do so. And although it's a small compensation, at least the bastards didn't rape her, though from what she said, had the mysterious Mick turned up, it might have been a different story.'

'That's a relief, I suppose.'

'I expect she told you about the guy, this Stefano person, being murdered.'

'What? No, she didn't, probably because I've been up giving some lectures in Edinburgh.'

'Apparently he tricked his way out of prison, and the next thing we knew, he was found beaten to death, right outside the back door of that wine bar where Kate first met him.'

'Good heavens.' He hesitated. 'I suppose I should say that's awful, but . . . Do they think it has anything to do with . . . with what happened to Kate?'

'I don't know. The police asked her if she had any idea who might have wanted to get rid of him. She thought they half-suspected she might have done it herself!'

'How ridiculous! It could as easily have been me, avenging my sister's honour.'

'Or me,' Janine said. 'On behalf of my friend.'

Magnus twitched awkwardly, tugging at his grey cardigan (should she offer to sew the missing button on for him now or wait for a more apposite moment?), touched his hair, unwound his long legs and wound them up again, and she had an absurd urge to stroke him, calm him down. 'Look, I haven't eaten yet,' he said. 'Would you like to find somewhere, nothing fancy, we'll do that another time, where we could have a curry or some pasta or something?'

'But aren't we coming to your house for dinner tomorrow?'

'Supper,' amended Magnus, 'I'm keeping it simple, but Kate will be there, which means we shan't be alone.'

'In that case, I'd love to,' Janine said, thoughts skittering round the pleasure of the phrase 'we'll do that another time' like an Olympic freestyle skater, 'we shan't be alone', oh lovely. 'There's a nice Italian place just a couple of blocks from here. They do wonderful veal.'

'Terrific,' Magnus said. 'Get your coat and let's go.'

Jefferson
Twenty-Three

'Hi, Gordon, it's Jefferson.'

'Jeff, me old son, how the hell are you? Enjoy your holiday?'

'It was fantastic. Thanks so much for arranging such a marvellous hotel for me – they wouldn't even let me pay the bill!'

'All part of the service, dear boy. How about the blue-shoed boobies, then?'

'Elvis, eat your heart out.'

'Nice one,' Gordon chortled.

'Look, I'd like to come down and have a chat with you.'

'What about?'

'I think it would be better if I came down, rather than talk about this on the phone.'

'That serious, eh?'

'Yes.'

'When would you like to come?'

'As soon as possible. Oh, and Gordon, did you have any chance to find that police report you mentioned?'

'Not yet. To be honest, I'm not even sure I've still got it. I dumped a lot of stuff from those days – too upsetting, considering what happened to your mum, didn't want the reminders.'

'I can understand that. But have another look, if you can. By the way, would it be all right if I brought a friend?'

'The more the merrier. Come for lunch.'

Jefferson picked Magnus Lennox up at eleven o'clock the following Saturday morning. Magnus had suggested bringing his sister along, as she was so closely involved, had actually survived the crash, but not knowing the woman, Jefferson said he thought it better not to overload Gordon with guests, though this was not the real reason, his stepfather's hospitality being boundless. The fact was that he had at least met Magnus, and knew he would provide moral support, whereas the sister was an unknown quantity and could well be the sort to get up Gordon's nose in some way or another, thus damming up any stream of information that might have otherwise been supplied. He could picture her clearly, a female version of Magnus, an angular bluestocking with severe hair and dull clothes (another grey cardigan?), a gummy smile, talking too much and trying to challenge Gordon, which Jefferson knew from past experience was a lost cause. Gordon was genial most of the time, but could dig his toes in if he felt threatened, and besides, his attitude to women was very far from reconstructed, and Jefferson could just see the sister bridling as Gordon called her 'dear' and asked her to clear the table, on top of which Magnus had embarrassingly implied that she was one of those women who suffered from PMT, might even be doing so at this moment; he *really* didn't want to go there.

Lunch awaited them in Gordon's surprisingly restrained dining room, fire burning in the grate (*'I like to be warm when I'm eating, old son'*), dark green wallpaper with nothing more extravagant on the walls than what looked like genuine antique prints of birds (though Jefferson seriously doubted whether Gordon knew a kingfisher from a kestrel), a fine mahogany table and a couple of beautiful sideboards. He wondered whether his mother had chosen them, and the *toile de Jouy* drapes over the French windows leading out into the garden.

'I've gotta mate with a restaurant in town, got him to send some stuff over and Trudi, my housekeeper, she's Austrian, organized the rest,' Gordon explained to his guests as they appreciatively ate home-made mushroom soup laced with sherry and mustard, followed by cold poached salmon with an avocado and lemon sauce, freshly baked bread, a Brie and a Bresse Bleu cheese, a platter of fruit, and a dish of kumquats soaked in a Cointreau-flavoured syrup. They did not talk of the reason why they had come, instead touching lightly on Russian orthodoxy (Magnus), makes of cars (Gordon), England's chances on the rugby tour of South Africa (Jefferson), and the current economic climate (all three of them, heatedly and with varying indication of stress).

'Very nice indeed,' Jefferson said, as finally they were drinking coffee in Gordon's study. 'What's the name of your friend's restaurant? I'll have to go there next time I'm in the area.'

'It's called Mango, down that side street by the Town Hall. I'll get him to give you dinner on the house,' Gordon said.

'That's not necessary,' said Jefferson. 'I can perfectly well pay my own way.'

'I'm sure you can, old son. But a freebie never hurts, does it?'

'I suppose not.' Though Jefferson had a powerful feeling that a freebie from Gordon might hurt quite a bit if he wasn't careful. If there was one thing he'd like to avoid, it was being beholden to Gordon, and he was already regretting the fact that he hadn't been more insistent on paying for his hotel in Quito, though on the other hand, since the management had been careless enough to let a sneak-thief or cat-burglar get into his room, he figured they owed him one. Looking back, he was quite certain they'd known all about the break-in, just from the way they glanced at him and then away, watching him in the mirrors of the foyer, just as he'd watched them.

'Right, shall we get down to business?' Gordon opened a box and brought out a cigar which, after a lot of fussing about with a multi-pronged silver (or possibly chrome) utensil and much unnecessary chat about the thighs of Cuban virgins, he lit.

'Well . . .' Jefferson looked at Magnus, who nodded encouragingly. 'I don't want you to be upset, but it looks very much as though my mother, Rhoda, was . . .' He paused, feeling a sudden lump in his throat. 'Was murdered.'

Gordon pulled himself upright. 'Murdered? Your mum? You're having me on.'

'Not her specifically, I don't mean, but she and the people in the car with her.'

'But why?' Gordon waved away the blue smoke which had gathered in a nimbus around his head, his expression, when it finally emerged, pretty much duplicating the look on the face of the blue-eyed duck-billed platypus. 'Who'd have it in for your ma, what did *she* ever do to anyone?'

'She was with *my* father – and his wife and child,' Magnus explained. 'Plus my other sister, the only one to survive the crash, and she doesn't remember anything at all about the accident, but it's beginning to look pretty obvious that their car was deliberately caused to swerve off the road.'

'That's terrible.' Gordon held his cigar away from him. 'Really awful. I'm so very sorry, not just for you, but for me, too.' He stared down at the floor. 'She was a good old girl, your mother, broke the mould when they made her, you wouldn't believe how much I still miss her.'

Not that much, Jefferson thought, recalling the hard-looking white-stiletto-wearing blonde who'd arrived as he was leaving last time he was here – or was that Trudi the Austrian housekeeper? 'I'm sorry, Gordon,' he said sympathetically.

'It was a long time ago,' Magnus added. 'I doubt if anyone will ever be brought to justice for it – even if we're correct in thinking it was deliberate.'

'Did you ever find the report you had from the police out there?' Jefferson asked.

'Matter of fact, I spent quite a bit of time looking for it, after you rang.' Gordon shrugged, spewing more cigar smoke. 'But no go, I'm afraid – I must have thrown it out. What about your dad's papers, is there anything among them?'

'I haven't finished going through them completely, but at first glance there's nothing resembling an official report. I've still got a few pages to wade through, though.'

'At the time it happened, there was some talk of gunshots,' said Magnus, 'but the only witness, a young boy, subsequently disappeared.'

'Someone probably paid off his parents,' said Gordon. 'Or the police. Or both.'

'The thing is,' Jefferson said, 'gunshots or not, why would anyone want to cause such an accident in the first place?'

'Exactly.' Gordon looked baffled. 'I mean, they were nothing more than a bunch of boffins, weren't they, zoologists, marine biologists, whatever they were, 'scuse me, both of you, no insult intended, but why would anyone want to eliminate people like that, scientists, more interested in seaweed and turtle eggs than anything else?'

'It could have been anything; the only thing we can think of is that my father was embroiled in some kind of dispute with someone who was despoiling the natural habitat of the Islands by illegally harvesting sea-cucumbers.'

'Sea-cucumbers, you having me on?'

'Not at all.'

'It seems a bit drastic,' said Gordon. 'I mean, who's going to cause the deaths of four people over a few sea-slugs . . . even if they do make Viagra look a bit pointless?'

'The aphrodisiac aspect isn't really proven,' said Magnus.

'Back then, it was a pretty lucrative trade,' Jefferson pointed out. 'Still is, to a certain extent.' He raised his eyebrows. 'Magnus's father was obviously spoiling their profitable little game – what you referred to the other day as a "loose cannon" – and they just wanted to get rid of him.'

'So basically you're saying that my wife died a hideous death, just because she was in the wrong place, with the wrong people, at the wrong time.'

'I suppose we are,' Magnus said.

'This police report you saw, Gordon, I don't suppose it had any of this information in it, did it?'

'You're not wrong there, Jeff. If I'd known anything of what you're telling me now, I certainly wouldn't have let the matter rest, no way.' Gordon frowned. 'Bugger it. If I'd only realized how important it could have been, I'd have taken a lot better care of that report than I did. Not that it said anything, not at first sight, anyway, and like I said, my solicitor fully agreed.'

'It wouldn't have mattered anyway,' said Magnus. 'It sounds as if it didn't begin to get anywhere near the truth, almost as if they didn't care about the truth, just wanted to get the ends tied up, sweep the awkwardness of it all under the carpet.' He was aware of metaphors being mixed, but ignored them. 'The only way we'll ever know now is if my sister remembers what happened, and she's not likely to do that, not after all this time.'

'Probably better if she doesn't,' Gordon said, which Jefferson found remarkably astute of him, even compassionate. In fact, he thought, driving Magnus back, over the past few weeks he had found himself revising his opinion about Gordon: he might confuse Ecuador and Peru, but he had been a good husband to Jefferson's mother, and what more could anyone ask?

Later, he sat in the huge area which constituted his living space, contemplating a glass of La Mouline Rhone, a treat he rarely allowed himself but which he tasted tonight because not only had he already had alcohol at Gordon's house (though it had been somewhat inferior to the wine which he held in his hand) and a glass or two more wouldn't hurt, but also because he felt he needed to. He had done all the embarrassing kind of wine-taster's stuff like sniffing, rolling, shooting out his lips like a carp and pulling air back in over it, tasting with mouth open, swallowing with mouth closed (it was almost impossible to do otherwise), the kind of behaviour in which he would never have indulged in public, and now he gave way to thoughts of his mother, a woman who remained dimly in the distance, disliked rather than liked, and definitely not loved, who had swum into his consciousness more clearly this afternoon than she had in the whole of the near-decade since her death. It was Gordon's curtains, he decided, which she must have chosen. She'd had a surprising weakness for *toile de Jouy*, those crinolined ladies and flute-playing shepherds in vaguely Chinese settings which seemed entirely at odds with the combative, almost masculine persona she presented both to her family and to the world. Looking back, tears pricked his eyes. Rhoda Bailey – Mum – fiercely resisting convention, sternly refusing to take the name of either of her husbands on the grounds that to do so would diminish her (*'Why shouldn't* they *take* my *name?'*), had always been out there fighting for the things she believed in, be they whales, gay marriage, establishment prejudices, or even sea-cucumbers. She should have lived in another epoch when there were real struggles to be fought, standing shoulder to shoulder with Annie Besant (*'no more hungry children'*), working with Marie Stopes (*'no more unwanted children'*), throwing bricks alongside the Pankhursts, chaining herself to railings. And like a damascene flash, he wondered whether the attraction of Gordon was the fact that he had plenty of money to fund her Causes; it would explain an awful lot.

But there was another reason he sat contemplating the wine and his mother, and that was the reactivated itch which he recognized as having lain unscratched for far too long, one which he had long ago categorized as 'the thrill of the chase' – in other words, a sense that if he could only put together details recently seen (or heard), he would have the answer to at least one of the puzzles which currently confounded him, though for the moment he could not quite focus on what any of them were. Something half-heard, half-glimpsed, half-*observed* – what the hell was it? He knew from experience that it would eventually come to him, if he would only stop picking at it.

In the neighbouring flat, Jean-Claude Bisset, a banker from Bordeaux, began his nightly ritual of loudly playing music composed by his fellow-countrymen, mostly St Saëns, Debussy, Satie, Messaien. Jefferson poured a careful half-glass more of wine – he preferred to sip it slowly, charting the way the wine evolved over an evening, perhaps not in such spectacular fashion as a Bordeaux but nonetheless in a manner which proved greatly pleasing – and dropped briefly into a daydream of the cellar he would one day own, temperature controlled, professionally racked, its slate-shelved magnificence filled with wondrous and mostly unobtainable Haut-Brions, Chateau d'Yquems, Chateau Pétrus, Lafite Rothschilds, Margaux, and lesser wines, St Emilions, La Rhônes . . . Stop! He could do this for hours.

Most of the rest of the La Mouline failed to dislodge the fly in his ointment (how exactly flies get into ointment in the first place was a question he had often pondered, suffering, as he had in his youth, from flexural eczema which involved large tubs of tar-smelling unguent of the appearance and consistency of fresh hummus, standing open while Matron at school applied the stuff to the insides of his elbows and the backs of his knees, but for which flies never once made a beeline, or even a fly-line) and eventually it occurred to him that he ought to take advantage of the evening to complete the task of trawling through his father's papers, anything rather than go on listening to Satie filtered through a double thickness of brick wall. But with rather more drink taken than he had intended, by the time he had risen to his feet and walked somewhat unsteadily towards the bathroom for a pee, sleep seemed a softer and far more pleasant option.

The Headmaster's secretary moved clumsily through his slumbers, a dumpy woman in slightly musty skirts made of brown or bottle-green serge (another small puzzle: why would the French name their sons after a type of cloth, it would be like christening a child Corduroy or Seersucker) and blouses of some man-made material which clung unappealingly to her upper body, revealing far more of her underwear and what it contained than Jefferson had ever wished to know, a woman, moreover, to whom the world seemed little more than a vehicle for furthering the welfare of her unprepossessing son.

What was Melvin Buonfiglio up to now? Behind bars, probably, Jefferson thought hazily, rising out of wine-tinged sleep as a car-alarm klaxoned in the street below and continued to do so until slumber was no longer possible. He'd read somewhere that after twenty minutes any alarm will stop, but by that time, the thieves, if that's what they were, would be long gone, though it was quite possible that thieves had nothing to do with the infuriatingly continuous noise outside. He'd once had an alarm system installed which literally, according to the salesman, would go off if a spider tiptoed past, which indeed it did, so often that Jefferson had come to the conclusion that his new home was infested by a contagion (or possibly an entire subspecies) of tiptoeing spiders and he had, in the end, been forced to change to a different system altogether.

Why had Buonfiglio's mother been in his thoughts, even subconsciously, he wondered, and reached for the bedside light with a view to starting the book he'd bought that very day at the bookshop next to TaylorMade Travel (chosen in the hope that he might see Kate as he passed, in fact the only reason why he had suddenly decided to buy the book at all), highly recommended as it had been during his flight home from Quito by an American student studying English literature at Brandeis, and perhaps it was the image of Kate, flitting like a melancholy Victorian heroine through his mind which brought back his trip to Ecuador, the hotel room from which his file had been stolen (for what purpose?), the man in the restaurant whom he knew he'd seen somewhere before.

Abruptly it came to him. The man he'd seen in Quito (probably devouring not just one but *several* guinea pigs) was Melvin Buonfiglio, of course he was. Older, fatter, and undoubtedly nastier (and, incidentally, as close to being the human embodiment of a sea-cucumber as any man could be), and though disguised (disfigured?) by the black beard, instantly recognizable, once you realized who you were recognizing. What the hell was someone like him doing in Quito – though he had, Jefferson was fair-minded enough to concede, as much right to travel to all known parts of the earth and beyond as Jefferson himself – but somehow it now seemed like a coincidence too far, that's all he was saying. But flipping the pages of the Brandeis-recommended novel (*'ohmigaaaahd, it's like, totally awesome!'*), the back half of his brain still churned and he knew it had little, if anything, to do with the resurrected memory of Melvin Buonfiglio.

Eventually, noting that it was still barely half past ten, he placed the totally awesome novel neatly beside his bed, got up and walked more or less straight towards the small office where he kept his business papers, with a view to finally completing the task Romilly had set him some weeks before.

The car alarm suddenly stopped, its echo ringing round the wharf area like ripples in a pond, and he heard unmistakably the sound of someone whispering near at hand, followed by the irritating little squeak one of his desk-drawers gave when pulled out; he'd been meaning to dab some oil on it but only remembered when he was on the train to London or standing in the checkout queue at Sainsbury's, his forgetfulness now proving a blessing, as he grabbed the heavy wrought-iron candlestick which he and Mary-Jane had bought years ago in Habitat, and tiptoed (like a spider) across the living room towards his office. He could see shadows against the light from the street, two men bending over his desk and he knew at once that they must be after his father's papers.

'*Pak choy!*' he yelled at the top of his voice, praying that they weren't armed, at least not with guns – or knives, come to think of it. '*Choo chee plah ga-pong!*' – ingredients he remembered from a Thai cooking course he'd taken once, which sounded far more menacing, he thought, than plain English (unless you were a Thai gourmet). He stood back from his office door, giving them a chance to make a break for the entrance to the flat. '*Pad Thai!*' he roared, smashing his candlestick hard against the floor, as the two of them looked up, startled (*'Bloody 'ell!'*) and then made a rush for the door of the office, temporarily log-jamming as they both tried to get through at the same time, leaving behind them a thick scattering of papers which fell to the carpet like pollen. One of them did indeed produce a gun and once through the door of the flat, leaned back inside and let off three shots, all of them well wide of Jefferson, while his companion, still racing towards the exit, took the opportunity to fly at Jefferson and strike him hard across the face, knocking him to the ground, and kicking him painfully in the ribs several times, but not before Jefferson had managed an almighty sweep with his wrought-iron weapon, which caught the man painfully across the forearm and resulted in a loud crack. 'Buggering scumbag,' the man swore, clutching at his elbow, 'he's broke my fucking arm, Jase,

I'm outta here,' then the two of them were racing down the stairs to the ground floor one storey below.

Jefferson writhed a bit, blood pouring from his nose. His ribs hurt, one at least must be broken, he thought, and he could see shards scattered like flowers across the parquet, the remains of a brilliantly coloured Italian ceramic dish which had been a gift from Romilly and the children and upon which the gunman had scored a direct hit. 'Fuck it!' he said, and decided he had been quite correct in calling upon his limited store of Thai, the English expletive sounding feeble and undangerous in comparison with a *choo-chee plah ga-gong!* ('snapper in thick red curry sauce') uttered in a sufficiently explosive manner.

He pulled himself upright, and limped towards the kitchen, where he took a packet of frozen peas from the freezer and applied them to his nose. Not broken, thank God – he moved it carefully from side to side but felt no grating of bone or cartilage – though some of his teeth seemed to stir loosely in their sockets. In a minute, he would begin to sweat and shake at the realization that he had actually been standing directly, or almost, in the line of fire from a *gun* armed with live *ammunition*. Holy fucking cow! he would think.

Moving painfully into his study, he surveyed the mess there, breathing stertorously through his mouth, kicking now and then at the pieces of old paper which littered the floor, some of which rose languorously into the air and fell back, the rest of which just lay there, clotted with rusty paper-clips, or half stuck together with something sticky (Dad liked to eat jam tarts when he was working, perhaps to make up for the otherwise sour atmosphere generated by Jefferson's mother). It gave him a different kind of pain from the one currently attached to his nose to see, here and there, fragments of his parents' writing, annotations, handwritten letters, memos, envelopes.

Bending painfully (thanks to a broken or certainly cracked rib), he plucked a sheet of paper from among these, glanced over it and immediately a great many things suddenly became clear. In the past few weeks, his powers of observation had not served him as well as he might have expected, but were now able to be brought fully into play. He looked at his watch, it was 22:49, an hour too late to telephone people except in an emergency, which this, he decided, most definitely was, though it came to him that if he did, he might not be understood. '*Mamma mia*,' he tried experimentally, '*here I go again*,' and heard the plaintive echo of his voice, filtered through a bloody pack of by-now half-frozen peas. *Babba bia, here I go aggedd* . . . so not the phone, then.

All Together Now . . .

Twenty-Four

'Magnus, that was delicious.'

'Yes, indeed,' agreed Janine. 'Thank you very much.'

Kate closed her eyes. 'I've drunk far too much, so if I fall asleep and start snoring, you'll have to be tolerant.'

'Aren't I always?'

'I envy you two.' Janine flipped back her black hair, smoothed her leather trousers. 'I've got a brother too, but I haven't seen him for years, and don't want to, either. Funny thing is, my mother dotes on him; even when he was sent to prison, she never stopped saying how wonderful he was.'

'Prison? Wow,' Kate said, and closed her eyes again.

'Doting is what mothers are for,' Magnus said, though how he knew with such certainty was difficult to say since he hardly ever thought of his mother, dead so many years ago; he just *knew*, that was all, in an entirely non-academic, purely instinctive way, that whatever depraved or crooked thing he did, his mother would still have doted on him, not that he was given to depravity or crookedness, but he could have 'gone to the bad' in his teens – smoked, shoplifted, done drugs – and she would still have been there for him. She'd been half-Finnish and he saw her now as one of the icons of the Madonna which hung on his walls, pale-faced, sombre-eyed, all-loving, ready to forgive if ever forgiveness was needed.

'Siblings have to stick together,' declared Kate, 'especially when there's no-one else.'

'If you'd ever met my brother, I doubt if you'd want to stick to him,' Janine said.

'If he's anything like you, I'd be quite happy—' Magnus began gallantly, then stopped, pushed his half-moon glasses back up his nose, and nodded vigorously. 'That's right, Kate. Stick together we must, we're all the family we've got now.'

'Once, though, there were more of us,' Kate said, words slurring gently, addressing Janine, who seemed to waver a little between the tall candles Magnus had set on the table, though whether the wavering came from Janine or from herself, Kate was not entirely sure, for all at once, as though someone had flicked a switch and turned her memory on, she was on holiday again in Quito, at the end of her second year at university. She saw the streets outside Dad's apartment, the spiky black shadows thrown by the palmettos, brightly shawled peasants in black felt hats mingling with businessmen in razor-sharp suits and secretaries in high, high heels and pretty blouses, all sparkling in the sunshine. Brown skin, dark eyes, and that indefinable, exciting menace hidden behind the smiling faces, and she saw, too, the winding road up into the mountains, the parrots among the creepers, Annie's hot little hand on her knee (*'It's ever so 'citing, Katie, isn't it?'*), the faint scent of Luisa's perfume from the seat beside her, Ms Bailey in front, and Dad driving so slowly through the heat, along the pitted road, trying to avoid the potholes, the group of men suddenly materializing from the shadows, one of them stepping forward and raising an arm, raising a *gun*, oh my *God!*, aiming it through the windscreen, Luisa screaming as glass shattered, the man aiming again, a boy peering huge-eyed round the corner of a whitewashed house, and in the front seat, Ms Bailey clutching at her chest, keeling over against Dad (*'I knew it, I knew i—'*), a third shot, Dad's tiny indrawn *'pffft'*, and a fourth and then the car swerving over the edge of the road, and the stink of burning rubber, the sound of exploding glass, blistering metal, fire, flames rushing into the sky, her leg, the smell of roasting meat . . .

'Oh, God!' Kate suddenly stood up, pressing her palms hard against her heart. 'Oh, my *lord.*' She walked distractedly over to the window, breathing hard, her fingers clamped tight against her temples, as though she had been struck on the head. 'What the hell happened, did somebody hit me on the head or something, it's all come back . . .'

Janine and Magnus had risen to their feet.

'What's on earth's wrong, Kate?'

'What the matter?'

She walked unsteadily to the table, held on to the chair-backs for support. 'After all these years . . . I knew I'd seen him before, I *knew* it, only I thought it was George Clooney, you see, oh God, oh *God*, it's like seeing a ghost, it was the same guy, out there in the village.' Her legs wobbled and she clutched tighter at the back of Janine's chair. 'He was younger then but I know it's the same guy, and I thought his face was *kind*, I can't believe it, I just . . . it wasn't Dad at *all*, oh shit, I'm going to throw *up* . . .'

Janine pushed her down into a chair. 'Sit with your head between your knees,' she ordered. 'Magnus, get a bowl or a bucket, quick.'

Magnus rushed to the kitchen and came back with a yellow plastic pail, and a glass of cognac.

'Be sick into this, or drink that,' he said.

Kate tried to grin. 'Hope I get it the right way round.' Her head felt like a pillow, stuffed with green feathers, blood, Annie's leg, the thick thud of something hitting Ms Bailey's T-shirted chest, Dad's head spilling over the back of his seat, Luisa's screams suddenly cut short, no time to say goodbye, oh God, and she bent horribly over the pail, clutching at Janine's hand, Janine who had somehow got hold of a wet tea towel which she was pressing against Kate's forehead, murmuring softly, reassuringly. She'd make someone a good wife, Kate managed to think; she'd make *Magnus* a good wife . . .

Eventually she sat up and sipped slowly at the brandy. 'Sorry about that,' she said, though Magnus wasn't really listening as he watched Janine efficiently remove the bucket. 'Magnus . . .'

'What?' He dragged himself back to his sister.

'I'm sorry about all your lovely food.'

'As long as you're OK.'

'Yes.'

'I presume you're going to explain what that was all about.'

'Yes – maybe I'd better have the bucket again. It's all so utterly, terribly *awful*.' She pressed her palms against her stomach, shuddering as she tried to marshal her thoughts.

Finally, as they sat over coffee, Magnus said, 'OK . . . we're listening.'

Kate nodded, swallowed. Her throat was sore, her eyes felt like craters, her mouth seemed raw, as though the words she was about to utter were made of broken glass. She stared bleakly at her brother. 'I don't know what brought it all back – you talking about family, I think, or the police talking about Stefan Michaels' father being a criminal, but I suddenly remembered where I'd . . . It was him, you see, the man who killed Dad, not just Dad but all of them, Annie and . . . He was the one who caused the accident, not Dad's driving; he *shot* them, he fired directly at Ms Bailey, he's Stefan's *father*, if you can believe it.'

'Who is?'

'The man who killed them all in the accident, all except me, he's Stefan's father, he was younger then, of course, he's hardly changed at all, just a bit greyer . . .'

'I'm getting lost,' Janine said. 'Are you still talking about the George Clooney man?'

Kate gulped in a deep breath, pressed her palms together. 'Sorry . . .' Tears began to roll down her face and she shivered. 'He came into the wine bar, into Plan A, one night, with his two sons, and I was sure I'd seen him before somewhere, but because he's handsome, and the same colouring, I just thought it must be because he reminded me of George Clooney.'

Magnus cleared his throat. 'Uh . . . do I know this Clooney?'

'For God's *sake*, Magnus!' Kate said forcefully. 'Get a *life*!'

'He's a film star, famous,' Janine said, smiling at him. '*Ocean's Eleven*.' Words which left Magnus almost as mystified as Jefferson Andrewes' remark about taupe sofas (*taupe sofas* – could he have misheard?). Sometimes he worried about early onset Alzheimer's, he seemed to live in a different world from most people, and he thought how much clearer things had been in pre-revolutionary Russia, how much more certain the uncertainties were then; no global warming to worry about, for instance, or the rights and wrongs of turning off gas-flows in the Ukraine or invasions in the Middle East, nor, indeed, parents driving over a cliff and burning to death.

'Magnus, *everyone* knows George Clooney.'

'Except me.'

'You need to get out more.' Kate thumbed tears from beneath her eyes, and she shivered, let them fall. 'Anyway, what I'm trying to say is that today, two police officers interviewed me while I was having lunch, and if you can believe this, they said this guy, him and his sons, they're career criminals – he came from Ecuador with his family years ago, is heavily involved in half a dozen businesses, all highly illegal, and the only reason he's still out on the streets is because they're hoping he'll lead them to the big boss, the guy behind these so-called companies, who is a *real* badass.' She swallowed hard. 'It's his son – the George Clooney guy's son, I mean – is Stefan Michaels, who . . . who . . . you know.'

Magnus looked puzzled, as well he might. 'Let me get this quite straight. You're saying that as well as Michaels *fils* . . . doing what he did, Michaels *père* also killed Dad and Luisa and Annie, all those years ago?'

'Yes, yes I am. Looking back, putting two and two together, I'm pretty certain. I saw this man, you see, step forward with a gun in his hand, that little boy was right about the shots, and aim right at us. And his name isn't Michaels.'

'Didn't you say he was Stefan Michaels' father?' said Janine.

'Yes, but they all seem to change their names all the time, anglicize them; they all come from Latin America, you see, the names are too difficult, all those Ramirezes and Fernandezes, this guy's called – um – Carlos Pedro de Something de Léon, near as I can remember, too big a mouthful for the British criminal fraternity to handle.'

'And is this Mr Big also from Ecuador?'

'The police seem to think he's actually English. George Clooney and his sons all work for him, as does horrible Mick – whose name isn't actually Mick at all.'

'So it's not just guys with difficult names who change them!' Janine said.

'I gather his *was* pretty difficult, actually! Anyway, the police told me that he, the Clooney character, I mean, was wanted for murder, back in Ecuador. And it was definitely him who fired those shots at the car; I know it was, I can see his face clearly in my mind.'

'You said it was Ms Bailey he fired at,' said Magnus.

'I think so, not Dad, at least not to start with. It's all coming back to me. She said something like "I knew it," and then . . . then . . . God, it was all so dreadful, I almost wish I hadn't remembered.'

'But why would anyone want to kill *her*?' asked Janine.

'I don't know.'

'Did I tell you, by the way,' Magnus continued, suddenly remembering, 'who Ms Bailey is, or was – or would be if she were still alive?'

'Dad's summer assistant,' Kate said impatiently.

'Yes, but she is – was – also the mother of your friend Jefferson Andrewes!'

'My *friend* . . . I hardly know him.'

The two women goggled at him, eyes wide, phrases like 'small world', 'I can't believe this', 'weird', 'how strange is *that*?' drifting behind their eyes, but remaining unvoiced until finally Magnus said, 'Yes, I thought you'd find that interesting.'

'This is all too much of a coincidence,' Kate said slowly. 'It's practically incestuous. I don't think I can believe it.'

'I'm beginning to. I went down with Jefferson Andrewes – nice chap – to meet his stepdad – the man married to Ms Bailey – the other day,' Magnus said. 'Apparently this man – Gordon Campbell – had been sent a report from the local police in Ecuador when his wife was killed in the accident, along with Dad and the others, but now he can't find it and he's afraid he may have thrown it out. But he seemed adamant that it contained no mention of gunfire. So in one way, we're no further on.'

'I *saw* him with a gun,' Kate said. 'And the little boy, hiding behind the wall of a house.'

'So where did *he* go?'

'Apparently he was sent away to the city and no-one seems to have seen him since,' Magnus said.

'But what *you're* saying, Kate, about hearing shots and seeing a man firing at the car, that backs the boy up, doesn't it?' asked Janine.

'It certainly seems to.'

'Which implies that the police were lying,' Magnus said slowly. He spoke to Janine. 'Everything was cleared away so quickly after the accident that there wasn't time for any independent person to check the bodies, even if there was enough left – sorry, ladies – to check.' Kate paled, moved closer to the plastic pail, sat with eyes and jaw clenched shut. 'Andrewes told me that Dad had been involved with some altercation with the local bad guys,' Magnus continued. 'Some juicy little racket involving sea-cucumbers.'

'Sorry to be flippant,' Janine shuddered, 'but please don't put "sea-cucumbers" and "juicy" in the same sentence.'

'*Bêche de mer*, to use another name, supposed to be a gastronomic delicacy,' said Magnus. 'Trouble is, we have so little information. We've always assumed that it was a straight accident, until very recently, when it started to look as if the local malefactors were after Dad all along, because he was trying to prevent them from illegal harvesting of these . . . er . . . creatures. But let's try another hypothesis.' He nodded professorially at them both. 'Suppose it wasn't Dad they were trying to get rid of at all, but someone else.'

'Someone else in the car, you mean?' Janine said.

'Exactly.'

'It could hardly have been Annie, or Ms Bailey, could it?' Kate said. 'Annie was only eight, and Ms Bailey was only there for a few weeks; she can't possibly have had time to annoy anyone enough to want to kill her.'

'But you said she was the one they shot at first.'

'Maybe she was just the nearest.' Kate sipped at the glass of brandy Magnus had poured. 'And *I* wasn't doing anything that could make anyone want to remove me from the scene.'

'Except demonstrating all over the place at university, getting up peoples' noses.'

'Pretty harmless stuff, Magnus. Besides, if so, why single me out?'

'Suppose,' Janine said, 'I mean, I don't know the circumstances, but suppose, just by pure chance, someone who'd seen you in England protesting against something he really believed in, and just happened to be in . . . um . . . Ecuador and saw you there, and decided that . . . um . . .' She looked at them both. 'Sorry, pretty feeble, really.'

'Not at all,' Magnus said, in the encouraging tone he used for the kind of student who could hardly remember his or her own name but who nonetheless had demonstrated a real enthusiasm for the subject under discussion. 'But what about Luisa?'

'What about her?' Kate refilled their glasses.

'Supposing we're right about all this, could *she* possibly have been the intended target? Dad met her when he was working out there and, after all, we never really knew that much about her—'

Kate glared at her brother. 'Except that she was lovely, and loved us, and we loved her.'

'Of course. I meant that maybe she was, or her family was – maybe quite innocently – mixed up in something we knew nothing about, and someone was taking revenge or something. After all, they're a fiery lot in Latin America, aren't they?'

'That sounds hugely xenophobic,' Janine said.

'I don't mean it to be but—'

The doorbell pealed suddenly, and Magnus sighed. 'Oh ha, ha,' he said. 'The local peasantry think it's hilarious to ring the door and run away.'

There was more pealing, accompanied by heavy thumping and the rattling of the letter-box, followed immediately by muffled shouts.

'That's not yobs,' said Kate.

Magnus got unwillingly to his feet. 'All right, I'll go, but don't blame me if we're overrun by the screaming hordes intent on rape and pillage because there won't be an awful lot I can do to—'

'Oh, get *on* with it, Magnus,' Kate said. She picked up a knife from the dining-table and followed her brother to the front door, where a figure could be seen gesticulating behind the stained-glass.

'Who is it?' Magnus shouted.

An indistinct cry made itself audible.

'*Who?*' Magnus said, but Kate marched ahead of him.

'It's Jefferson Andrewes,' she said, pulling the door wide, then standing back as a bloodied figure lurched into the hall.

'Jeez, what on earth happened to you?' Janine cried.

'Kade,' the newcomer said, his features smeared with dried blood, 'whodd are *you* dooigg here?'

'I live here, or used to.'

'*You're* Bagnus's sisder?' Jefferson said, still thickly but at least sounding human. 'You *cahd* be.'

'Why not?' Kate got Jefferson's arm round her shoulder (*'Warm water in a bowl, Janine, please. Magnus, get some of your brandy and some codeine from the first-aid kit.'*) and guided him into the sitting room.

A look of pained irritation crossed Jefferson's battered cheeks as he thought of all the time he could have spent with Kate if he'd only realized. 'Ouch!' He held his side, looking piteously at Kate, who remained relatively unmoved. 'I think I've got a broken rib or two,' he said, more or less intelligibly, 'but I thought you were going grey, you see, and wore an awful cardigan like your brother's, and suffered from period pains and – and . . .'

'Why would you think that?' She patted his face dry with a damp towel. 'What on earth have you been saying about me, Magnus?'

'What's wrong with my cardigan, anyway?' Magnus said, giving Janine the opening she'd been longing for.

'There's a button missing,' she said quickly, 'but I could easily sew it back on for you – there'll be a spare one on the label, most likely, down on the left side.'

Magnus checked, and indeed there was. 'How do you know that?' From his admiring tone, Janine might have just turned in a thesis which proved beyond all possible doubt that Tsar Nicholas II was the love-child of Queen Victoria and Rasputin.

Janine smiled. 'Take it off and hand it over.'

Jefferson sipped cautiously at his brandy, wincing as the spirit stung his bruised lips, but making it easier to enunciate. 'Sorry to come calling so late, but I think I have some information you might like to hear.'

'We think we may have some too,' said Kate. Briefly she reprised what she had just told Magnus and Janine. 'The police are keeping their hands off this Charlie Lyons character – or Carl Someone, as he's also known—'

'What?' Janine stared at her.

'I don't know. They didn't say.'

'You said something about someone called Carl.'

'Yes, one of Stefan Michaels' father's many aliases.'

'Carl? Are you sure?' But Janine knew she was right, the likeness to George Clooney was only one of the many links to her lover, and she'd always suspected him of operating on the wrong side of the law; perhaps in her heart of hearts she had *known* it. But killing people? Oh God, what had she been doing all these years? Would she be hauled into the dock for consorting with criminals and murderers, put away for years? What would Mum say, and *Magnus*, how would he feel about her if he knew?

'Absolutely,' Kate was saying. 'Apparently the police are hoping he'll lead them to the Boss, name so far unknown.'

'Actually,' Janine said, her voice tremulous, staring down at the cardigan in her lap. 'I think I met this boss once.'

'*You* did?' Jefferson asked.

'He was a nasty little creature, gingery sort of moustache, wore cowboy boots and kept trying to feel me up.'

'Cowboy boots? Oh Christ, that just codfurbs it,' Jefferson said, waving a sheet of paper at them.

'It's because of . . . of Carl,' said Janine. A tear fell on to the grey cashmere, followed by another, and then a whole flood of them. 'I simply had no idea he was anything to do with Stefan.'

'Why should you?' Magnus said forcefully, finding her hand and grabbing it tightly, only to pull rapidly away as his palm was painfully stabbed by the needle she was using to attach the button to his cardigan.

'Exactly. Why should you?' Kate echoed. 'I'm not following any of this.'

'Carl,' said Janine.

'What about him?'

'He's . . . um, my . . .' Janine looked piteously at Kate and down again at her lap, while Kate rapidly reviewed what she knew of Janine and concluded that for some bizarre reason, which would need to be clarified at a later date, the mystery lover in London was the same man who had been responsible for the deaths of her family ten years ago on Galápagos, the nice man who was also the father of her own abductor and who had, apparently, shed tears at hearing that his son was dead. 'I see,' she said, 'I think,' nodding wisely while Magnus smoothed the black hair away from a by-now sobbing Janine's forehead.

'Janine isn't responsible for anything,' Jefferson said, a remark which, once his listeners had translated *Jadide isud respossible for eddithig* into normal English, had them nodding in agreement. 'But I know precisely who *is*, the filthy murdering rat-arse.'

'You've lost me,' Kate said. 'I thought we were talking about . . . um . . . this Carlos man.'

'Carlos the Jackal,' said Magnus, pleased with the contemporary take on things he had achieved, his mind then meandering, for some reason, towards the paper he had recently contributed to one of the learned Romanov-specific journals, his thesis effectively demythologizing Grigori Effimovich Rasputin *('More Sinned Against Than Sinning')* offering a rehabilitative interpretation of the red-haired holy man and healer from the Caucasus who had generated so many legends about his abilities and turned an entire empire against him.

'Not quite,' Jefferson said thickly, though alcohol was definitely clearing the congestion in his nasal passages. He gulped down the brandy and held out his glass for more. 'But Mr Big, the Big Boss, is . . .' He shook his head. 'Even now I've had time to think about it, I still can't believe it. Jesus Christ, I've eaten the man's bread and drunk his bloody wine, for heaven's sake. Listen to this, I should have realized yonks ago . . . the sea-cucumbers, he pretended he didn't know anything about them, but he was well aware that they had aphrodisiac qualities, and then he pretended to mix up Ecuador and Peru, in case I realized he knew perfectly well, and it was probably him who got the hotel staff to steal my papers, lucky I'd got copies . . . and then all those sodding crocodile tears for my mother, how he missed her so, when it was perfectly obvious that he almost certainly arranged to have her killed out in the Galápagos, and the hell with anyone else in the car.'

'What's he on about?' Janine said.

'Look!' Jefferson spread out the page he had been holding, while Magnus pondered the exact meaning of bread and wine in the context of Jesus Christ (the Last Supper?) and whether Jefferson was in fact a renegade priest or something similar – stranger things had happened, though the man had evinced no particularly religious leanings on their way to visit his stepfather, nor indeed on the way back. 'I found this among my father's papers, stuck to the back of a report on global warming.'

'Would you like me to read it for you?' asked Kate, noticing that he was finding it painful to take the copious breaths which his heightened emotions were causing him to draw. He said that he would, please, his eyes reddening as he handed over the page. It was all very emotional, especially after all these years, his poor mother, never did anyone any real harm, and as for that little cowboy-booted ponce . . .

'"Truman,"' Kate began. (*'That's buy father.'*) '"Truman: I have no right to ask anything of you, but I can't see where else to turn. I won't trouble you with the details, but I've discovered that G is—"' (*'Gordon, that is.'*) '"—is, not to put too fine a point on it, a big-time crook, maybe even worse. You know me, I've never been one to hang back when it comes to exposing matters I perceive as wrongs, but I'm actually frightened for my own safety, now that he knows I know. Of course I ought to go straight to the police, but he is my husband, for better or worse, and I find it hard to do this, which is why I'm turning to you for advice. I'm leaving tomorrow for the Galapágos Islands – I managed to get a grant to work with a Professor Lennox there – and shall be away for six weeks. I should be safe out there, at least, but can we talk when I get back? I should really value your input. Rhoda. PS I've been SUCH a fool."'

There was silence when she had finished. Then Jefferson said, almost weeping, 'The bastard, the double-crossing, murderous bastard; it was him who killed her all along.'

'Is this the . . . uh . . . "Big Boss" we've been talking about?' enquired Magnus, feeling that if he could only hang on long enough everything would be made clear, while Kate remembered Ms Bailey saying 'I *knew* it . . .' as the gunman stepped forward. She had wondered not long ago whether all the pieces would come together if she only concentrated hard enough. They were doing so now with an almost careless abandon, everything connecting with everything and everybody else. Did the fact that Jefferson's stepfather had apparently been responsible for wiping out most of her family alter in any way how she felt about Jefferson himself at this moment or might feel about him in the future, were she to feel anything at all, a possibility about which she was fairly certain she currently had no opinion? As for Stefan's father – Carl or Carlos – who was also the London Lover, how would that affect her relationship with Janine? It wasn't as if either Janine or Jefferson was in anyway culpable themselves, yet somehow it all seemed a bit too pat, as though someone had deliberately withheld the final pieces of the jigsaw (Jefferson's stepfather, Janine's boyfriend) until the very end and then flourished it triumphantly (*'ta da!'*) before irritatingly pressing it into place, something no jigsaw-puzzle-solver could easily tolerate.

Flourishing the Armagnac bottle, Magnus said, 'I think we all need a drink.'

Melvin
Twenty-Five

'And a cognac to finish with, Philippe.'

'That'll be on the house, sir.'

'That's very good of you.'

'It's a pleasure to have you back, sir.'

'It's a pleasure to *be* back, I can assure you.'

He meant it. He had been away for far too long.

'That's good, sir. Would you perhaps like your cognac in the lounge? There's a nice fire in there.'

'Excellent idea, Philippe. I'll do that.'

In the lounge, Melvin sat back, looked around at the heavy furnishings, the red marble fireplace, the elaborate ceiling rose (plastic, almost certainly), and felt at peace with the world. There were newspapers on a side table, plus the upmarket magazines and for a moment he contemplated getting up and bringing a couple back to the sofa he was occupying. As he'd passed he had noticed the big headline in the local paper, *Widow Butchered in Own Kitchen*, which titillated him; he always enjoyed reading about really horrific murder cases, particularly if they took place somewhere he actually knew. He loved those misery memoirs about some kid forced to drink bleach and having his hand held on to a red-hot oven plate, or being raped by her father before being hired out to service all his friends, and, equally, it always looked good to be seen reading *The Economist*, you never know which of the guys in the lounge might not end up being people he'd do business with, but in the end he felt too lazy to get up; he really had to do something about his weight, even the woman he loved had said something about it last time they'd met, wiggling her bum at him, white stilettos showing off her legs as she crossed them and leaned forward, her brow wrinkled in that cute way she had. (*'Oh Melvin,* mein liebchen, *you really are getting chunky, aren't you, not that it matters to me, I like it, I'm just concerned about your heart, carrying that extra weight.'*)

This was one of his favourite things to do: have dinner in a top-notch place, all by himself, wearing good clothes, knowing that people looked at him and thought, *I bet he's someone*. Well, of course he was someone, but *someone* someone, not necessarily a celebrity someone, but certainly a man who was doing well, came from a good background, had the world at his feet, someone people looked up to and admired.

He had Mum to thank for that, of course, as for most things. No state comprehensives for her boy. The fees at Haddon Hall weren't cheap, second-rate little public school though it was, but she'd managed to find the money somehow, bullied Dad, most likely, plus working like fuck at the job there, and like she always said, it got him mixing with the right kind of people, adopting the accent, not that he ever used it at home, except to Mum, to make her laugh – he could just imagine what the rest of the family would have said if they'd heard him speaking posh, trying to pass himself off as one of the boys at school, even though they went home at the end of the day to some choice farm in the country, or at the very least a large detached house in the best suburbs, while he made his way back to their cramped little semi on the far side of town, he'd love to see the look on their faces if they could see him now, that po-faced Jeff Andrewes, for instance.

He couldn't wait to take Mum to the house he'd just bought, show her that her sacrifices had been worth it, introduce her to the woman he intended to marry. He hoped she and Mum would hit it off. If not, then he'd have to ditch her. After all she'd done for him, Mum had to come first. Stubborn old cow, he thought, with wry appreciation. He'd bought her the house, paid enough money into her bank account so she'd never have to work again, but she insisted on going out every day to that crap job of hers at the baker's shop, you had to admire her, taking the bus, said she couldn't be doing with a car, said she'd go bonkers if she didn't have something to keep her occupied, she wasn't the sort to be tidying up the herbaceous borders or taking up golf, that was for sure. There'd be grandchildren before too long, though, with any luck, and that might change her attitude a bit, and he was planning to convert the stable block, move her in, whatever she said now he knew she'd love it; when he was inside, the first time he got sent down, for stealing cars, some seasoned old lag had told him the first rule of success was never to trust anyone, not even your sweet old white-haired mother, but he knew that his mum would die before she betrayed him.

He sipped his cognac appreciatively. The waiter who'd brought it to him was now leaning one elbow on the counter, chatting to the bartender about the murder, bloody shocking if you ask me, poor old girl, more or less cut her to bits, wonder who they was after, police seemed to think nothing was taken, one of them big forty-two-inch-screen TVs still there, plus her handbag, jewellery, disgusting, really, what people get up to these days, bits of the poor old biddy all over the kitchen, her own kitchen, think you'd be safe there, wouldn't you, nowhere's safe these days, mate, bring back the death penalty, I say.

He knew he'd been stupid, fucking stupid, helping to snatch a girl like that off the streets, taking that little fucker's word for it that she was just some bint who'd dissed him and needed to be taught a lesson. And then the stupid arsehole only has to let her escape, doesn't he, and then the shit really hits the fan. He himself had managed to get away, though it meant spending six bloody weeks cooling his heels in bloody Ecuador, Boss's orders, waiting for the fuss to die down. Sometimes he'd thought he'd rather have turned himself in, taken his chances in an English nick: at least they didn't have bloody mosquitoes in HM's prisons, nor would he have found himself using an insect repellent which brought him out in hives, and swelled up his lips until he looked like he'd been kissing bloody wasps, let alone his eyes came across like he'd gone ten rounds with that big American boxer, Michael Something, having to grow a beard, for Chrissakes. And on top of that there was Montezuma's Revenge, malaria, dysentery, hepatitis A, you name it, he got it. He'd been lucky to miss out on cholera, dengue fever and housemaid's knee. He'd visited the country many times before, on business for the Boss, but never long enough to see what a hell-hole the place really was, or he'd certainly have thought twice about decamping to South America, Latin America, whatever, even under orders.

He'd known all along it was a mistake, snatching her, someone classy like that. He'd have done better to trust his instincts, just dump her somewhere and head off as fast as he could in the opposite direction, ditch the van as soon as possible and keep a low profile for as long as it took. But what could he do? He was supposed to be keeping an eye out, give the little wanker what he wanted, within limits, yada yada yada, at least until the business with the guy's father was completed. And to be honest, it had been fun, what a turn-on, off at work, knowing she was back in the house, waiting, terrified, his to use whenever he wanted, and not a fucking thing she could do about it, for all her stuck-up ways, not, of course, that he ever got to make use of her being there, and it was pretty clear that Stefan Wanker hadn't, for all his talk; he was more into porno mags and Internet sites, dirty little bugger. Melvin had been round to his flat once, message from his dad – 'I'm no messenger boy,' Melvin had said, but the Boss had made it clear that if he knew what was good for him . . . So round he'd gone, nice enough place but dirty? My *God*, crusty little screwed-up bits of Kleenex full of cum all over the place, TV blaring away at ten o'clock in the morning, Melvin never put the telly on until six p.m., unless it was sport – football, maybe, or the golf; he was planning to join the local golf club soon as he was settled, got his name down already.

He could feel himself harden, just at the memory of the girl. Maybe one of these days, he'd try it again, pick some bitch up and really enjoy himself. He'd read a book once about this guy who kidnapped girls, one at a time – *The Collector*, it was called, by John Somebody – and kept them in his cellar until they died, at which point he went out and got another one. And he knew just the right place for a bit of fun and games – though the girl might not think it was as much fun as he would! Sound-proofing round the doors and windows, proper bondage gear this time, cuffs and chains, leather masks, whips, there were shops for all that kind of stuff, not to mention the Internet. Yeah, one of these days he'd definitely get that sorted. He thought briefly about the woman he intended to marry: would she go in for that sort of thing? Probably not, and anyway, could he do it to her, hurt her? Could he bear to catch contempt, even hatred, in her eyes instead of love? Nah . . . he'd keep her right out of anything sordid. It was brilliant enough that she seemed to love him, too. God only knew why, but that German – *Austrian* – accent, that gold chain round her ankle, sexy, he really liked that.

He swallowed more cognac. Apart from the exile in fucking Ecuador, it had been a pretty good life. So far. Touch wood. He resolutely thrust aside the faces of his sister, younger boys at school, Mum that one time – what kind of man mugged his own mother, especially when it all came to nothing, that bloody Andrewes making him pay it all back? If you can't stand the heat, he told himself, survival of the fittest and all that, *caveat emporator* or whatever it was, never had much time for Latin; he'd only managed one year of it and then he was out of there, doing something useful like double maths, and he remembered his sister's dog with a touch of shame, shouldn't have done that, bloody animal, crapping on Mum's new carpet, definitely out of order there, him *and* the dog, at least nobody knew it was him who'd cut the thing in half – what did she call it? Cary, after Cary Grant, didn't look anything *like* Cary Grant. And now there was the money, stashed away, all cash, thank you very much, no bank accounts for him – bank records could be hacked into, bank accounts tracked down – nice packets of untraceable tenners, that's what he liked, money carefully creamed off the top of the profits, never too much, never enough to make them suspicious, the bloody Latinos hadn't a fucking clue, and they'd never find the place he'd stowed it, all packed away in his good-quality briefcase, couldn't be safer, and once he'd pushed it through the system, they'd never even realize it had gone. Besides, thanks to Silvio and his magic fingers, he had any number of identities to fall back on, all the documentation fair and square, social security, birth certificate, credit cards so good even the issuing companies could hardly tell them from the real thing, plus a couple Silvio knew nothing about, had them done in Quito, which was how he'd managed to get back to dear old Blighty without being collared, the only good thing to come out of his 'exile', every cloud has a silver lining. Not that there was too much of a lining, since the Boss had made it clear he was only to come back for the one job, fly into Paris, get the ferry from Boulogne, train up here, top bloody Stefan, and heigh-ho for Edinburgh and back to Ecuador for however much longer was necessary.

Briefly, he felt a frisson of unease as he thought of American thrillers he'd read, gangster movies watched with half an eye on long-haul flights to Quito and back, remembered grim tales of the mob bosses never resting till they'd tracked down those who cheated them, torturing them with knives and branding irons and the like, and for a long moment, he saw himself naked, tied to a chair in some dark warehouse, while they ripped out his balls or snipped his fingers off one by one with a wire-cutter.

Naaah . . . never going to happen. Not to him. He'd been much too careful.

He paid the bill, left a big tip, as usual, strolled outside. Daylight was only just fading behind the rooftops, illuminating the sandstone facade of the Town Hall and the gothic architecture of the Butter Market. He tried to visualize the farmers' wives in the olden days, sitting underneath the curiously arched roof, bonnet strings hanging down, baskets of butter between their knees, and gave thanks that he'd been born into a civilized century. He'd decided to stay at the Grand tonight, rather than out at his hidey-hole. He retrieved an overnight bag from the boot of his lovely new Merc, always wanted one of them, always promised himself he'd have one eventually, and now he had, and walked on down the street for a while. It was too nice an evening to go back to the hotel just yet, so he dropped the bag off with the porter then sauntered on, down towards the river.

Across the water he could see the warehouses, cranes hanging above them like lovers, yellow and red in the spring dusk. All being converted now, some already occupied, classy high-ceilinged flats, criss-crossed with girders, huge windows letting in a panoramic view of the city. He'd looked at one once, but decided it was more like a haven for dust and spiders than a home for respectable human beings. He never could abide spiders, couldn't imagine sitting there of an evening watching the light on the water while they span and wove and caught flies above his head, just imagine them getting careless, dropping the fucking things, one of those wrapped flies, right into your glass of good wine. He shuddered in prospective disgust. Once he'd moved in to his new place, there'd be a regular cleaning service, thanks very much.

He turned left where the river did, the lock dark on his right, and beyond it, the canal. Up the little steps carved out of the bank by people wanting a short-cut, down to where the bigger houses began, stroll along Bathurst Avenue admiring the plantings in the front gardens, down Greenfield Avenue, cross the road towards Maitland Park Road, with the museum at the end of it.

It was as he stood waiting for a gap in the traffic so he could cross the road that he thought he saw something out of the corner of his eye. He was too canny to turn round, let them see he'd noticed – if indeed there was anything *to* notice. He'd look into the window of the big carpet wholesalers opposite, see if there was anything reflected in the glass and if it turned out to be *some*thing, then he'd have a chance to turn the corner and then run like hell. He danced dangerously between the cars, and fetched up on the other side of the road, stood staring in at the window – and there they were, the two of them, the fuckers, looking to right and left, waiting to get across after him.

He dismissed the flicker of fear which heart-burned in his chest, walked nonchalantly to the corner of the street and then took to his heels, running for his life, thinking that's what it might very well be, his fucking life, and no way was *that* going to happen, not now, not after all he'd done to get where he was now. He wasn't worried; he might be big but he kept himself in good shape, down the gym working out most weeks, regular check-ups, strong as an ox, his doctor down in London told him, never had so much as a filling at the dentist.

Panting, he paused at the junction of Maitland Park Road and Chillenden Street. He could hear them now, coming after him, their footsteps echoing on the empty pavement as he turned down Chillenden Street, hurrying between the blank, closed facades of houses whose inhabitants were watching telly or already tucked up in their beds. He was heading in a roundabout way back towards the canal; there was a cop-shop just over the footbridge and round the corner, a couple of blocks down: he'd drop in there, say someone was following him. He could just imagine their cynical reaction. (*'Following you? Following* you, *Micky lad? 'Ere, Sarge, can you believe it, someone's got the bleeding nerve to be following young Michael, or should I call you Melvin, or is it Martyn these days, Martyn-with-a-Y, better call in Scotland Yard on this one.'*) He smiled quizzically to himself – who'd ever have thought that he'd feel safer among the pigs than among his former associates? But he'd seen enough of that lot and the way they could use a knife to extract information: he preferred to keep his Johnson in good working order, thank you very much, plenty of life in the old boy yet, and he liked the way his face looked, especially now he'd lost the beard, didn't want it rearranged by those crazy Latinos; he'd seen one of them take off a nose and a lower lip before the victim even realized the knife was out. There were guys down in London whose only reason to be thankful was that they were still walking round, despite the fact that their faces looked like something that would've turned even Hannibal Lecter's stomach, and he experienced a faint flash of sympathy for the poor old cow who'd been butchered in her own kitchen. You never knew these days, old girl living on her own, one more reason to persuade Mum to come and live at his new place.

He stopped for a second to listen, then ran on: they were still coming for him and he cursed himself for leaving his gun at the boarding house. With that in his hand, he could have easily picked them off, but he was so close to fulfilling his dreams that he hadn't wanted to risk being picked up by the rozzers and be done for illegal possession. In this town, they all knew his face: if they caught him on the streets they'd have him for sure. Bloody hell. Everything was in place, everything fucking sorted; he'd got the dream house, the dream bank account, even the dream woman. And then he'd been stupid enough to believe what the Big Boss told him, fucking little dwarf in his fucking cowboy boots, stuck all over with bits of blue stone and chicken bones (*'No danger at all, me old son, you'll be gone again before they even realize you was here.'*), and even more stupid to drive over to visit Mum, explain that he didn't know when he'd be back, but soon, once again, thanks for everything, Mum, take care. They must have followed him down from Edinburgh, only explanation, he'd been fucking stupid not to check, and of course the little wanker knew all about the Manor, probably caved in on one of his Dad's visits, knowing it was 'admit everything or enjoy your time inside, son, long as you last'. Perhaps the Big Boss thought he'd cave in himself if the cops caught up with him, as if he would. Fuck him, he'd even stuck tape over those stones at the entrance, hidden the name, Stefan must have peeled it back on one of his visits to the girl, and they'd have traced the purchase back to him, started asking themselves where he got the cash, had a closer look at the books . . . Oh bloody hell. Still, he'd been in worse holes, had closer shaves.

He wondered who could have tipped them off about Mum – someone must have, that was for sure, unless they'd been following him since he got back, because if there was one thing he'd never let on about, it was Mum's address, not to mention the boarding house; most times he stayed at the Grand, it was only now and then he went to Cora's, just to fool them, and if he ever got his hands on whoever had grassed him up . . .

He pounded down Spifford Road, a hundred yards to go and

round the corner, and he'd be heading straight for the footbridge. Already the air was thick with the smell of decay and leaves and green slime which always came off the canal at this time of night, at this time of year, when there weren't many cars around, and he could hear the wind moaning in the poplars which lined one side of the towpath. He reached the corner, turned right, and ran across the road, ducking down into the alley between two of the houses. He had a big advantage over them, he knew this place like the back of his hand, being in and out of these streets since he was a kid, first when he was still ignorant enough to be doing it the hard way with his paper round, then, when he wised up, as a runner for that stupid Irish prick, 'Four Eyes' O'Grady. *Four Eyes*, I ask you, whoever heard of a dealer wearing specs? You couldn't take the guy seriously; he could've afforded contact lens any day of the week, never seemed to realize that it made him look like a proper woofter. He'd enjoyed that, dodging through the backstreets, down the alleyways, kicking over the dustbins as he went, too young to be nicked, always a step or two ahead of the cops, sometimes on his bike, sometimes on foot and once he'd delivered it was back again to Four Eyes for another errand and a handful of money.

He tore out of the alley into Melford Street and straight across into another one, the smell of the canal receding for a moment then returning full force when the narrow passage turned at right angles and there it was ahead of him, just across the road, the glare of the neon lights sending orange ripples across the filthy water. He wouldn't drink a glass of that for a thousand quid, he thought, maybe not even a million, though with that much cash you'd be able to afford the top specialists to cure the effects of the muck which went down your throat. He'd seen a dead dog floating down there one morning, swollen and matted, one blank eye facing the sky, and thought *what a way to die, what a horrible end.*

And then, as he came to the opening on to Canal Side Lane, a black shadow stepped out from behind the side wall and stood there, blocking his way. Bloody fucking hell . . . He had to think quickly because he only had two choices; he could either barge on through the bastard at the mouth of the alley and take his chances, or he could run back and do the same thing at the other end, because you could bet your grandmother's tits that the other one was there, waiting for him.

Cornered like the proverbial rat . . . He didn't hesitate but pushed on, hoping to catch the guy by surprise so that he would at least pause. He held his full weight poised to knock the fucker out of the way, which he did, though not before the guy's arm had thrust at his upper leg. He kicked out, at the same time smashing his fist in the other man's face, heard the crack of breaking bone and a grunt as the guy dropped to his knees, clutching at his nose. It was the older one – for a moment he was tempted to turn and race for the other end of the alley; the other guy worked for the Big Boss only occasionally – driver, or something – and he personally knew him to be a fucking wimp, unlikely to stand in his way. Matter of fact, it astonished him that he had summoned up enough courage to dare chase him, as though the threatening pressure he'd always applied – only way he'd managed to keep his head down for so long – no longer prevailed. Funny that, and then it came to him that maybe it wasn't the boss, fucking Carlos de Poncing Doodah y Macaroni or whatever, but the Big Boss himself who was behind this, tidying up loose ends. In which case . . .

A tearing pain bit into his leg as he ran across the road and on to the canal path, limping now; bastard must have stuck a knife into his thigh. He pushed one hand into his pocket, wincing as he felt the wound, trying to judge how serious it was. A lot of blood, he thought, but he'd survive, not a severed artery or anything, and then felt the rounded shape of his key ring. Christ, if by any chance they caught up with him, they wouldn't rest until they'd forced him to say where the money was. His mouth twisted at the thought of the pain they could inflict with one of those thin blades they always carried. He pulled out the key ring, slippery with blood now, and jogged on to the grass verge, dropped it into a clump of grass – he'd come back tomorrow and retrieve it – and then he was taking the four shallow steps two at a time on to the footbridge, breath coming gaspingly now, but full of elation because he'd outwitted the cunts, they hadn't expected him to keep coming, and he was pounding towards the last yard or two before he reached the other side of the footbridge when something grabbed his hair, an arm came round his neck like an iron bar, forcing him to his knees; his head was yanked backwards, neck stretched. In those final moments, the future he'd envisioned for himself rushed past him like a series of flash-forwards – the yacht moored at Cowes, the fancy sports car, Mum on his arm at Ascot, kids running across a wide green lawn, respect of the community – then there was a blade flashing like a slice of melon in the carroty glow of the tall neon lamps, the water frog-green through the cracks of the planks. Was this how it was going to end? He saw Mum sitting across the table from him, smoking her fags, laughing at something he'd said. 'You're a real man,' she used to say, 'a real man, not like your Dad,' even after he was sent down, visiting every week, never missed, and then they were kicking him as he clutched at his leg, kicking his head so that little lights exploded like Catherine wheels behind his eyes, stamping on his fingers so the bones cracked like walnuts, kicking his kidneys – he'd be pissing blood for a month at this rate. He tried to scream – where were the fucking cops when you needed them? – but no sound came out of his mouth. He could smell sweat and piss and that god-awful aftershave they wore, stank like a pox-doctor's clerk, something the whores wore in that Quito brothel, which is probably where they bought the filthy stuff in the first place.

He found some strength, kicked out, caught one of them on the knee, heard a high-pitched squeal. The younger one . . . good. When this was over, the jerk would wish he'd never been born. He'd already done his brother, soon as he got back – can't have a loose cannon running round, the Big Boss had said, so he'd waited for Stefan near that wine bar he liked, already chatting up some other tasty bit as though the last one hadn't landed them all in trouble, hung about until he came out then caught him round the back of the head with an iron bar, dragged him round the back, chucked the weapon in the canal immediately afterwards and was off back to Cora's.

He managed to get to his feet and tried to run down the steps in a half-crouch, pain burning in his gut, blood pouring down his leg and into his shoe, and then they were on him again and he knew there was no hope left, no fucking hope at all, as they snapped his head back and the blade slid once more across his throat. *Mum!* he tried to scream. *Mum*, like he was a kid again, but the word wouldn't come out, only a bubbly sound.

Mum! Was she OK, had the bastards got to her, had they used their knives on her to get her to tell them where he was, not that she knew? Oh Jesus God . . . the old girl butchered in her kitchen, that was Mum – it was *Mum*, wasn't it? He'd kill them for it, he'd fucking *kill* them, mad foreign bastards – *bastards*! They were going through his pockets, removing everything, and his penultimate thought was *they won't find the key and even if they did* . . . As one of them swung a baseball bat at his skull, over and over again, until his face was a crushed mess of blood and bone and teeth, and as they got him by the arms and legs and started swinging him from side to side, they never knew that his final conscious thought was *please not in the fucking canal.*

Dora

'Morning, Dr Lennox, how are you?'

'Just fine, Mrs Harding, and you?'

'Lovely, thanks. How's the baby?'

'Still a bit new, really.'

'What's her name?'

'We decided to call her Anna-Margarita.'

'Ooh, that's ever so nice. And Olga and Alexei not jealous of her?'

'Not as far as we can tell.'

Mrs Harding watched him walk further along the towpath. That poor wife of his, awful about her mother being murdered like that, all over the papers, it was, sliced to pieces if you believed what you read, couldn't trust them journalists further than you could throw them, in Dora's opinion. Mafia, that's what it was all down to, people dying left, right and centre; that chap found outside a wine bar, what was it, months ago now, skull split, so they said, then his father, someone had done away with him too, and then that gang boss further south, big trial there'd been, he'd gone down for twenty years, though it probably wasn't long enough for someone like that – still it was some time ago, well over a year, more like fifteen months, and there'd been peace and quiet up here since then, though they'd never found out who that was floating in the canal all those months ago – Mrs Harding knew that for a fact, because she'd rung the police station herself to ask, seeing as how she was the one called the police in the first place.

'Have a bit of sponge, Cora, I made it for you special.'

'Mmm . . . not bad, though you always was a bit heavy-handed when it comes to beating.'

'Do well in one of them terrorist prison camps, then,' quipped Dora, while Cora passed over a plate of fancy biscuits, saying, 'Try one of these – one of my Guests bought them for me.' Cora always called the people who stopped at her tiny B&B her Guests, audibly including the capital G.

'Lovely.' Dora's fingers hovered over the selection – ginger nut, creme sandwich, milk chocolate digestive, caramel waffle, lemon crisp and lovely sugary Nice – which wobbled in front of her, Cora's hands being none too steady these days. Personally, Dora put it down to the Demon Drink, a glass or so every now and then never did anyone any harm, but judging by the empties in the kitchen, Cora was going at it like a sailor, if it was sailors who went at it, though she always insisted that she was under the doctor for it because *he* thought the tremor might be the onset of Parkinson's and a bit of sympathy would be nice, chance would be a fine thing. Dora thought Parkinson's was unlikely – you didn't have any facial expression with Parkinson's, did you? Cora had far too much expression, most of it nasty, in Dora's opinion, still they were twins, after all, and now that their big sisters, Thora and Nora, were gone, not to mention their husbands, each other was all either of them had. 'I'll have the lemon crisp.'

'Why'd you choose that, you know it's my favourite?' Cora said, sniffing, and pulled the plate out of Dora's reach before plonking a Garibaldi in front of her, not Dora's biscuit of choice – they used to call them squashed-fly biscuits when they were little and she'd never really fancied them after that.

'I'll leave the cake for you when I go,' Dora said. 'Can't stay long this time, Livingstone's been a bit off colour,' and while she waited for Cora's inevitable response when Livvy came into the conversation (*'You and that dog'*), she opened her big black handbag (bought on sale, must be six years ago, and still going strong, which just bore out what Dora always said, that it pays to buy good stuff) and searched around for the bus timetable, pulling out her purse, her keys, a packet of menthol cigarettes ('*Ooh, Dora, you're not still smoking, are you, give you cancer soon as look at you, thought you gave them up years ago.*') and the Quick Crossword from the *Mail*, which she'd cut out and folded neatly, intending to do it on the way home, the bus taking forever these days, winding through the villages and meandering all over the place. She was about to run her finger down the columns to check what time the next bus was when Cora pointed at the bunch of keys which now lay splayed on the tablecloth Cora had embroidered for her bottom drawer (Mother had insisted that they all did one). 'Like your key ring,' she said. 'That's new.'

'Not really, I've had it at least a year now,' Dora said. 'Sally gave it to me,' guiltily remembering that to all intents and purposes she'd stolen it – you could hardly call it borrowing when you didn't know whose it was. And Cora asked if she recalled that Guest she used to have, came every now and then, very dark hair, stayed a night or two and took off again, well, he'd had a key ring just like that, she remembered the dolphin particularly because she'd gone on the coach with the Over-Sixties to one of them amusement parks, not that there'd been much amusement about it, everything cost the earth and she'd ruined a perfectly good pair of fur-trimmed ankle boots in the mud, but there'd been dolphins there, ever so nice they were, always smiling at you, not really smiling, of course, it was the way their mouths were, but anyway, this Guest – Mr Buono, he called himself; funny sort of name, but a nice sort of chap – *he'd* had a key ring like this one. And what's more, Cora went on, last time he came was – oooh, *months* ago, more than a year, haven't seen hide nor hair of him since, but he'd left a briefcase with her, that last time, for safe-keeping, he said, and seeing the dolphin reminded her.

'Ever looked inside, Core?' Mrs Harding asked, and Cora said of course not, what did Dora take her for? But it would be interesting to know, wouldn't it? 'So where is this briefcase?' asked Dora, and her sister explained it was under her own bed. 'And you never even tried to see what was in it, Nosey Parker like you, pull the other one,' Dora said, 'come off it, I know you too well.' Cora conceded that she might have tried to open the case (must be nearly fifteen months since he was last here, now she came to think) but it had been locked and though she'd tried to prise it open with a screw-driver, she hadn't succeeded. 'For my own protection, of course, you never know, might have been a bomb in there, or *drugs*, you wouldn't want them drug dukes after you, would you,' at which point Dora recalled that there had been a key on the key ring she'd found in the grass more than a year ago or, more correctly, *Livingstone* had found, a small key which at the time she had guessed was for a suitcase or something similar.

'Is it heavy?' she asked, but Cora couldn't really say, what with the Parkinson's and everything, not that she got a drop of pity or consideration from anyone, especially her own family. Dora watched Sooty the cat stalking a sparrow across the grass outside the window, body elongated to twice its normal size, like a telescope or something, then said why didn't she, Dora, nip upstairs and have a look at it? Like Cora said, you didn't want to be harbouring Mafia money or drugs unbeknownst, did you – 'and it's *barons*, Cora, not dukes.'

'Why not?' Cora shrugged and mentioned her legs, which had apparently been playing up, making climbing the stairs more of a problem than they used to be – Mum's were the same, Dora might remember. Upstairs, Dora sniffed the stuffy air of Cora's bedroom: mothballs, stale scent (Cora liked Chanel No. 5, which Dora found too rich, preferring Anaïs, but happy with whatever Sally or Lizzie bought for her in the Duty Free shop at Heathrow), unwashed tights and sweat (Cora had always had a problem with body odour, even as a girl) and a chair strewn with surprisingly sexy underwear. (Cora hadn't gone and found herself a *man*, had she, after all these years of widowhood?) She peered under the bed, wrinkled her nose at the dust balls gathered there (at least there wasn't a chamber pot, like Mum used to have. *Goosey Goosey Gander*, it used to say round the rim, half-full, like as not), pushed aside the pink marabou-feathered high-heeled slippers (when in the world would Cora ever wear *those*?) and pulled towards her a handsome briefcase made of soft light-brown leather. Locked, as Cora had said. Dora tried to imagine what was inside. Dozens of small cellophane packages containing a suspicious white powder, or diamonds stolen from – where was it? – Hatton Gardens in London, or bearer bonds (whatever they might be) with a face value of millions, or even souvenirs of recent grisly murders – a hank of hair here, a pair of lace knickers there, a locket containing a photograph of the victim's boyfriend. But when she lifted it on to the bed, nothing rattled or shook. She could see the scratches on the lock where Cora had used the screwdriver and wondered what the lodger – sorry, the Guest – would say when he returned, but it had been fifteen months, seemed a long time to leave anything for safe-keeping with anyone, especially not a landlady or whatever you called a woman who ran a B&B.

'It's worth a try, Core,' she said, carrying the case downstairs. 'Let's have a look, see if we can open it, find out what's going on.'

'Maybe Mr Buono was in an accident,' Cora said. 'Maybe we should call the police.'

'And maybe we shouldn't,' Dora said. 'It's waited this long, and nobody's come asking about it.' She recalled the corpse in the canal and wondered if this Mr Buono had met a similar fate somewhere. She found the small key on her dolphin ring and pushed it into one of the two brass locks, listened to the click as it turned, did the same with the other, and watched with satisfaction as Cora's mouth dropped open.

'There you go, Cora,' she said, 'you get to lift the lid, seeing as how it practically belongs to you now – finder's keepers.'

Cora stared at the case. 'Supposing he comes back, asking for it,' she said, to which Dora briskly responded that she was well within her rights and she could tell him that she'd opened it (not that she yet had) in the hope of finding some kind of identification which would enable her to return it to him, in case he'd forgotten about it – or else you could say that after twelve months, let alone fifteen, any property left unclaimed reverted to the 'landlady' and she was very sorry, Mr Buono, but she had a legal right (*'Do I really, Dora?'*) to look inside and take possession of the contents.

'Go on, open it, Cora, the suspense is killing me.'

'Here goes,' Cora said and slowly lifted the lid of the briefcase to reveal dozens – hundreds, *thousands* – of ten-pound notes loosely packed together. 'Bloody hell!' Cora said. (Mother would have turned in her grave) 'What are we going to do with it, take it to the police?'

'The police? Not on your nelly,' Dora said. 'First we're going to count it and then we're going to . . .'

'What, Dora?'

'. . . *spend* it.'

Visions of the midnight-blue satin evening dress with diamanté scattered all over the bosom which she'd seen on sale in Thornton's only four days earlier danced in front of Dora's eyes, then rippled, spread, expanded into further images: a cobalt sea, herself perched beguilingly on a high stool daintily sipping a cocktail from a Y-shaped glass, besieged by not one but two – make that *three* – grey-haired Texan billionaires while the Captain entreated her to sit at his table for the duration of the cruise and . . .

'My Boutique B&B,' said Cora softly.

'You could come on a cruise with me first,' Dora said generously, 'and then you'd have to move somewhere else, can't stay here in case your Mr Buono takes it into his head to come looking for his case – or you could simply tell him, if he does, that you took it to the police. That'll stop him because you're not going to tell me this is – what do they call it? – legit. It's not legit, no way, so you're safe, Cora, and so am I. It's a dream come true, that's what it is.'

And think of the good that could be done! Mr Gilmour and his dog, she could give a huge donation to the Guide Dogs for the Blind, and Cancer Research, and build wells out in Africa, pay for operations on some of those poor little kids in the Sunday newspapers with horrendous harelips, there were so many things you could do, as well as having some fun.

'Tell you what, Dora,' Cora said, getting up and moving towards the green-painted dresser. 'There's a bottle of wine I opened this— last night, why don't we have a drink, celebrate, what do you think?'

'Good idea,' said Dora. 'Cheers.'